My Daughter's Army

Greg Hogben

DSP PUBLICATIONS

Published by
DSP PUBLICATIONS

5032 Capital Circle SW, Suite 2, PMB# 279, Tallahassee, FL 32305-7886 USA
www.dsppublications.com/

My Daughter's Army
© 2015 Greg Hogben.

Cover Art
© 2015 Greg Hogben.
Cover content is for illustrative purposes only and any person depicted on the cover is a model.

ISBN: 978-1-63476-192-5
Digital ISBN: 978-1-63476-193-2
Library of Congress Control Number: 2015908399
First Edition December 2015

Printed in the United States of America
ⓧ
This paper meets the requirements of
ANSI/NISO Z39.48-1992 (Permanence of Paper).

For the voiceless, those who have found their voices, and the army of dedicated advocates fighting tirelessly to make those voices heard.

Acknowledgments

A very special thanks to Kenny and Umi for everything you have done. Also, thanks to Randy, Chris, Elizabeth North, Tracy E., and Frances M. for all your support.

PROLOGUE

WE ALL have our own personal saviors. They are the ones who rescue us from life's worst moments through acts both great and small. By chance, or maybe it was fate—if you believe in such a thing—I raised the young lady who became mine.

I shared my personal savior with millions, but no one knew at what cost.

CHAPTER ONE

August 1990

THE TRAIN journey from Buffalo was almost unbearable. Every rumble of the tracks made me nauseous as it carried me home to New York City. I'd spent the journey replaying the last moments of Michael's life over and over in my head.

I was jolted back to reality as the train's engines slowed. The people around me gathered their belongings and stood as the train arrived at our destination. Within minutes of the doors opening, every passenger had disembarked except me. A conductor called for me to exit the train as he walked through the carriages to check for stragglers, but I didn't move. He turned, aware I hadn't responded to his barked order. He must have seen the sorrow on my face.

"Sir, I'm sorry, but we've reached Grand Central Station," he said, more kindly. "This is our last stop, so I'm afraid I have to ask you to make your way to the terminal."

As I reached for my bag and felt how light it was, another punch of grief hit me. Michael's ashes were gone, left in Buffalo in the care of his mom and dad.

I made my way from the platform through the concourse of Grand Central Station. Nothing but my mind's darkness guided me down the stairs and onto the subway platform with a determination that both frightened and calmed me. Soon this desperate feeling would be gone and I'd be free of the pain.

A small bead of summer sweat ran down my back as I bowed my head and stared at the bare subway tracks. I shifted my weight from foot to foot and felt the raised dots on the yellow line that warned of the platform's edge. They pressed into the soles of my shoes when the ground trembled as a train on the platform behind me rushed into the station. If I'd gone to that side first, it would already be over. But out of habit, I'd headed to the platform where the Number 6 train would usually take me to the City Hall stop near my home on the Lower East Side.

From the corner of my eye, I could see the first haze of yellow light growing wider in the tunnel and realized my position on the platform was wrong. I was in the middle when I should have been closer to the end where the train would appear. If the driver saw me and applied the brakes, the train might not be going fast enough for the impact to kill me instantly. I might experience the whole thing in slow motion before the weight of the front carriage crushed me. The light vibrations on the platform became tremors. The shiver in my body turned into a violent shake as I felt the warm, stale air pushing toward me from the tunnel by the oncoming train.

Just one step, Adam. That's all.

The ice in my knees cracked as my legs began to move. My eyes darted between the finality of the oncoming train and the safety of the exit. For a split second, I didn't know which way my legs would carry me, but my turning foot gave away its intention. I rushed back up the stairs and into the concourse of Grand Central Station before my mind sank into darkness again.

The late afternoon daylight shone through the cathedral-style windows, illuminating and side-blinding people as they made their way out of the terminal. The brightness gave me an excuse to dip my head and look at the ground as I made my way across the hall and toward the Forty-Second Street exit, where I could hail a cab. Echoes of hundreds of conversations, raggedy wheels on old suitcases rolling across smooth tiles, spinning flaps on the constantly changing destinations board, and the general chaos of a Friday afternoon in New York's busiest train station all blended in my ears, a steady roll of commuter thunder.

Over the years, I'd grown deaf to the din, but today something stood out. I heard crying. For a moment I thought the sobs might be my own. I walked briskly past the information kiosk in the middle of the concourse and headed for a solitary bench against the wall opposite the ticket counters. I sat and buried my head in my hands, hoping to stifle my tears and keep it together long enough to get back to the apartment. As I tried to settle myself, I heard the cry again. But it was clearer and much higher than the muffled grizzle a thirty-two-year-old man would hear in his own ears. The pitch of the cry grew higher and higher, so I looked around for toddlers or babies in strollers. But there were none—

at least none close enough that I should hear so clearly. Then I realized the noise was coming from beneath me.

I stood and then crouched to look under the bench. There, wrapped in a plain white cotton towel, was a baby. It couldn't have been more than a few weeks old. Gingerly, I picked up the bundle and looked around, searching for its mother. But people carried on walking as though they hadn't noticed. I sat and carefully lowered the baby onto my knees, continuing to scan the area for someone—anyone—who looked hysterical. Not a single person looked interested or even remotely concerned. When I looked down again, the baby had stopped crying, and its right arm had broken free of the toweling. Its tiny hand grasped at the air, desperate to catch hold of something. I held out my little finger and felt the tiny hand grip it, stronger and tighter than I would have imagined possible for a baby so young. For the first time in five weeks, a sense of calm and peace washed over me.

Of course I was shocked and somewhat panicked at finding an abandoned baby. Anyone would be. But amid those feelings, there was a moment to step outside myself, to care about and concentrate on someone with bigger problems than my own. And, however selfish it might sound, I was relieved to have a respite from my grief.

I knew the NYPD patrolled the entrance to the terminal. I didn't want to carry the baby outside in case its mother came back, so I tried to flag people down as they passed. I managed to catch the attention of a young woman in a business suit and asked her to alert the police. She was just as horrified as I was and looked around, expecting to find a frantic woman in the area, before hurrying away to summon the cops.

"Who would leave you?" I cooed as I stroked the baby's plump cheek. Its eyes were a beautiful shade of aqua blue and followed every movement of my face. When I looked up again, I saw two officers heading toward me. The older, more experienced cop walked at a stroll. The other, who looked fresh from the academy, approached with a little more urgency.

I explained how I'd found the baby, and the older cop stepped to one side to speak into his radio. The younger cop sat beside me and pulled out a small pad and a pen from his pocket.

"Can I take your name, sir?"

"Adam Goodwin," I replied. The young cop introduced himself as Officer Marino and jotted in his notepad as I spoke.

"Is it a boy or a girl?" the older cop called out to us. I opened the towel to find the baby was naked.

"It's a girl," I called back. "She must be older than I thought. She has to be at least several weeks old. Her navel is completely healed."

"Can you hazard a guess at her ethnicity?"

I looked down again. Her skin wasn't pale enough for a Caucasian baby nor dark enough to be black. It appeared to be light olive, but it was difficult to tell in the mix of natural and artificial light in the concourse.

"Maybe Hispanic?" Officer Marino called out to his partner. "But then again... I don't know. She kinda looks like my sister Lucia's kid when she was a baby. Could be Italian, but you don't often see kids like that with blue eyes."

"All babies are born with blue eyes," the older cop called over with a look of exasperation at his partner's unhelpfully vague description. He continued speaking into his radio.

"Okay, sir," Officer Marino continued. "Can I get some contact details from you? You know, just in case we need to get in touch with you or call you as a witness at a later date. I'm not too sure of the procedure for lost babies."

"I don't think she's lost, officer. She's clearly been abandoned."

"Oh yeah. Sure," he said awkwardly, as if he thought it was the second stupid thing he'd said in as many sentences.

"And not all babies are born with blue eyes," I added to be kind. He looked embarrassed, so I continued. "The police will contact Social Services and Child Welfare, who will file a report and take custody of her." I don't know why I smiled as I explained the chain of events to come. I guess I thought it might soothe her or make it easier for her to hear, even though she couldn't understand a word of it. "Then a social worker will be assigned her case and will attempt to find her a temporary foster home until her mother is found or comes forward. Then they'll have to evaluate the mother's state of mind, decide whether any charges should be filed, and conduct home visits to see if she might remain in danger." I stroked the side of her chubby little cheek again. "She's obviously been well cared for. Even this toweling looks brand new."

"You know a lot about this, huh?"

"I'm a Legal Aid attorney. I work with Social Services and the Family Court a lot. I have an idea of the procedure, but I've never actually dealt with it myself."

The young officer nodded, then shook his head in disgust. "What kind of woman leaves her baby, huh? Some people don't deserve to have kids. I hope they don't ever find her." He pointed the top of his pen at the baby resting quietly on my lap. "Lucky you found her. Perhaps she'll stand a chance without a woman like that as a mother."

I tried to keep an even tone. "Officer, you don't know the mother's situation. There could be a dozen reasons why she left her baby here. She could be in trouble. She might recognize that she can't cope. She may think the baby's father is dangerous and is trying to get her away from him. You shouldn't jump to conclusions before you know more."

"Nah, I don't buy it," the young officer said dismissively. "Why not leave the kid at a hospital or a police station? Or just give it up for adoption? Why leave it under a bench in a train station? That proves to me she don't give a damn."

"You're right, there are safer places. But isn't this situation better than you or one of your colleagues being called to a back-alley dumpster to investigate a dead baby that's been thrown away?" It came out far more bluntly than I'd intended. The cop was young and obviously new to the beat. He hadn't yet been exposed to some of the horrors uncovered in the city on a daily basis.

"Yeah, I suppose so. I just find it hard to believe someone would do something like this, ya know?"

The older officer came over and informed us that no one had reported a missing child in the area and prepared to take the baby.

"Do you want me to bring her down to the station?" I asked hopefully.

"There's no need. We'll take her until Social Services arrive. The patrol car ain't fitted out with seats to take a baby, so we're gonna hang on here until then. You're free to carry on with your day, sir, but we may be in contact again soon."

I nodded, feeling oddly bereft, and wrapped the little girl tightly in the toweling again before I stood and gave her a quick cradle in my arms. "Look after her," I said, preparing to hand the baby over to the older, more experienced cop, since Officer Marino looked scared to handle her.

He unclipped the radio from the front of his shoulder and handed it to his partner before awkwardly taking the baby from me. He held her up to his chest and wrapped his arm around the bundle.

As I started to move away, she began to whimper. I had walked just a few steps toward the exit before her screaming cries dominated the sounds of the station. By the time I got outside, my grief and sadness had returned, and I was on my own again.

AFTER PAYING the taxi driver for the ride to my apartment building, I took a deep breath before opening the glass doors that led into the lobby. I headed up two flights of stairs and down the short hallway, passing my neighbor's door. It was slightly ajar, clearly left open to listen for my return.

Della Walker, or "Miss Dee" as she was known in our four-story apartment block, was a retired nurse. She was one part Maya Angelou and two parts Whoopi Goldberg, though in recent weeks that mixture had been inverted. I knew she'd appear the moment my keys jangled as I pulled them from my pocket. And true to her Georgia roots, I also knew that her hands would be full of Southern comfort food. I wasn't disappointed.

"My spiced chicken, fried confetti corn, and mashed potatoes with cream gravy," she called with a smile as she walked toward me with a covered plate. "And buttermilk biscuits, freshly baked today," she added as she handed me a small Tupperware box.

"Thank you, Miss Dee." I bent down and gave a peck on the cheek to the woman who'd fed me both food and advice for the past five weeks. "You really are a godsend."

"Now, honey, tell me how it went today. I know it had to be tough."

I slowly nodded. "It was, but at least it's over now."

"And tell me, how were Michael's momma and daddy?"

"They were okay. I think they were a little worried that it had taken me two weeks to give them the ashes. But I think they realized that it was hard—"

"—hard to let go," Miss Dee finished my sentence. "But you gave them what they needed to grieve, a chance to have their child with them forever."

"Yeah, but what about me?" I asked hopelessly.

"You get to keep all those memories in your heart where they belong, honey. They'll never be relived or felt in an urn. An urn don't feel nothin'."

I gave her a brave smile. I knew she wouldn't leave until she saw one.

"Now, baby, if there's anything I can do for you, you let me know, ya hear? Just you holler."

I leaned down and gave her another peck on the cheek before she wrapped her hands around my face, gave it a little shake, and headed back down the hall and into her apartment.

I unlocked the door and walked into my empty home. It was a modest two-bedroom apartment, but without Michael, it felt as if the space could fill a mansion. I walked through the open-plan living room and kitchen and dropped my empty bag onto the counter. I drew back a chair from the dining table, uncovered the food, and began my recently developed ritual of getting halfway through Miss Dee's meal before my throat closed up and tears ran off my cheeks and onto the plate.

I didn't want to leave the table because I knew what was coming. It was the same thing every night. But tonight—especially tonight— without even Michael's cremated presence in the apartment, I knew it would be worse, and it terrified me. I would lie on our bed alone and surrender to impossibly dark thoughts. They'd hold me hostage until I finally succumbed to sleep. I'd have a few hours of sweet unconscious release, but eventually, the nightmares would recapture me as I recalled saying good-bye.

"I love you, Michael. You are and will always be everything to me," I'd said over the hospital bed as the artificial sound of his heartbeat slowed. Then I whispered the same thing I'd whispered every night before we went to sleep.

"Dream of me, Mikey."

I never knew if he heard me that last time I said those words out loud. Only once, in a precious dream, I heard the words Michael said back to me every night. *"Why dream when you're here next to me?"*

Chapter Two

"I'm sorry, but I really need to get to another court," I said to the parents who'd just watched their son get six months in prison for assaulting his girlfriend. I gathered my papers and slid them into my briefcase. It closed with a snap. "Try not to worry. He'll probably be out in three if he behaves himself."

The parents had been polite and thankful the sentence wasn't as harsh at it could have been. But their son, my client, continued to rant, rave, and threaten me the way he'd done from the moment I'd received his case. He had what I considered "angry young man syndrome." He believed the whole world was out to get him, nothing in life was fair, and that he was the sole target of a universal conspiracy that wouldn't allow him to be innocent, since he wasn't what society thought he should be. Of course, the video footage of him breaking the young woman's jaw outside a nightclub—and the ensuing brawl with the club's security—hadn't helped. Despite my maneuvering to get his sentence reduced, he still railed against me since he thought he should've walked away scot-free. If I'd been the judge, I would have thrown the book at him, and hard. But defending him was my job and what I was sworn to do.

My career hadn't always been like this. I'd been an associate at a successful firm in the city after I graduated law school. But after five years of long hours and meetings that never seemed to end, the sense of never achieving anything of importance took its toll. I hadn't made the decision to work for Legal Aid lightly. It paid a lot less money, involved more hassles and even stranger hours, and the clients no longer sent gifts for my efforts. Instead I often was seen as the enemy, even by those whom I was dedicated to helping. But in most cases, I felt a real sense of achievement. Though I sometimes had to defend people I neither trusted nor liked, I was also able to help innocent victims or charitable organizations who otherwise would have been thrown to the wolves.

As I reached family court, I heard the quickening taps of high heels behind me.

"Adam!"

I turned to see Donna Wilson hurrying behind me. She was a department head for Child Protective Services, with whom I'd worked closely on other cases. She had an extraordinary gift of balancing professionalism with unbridled compassion for the families with whom she worked, and I admired her tremendously. I stopped and waited for her to catch up.

"Has the mother come forward yet?" I'd spoken to Donna regularly since that day in Grand Central Station. She'd contacted me to ask if I was the same Adam Goodwin who found the baby girl. She wasn't able to give me all the information on the baby's case, but she coughed in the right places if any of my leading questions risked confidentiality.

"No, and we've had no luck locating her, even with media help. She seems to have disappeared off the face of the planet."

In the past eight weeks, I'd thought about the baby girl every day. I watched the news and read the headlines in the papers, becoming more and more disheartened that she was still in the care of the state. I don't know if it was because I was the one who discovered her, but I felt responsible. What I hadn't learned from Donna, I'd learned from the press. Each morning I glanced at the newspaper article I'd saved about the baby. A photo showed her little face peeking over the CPS-issued blanket and, even through my settling grief, the little face managed to pry a smile from me.

I'd been called to court to give my account of the events that led to the baby's discovery. It would only be a brief statement, but I was happy to attend, since it felt like I was helping her in some small way.

As I took my place in the gallery, the judge came out of her chambers, and we rose. I was happy to see Judge Adesso, an older, no-nonsense Italian woman who was nearing the end of her time on the bench. As she took her seat, she spotted me, raised her eyebrows, and smiled. She gave me a little wave and mouthed *"What are you doing here?"* She donned her large crimson-rimmed spectacles dangling by a chain around the neck of her robe. The court fell silent as she quickly read over the papers in front of her, only stopping at what must have been the recognition of my name. She glanced at me over the top of her glasses.

I'd appeared before Judge Adesso more than any other judge over the past five years, and we'd developed a professional friendship. Not that this helped me in any of her rulings. She'd often been curt to me during proceedings and spoke her mind without filter. But she was also quick to stop me after a session, especially if I'd lost the case, to let me know where I'd gone wrong, to explain where I could've been more convincing, or simply to share a joke to keep our relationship intact. After Michael died she was the first to find me in court to offer her condolences.

When she finished reading the brief, she took off her glasses and surveyed the court.

"Okay, we're here to discuss the continuing custody of the infant known as Baby Doe 6575," she announced in a loud, authoritative voice that didn't match her slight stature. "Now, as I understand it, the child is still in the care of social services. So, I'd first like someone to explain how she was found, and why, after two months, she isn't with a family in foster care."

Donna stood and addressed the judge. "The baby was found at Grand Central Station August 9, at approximately 5:30 p.m., by Mr. Adam Goodwin, who immediately reported the discovery to Officer Morris and Officer Marino of the NYPD, who were patrolling the station that evening."

Judge Adesso held up a hand to stop Donna and looked in my direction. "When you found the child, did she look healthy? Did it appear she'd been cared for?"

I stood to respond. "Yes, Your Honor."

"Thank you, Adam. She was lucky that you were the one to find her," she said in a businesslike tone laced with kindness. "And I assume there was no indication of the child's mother being present in the area?"

"No, Your Honor. It was a Friday evening, so the station was busy. But no one in the vicinity seemed to be acting in a way that would indicate they'd lost their child. Nor did the officers or I see anyone acting suspiciously or watching to see if the child was found."

The judge nodded and turned to the other side of the aisle. "Now, Officers, tell me what happened next."

I hadn't noticed the two uniforms in the court, but they were instantly recognizable once they stood. The older cop, who I now knew was Officer Morris, was the first to speak.

"After taking Mr. Goodwin's statement and details, we proceeded to contact Child Protective Services and were given instructions for the chain of custody to begin."

The cop stopped and looked behind him as he, and everyone else in the room, heard the muffled sound of a screaming baby getting louder. He turned back to the court. "We were met by the social worker on duty, a Ms. Nash, who took custody of the child at Grand Central. She then followed us to the station, where the relevant reports were completed."

"And where is Ms. Nash?" the judge asked, looking over the people in the courtroom, waiting for the social worker to identify herself.

"Judging by the noise, Your Honor, I think she's outside," Donna said, pointing a thumb over her shoulder.

The piercingly violent cries of a baby reverberated in the corridor. Many in the court, including the judge, winced with every breath of fresh hell she screamed.

"Why on earth has she brought the child with her?" the judge asked before turning to the court officer. "Could you go and fetch them? Let's make this quick before all our eardrums burst."

Ms. Nash entered the courtroom holding the baby balanced on her hip. The middle-aged social worker looked haggard, with dark circles under her eyes magnified by her thick glasses. Her frazzled ponytail clearly hadn't seen a brush in days. She looked on the verge of cracking up. The baby wore a pink felt onesie and had grown a little since I'd found her. She had a light dusting of dark brown, possibly auburn, hair that curled in all directions. Her right arm was squashed against Ms. Nash's gray cardigan while the left one hung motionless.

As they walked down the center aisle, people turned to shield their ears from the sound. I caught the baby's eye and smiled sympathetically. I'd cried enough recently to have some sympathy for her distress. The moment her eyes locked on mine, the crying stopped.

Ms. Nash froze in her tracks. "Oh thank God!" she said with a look of absolute relief. But as she began walking in the judge's direction again, the baby started to howl once more.

"Ms. Nash," the judge began, raising her voice over the screams, "why isn't this child in a foster home?"

The baby girl began wriggling and tried to climb, one-handed, up onto Ms. Nash's chest. Ms. Nash struggled to keep the infant on her hip but gave up and raised the baby onto her shoulder.

"Ms. Nash, this child has been in the custody of the state for over eight weeks. Why haven't you assigned her to a temporary foster home? She is clearly...."

The judge stopped. Something caught her, and my, attention. The baby's hand grasped the air in my direction over the social worker's shoulder. She began kicking with what looked like a wild attempt to get closer to me.

Judge Adesso looked back and forth between the baby and me. She paused for a moment before saying, "Adam, would you be a dear and take her for a moment? She seems to have taken a shine to you. Perhaps you can keep her quiet while we get through this?"

I nodded, feeling a bit bemused. As I took the baby, she stopped crying and wrapped her little arm around my neck. And, just like the moment I found her, an overwhelming sense of calm and peace revisited me, though at the time I assumed it was nothing more than the relief of silence. As I retook my seat, Judge Adesso eyed me carefully before returning her attention to the social worker.

"Now, Ms. Nash, why is this child still with you?" she asked, clearly tired of having to repeat herself.

The social worker straightened her clothes before taking a deep breath to compose herself.

"She has been impossible to foster, Your Honor. She's been in the care of four sets of foster parents, two of whom have had ample experience of dealing with difficult children. But not even they could cope with her."

"What are her difficulties?" the judge asked.

"Well, she has a moderate form of Erb's Palsy, but–"

"—and what is that?"

"It's a kind of paralysis caused by nerve damage in the neck. The most common cause is an abnormal or difficult childbirth or labor. It can happen if the infant's head and neck are pulled to the side at the same time the shoulders pass through the birth canal. It can also be caused by excessive pulling on the shoulders during a head-first delivery or by pressure on the raised arms during a breech birth."

"Is the child in pain? Is that why she's crying?"

"No, not at all. She can't feel anything in the affected arm."

The social worker walked over to me, took the baby's limp arm, and shook it before bending her elbow like a rag doll. The baby didn't respond to her gestures at all. "See?"

Blood rushed to my face as I removed her hand from the baby's tiny disabled arm. I have the utmost respect for social workers—they are overworked and ridiculously underpaid for a job that is, more often than not, difficult and thankless. While the overwhelming majority of them work in a caring and professional manner, there are some who simply carry out their duties as a means to collect a salary or have been in the job so long they've lost all compassion. I didn't know if Ms. Nash fell into either of those categories, but I didn't like the casual way she handled the baby's arm.

"It'll usually resolve itself as the nerves repair, but it sometimes requires surgery or physical therapy," Ms. Nash said as she walked back in front of the judge.

"So what's the problem, exactly?"

"She simply won't stop crying. What you heard just then, that's all she's done since the moment we picked her up. She barely sleeps and only stops crying when she feeds. We've had her examined by a doctor, but he can't find anything wrong with her. No colic, no skin irritation or allergies, no infections. Nothing. He can't explain it. Even when we try to rotate her care within our department, it becomes impossible, since she refuses bottles from anyone other than me. Then, the moment she's fed, she starts crying again."

"Well, she seems okay at the moment," Judge Adesso said, pointing her pen in my direction.

"Honestly, Your Honor, this is the first time she's stopped. I know it sounds like I'm exaggerating, but she never stops. She never, ever stops!" She seemed angry, as if the baby's sudden silence was a deliberate attempt to make her out to be a liar. It was clear she desperately wanted—needed—to be believed. "It's a miracle her throat isn't red raw from all the crying. Considering how much she screams, she should have gone hoarse weeks ago. But no such luck!"

I adjusted the baby so she sat facing me in my lap. Once again, I knew it was impossible for her to understand the words, but I felt I needed to protect her from even seeing Ms. Nash speak about her in such an ugly way. I leaned forward and touched her head with my nose while I gave her a little shake and made googly noises. She smelled exactly how babies should smell, a mix of new skin, baby lotion, and no-tears shampoo.

She reached up to my face with her right arm and walked her little fingers over my chin and up to my mouth. I hummed as she flapped my bottom lip to change the sound. She was so beautiful. The redness of her face was clearing, and I could see she had flecks of green in her big blue eyes. I picked up my tie and waved the end in her face, and she shrieked with delight as she tried to catch hold of it. The people around me began to laugh.

"*Mr. Goodwin!*"

I didn't know how much I'd missed. The conversation between the judge, the police, and the social workers had continued, but I was oblivious. The sharp use of my surname got my attention, and when I looked up, I expected to see the judge angry at my apparent lack of concentration. But instead she was smiling.

"Sorry, Your Honor."

"I asked whether you would be interested in taking temporary custody of the baby."

Shock must have registered on my face, as Judge Adesso began to laugh. I looked over at the social worker. She wore an apprehensive expression, as though the next words from my mouth would decide her sentence or release.

"Me?"

"Yes, you," the judge said a little more seriously. "The child obviously likes you, and you've already seen how she behaves with others."

"No," I said, shaking my head and laughing nervously. "No, no. Your Honor, you can't be serious."

"I'm being perfectly serious. You'll have to go through the same home inspections that any other prospective foster parent would go through, but I'm sure Ms. Nash will be more than willing to help you with that."

The social worker quickly nodded.

"If you pass that, I don't see why you shouldn't be granted temporary custody. The question is—would you consider taking on the role?"

"But I'm–"

"You are a single man, well regarded by the state, with no criminal record and an exemplary reputation. I think that more than qualifies you to be this little girl's guardian."

"But you know I'm—"

The judge cut me off. "I know all that I need to know. The question remains whether you are willing to take care of this child until a suitable and more permanent home is found." The judge turned to Ms. Nash and Donna. "Do either of you have any objection to this?"

They both shook their heads.

I looked down at the baby again and saw her big eyes staring up at me. She looked so damn helpless.

I shook my head slowly in disbelief as the word "Yes" spilled from my mouth.

"Trust me, I know it's a lot to get your head around with so little time to think about it. But you're doing the right thing. I know you'll do what's in the best interest of the child, or I wouldn't have even considered it."

The judge turned to Donna. "Could you please walk Mr. Goodwin through all the necessary papers and petitions so we can get this child placed as soon as possible?"

Donna smiled and looked in my direction. "Yes, Your Honor."

ONCE THE hearing was over and I'd had a few private words of encouragement from the judge, Donna and Ms. Nash came over to collect the baby from my lap.

"You have no idea how much you're helping us by doing this," Ms. Nash said, hardly disguising her excitement.

Even though I understood her relief, my hackles rose again. I hated hearing her speak of the happy baby on my lap as some kind of unpleasant chore. Worried that I might say something I'd regret, I turned my attention to Donna. "So what happens now?"

Donna sat beside me, pulled a blank sheet of paper from a file, and started to make notes.

"The first thing we should do is name her. We can't keep calling her Baby Doe, and none of the other foster families had her long enough to name her. Since it looks like you'll be her first real parent, I guess you should be the one to do it. Any ideas?"

"Of course not! Most people have months to think of one. Is it even right for me to name her if this is only a temporary thing?"

"I think so. We can't give a definite timeline on how long it'll take to find a home for her. It could be weeks, it could be months. Either way, we have to name her."

I looked down at the top of the baby's head resting against my chest. She had fallen asleep, though her tiny right hand still gripped my shirt with all its might.

"How the hell are you doing that?" Ms. Nash whispered in disbelief. I continued to ignore her.

"Do you want me to come up with a name?" Donna asked.

"Actually, would it be okay if we call her Sarah?"

"Of course!" Donna said, taking her pen to the paper. "Do you want it spelled with an 'H' on the end?"

I placed my hand on the little girl's back and felt her tiny breaths. I smiled as a memory passed through my mind. "Actually, can you spell it S-e-r-a?"

"Seh-Rah?" asked Donna.

"It'll still be pronounced 'Sarah.'"

"Okay. I've never seen it spelled that way before."

I looked at the sheet of paper and saw Donna write two names a few inches apart: "Sera" and "Goodwin." She underlined them for emphasis. Seeing my surname so close to the baby's newly given name unexpectedly filled me with delight. And absolute terror.

"So what happens next?"

"Well, we'll expedite the usual proceedings, since she's a special case. This afternoon I'll mail you a booklet that has all you need to know about becoming a foster parent. You'll have to follow the instructions before we come over for a home inspection. I'll also mail you the relevant forms you'll need to complete, but don't worry about that. I'll go through all the questions, one by one, over the phone with you sometime this week."

Reality suddenly hit me. "What about work? Donna, I can't do this. I have to work. I can't take any more time off."

Donna put her pen down and looked at me kindly. "Adam, I know what a big deal this is. I know we're asking a hell of a lot of you, especially with all you've been through recently. But you have my word that we'll do whatever we can to help you out, including helping you pay for a childcare service at your home during the day. I promise you, we'll come up with a solution."

"And I'll do anything I can to help! We have plenty of resources to assist you," Ms. Nash added. My attitude softened toward her a little, if for no other reason than I knew she'd go out of her way to ensure this arrangement succeeded.

"How long have I got to sort all this out?"

"We could place her in your care within two weeks, so long as you're prepared to undergo the compulsory thirty hours of parenting sessions. Usually you'd have much longer, but in this case we can work you into ongoing sessions if you can attend every evening and for the next two weekends." Donna furrowed her brow and narrowed her eyes as she awaited my reaction, anticipating shock or refusal. But I'd already started to feel like I didn't want to hand the little girl back to Ms. Nash.

I held the baby even closer to me and nodded.

"It'll be okay," Donna said, clearly relieved. She moved off her seat to give me enough room to pry the sleeping baby from my chest. Donna carefully passed the child to Ms. Nash, who looked apprehensive as she took her, desperately trying to stretch out the nap as long as possible.

But Sera woke just as Ms. Nash opened the door. My heart ached as I listened to her screams as they left the building.

CHAPTER THREE

"WHERE DO I start?" I asked, scanning my long list in the Babies"R"Us Superstore in Brooklyn. The wall before us held every kind of stuffed animal imaginable.

"What the hell are you asking *me* for?" Aaron asked, wide-eyed. He began to laugh. It was the same laugh he'd given when I told him I was fostering a baby, and when I told him I needed him to cancel his Saturday plans to help me prepare for the home inspection. "I *still* can't believe we're here!"

My younger brother Aaron worked in downtown Manhattan, but he'd recently bought a house in Brooklyn Heights just across the East River from the city's financial district. He had the cockiness and swagger you'd expect from a carefree guy with youthful good looks and the abundant Wall Street cash he earned. But at heart he was a genuinely good guy. He'd been an accountant for the first few years of his career before he discovered that designing and running accounting software systems for banks yielded a much higher salary. The company for which he worked was a leader in the city, and Aaron was one of their most valued employees.

"You're wasting your time in here. You should be at a pharmacy getting yourself some Xanax, because you sure as hell won't be sleeping anymore," he said, launching stuffed bears at me like they were footballs. He only stopped when he saw an attractive young woman walk past. He cocked his eyebrow and looked her up and down from behind like a cartoon wolf at a burlesque bar.

"Aaron, she's pregnant."

"Yeah, but did you see her...." He cupped his hands in front of his chest. "What I wouldn't do with those things." He winked.

"You're twisted. I'm telling you, Aaron, you're not right in the head." I laughed. "You need to see someone."

"I already am. She's a receptionist at work. Long blonde hair and an ass that—"

"I meant a professional, with a clock and a couch. Anyway, what happened to the girl you were seeing from the Upper East Side?"

"Paige?"

"No, the other one." I nodded at a small stuffed lamb Aaron was holding out for approval.

"Oh, Melanie! It was fun while it lasted but things started to get heavy. She wanted me to spend the whole night at her place."

"Oh no! Not the *whole* night!"

Aaron lightly punched my arm. "You're such a smart-ass. But I'm telling you, I'm far too young to be tied down."

"You're twenty-seven!"

"Exactly! I'm still sowing my wild oats! And I have a hell of a lot of oats to sow."

I laughed and shook my head. I'd seen my younger brother in action. He was handsome, witty, obviously successful, and if all that wasn't enough, he was able to charm himself into almost any woman's good graces—or bed.

Aaron appreciated that I was laughing again. Since Michael died he'd taken to starting every conversation with a somber "*Hey bro, how you doing? You okay?*" He'd had good reason to worry for the first few weeks after the funeral, but as he threw cuddly toys at me, I could tell a weight had lifted from his mind.

"I'll buy this one for her," he said, setting the stuffed lamb in the cart, apart from the others. I appreciated the gesture.

"Right, we need to get a crib, a mattress, bedding, a bottle sterilizer, diapers, a car seat—"

"But you don't drive in the city," Aaron said, joining me and looking over the list.

"No, but they seem handy. You know, you see people walk around with them when they have nowhere else to put their kid. Besides, you have a car here in Brooklyn, so when you babysit you'll need one." It was worth saying just to see the look on his face. "Then we have to get a changing table, a stroller, a mobile, clothes, blankets, and a baby monitor. Oh, and the stuff to babyproof the apartment."

"Seriously? You need all of that? Doesn't Child Protective Services provide you with at least half of this? I mean, you're doing them a favor."

"They help out, but I hate the idea of Sera being in anything secondhand or state-issued. I don't know, it seems right to buy the poor little mite new things. She's been through enough without having to sleep in a secondhand crib." I looked down at my list again. "Besides, I may as well do this right. I've spent every night for the past two weeks learning how to deal with a baby." I sighed before adding, "I wish Mom and Dad were still around. At least they would've been able to help out if I got anything wrong."

Aaron nodded slowly. "And Michael."

He looked for my reaction. I couldn't fault him for it. Aaron was the one who'd introduced us, as they'd worked together at one of the large banks. They'd become friends and he was eager to set us up, as he rightly thought we'd make the perfect couple. I sometimes forgot that he mourned Michael too.

"Are you kidding? Michael would've been as terrified as I am!"

"Are you scared?"

"Of course I am. I'm going to have a little person who depends on me. What if I mess it all up? What on earth was I thinking?"

Aaron slung his arm around the top of my back and squeezed my shoulder. "You're going to be great. It's only temporary. And I'll do anything I can to help."

"I'm not letting you take this baby to the park so you can pick up women."

"Aw, c'mon! Not even the nannies? Or maybe a hot little au pair?"

"No!"

I ducked as a large stuffed elephant flew at my head.

DONNA ARRIVED the following Thursday evening to conduct the home inspection. I'd followed all the instructions to the letter, apart from buying food, as I didn't know whether there was a particular brand of formula Sera was used to. As Donna ticked off her checklist of requirements, she remarked at how impressed she was at the effort I'd put in.

Aaron had helped me set up, and by the end of the weekend I could tell he was feeling a little excited about being a temporary uncle. But even more than Aaron, I'd had help from Maggie O'Dowd, a retired schoolteacher who lived in the apartment next door. She gave me advice and a bit of a head start when it came to my parenting classes. The classes were long, and while others had their husbands or wives to depend on, I often was alone in my attempts to dress, burp, bathe, and take the temperature of the baby doll, with no class partner to remind me what we'd just been taught. The instructor took pity and joined me when she could, but in the scheme of things it was probably better that I got used to being on my own.

"Ms. Nash has asked whether it's possible to drop the baby off tomorrow evening instead of Saturday," Donna said with her brows high. Once again she expected me to protest over the late notice. "It seems that Baby Doe—"

"Sera," I corrected her.

"Yes, of course. Sorry. It seems that Sera still isn't settling with anyone else."

"Sure, bring her along. I finish work at about five, so any time after five thirty should be okay. Have you got the contact numbers I need for childcare next week?"

Donna pulled out a list of names and numbers. "A couple of them might put up a little resistance. Unfortunately Ms. Nash has been rather vocal about this particular child," she said sternly before looking resigned, "but her contacts in the community are invaluable, so I've had to let it slide with no more than a light reprimand."

I couldn't help feeling resentment at Ms. Nash for issuing warnings about Sera, but at the same time, I also worried about what I'd do if Sera didn't settle with me.

"How did the meeting with the Erb's Palsy support group go?" Donna asked.

"It was good. The doctor showed us how to massage and stimulate the muscles in the arm and shoulder. He said that there's a good chance Sera will get the full use of her arm back if I keep up the techniques he showed me. I've got his number, so whoever takes over from me as permanent foster parents can go along and see him. Or I can show them myself."

As I showed Donna out, she said, "Adam, I know you've been though a rough time recently, and I know I've already said this, but thank you. I'm not blind to what you're taking on for us. If you have any problems, any problems at all, contact me directly and I'll sort them out."

I WRAPPED up work at four thirty on Friday to give myself enough time to get home and wait for Sera to arrive. As I pushed through the communal glass doors at the entrance of my building, I heard the echo of a baby crying. I hurried up the two flights of stairs to find Ms. Nash looking impatiently at Sera, who suddenly fell silent, apart from the odd post-cry hiccup. Ms. Nash looked annoyed that once again I'd calmed the baby apparently by doing nothing at all.

"I didn't expect you until after five thirty," I said, pulling the keys out of my briefcase.

"I thought I'd arrive a little early to make sure I was on time," Ms. Nash said, holding Sera out to me like she was an unexploded bomb.

"Would you like to come in?" I asked, dropping my briefcase and taking Sera onto my hip while I watched Ms. Nash furiously search her large satchel. She shook her head and retrieved her clipboard.

"I just need your signature here, Mr. Goodwin."

I signed the form and handed back her pen. "She's due for a feed in about half an hour," Ms. Nash said as she buttoned up her coat. I didn't know whether the "Good luck!" and little wave she gave as she turned and walked away were intended for me or the baby.

I pulled Sera up onto my chest and held her with one arm while I opened the door and kicked my briefcase into the short hallway of the apartment.

"Hello, sweetheart!" I said, and I nuzzled my nose against hers. The fears I had that it may have just been a fluke that she'd taken to me were gone in an instant when she giggled. In fact, all my worries disappeared the moment I saw her outside my door. I sat on the couch and perched her on my lap.

"Have you missed me?" I gently poked at her belly with every word. "Have. You. Missed. Me? I've. Missed. You. Yes. I. Have!"

When she stopped giggling, she looked at me and waited for me to say or do something else to make her chuckle. I clamped my hand over my eyes. Not because I was about to play peekaboo, but because I'd just remembered I hadn't bought baby formula. I'd been so excited about seeing her that I'd completely forgotten to ask Ms. Nash what brand she was used to. I looked at Sera, full of apology.

"Oh dear, I've only had you for five minutes and I'm already neglecting you. I have to go out and get you some food, sweetheart," I said, trying to figure out where the nearest store was. A Chinese family ran a convenience store across the street that I dropped by every morning on the way to work. I was almost sure they'd have baby formula. The owners, Lei and Choi, had recently had a baby themselves, so I took a chance.

"Let's go and see if Miss Dee can hold you for a couple of minutes while I run across the street and get you some food."

It was the first time I'd ever been left alone with any baby, let alone Sera. With her arm as it was, I needed to figure out the best way to carry her before I took her outside. It was rush hour on a Friday evening, and I wasn't prepared to take any risks.

I knocked on Miss Dee's door, but there was no answer. I walked next door to Maggie's and knocked. Maggie had been such a big help to me already and, like Miss Dee, had expressed excitement at meeting Sera. They'd both been counting down the days and often reminded me how long I had left until Sera arrived whenever we passed in the hallway. Surely Maggie would be more than happy to hold her for a few minutes. But, again, there was no answer.

As I turned and settled into the realization that I might have to bite the bullet and take Sera into the nightmare that was "outside," I heard laughter coming from behind Maria Fuentes's door. Maria was also retired but still worked as a volunteer at Amnesty International in Midtown four mornings a week. She was as sweet as could be, and we'd gotten to know each other well. Like my own work, the subject matter she dealt with on a daily basis sometimes weighed heavily on her.

I knocked, and when Maria opened the door, her eyes widened and she gasped. "Is this her? Is this the little one?"

"No, I just stole this one from outside Macy's. You know, for practice."

Maria was about to give me a well-deserved slap on my arm when I saw Miss Dee and Maggie rise from the kitchen table, dropping the cards they held and abandoning their weekly gin rummy game.

They both hurried to the door, only to be shooed back as Maria beckoned me in.

"Ladies, this is Sera!" I said, presenting her like a proud father to a packed maternity ward waiting room.

Almost immediately three pairs of arms rose, ready to take her from me.

"Now, ladies, I'm a bad person, and I have forgotten to get her formula."

"Oh, Adam," Miss Dee said in mock disapproval, the kind that showed forgiveness for my bad parenting would only be granted if she was the first to hold the baby. "You want us to hold her for you while you go get some?"

"Would you mind? It's only across the street. I'll only be a few minutes, I promise," I said, handing Sera into her arms. I paused for a moment to make sure Sera didn't start screaming like she did with Ms. Nash. Thankfully, though, she quietly stared up, her gaze darting among the women.

Maria and Maggie stood behind and looked upon Miss Dee as she raised Sera up in the air. "Oh, child, we've been waiting for you!"

WHEN I returned I found the ladies cooing over Sera, whom Maggie was holding propped up on the table. I looked to see if her eyes were red but she seemed bemused, though happy, with the three women, and they seemed completely mesmerized by her.

"She is just the most beautiful little thing in the world," Miss Dee said, taking the bag of formula from me. "I got this, honey. You sit down and relax."

"I haven't got time to relax," I said as Miss Dee opened the tin of formula and began to prepare it. It was a relief to get hands-on instruction on how to feed a real-life baby instead of a plastic doll. "I have a list of numbers I have to get through to arrange childcare next week. I'll probably spend the entire weekend trying to sort out a schedule."

"I can look after her during the day while you're at work!" Miss Dee exclaimed.

"Thanks for the offer. I really appreciate it, but I couldn't impose on you like that."

"Oh, child, don't be silly! It's no imposition. If I could handle my two girls when they were babies, I can handle this sweet little thing."

Miss Dee could see my concern. She might have been an active woman, but she was in her early sixties. It would be far too much to take on at her age.

Maggie broke the awkward silence. "Why not let Miss Dee take her two days a week and let me take her two days a week too."

"Thanks, Maggie. Again, I really do appreciate the offers, but she's going to take a lot of—"

"—looking after? Adam, I looked after a classroom of six-year-olds for thirty-seven years. Do you think I couldn't handle one baby?"

Maria looked on. I raised my eyebrow, expecting her to show solidarity with her friends and encourage me to give Miss Dee and Maggie a chance. Instead she slowly dipped her head. "I know I've never had any children myself, but I'd love to take her on Fridays when I'm not working. I may not have as much experience, but Maggie and Miss Dee are just down the hall should I need any help."

I could have argued with Miss Dee and Maggie, but Maria was different. Widowed at a young age, she had never remarried or had children. I knew having time with Sera could bring her a joy she'd never had the chance to experience.

"Adam," Maggie said softly. "We think what you're doing is just so... so admirable. You've been through so much lately, and we've had to stand by helpless."

"But you've all helped me, ladies, and I can't thank you enough."

"Please, Adam, let us help you with this," Maria said with the same soft pleading tone. "This is what we want."

"But my hours can be strange. I could be called out in the evening to go defend someone who's just been arrested, or I could be kept late at work."

"Then doesn't it make sense that you have three women in your building who can be on hand to take her when you need it, rather than waiting for babysitters to arrive?" Miss Dee reasoned.

I had to admit it made sense. The convenience of having three babysitters so close, and ones I knew and could trust, was too tempting an offer to refuse. I also wondered whether, as retired women, they could use the extra cash Donna had promised to help with childcare. I explained they would all be subject to home inspections by CPS and that they would have to fill out paperwork, but they waved that off as no big deal. When I agreed that I couldn't find fault with their idea, the women beamed and turned to Sera, who happily shook her good arm up and down, causing her whole body to bounce on the table.

"Before you go, I remember you said the social worker told you she had trouble sleeping. So I bought her this," Maria said, handing me a bag. "It's a pillow filled with lavender. Put it somewhere in her room. It will help soothe her to sleep."

"Thank you so much, Maria," I said as I held the pillow up to my nose and took in its scent. "I guess we'll soon find out if it works."

I took Sera home and put the padded baby-changing mat on the dining table. I carefully took off her little state-issued onesie and softly massaged her palm, arm, and shoulder with a touch of baby lotion. Though I'd been through the training and the demonstrations with the doctor, I was nervous I would somehow hurt her, despite knowing she had no feeling in her arm. With two fingers I gently rubbed in a circular motion as she stared up at me. I carefully bent her elbow several times, raised her arm above her head as I'd been instructed, and massaged the outside of her tiny bicep. When I finished, I delicately pulled her arm back through the sleeve of a new fleece onesie I'd bought on the trip with Aaron. I gave her belly a little shake for being so brave. Then, in a moment that felt like a barrel of pure joy had been poured over me, she smiled at me and the apartment felt full again.

Later that evening, as I lay on the sofa with the television volume turned down low, Sera fell asleep on my chest. As her little back rose and fell in a deep slumber, I wondered whether it was the first time she felt safe. I should have moved her to the crib, but she looked so peaceful. I pulled the throw cushions from the sofa to my side to box us in. Without the use of her left arm to help her turn, it was unlikely she'd roll, but I didn't want to take any chances.

I hadn't meant to, but Sera's calm somehow transferred to me, and I reluctantly fell into my own deep sleep. It was the first time in months the usual nightmares didn't appear to torture me. I woke in the early hours as I felt Sera shift on my chest. I raised my hand to her back to steady her, panicked for a moment that she might fall.

"It's okay," I whispered as we both drifted back to sleep. "Daddy's got you."

CHAPTER FOUR

"AB-BA!"

"No, sweetheart. Da-da!" I said as I zoomed a spoon heaped with applesauce toward her mouth. She smacked her lips, ready for the last spoonful. Her left arm bobbed a little at her side. The massage was working. Though her arm still wasn't completely functional, she'd managed to create a fist with her hand. I encouraged her determination by holding her near the wooden handles of the kitchen cabinets. I knew it wouldn't be long before she could show her strength by opening a door by herself.

"Ab-ba!"

"It's okay, sweetheart, you'll get it," I said through a smile as I wiped her face. "Let's get you ready for your big day!"

I looked at my precious little girl and let out a happy sigh. Everything in my life had become better with Sera in it. The arrangement with Maggie, Miss Dee, and Maria had worked out perfectly. They'd been invaluable over the past nine months, something I tried to remind them of every day. And looking after Sera had become what they described as a highlight of their lives. They simply adored her.

Coming home to Sera every evening also affected my daily work life in a positive way. In the years I'd been a Legal Aid attorney, I'd seen truly terrible acts of neglect, violence, and cruelty to both children and adults. Before Sera, these ugly acts had played on my mind and often dragged me down for days. But seeing that little face lighting up each evening when I picked her up from the ladies put everything I'd experienced that day into the shade. If anything, being a parent made me better at my job, as I developed more empathy, especially with families going through hardship. Sera made me want to do more to help, to try harder so I could give others just a touch of the happiness she gave me.

One of the biggest surprises came from Aaron, whom I hadn't expected to take to Sera so strongly. I assumed the novelty would wear off and I'd see less of him, but I was wrong. He often came over to the apartment and demanded that we take Sera out for the afternoon or to the zoo or the park on the weekends. He even offered to babysit to give me a chance to go out with friends and relax a little.

Listening to friends with kids over the years, I'd heard you don't know what love is until you have a child. It's an absolute, whole, and unconditional love. Even though Sera wasn't of my blood, I found it impossible to believe I could love her any more than I did. She brought me a joy I never thought I could feel and a sense of purpose and responsibility that I cherished. So when Donna suggested I apply to adopt her, I didn't even have to think about it. I knew there would be massive hurdles to overcome, but I also knew having Donna and Judge Adesso on my side gave me a good chance. As I expected, Ms. Nash hadn't made much of an attempt, if any, to find Sera another home anyway, so there was no competition when it came to my application.

"Where's the birthday girl?" Aaron called, pretending not to see Sera. He breezed through the door without knocking, bearing an armful of stuffed animals and a wrapped box with a giant pink bow. He was accompanied by a beautiful young woman who walked behind him looking a little embarrassed and nervous. This was his latest squeeze, whom he'd met at a club in Hell's Kitchen and with whom he'd had an on-and-off relationship for the previous few months. It was mostly "on" when it suited him.

"I don't know why you keep buying her those animals, Aaron. She never lets go of that lamb you bought her," I said, nodding to the slightly tired-looking cuddly toy that was wedged in Sera's high chair next to her. Aaron walked over and kissed the side of her head with such affection that her head bounced back a little. She giggled, as she always did.

"I had to get her something. It's her first birthday!"

This wasn't strictly true, since we didn't know exactly when she'd been born. Rather than give a rough date, I'd decided to make her birthday the day I discovered her. I might have been a number of weeks off, but the day we found each other was just as worthy of a celebration as the day she came into the world. Perhaps even more.

It wasn't long before the apartment became cramped. Miss Dee sang in the kitchen area as she prepared food, while Maria and Maggie decorated the dining table with party hats, streamers, and colorful paper plates. Aaron and his girlfriend helped with the drinks. Lei and Choi, the owners of the convenience store across the street, looked after Sera and their own little girl, Meena, while I welcomed guests.

With my friends, neighbors, and colleagues in the room and Sera in my arms, we all sang "Happy Birthday." Sera looked utterly bewildered, which I kind of understood, as I'd never heard a group of people sing with so much enthusiasm before.

We were midway through the tune when the apartment door opened and Donna's head popped around. I waved her in, and she sheepishly joined in with the last line of the chorus. As people clapped and cheered, I handed Sera to Aaron and went to greet her.

"You made it!" I said before giving her a quick peck on the cheek. In recent months I'd grown much closer to Donna, as we often met for updates on Sera over lunch. "I thought you had to work."

"Is there somewhere we can talk?" she asked, looking around the crowded apartment.

"Sure. It's getting loud in here."

"Can we go outside into the hallway?"

"What is it? Have they rejected my application?" I asked. I'd tried to prepare myself mentally for this. I knew there was a chance someone else might apply to adopt her, but I couldn't bear the idea of Sera being anyone else's child.

"Your application has just been put on hold. I'll explain more outside."

I followed her into the hallway. Each step felt like an emotional stab at my heart.

AARON MUST have seen how pale I was when I walked back through the door, as he immediately handed Sera to Miss Dee. He held his palms up and shuffled me back into the hallway. Once outside I fell against the wall and slid down onto my haunches, burying my face in my hands.

"What's wrong? What's happened?"

"A girl has come forward claiming to be Sera's mother," I said, desperately trying to keep control. "But there seems to be some confusion as to whether it's her or not."

"What do you mean?"

"Apparently a young girl went to Social Services and the police to report that she'd abandoned her baby in New York about a year ago. Donna, the woman you just saw, works at CPS. She said this girl has some sort of mental health issue and has admitted to being a former crack addict. Apparently she was so doped up on antipsychotic drugs, she can't remember where she left her baby. They obviously had to look into it, and the only baby found around that time that hasn't been returned or identified is Sera."

Aaron slid down the wall next to me and put his arm across my shoulders. "But if she has mental health issues and she dumped her baby somewhere, surely they're not going to just give her back to her. If she's unstable or a drug addict, there's no way they'll put Sera back in her care."

"Donna said that there's a chance this girl wasn't even pregnant. She may just be having a psychotic episode or recalling a bad trip when she thought she gave birth. Whatever happened, she's convinced she's had a baby and has gone to Legal Aid to get representation."

"Would they represent her? Knowing her background?"

"Mentally unstable or not, she still has rights."

"But even if Sera is hers, there is no way—"

"Aaron, it's not that simple," I said impatiently. "If they do a DNA test, which they'll no doubt insist on, it could prove Sera is hers. Even if the state decides she isn't capable of looking after her, the girl's parents could step in. I've seen this a hundred times before. The courts always grant custody to the maternal grandparents if they've filed for it. So it's not even about the girl, it's about her family."

"Selfish bitch," Aaron spat angrily.

"Aaron, don't be like that."

"But you said she was a crazy, whacked-out drug addict. I think it's pretty clear she didn't give a damn about Sera. Anyway, why come forward after all this time?"

I shrugged.

"Try not to worry," Aaron said, softening his tone. "We'll get through this."

I RECEIVED notification to present Sera for a DNA test four days later. It would be a quick swab of her mouth, and the court would be notified of the results once the possible mother had produced her sample. I should have been worried, even terrified, but Sera, as she'd done since I first laid eyes on her, gave me a sense of calm that everything would work out.

Unfortunately I only felt that way when I was with her. The moment I dropped her off to Maggie, Maria, or Miss Dee to head to work, each step away from her wore away my confidence. By the third day, I was at my wits' end. I finally couldn't take the uncertainty and paid an unannounced visit to Donna's office, worried she might try to put off seeing me, as we both knew there was only so much confidential information she could share.

When I arrived I stood at reception in the communal room that held people waiting to see various social workers.

"Can I help you, sir?" asked the young receptionist.

"Is Donna Wilson available?"

"She's with someone at the moment but shouldn't be too long. But she's at lunch straight after. Do you have an appointment?"

"No, I'm a friend. I'll catch her when she comes out, if that's okay?"

The receptionist nodded and continued her work.

I hated putting Donna in such an awkward position, but if she could tell me something—anything—that could give me a little peace, it was worth it.

I'd just turned my head after reading a "Suicidal? Call the Samaritans" poster when I saw Chris Randall, a bright young Legal Aid attorney with whom I'd worked in the past. He walked through the waiting room and, after a quick knock, entered Donna's office.

After what seemed like an eternity, the door to Donna's office opened and she and Chris stepped out, closely followed by a young white girl in her early twenties. An older, well-presented couple who looked as if they could be her parents accompanied her. Donna froze when she spotted me but managed to compose herself quickly enough not to alert Chris, who was in the process of showing the family out. Her look was enough to tell me whom she'd been meeting.

I turned my eyes back to the girl. She was pale, and her skin was worn and leathery and scarred with pockmarks. I knew this wasn't unusual for a drug addict or someone suffering from a mental disorder. Hygiene was often the first thing to go when they entered the downward spiral. But she was dressed well and didn't have the hollow cheeks of someone who'd just come in off the streets, so I assumed her parents were caring for her. The only thing I noticed that could connect her to Sera was her long, curling auburn hair. I wondered whether she could have been with a light-skinned black or Hispanic man—a mix that could have given Sera her light tan color.

"Chris, you go on ahead. I'll see you at Starbucks. I've just remembered I have to make a quick phone call," Donna said. She watched without expression until they left the waiting room, then turned and signaled me to follow her into her office.

"I'm so sorry, Donna. If I'd known you were busy—" I said as I closed the door behind me. Donna sat back on her chair and sighed as she massaged her temples. "Was that…?"

Donna nodded. "If that meeting had gone another way, your presence here could have been incredibly awkward," she said severely. Then she smiled. "But it seems that you don't have anything to worry about. The claim has been retracted. She's refused to give a sample for the DNA test and told me that she never had a child. She apologized profusely for all the trouble she's caused."

I looked blankly at her. We both knew that wasn't characteristic of a girl with the kind of issues she had. She must have been coached in some way.

"There's a good chance she never had a baby. But if she did, it seems that her parents have convinced her to withdraw her claim." Donna sighed. "To be honest, I feel sorry for the girl. She's obviously very troubled. But from what I've just seen, she's lucky to have a great mom and dad who are there for her."

"So what was said?"

Donna took a moment, as if contemplating whether to confide in me. It seemed since the girl had withdrawn her claim, she decided to tell me what she knew.

"Apparently the girl went on a bit of a binge. She stocked up on her legitimate antipsychotic medication and decided to take off. It took her parents months to find her and bring her home. She has her ups and downs, like most people who suffer from her type of issues. They take their meds, which makes them feel better. They feel better so they think they no longer have any problems and stop taking the medication. Then, of course, the medication wears off, they have a dip in sanity, start taking risks and making bad choices, and then it's drugs and hitting rock bottom before being committed to a psych ward. They get evaluated, medicated, and released back into the community. Then the cycle repeats itself."

"But they must've done a physical on her when she was committed."

"They don't look for evidence of past pregnancies, Adam."

"So there's no chance she'll come back?"

"I doubt it. And between you and me, I think Chris probably knows a lot more than he's letting on and has nudged her in the right direction. False reports to the police will land her in trouble if she wasn't pregnant, and she could face abandonment charges filed by CPS if she was. At the end of the day, it seems the matter is settled. I'll make sure that your adoption application isn't held up anymore. In fact, I'll see what I can do to get it bumped up just in case. I can't tell you how much it's stressed me out, thinking you could lose her."

"But if Sera is hers—and I can't believe I'm saying this—don't you think she has a right to know where her child is? Or at least know that she's safe? If she truly believes she gave birth, not knowing what happened to the baby would surely just send her into an even worse spiral. I know it would kill me not to know."

"I think between her lawyer, parents, and her own uncertainty, she's come to terms with the fact that she never was pregnant."

"I'd still like to be sure."

"Adam, I can't order the girl to go for a cervical exam! Let it go and get on with your lives. If you want confirmation that Sera isn't hers, take it from me. In her original statement, she was confused about the dates anyway. To be honest, I'm pretty sure she made the whole thing up to emancipate herself from her parents and apply for housing. The application would have been easier for her if she had a baby."

Donna looked sympathetically at me.

"I know you've been worked up in knots over this, and I can't say I blame you. But really, you have nothing to worry about. As far as I'm concerned, Sera's mother still hasn't come forward, and the chances are she never will. Now go home and enjoy being with your daughter and stop overthinking this."

THREE MONTHS later, amid cheers and tears of joy in the courtroom, the adoption was complete and Sera was legally declared my child.

CHAPTER FIVE

IN THE three years since the adoption, Sera had grown into a proper little girl with long dark locks of unruly auburn hair and half a dozen tiny freckles on each cheek that darkened in the summer. I'd decided from the beginning to be honest with her about the circumstances that led to us being together. At every bedtime I read her a story, deliberately including characters who were adopted, brought by storks, or found in a cabbage patch, but all of whom ended up in happy families.

Though the movement in her left arm had returned, she still had to work hard to strengthen her hand. She grasped at every door handle to show her continued improvement, even managing to turn the solid brass handle of the front door when she reached up on tiptoes. Miss Dee, Maggie, and Maria managed to keep up with her as she learned to walk and then to run. She'd become a confident and gregarious little girl who people warmed to instantly. She'd started pre-K and was not only adept at learning but also popular. The other kids in the school, including Lei and Choi's little girl, Meena, were so taken with her that they competed, sometimes violently, for her attention. But Sera was happiest when she was at home.

I never would have imagined giving up my job at Legal Aid to return to the world of corporate law, but the odd hours the city had me working were too hard to juggle with a small child who now had her own schedule. Besides, I missed her terribly when I was called out in the evenings. Also, since I'd formally adopted Sera, I was no longer entitled to financial help from the state, and the much-improved salary would more than cover the money I paid to the three ladies who cared for Sera during the day, though each week brought a battle to get them to accept it.

Aaron had heard of an opening at a firm in the city with a reputation for treating their attorneys well and not discriminating against those who didn't work the usual seventy-hour weeks most other law firms expected. Of course working nine-to-five would make the partnership track longer, but it allowed more time with my daughter. The firm offered me some pro-bono work for the city too, so I was able to keep up with old colleagues, cases, and friends. This benefitted them too, as the firm was able to take advantage of my contacts at the prosecutor's office.

Everything was working out well. The only thing that gave me pause in those early years was that Sera often seemed distracted and sometimes looked as though she was in a trance, as if she was paying attention or listening to something that simply wasn't there. Occasionally she erupted into laughter or her eyes wandered like she was following something invisible in midair. I took her to the doctor, but he found nothing to indicate she suffered from epilepsy or any other disorder.

The mystery of these mini states of invisible distraction stopped one day when, out of nowhere, she pointed to the wall and shouted "Sophia!"

This was my first introduction to my little girl's new friend.

"ADAM, YOUR daughter is fearless!" Aaron said as he walked in the door with Sera, who was holding an ice cream and smiling. "You should've seen her. There was a huge dog at the park, and this one—" He stopped and pointed to Sera, who now had ice cream all over her hands and running down her cheeks. "—she goes over and starts petting it like it was a bunny!"

I tore off a strip of paper towel and wiped Sera's face and hands before Aaron put her down.

"How's your arm?" I asked Sera, who was flicking it out as if to stretch the muscles. She'd worked so hard to overcome all the symptoms of the Erb's Palsy, but the exercises left her with muscle cramps and tremors in her biceps and forearm that flared up occasionally.

"It hurts a little bit."

"Go get the bottle, sweetheart."

Miss Dee had bought Sera a bottle of chamomile lotion when she was a baby, saying that it would help soothe her muscles. As a gift for her first birthday, she'd given Sera a ceramic bottle to refill with the lotion, on which she'd hand painted a single small white flower. Each following year, on her birthday, Miss Dee would paint another one onto it, adding to the bouquet. Of all the things she'd received over the years, Sera was most careful with this. Even I was nervous of handling the bottle for fear of breaking what I'd nicknamed Miss Dee's Daisy Dispenser.

When she returned, Sera gave the bottle to her uncle to apply. Aaron pushed the little sleeve of her Muppets T-shirt up over her shoulder and began massaging the lotion onto her muscles. He couldn't resist tickling under her arm to make her scream with laughter.

"Go play in your room," I said as Aaron pulled her sleeve back down.

She wanted to stay with her uncle but didn't argue. She rarely did. Once she was out of earshot, I turned to Aaron. "What the hell were you doing letting her play with dogs at the park? Why did you let her get close enough to the damn thing in the first place?"

"Well, I was chatting with this hot au pair. She was gorgeous... European... French, I think. Anyway, she didn't speak much English. Not that she needed to speak English, having such a massive set of—"

"So you let Sera run around while you were trying to hook up? What the hell is wrong with you?"

"No, it wasn't like that. I was watching her! There were loads of kids running around and on the monkey bars and swings. Then some asshole walking his dog let it off the leash, and it ran into the playground. All the kids scattered. Sera was on the top of the slide, so she was out of reach. But then she slid down and charged toward the dog and started petting it. I ran over, half expecting the damn thing to rip her arm off, but it just laid down in front of her and bowed its head. It was unbelievable."

"I'd better talk to her. She's too brave for her own good sometimes," I said, shaking my head. Hardly anything fazed her, even things that would scare any other kid.

"I know it's not my place, but I did tell her off a bit." Aaron looked a little sheepish.

"No, it's okay. It needed to be said there and then, so you did the right thing."

"She kept saying she knew she'd be okay because Sophia was there. Who's Sophia?"

"Sophia is her imaginary friend. She's been around for a while, and apparently I trip over her all the time," I said, remembering Sera pushing my legs because I'd supposedly bumped into the invisible child.

"Well, Sera wants me to buy her and Sophia a puppy."

"That conniving little—" I laughed. "Still, I have to hand it to her, she's consistent with her demands. She must've asked me a hundred times. Maybe she thinks you're a softer touch."

"Let me buy her one!"

"And it seems she's right."

"Please!"

"Hell no! The last thing I need is a puppy tearing up the place. Sorry, you'll have to be the bad guy on this one."

Aaron looked crestfallen that he wouldn't get the chance to earn Greatest Uncle of All Time status from the little girl he adored. "So what's the deal with this Sophia?"

"Oh, she goes everywhere with her—the park, the toy store. Miss Dee takes Sera to a gospel church in Harlem every other Sunday. She absolutely loves it there. Apparently she even sways and claps her hands when she sings. She comes home like she's high on sugar. Sera says she takes Sophia along so they can learn the words to the songs together."

"You let her go to church?" Aaron said, astonished.

"Yeah, why not? She's still only a kid. Besides, she only likes it there because of the singing. It's not as if she understands anything about the sermon."

Aaron still looked surprised. "I didn't think you'd raise her with the whole religion thing." Though we were both raised in the church, it had never been important in our adult lives.

"I didn't think I would either, but I was chatting with Maggie recently, and she said that I should start thinking about where Sera will go to school. She used to teach at St. Katherine's Catholic School, which is only three blocks away. It's a private school with a great reputation. Apparently it's quite hard to get into. But she said once she explains the circumstances, there's a good chance she could get her in there."

"What's wrong with a normal school?"

"It is a normal school. But I have to think about what's best. If it's only three blocks away, I can take her to school every morning before I go to work. Maggie, Maria, and Miss Dee are pretty old,

Aaron. They can manage a three-block walk to pick her up every day, but not a trek across the city. It's more out of convenience than anything else."

"A private school? That's gonna cost some money."

"That's another reason I went back to working for a firm."

Aaron nodded. "I suppose that makes sense. Did you want me to look into college funds?"

"Can you believe we're talking about this now?"

"We have to," Aaron said, giving a mock wistful look. "They grow so fast."

MAGGIE PULLED some strings and fought in my corner with the dean and a mix of nuns and civilian teachers and finally managed to secure Sera a place at St. Katherine's. I knew it couldn't have been easy, especially given the church's view of gay men. I don't know whether they'd taken pity at the story of Sera's start in life, or whether Maggie, being held in such high regard, had simply insisted on it.

Life took on a whole new routine. I looked at my little five-year-old in her pint-sized royal blue blazer and her striped blue-and-gray tie and wondered where the time had gone. The first morning I dropped her off at school I welled up. The nun teaching her class said she would address the subject of adoption when the kids introduced themselves and talked about their families. I struggled over whether this was necessary, but I didn't want Sera to have to explain to each child individually why she only had a dad. I hated the idea of her being bullied or sneered at for not having a mom. But that fear proved needless. Just like pre-K, she was immediately popular with every kid in her class.

SERA RAN into the kitchen on Monday morning, where I was preparing her lunch for school. "Girl power!" she screamed and struck a pose with her hip jutted out to one side. Her hand punched into the air and her fingers gave the peace sign.

"Sera, please!" I dropped to my knees and pretended to beg. "Not again. Please, not again. Anything but the Spice Girls!"

"Girl power!" she screamed again and then ran back into her room before playing the songs I'd heard a hundred times over the previous month.

"Are you ready? We're going to be late!" I yelled over the noise before muttering, "Damn you, Geri Halliwell, you have a lot to answer for."

The music switched off, and I leaned back against the counter and sipped my coffee. Sera walked in with her tie loose around her neck.

"There's another girl in my class called Sera," she said as I lifted her onto the kitchen island. "But she spells her name Sa-ah-rah-ah-huh."

"And how do you spell your name?"

"Se-eh-ruh-ah," she said, looking pleased with herself. "Daddy, why did you call me Sera?"

"It was my mommy's name. But she spelled it the same way your little friend does," I said as I grappled with the knot of her tie. I wanted to make it perfect, lest the nuns judge me.

"Why is mine spelled a different way?"

"Well, when Grandma was unsure of something, she would shrug and say, 'Oh, que sera!' When I was your age, I thought she was just putting on a funny voice and talking to herself, saying 'Okay, Sarah!' But if she was nervous or worried about something, or wasn't too sure of what to expect, instead of saying it, she would sing it. Years later I found out that it was a song called *Que Sera, Sera*, and the words she was singing actually meant something completely different, because they are Spanish."

"What do they mean?"

"Whatever will be, will be."

"Sing it to me, Daddy!"

I picked Sera off the counter, held her at my hip, and extended her little arm out. I spun us around once, then began our short dance across the kitchen like ballroom partners as I sung the classic Doris Day song.

At the end of my rendition, I sat her back on the island and straightened her tie again. "So, sweetheart, when you were just a baby and I got the chance to look after you, I was nervous because I wasn't too sure if I would be a good daddy. And that song popped into my head. So I called you Sera."

She smiled at the story.

"You're the best daddy ever."

"You think?"

"Yes, and Sophia thinks so too."

"Really? And what else does Sophia tell you?"

"Lots of things."

"Like what?"

"That I'm special."

"Of course you're special!" I said, attacking her with tickles under her arms. "Sweetheart, you know I love you, right?"

"Yes."

"So don't be mad when I say this, but we have to talk about Sophia. You know, you're getting to be a big girl now. I don't think your friends at school will understand about Sophia because no one else can see her. So I think it's time you stopped talking about her. Do you understand?"

She looked utterly confused. I didn't blame her. In the past I'd sat down for tea with Sera, three dolls, a stuffed lamb, and Sophia, and had partaken in perfectly normal conversations with every one of them. I chastised myself for practically encouraging it for so long.

"But she's real, Daddy."

"No more, Sera, okay?"

Sera nodded sadly and shifted herself off the counter.

"Go get your satchel for school."

"Yes, Daddy," she said in resignation. She turned to her imaginary friend one last time and held her finger up to her lips as if to shush her once and for all.

SERA TOOK my hand as I walked her to school. She'd remained quiet since our talk but looked like she was on the verge of blurting something out. As we passed St. Katherine's Church, I felt her hand pull as she began to trail behind me. Her head was turned, looking at a disheveled man in his early thirties who sat on the steps leading up to the church doors. He wore a ragged old parka jacket, a pair of mismatched sneakers with no socks, suit pants, fingerless gloves, and a woolen hat. His dark stubble framed a mouth that didn't even hint at a smile. I didn't like the way he stared at Sera so intently, so I shot a look in his direction to show I'd noticed him. He turned away.

Outside the school gates, I looked Sera over to make sure she was presentable. I checked that she had her brown bag lunch, rebuttoned her blazer, and gave her a hug. I knew she was still angry with me, but I couldn't bear the idea of her spending the day resenting me.

"Now, you remember what I said about Sophia?"

"Yes, Daddy."

"Good girl. You know Daddy loves you more than anything in the whole wide world?"

She nodded a little grumpily, so I gave her a raspberry on her cheek until she smiled.

I watched as she skipped toward the school gates.

"Sera," I called after her, "come back!"

I crouched down as she skipped back to me. I pointed at her shoes, which were untied. She wobbled as she balanced her foot on my knee.

"Is that too tight?" I asked as I tied her shoelace into a double knot. She shook her head. Sera knew how to do this herself, but she occasionally had some residual awkwardness in her hand from the Erb's Palsy, so she often didn't tie them quite tight enough.

"Come on, Sophia," she said as she headed off.

"Sera!"

She turned, guilt plastered all over her face. "Sorry, Daddy!"

CHAPTER SIX

THE END of 1996 brought heavy winter snow. The tourists delighted in the pre-Christmas fairytale of New York, but we residents barricaded ourselves out of the bitter cold into the warm sanctuaries of our homes. With not much else to do on a Sunday afternoon, Sera entertained herself while I caught up with work I needed to complete before we braved the outdoors on Monday to return to school and office.

I'd set up a desk and computer in front of the kitchen island as a kind of home office and was busy on a brief when I overheard Sera talking. I turned to see her watching *The Lion, the Witch, and the Wardrobe* on TV.

"Sorry, sweetheart, I missed what you said."

She laughed. "I wasn't talking to you, Daddy!"

Assuming she was talking to Aslan on the screen or expressing her fears that the White Witch was going to do something terrible to the lion, I returned to my work.

"Is Uncle Aaron coming over at Christmas?"

"Yes, he'll be here to bring you the extra presents that Santa couldn't bring."

"Santa's not real."

I had to laugh. It was the way she said it, as if I'd said the most ridiculous thing she'd ever heard.

"Well, little girls who don't believe in Santa don't usually get presents. You have to believe in him or he might skip you!"

Sera turned and climbed onto her knees so her head looked at me over the back of the sofa. "I'll believe it when I see a puppy. Otherwise I ain't buying it!"

I clamped my lips shut to stifle my laugh. Every so often I'd hear Maggie's or Maria's voices come out of her mouth. But when Miss Dee's appeared, or rather Sera's deliberate impression of her, it usually meant she was in a mischievous mood or wanted something. *"You understand me? Child, I ain't playin'. I ain't playin'!"*

Ordinarily she would have me in tears of laughter as she nailed Miss Dee's mannerisms. She could usually count on me to give way— it was hard to say no when I was doubled over in hysterics—but this time I had to remain strong. I turned back to my desk so she couldn't see me smile. "Okay, but don't blame me if you get a lump of coal in your stocking on Christmas morning."

I wanted just one more year of seeing her excitement build as the days led up to Santa's visit.

MONDAY MORNING came, and I bundled Sera up in her uniform, coat, scarf, hat, and gloves. We walked briskly to school, passing the homeless man on the steps of the church. He watched us as he pulled down the scarf wrapped around his mouth to take a swig from a cheap bottle of wine. Sera saw him watch us too, but rather than shy away, she let go of my hand and turned on the sidewalk.

"God loves you, Oscar!" she cried out before taking my hand again.

I looked over just in time to see the man replace the scarf around his nose and mouth and pull down the front of his knitted hat. For a moment I expected some abuse, the rant of a homeless man drunk at eight thirty in the morning. Instead I saw his eyes smile as the exposed tops of his cheeks rose.

We got to the school gate but I kept hold of Sera's hand. The other parents looked as if they couldn't say good-bye fast enough and get into their warm cars.

"Sera, do you know that man?"

"No."

"So what does that make him?"

She knew what was coming. "A stranger."

"And what don't we do?"

"We don't talk to strangers. But Daddy, you were with me, and he looked so cold and unhappy!"

"Why did you call him Oscar?"

"Because he reminds me of Oscar from *Sesame Street*. He looks grouchy, but I'm sure he's nice, really."

The bell rang, and the other children started running toward the main doors of the school. "Sera, promise me you won't talk to him again. Okay?"

She nodded and, satisfied that I wasn't too angry with her, got on the tips of her toes to show she was ready for her kiss good-bye.

FOR THE next two weeks, the citywide freeze didn't let up. It was colder than I'd ever known it. The day school broke for the Christmas holiday, I was in my office running through a client brief and about to head into a meeting when my phone rang. It was Sister Rose from St. Katherine's, asking whether I would be picking up Sera from school and if I wouldn't mind dropping by to see her.

"Is everything okay?" I asked as I scrambled for the papers I needed.

"Yes, Mr. Goodwin. Sera's absolutely fine! I'd just like to have a little chat, if that's okay?"

"Sure. Sister, I'm so sorry but I'm late for a meeting. Sera's usually picked up by a neighbor, but I'll make sure I leave early to get there myself."

I REACHED the school just as the kids ran out to their waiting parents, satchels bouncing off their hips, barely containing their excitement. It was just as I remembered when I was their age. The end of school meant Christmas morning was close enough to taste.

Sera and Sister Rose were sitting in the classroom waiting for me. Bright numbers and a chain of pictures covered the walls, each picture representing a letter of the alphabet in a frieze around the room. The only difference from a typical public school classroom was the large wooden crucifix on the wall.

The nun stood and greeted me before showing me to a pair of children's chairs butted together to make a seat wide enough for an adult.

She raised her eyebrows at Sera, who sat with her ankles crossed, her hands in her lap, and a guilty look on her face. "Go on, Sera." The sister nudged her with a nod toward me.

"I'm sorry, Daddy."

"What for? What's happened?"

Sera turned away and looked at the nun.

"Mr. Goodwin. In the past couple of weeks, I've noticed Sera come to school five times without any lunch."

"Sweetheart, what's going on?" She remained quiet and chewed on her lip.

"We will usually provide a lunch for a child who comes to school without any," the nun said kindly. "We understand that sometimes children forget to take their lunches with them, or parents are so busy and rushed in the morning that it simply slips their minds. It's not uncommon, but it doesn't usually happen this regularly."

"But I've made her lunch every day," I explained, mortified that the nun might suspect me of neglect.

Sister Rose smiled. "I don't doubt that for a moment, Mr. Goodwin. But it seems that it doesn't always make it all the way to school. I sat down with Sera today, and she explained she's been giving it away."

"Sera, look at me," I said, calling her attention from the spot on the floor on which she intently focused. "Why have you been giving your lunch away?"

"He was hungry," she replied, wringing her hands together.

"Who was hungry?"

The sister leaned forward and spoke softly. "Sera, now I'm sure your daddy won't be mad. Just tell him the truth."

"Oscar," she said quietly.

"It seems she's been dropping her lunch behind her when you walk past the homeless man on the steps of the church. The school and church are aware of him and believe him to be harmless enough. He's not here every day. Sometimes he begs in the Financial District, and other times he begs or sleeps in the park."

"And sometimes he takes food off little girls on their way to school?"

The nun looked awkward. "I'll talk to him the next time I see him."

"Don't let Oscar get into trouble!" Sera cried out. "It's not his fault!"

"Then whose fault is it, Sera? I told you never to talk to him."

"I didn't talk to him!"

"Why are you leaving him food?"

"Sophia said he was hungry!"

"Oh for God's sake, Sera, not this again," I said, before throwing the nun an apologetic look for my poor choice of words. "Wait outside and let me talk to Sister Rose alone."

Sera slid off her chair and walked toward the door with her head down and her satchel dragging on the floor behind her.

"I'm so sorry, Sister. I'll make sure it doesn't happen again."

"That's quite all right, Mr. Goodwin. We do our best to encourage children always to help others, but sometimes we forget that it isn't always the safest thing to do. Her heart was in the right place."

"While I'm here, how's she getting on?"

The sister smiled. "She's a remarkable young lady, Mr. Goodwin, she really is. She's affable, her classmates adore her, and she's such a sweet child to teach."

"Good," I said, relieved that she was still fitting in okay.

"To be honest with you, I've never taught a child quite like Sera before. She has such a positive influence over the other children. We usually have a first semester pecking-order battle, which sometimes leads to bullying, but I can't think of one instance of it this year. It really is quite odd. Wonderful—but odd. I think the other kids know Sera wouldn't like it, so they don't do it. Not out of fear or retribution. They simply don't want her to be mad or disappointed with them."

"Oh," I said, surprised.

"She is also remarkably intelligent. I haven't had to explain anything to her twice. She picks things up very quickly." The nun paused. "Although, maybe there is one thing...."

"And what's that?" Despite being mad that Sera had been dropping food on the street, I was welling up with pride.

"Well, it's Religious Studies. She's having difficulty understanding the concept of God our Father."

"How so?"

The nun rose from her chair and beckoned me to follow her to a wall of paintings. The word "Family" arched over the gallery in brightly colored cutout letters. They were typical paintings for children of their age: one line of blue for the sky, a ball of yellow for the sun, and a box for a house or apartment building. Sister Rose pointed to the one marked "by Sera." There were seven stick figures drawn standing on a green line of grass and what looked like a bird in the sky.

"This is your daughter's painting. You can see three of the figures have triangle dresses on. Sera said these are the ladies who look after her when you're at work."

"Yes, they've helped me with her since she was a baby."

"And how wonderful that she considers them family!" The nun smiled. "Now, these two I understand are Daddy and Uncle Aaron," she said, pointing to the two male stick figures on one side of the house with the women. "And these two"—she pointed to the other side of the house—"these are her brother and father."

"Huh?"

"This is where we have our little problem, Mr. Goodwin. Sera is fiercely intelligent, but she seems to take everything we say in Religious Studies almost literally. She understands the ladies aren't actually blood relatives, and like I said, it's wonderful that she considers them to be a part of your family unit," the sister began with another smile. "However, when we pray and we say 'The Lord, our Father,' we obviously don't mean it in the literal sense." She pointed to one of the other two stick figures. "So, by her logic, if the Lord is her father, then this must be—"

"Her brother, Jesus?"

"Yes!" the sister exclaimed. "This isn't anything to concern yourself with. They're still only little, and we haven't really gotten around to explaining faith to them quite yet. But I'm sure she'll grasp it as quickly as she does everything else. But in the meantime, when you pray together, it might be worth trying to clear up the misunderstanding."

I didn't want to address the fact I never prayed with Sera; admitting my lack of faith to a nun didn't sit right. Maybe it was my own experience of Catholic school, but I couldn't help seeing her habit as magical clothing that could detect lies—and I wasn't about to lie to a woman of the church. Besides, I couldn't recall ever seeing Sera press her palms together, before or since she started school.

"Would you mind if I take this, Sister?" I asked, pointing to the painting. "I understand what you're saying, but I'd like to run through it with her myself. As you know, she was adopted, so I just want to make sure she understands."

"Yes, of course!" the nun said approvingly. She unpinned the painting from the wall before walking me to the door. "If I can be of any help, just let me know."

THAT EVENING, after a few hours of Sera being quiet and unresponsive, I sat her down on the sofa and put the painting on the coffee table.

"This is beautiful, sweetheart," I said, hoping a soothing voice would ease her into the discussion. But she was still mad at me. "Sera, we have to talk about today. Why did you give away your lunch, and why didn't you tell me?"

"Because you told me I wasn't allowed to talk to him. But Sophia said he was hungry, and I didn't want to ask you to give him food in case you got angry."

"We'll come back to Sophia in a minute. Why didn't you talk to me about this? You've always been honest with me."

"I didn't lie to you, Daddy. But you said not to talk to Oscar, and you told me not to talk about Sophia. I didn't want you to be mad at me."

"But he could be dangerous, Sera."

"But you said when I was little that when you had to work late it was because you were helping people. I was trying to help Oscar like you would."

"But I'm a grown-up."

"So I can't help people because I'm a kid?"

"No, you can. But you have to be more careful, sweetheart," I said. She looked crestfallen that her good deed had landed her in trouble, so on this occasion I compromised. "Okay, how about every morning we make an extra sandwich for Oscar? But on the condition you promise me that you will never go near him if I'm not with you. Do you understand?"

"Yes," she said, finally smiling. "I promise."

"Your teacher said you are such a clever girl. She said you were good in math and spelling and reading. Oh, and art!" I said, pointing at the painting. "She gave me this to bring home. Can you tell me who's in this picture?"

Sera pointed to each stick figure. "That's you, Daddy. That's Uncle Aaron. That's Maria, Miss Dee, and Maggie. And that's God, my Father, and that's my brother, Jesus." Then she pointed to the bird. "And that's Sophia!"

"But I'm your father, aren't I?"

"No, silly, you're Daddy."

"Sweetheart, when they say the prayer 'Our Father,' they mean God is like a father to everyone. But he's not actually your father. Do you understand? It's like Santa Claus. Lots of people call him Father Christmas, but he's not actually their father."

"That's what Sister Rose said, but Sophia told me that God is my real father."

There was a little stab at my heart, though I knew she didn't mean what she said, but I was also getting frustrated at her blaming her imaginary friend again.

"Sweetheart, you know that when you were a baby, I adopted you."

Sera nodded. I'd always tried to make adoption sound like a casual, normal thing—like it was nothing dramatic or out of the ordinary.

"It's one thing to think that your real mommy is a princess or your real daddy is a brave knight and they're having an adventure looking for you. But you can't think that God—" I stopped as a look of horror appeared on Sera's face.

"No, Daddy! I don't want anyone to find me! You're my daddy! I don't want anyone to take me away from you! I don't care if it's a princess or a knight."

I wrapped my arms around her. "I swear no one is going to take you away from me, sweetheart. Do you believe me?"

The fear faded from her face. I gave her a cuddle. "Listen, when the nuns say God is your father, they mean that he's someone who loves all of his children. And all of his children are everyone on earth."

"Was Sister Rose mad about me covering the cross?"

"What do you mean?"

Sera took a deep breath. "I took a towel to school and covered up the cross with Jesus on it."

"Why did you do that?"

"I don't like it, Daddy. They put nails through his hands and feet and they killed him. Sophia didn't like it, either."

I sat for a moment and wondered whether that was the real reason the young nun had shown me the painting. It was obvious that Sera had things mixed up, but was covering the crucifix a little too blasphemous for Sister Rose to address? Was that the real reason she'd called me in? Did she assume our conversation would lead to this?

"Have they explained to you why Jesus is on the cross?"

"No."

I thought about it for a moment. The unexplained image of a man nailed to a piece of wood must look macabre to a five-year-old kid. I guess the school assumed that parents who sent their children to a faith-based school had already given them some understanding of Jesus and the reason for his crucifixion.

"I'll explain about Jesus later, sweetheart," I said, wondering how I would.

"Okay, but I still don't like seeing it."

"I promise I'll explain, and you know if you have any questions, you can ask Sister Rose, right?"

Sera nodded.

"Now, about Sophia—"

"But she's real, Daddy!"

"Sera, I'm not going to tell you again. No more blaming Sophia for anything. In fact, I don't want you to mention her name again. Do you understand?"

Sera looked mutinous. "But—"

I held my hand up, deciding to leave the imaginary friend debate for another time. Besides, I'd recently caved in to Aaron's appeal to get Sera something special for Christmas—a gift that hopefully would blot Sophia from her mind.

ON CHRISTMAS Eve I took Sera out to see the window displays at some of the larger department stores in the city. As we weaved through the hordes of Christmas shoppers at Macy's, I finally spotted what I was looking for. I picked Sera up so she could look over the crowd and queues gathering at the makeshift grotto.

"Look, sweetheart. It's Santa!"

Sera immediately shot back, "That's not Santa! Santa's not even real!"

I turned and gave the many parents in the area an apologetic look as they dramatically covered their kids' ears and gave me stern looks. Although Sera sounded adamant in her statement, I could tell by her eyes she wasn't completely sure.

"He is real!" I said as I turned away and carried her toward the nearest exit before she could dash any other kids' dreams. "Why don't you believe in him?"

"He couldn't deliver that many presents in one night. It's impossible when he's spending so much time at Macy's."

I sucked the inside of my cheek between my teeth to stop myself from laughing. "Well, sweetheart, some of it's magic and some of it's good planning. Sometimes he leaves presents with moms and dads days beforehand to make sure every child gets something."

Sera screwed her nose up at me, as if she didn't believe a word I'd said.

"Okay, Sera, but I know for a fact that he tried to deliver something to me yesterday for you, but I was at work. So he left it with Uncle Aaron."

My little girl's eyes twinkled at the promise of a present. "What is it?"

"Well, Uncle Aaron asked Santa if you could have the present a day early. He said you'd been a very good girl and told him all about how well you're doing at school, so… Santa said yes!"

"Really?"

"Yes, and Uncle Aaron is at home now waiting to give it to you!"

FOR A little girl who didn't believe in Santa Claus, she sure did run up to the apartment fast enough. I was midway up the first of the two flights when I heard her squeal of delight echo down the stairs. I reached the next landing and watched as Sera rushed toward the top step with a wide smile. A chocolate Labrador puppy wriggled in her arms, his head bouncing as she carried him.

Then, it was as if it happened in slow motion: Sera's loose shoelace slapped wildly from side to side. I watched in horror as her other foot came down onto it, causing her knee to stop in midair before she began to tumble forward.

I leapt up the stairs to catch her, but it was too late.

She fell but thankfully was able to catch herself on the iron banister. But she let go of the puppy to grasp the rail. It yelped as it landed on the banister, and its clumsy legs scrambled to right itself; then it lost its balance and went over the side. It dropped two flights of stairs, hitting the banister railings like a furry pinball, until it landed with a sharp slap on the concrete lobby floor.

The sound that emanated from Sera sent chills down my spine. She thundered past me to get to the puppy. I tried to grab her but she ducked under my arms. "Sera, watch your laces!" I shouted after her, worried she would go headfirst down the stairs.

Footsteps rumbled in the hallway that led to our apartment, and I could hear Maria, Miss Dee, and Maggie come hurtling out their doors, alerted by Sera's scream.

I chased after Sera and reached her in time to see her pick the puppy's lifeless body off the floor. She looked at me, and I knew that she was desperately hoping I could do something, but it was obviously dead. I picked Sera up and carried her up the stairs as she held the puppy in her arms, crying into its fur.

Aaron stood at the top step. "I'm sorry. I didn't think she would run out the door like that."

I carried Sera into the apartment and set her down on the sofa. The ladies followed me in and quietly looked on as I crouched down next to my little girl, who was shaking.

"I'm so sorry, I'm so sorry," she whispered to the puppy. A few drops of blood trickled from its nose and onto her dress. It was lying on its back with its head flopped to one side like an oversized, yet much more lifelike, Beanie Baby. "I'm so sorry," she whispered again as she stroked its chest and belly. She began rocking and stroking the puppy a little harder.

"Sweetheart, it was an accident," I said, reaching out to take the puppy from her lap before she became too traumatized. "It's okay, baby."

Sera shot forward as if to protect the animal from my grip and continued to stroke its little chest.

I turned to see Aaron looking mortified, as if he'd been responsible for it. Miss Dee and Maggie looked at each other but didn't speak. Finally Maria came forward next to me.

"Sera, remember what we told you," she whispered before patting Sera gently on the shoulder. She kissed the top of Sera's head and stood to join the other women behind me.

"Come on, sweetheart, let me take him," I said, holding my hands out. It crushed me to see her so distraught. "He's gone."

"I'll get you another one!" Aaron exclaimed in desperation. "I'll get you another one today!"

Sera acted as if she couldn't hear anyone and continued to smooth the fur on the puppy's chest and belly with a firm, clumsy stroke, the remnants of her Erb's Palsy condition still evident in her hand. I stood up and tried to figure out what to do. I didn't want to pry it from her and upset her even more. But I also didn't think it was right to let her continue to pet a corpse.

Suddenly the puppy's head jerked and its little body flipped onto its stomach, like a falling cat righting itself to land. Its little tongue started licking at Sera's hand. Rather than being astonished, like Aaron and I clearly were at the sight, Sera laughed with relief.

"See, Daddy, he's not gone!"

"What the—" Aaron gasped before catching himself.

Miss Dee came over and knelt next to me. She patted the puppy's head, showing me that Sera had stopped being so protective.

"Sera, I have to take this little one to the animal doctor to get him checked over, just in case he's hurt somewhere we can't see," I said holding my hands out.

Sera nodded and passed the puppy over, still smiling. No sign of emotional whiplash over the dramatic shift from mourning to happiness. "Can I call him Buddy?" she asked.

"Let's name him when we get back," I said, hoping internal injuries wouldn't kill him before we arrived. I didn't relish the idea of coming back from the emergency vet and explaining that the puppy that had left the apartment alive and seemingly well had been put down. "Aaron, did you come over in the car?"

He nodded and began to put his coat on.

"Can you watch Sera?" I asked the ladies.

"We'll go play gin rummy until you get back," Maria said, taking Sera by the hand.

AS I came out of the vet's examination room, Aaron stood up, relieved that the puppy in my arms was still alive.

"He's fine. Apparently they have soft bones at this age and are quite resilient. He thinks he probably just had the wind knocked out of him."

"What about the blood?"

"They've x-rayed and examined him and can't find anything wrong. The vet said the impact might have bashed his nose. I didn't actually see him hit the ground, so I guess that could be right."

"Still," Aaron said with an odd look on his face, "you gotta admit, that was a hell of a drop."

"It was. The vet reckons that Sera stroking him so hard when she was upset may have stimulated his heart. Like a kind of puppy CPR."

"Christmas miracle." Aaron shrugged.

"At this point, Aaron, I'm willing to believe it. I wouldn't have been able to tell Sera he was dead," I said, shaking my head. "She's hypersensitive to this sort of thing. I don't think she would've been able to cope with it."

Chapter Seven

AARON BLEW a wolf-whistle at a pair of attractive women in their midtwenties who passed us as we walked along the Coney Island promenade. Buddy, now eight months old and seeing his first summer, stopped and turned in front of us. Thinking the whistle was for him, he raced toward us as Sera tried to keep hold of him on the leash. The women turned their heads and smiled. The blonde one bounced a flirty eyebrow at my brother.

"That one liked me," Aaron said, winking at Sera, who turned back to look at the women with confusion.

"Why did you whistle at her? She's not a dog," Sera said, crinkling her nose.

"Girls like it!" Aaron said, giving a cheeky swagger to mirror the swinging hips of the women who'd passed us. "Watch!"

A beautiful Italian-looking girl who'd just come off the beach was walking to the concession stand wearing a bikini top and sarong. Aaron wolf-whistled again as she crossed in front of us.

"Creep!" the girl called back.

I laughed. "You deserved that."

Aaron shrugged and muttered, "Probably a lesbian."

I was about to chastise him when Sera turned.

"No, Uncle Aaron!" she shouted as she took the stance I'd seen a thousand times. "She's got girl power!" She punctuated this, as she always did, with a peace sign and a proud smile.

Aaron cocked his eyebrow at me.

"Spice Girls," I said simply.

"Oh, and you got girl power too, huh? Let's see about that!" Aaron crouched down as if to chase after her. Sera shrieked with laughter as he shot forward. She tried to get away, but Buddy, being all paws, gangly legs, and excitement, took off in the other direction. I took his leash from Sera as Aaron hoisted her up onto his shoulders.

"Uncle Aaron, can I have an ice cream, please?" Sera asked, tapping him on his head. Aaron looked sheepishly at the nearest sign for gelato, where the Italian woman who'd just shot him down was standing.

"At the next one," he promised.

True to his word, Aaron stopped at the next ice cream stand. Balancing an extra-large vanilla soft scoop cone in her hand, Sera took in the view from atop Aaron's shoulders as we continued to walk along the busy promenade toward the subway. The light sea breeze separated strands of Sera's auburn locks as they whipped around her. The sun behind her shone through the wisps like a steady glow of embers behind her head. I loved seeing my brother and daughter so well bonded. They obviously adored each other. It made me a little sad Aaron wasn't yet a family man, as it was clear he would be a great dad himself.

"When are you going to settle down?" I asked as we strolled through the bustle of the boardwalk. "You're in your early thirties now. Don't you think it's about time?"

"Nope! I'm happy as I am. Besides, there are a lot of women out there who I have yet to charm. And when I say charm, I mean—"

"I know what you mean," I said, giving him a warning nudge before he could finish. "You could meet the right girl any day. I hope whatever it is you're trying to get out of your system is gone before she gets here."

"What about you? I don't see you dating anyone at the moment." He bounced his shoulders to get Sera's attention. "What do you think, pipsqueak? Do you think your daddy should get out there and date?"

"Yes!" she said encouragingly.

"And it looks like you're getting back in shape."

"Daddy's started running again, but it makes his eyes go red," Sera chimed in.

Aaron gave me a confused look.

"My allergies play up when I run."

"Even this late in the year?"

I shrugged.

"Well, you're looking fit. You should get out there and start mingling again."

I could tell I was about to get a lecture on dating, but something caught Aaron's eye. He was looking over to the beach, where a full-bodied woman stood over her two small children. She was applauding them as they presented their sandcastles.

"Would you look at the state of that? Women that size have no business wearing bikinis."

Aaron stopped abruptly. His chest suddenly rose as he drew air through his gaping mouth. "Sera!"

I looked up to see my daughter release Aaron's collar, where she had tipped the remainder of her ice cream down the back of his neck.

"Sorry, Uncle Aaron. I dropped it!" she said sweetly before looking down at me with a mischievous smile. "I'll try and scoop it out!" Then she prodded the ice cream farther around his neck until it dropped to the front of his chest, causing him to draw in another huge breath.

"Wait, wait!" I said, pulling my camera from my shorts pocket. "I've got to get a photo of this!"

With her hand dripping in cold white drizzle, she gave me the peace sign and silently mouthed "Girl Power!"

THE FOLLOWING Monday as I walked Sera to school, Buddy pulled on his leash toward the homeless man we had nicknamed Oscar. He ruffled Buddy's ear as Sera placed the brown paper bag containing a sandwich and an apple on the stoop next to him. She'd taken on the responsibility of making his lunch the night before, while I made hers. It became a routine that guaranteed us time together in the evening to talk about her day at school.

"Have you been to the shelter yet?" I asked. I'd contacted friends in Social Services to get information on local homeless shelters that accepted walk-ins. When I'd given the slip of paper with the address and phone number to Oscar, he simply took it with his fingerless-gloved hands and nodded. He never spoke to us—it would be a long time before I heard his voice—but he always smiled at Sera to thank her for his food. For the past two months, I'd asked him regularly if he'd contacted the shelters, but he always shook his head. "Please think about visiting them. It's warm now but it won't be long before the weather turns and the cold sets in again. Try and get down there at least to introduce yourself."

Oscar took a swig from his bottle and nodded again as if to placate me. At least he was wide-eyed of his own accord that morning.

I often had to pull Buddy away from him on our way to the school so as not to wake him. As with many homeless people, he slept lightly for fear of being robbed or having to move on when the police arrived. Sometimes he would pretend to be asleep and position a wine bottle in his hand as if he'd passed out. But I'd always see an eye open a little to watch us when we walked by. He might not want to be bothered, but I think it gave him comfort to see a familiar and caring face every morning.

I dropped Sera off at the gate. "I'm working from home this afternoon, so remember I'll be picking you up after school!" I called as she ran toward her friends in the playground.

"THANKS FOR coming, ladies," I said as Maria, Maggie, and Miss Dee filed into the apartment. Maria had taken a week off from her volunteer work at Amnesty, so I was lucky to get them all together at the same time without Sera being around. As we sat around the table, the three women looked at one another, not sure why I'd asked to meet with them. There was a slight nervousness to them all, like they were expecting bad news. They'd all grown so attached to Sera that I sensed each of them was worried I was going to change the arrangement.

"Have you noticed any problems with Sera recently?" I asked, checking the time on the clock. I only had half an hour before I had to pick her up from school. "I mean, has she said anything out of the ordinary lately?"

The women exchanged conspiratorial glances.

"I'll take that as a yes." I laughed. "I spoke to her teacher, who said that she excels at every subject. I know I have a lot to thank you ladies for because you've taught her so much yourselves. But when it comes to Religious Studies, she seems to be confused. It's been going on since before Christmas, and I just can't seem to get through to her. I've had to meet with her teacher again."

"What has she said?" Maggie asked. Her eyes darted to the other two women.

"She thinks God is her father. I've spoken to her about it, and so has her teacher, but she still doesn't grasp that 'father'"—I hated myself for doing it, but I added air quotes—"isn't actually father."

"She's such a good girl," Maggie said, beaming with pride.

"She's an absolute angel," I agreed, "but I'm worried that if she continues to believe this, or says it out loud, she might be bullied."

"We are all God's children," Maria said kindly, as if Sera's misunderstanding was perfectly reasonable.

"You see, I think this might be part of the problem, Maria. If you say things like that around her, she takes it literally. I need you to start calling her out on it if she mentions it around you. Because if it continues, I may have to think about having her see someone."

The last sentence sent a bolt through the room. All three women instantly straightened their backs and gave me a disapproving look.

"What do you mean, child? Like a psychiatrist?" Miss Dee asked, as if I was crazy.

"Nothing quite so extreme. I used to work with a woman who could put me in touch with a child therapist. She might be able to talk it through with her in a way that would be more successful than Sister Rose's and my attempts. But I don't think we've reached that stage yet."

"No, you mustn't do that," Maggie insisted. Miss Dee and Maria backed her up by shaking their heads. "She's still so young. We'll speak to her and make sure she understands."

I was relieved. "Ladies, each of you has helped me so much over the years. And I know you hear me say it a lot, but I want you to know how much I appreciate it. And you all know how much Sera loves you—"

"And we love her!" Maria interrupted.

"But I've seen how these things can manifest themselves if they aren't dealt with early on. I know she's still just a baby, and maybe I'm going a little over the top, but with this and her imaginary friend, Sophia—"

"She still talks about Sophia?" Miss Dee asked in surprise.

"Actually, come to think about it, she hasn't mentioned her for a while."

"I should think not," Maria said. "We all said good-bye to Sophia months ago, just like you asked us to."

"Well, there you go!" Maggie said. "You're worrying over nothing. She's just being a child. But we see your concern. You just leave it to us."

The women rose from the table together, as though the matter had been resolved.

"Is there anything else I need to know? Has she said anything else that's a bit… strange?"

"No," all three women replied in unison.

"Maybe you're right. Maybe I've just seen too many things in my years as a lawyer. I just worry."

"Of course you do, honey. And this is your first time being a parent," Miss Dee said as she reached over and cupped my hand in her own and shook it. "You're doing a great job."

I WAITED by the gates of the school with Buddy, mulling over what the ladies said and convincing myself that I had, indeed, gone way overboard even suggesting the possibility of Sera seeing a therapist. This was reinforced when my little girl came running out of school and into my arms.

"Daddy!" she cried in delight. Picking her up from school myself was a special occasion for Sera.

"What have you got there?" I asked as we began walking the short three blocks home. Sera pulled out a blank piece of white paper and a blue crayon from her satchel. She beckoned me down and whispered in my ear as we approached the steps of the church. I looked into her eyes and felt my heart swell. I was surprised the thought had crossed her mind, since I hadn't even considered it.

As we passed Oscar on the steps of the church, Sera took hold of Buddy's leash and walked on a few feet to give us a little privacy. I sat down next to the homeless man, the closest I'd ever been to him. I expected him to shy away or be uncomfortable with me being in his space, but he just sat and smiled over at Sera and Buddy until I spoke.

"Oscar, I'm going to draw you a map of how to get to the shelter," I said as I put the blue crayon to the blank paper Sera had given me. "All you need to do is follow the arrows."

He watched and listened as I tried my best to explain and draw the directions. I reached into my pocket and handed him two twenty-dollar bills, partly out of guilt that I'd chided this man for two months and missed the one thing a six-year-old could see. "Oscar, my little girl thinks a lot of you. Make sure you look after yourself so you're around to look out for her, okay?"

He smiled and gave a quick nod.

AS WE approached our apartment, I looked down at Sera, still astounded at her awareness. "How did you know that Oscar couldn't read?"

"I didn't. I just knew he needed help to help himself."

CHAPTER EIGHT

I EXCHANGED nervous looks with two other parents as we bounded up the stone steps toward the large wooden doors of St. Katherine's. It was clear from our quickened pace that we all wanted to run toward our children's classrooms, but we managed to contain the urge so as not to panic the kids who were already leaving the building with their parents. My strides became longer and faster as I reached the hallways. The ever-increasing number of sirens from the street echoed off the polished concrete walls. A man in a suit sprinted past me and into the doorway of a classroom ahead. Red-faced and gasping for breath, he harshly beckoned his kid in that way a father does when there will be no discussion or argument. I hit Redial on my phone and got voice mail for the fifth time.

"Aaron, call me as soon as you get this message." The desperation in my voice grew stronger with each message I left.

I found the classroom and walked through the door to find the teacher, a young nun, standing silently in front of Sera and the small class of other eleven-year-olds. They sat at their desks in their blazers with their arms folded, their satchels hung over their shoulders, ready to leave in an organized fashion. I gave the nun a solemn nod and called for Sera. "Come on, sweetheart, we're going to Uncle Aaron's house!"

The false cheerfulness in my voice didn't fool the other kids, who all looked anxious and confused. Just as Sera began to get up from her desk, a middle-aged woman rushed through the door behind me and headed straight for her daughter.

"We've got to get out of here... *now!*" She grabbed the girl's hand and yanked her up from the desk. Her panicked voice filled the classroom and trailed off as they disappeared out the door. The other kids were left looking like they were about to be trapped in a closet with the monster they feared the most.

"It's okay, children, you're all safe," the nun said kindly.

As Sera took my hand and joined me at the door, I noticed the other kids' faces. Their eyes begged her to stay. One girl called, "Sera, don't go!"

I wanted to comfort her, to tell her that her parents were probably already on their way, when Sera broke free of my hand. She walked over, bent down, and whispered in the girl's ear as she gave her a hug. The girl became noticeably calmer. Sera walked back to me and took my hand.

As we left the school, six fire trucks hurtled by. Sera pushed her hands onto her ears to escape the noise of the blaring sirens and turned away from the bright revolving lights.

"Dad, what's happened?" she asked as we hurried toward Madison Street. "Where's Buddy?"

"He's at home. He'll be fine, I promise."

Sera stopped abruptly as we turned the next corner. We both looked up at the blue sky and watched as two huge flumes of charcoal gray smoke snaked together, joining as one in the wind. I reached for my phone and hit Redial. Voice mail again.

"Aaron, for fuck's sake. Please! Call me!"

"Dad, what's happened?" This time I heard a definite quiver of fear.

There was no point in lying to her. I could've told her a plane had somehow managed to steer off course and crash into the World Trade Center, but with both buildings hit it was clear, even to a child, that this was no accident. Just as I left work to collect Sera, I'd heard the radio through the open window of a yellow taxi that had pulled over to allow a fire truck to pass.

"There are now confirmed reports of an explosion at the Pentagon," the radio presenter said in a grave voice. *"America is under attack."*

"Sera, listen to me carefully. I don't know what's happening. All I know is the city isn't safe to be in at the moment. I don't want to use the subway, so we have to walk over the bridge to get to Uncle Aaron's house."

My voice cracked when I said his name.

"Dad, is Uncle Aaron okay?"

"I'm sure he's fine, sweetheart. But we need to get to his house as soon as we can."

We joined hundreds of people as we made our way to the mouth of the Brooklyn Bridge. Sera knew what was worrying me: Aaron had clients in the towers, and there was a good chance he might have been working in one of them. Dark pictures of my brother trapped, or worse, crept into my mind. Each time Sera squeezed my hand, it felt like she was pushing yet another horrific image out of my head.

People filed eight across onto the footpath and began an eerie march across the bridge. Every kind of person imaginable was on the bridge that day: businessmen with briefcases, young mothers with strollers, construction workers in hard hats, tourists holding maps and sporting "I Love NYC" and Knicks T-shirts. The melting pot of colors, religions, and professions of New York walked in the same direction, with the same goal and the same look of disbelief. Only a few exhibited signs of panic, but most everyone understood that running or freaking out would hold up the stream of human traffic, therefore delaying their escape from the city. Cell phones were pinned against ears as people either tried to contact or were called by loved ones who were doubtlessly watching the attack unfold on televisions or through windows in high-rises across Manhattan.

With my mind so completely on Aaron, we were a little over halfway across the bridge before I looked down to check that Sera was okay. She was pale and looked anxious. Her lips were moving so fast it looked like her teeth were chattering. But I couldn't hear what she was saying, if she was saying anything at all.

"It's okay, sweetheart, we're going to be—"

I heard a collective gasp as I bumped into the businessman in front of me who, like everyone else on the bridge, had stopped and turned. I looked around just as the South Tower began to collapse into itself. My blood ran cold as the delayed roar of millions of tons of concrete and metal imploding on itself traveled far enough to hit my ears. Sera squeezed my hand as I stood transfixed by the sight, terrified that my brother had disappeared along with part of the New York skyline I'd seen almost every day of my life.

There was a rumbling of voices, each with a different tone and pitch, but all repeating the same thing with the same stunned inflection.

"Oh my God. Oh my God!"

Sera released my hand. I'd never seen her so distressed. She cupped her palms against her ears to block the desperate chorus.

"Oh my God. Oh my God!"

The pace of the crowd quickened as people started to make their way forward again, only with more urgency.

I hit Redial on my phone again. *"We're sorry, but we are unable to connect your call at this time. Please try again later."*

I wanted to go back to the city. I needed to find Aaron. If the worst had happened, I had to be there. I looked through the wooden slats of the footpath and tried to see the road below. Traffic out of the city was backed up while the other side was empty. They must have blocked the entrance from the Brooklyn end. There were thousands upon thousands of people on the bridge. A woman walking in front of us slid her arm across her young son's shoulders. "Don't look back," she said softly.

As I tried to figure out a way to go against the oncoming tidal wave of people to get back to the city, another terrifying thought hit me. What if whoever was doing this—those responsible for slamming planes into the towers—what if they tried to take out the bridges too? Wouldn't they start with the most famous in the city? I looked up to the sky to try to spot any aircraft, but there were only news or rescue helicopters, and they were all concentrated on and circling the south end of the island. There had been a confirmed report of an explosion at the Pentagon. Had it been a bomb? Had they rigged the bridge to blow too? I had to get Sera off it as soon as I could, and the fastest way to do that was to go with the flow of traffic heading toward Brooklyn.

I began to shake with nerves. I could feel myself beginning to sweat. I had visions of the bridge collapsing and all of us descending into the turbid waters of the East River, metal raining down on top of us. Were we walking toward the explosives? Would we be on top of them when they were triggered? What if I didn't survive but Sera did? Would Maria, Miss Dee, and Maggie look after her? What if I survived but Sera didn't? What if I lost her? With Aaron gone too, there wouldn't be any reason in the world for me to wait more than a moment to take my own life.

My downward spiral into the once familiar darkness was broken when Sera grabbed my hand again. It was if I'd come around from a trance. She took the lead and wove us between people in an attempt to get us across quicker. As the end of the bridge came into sight, particles from the World Trade Center that had escaped the higher winds but were caught on the river's breeze cloaked us like pollen from a woodland of cement cedar trees. The bridge behind us was full. In a twisted way, it resembled the starting corrals of the New York marathon, thousands of men and women walking patiently before having their chance to run. The idea of the bridge blowing up with so many people on it was too horrific to dwell on.

We walked quickly through the tree-lined avenues of Park Slope until we arrived at Aaron's house. I nervously fumbled with my fob to find the spare key to his door. Sera tugged at the key ring and found the right one before slipping it into the lock. I stormed through the front door and straight into the living room, hoping to find one of Aaron's many laptops so I could check my e-mail and see if there had been any word from him.

A young woman with tousled brown hair stood in the kitchen, wearing nothing but one of Aaron's long work shirts. Her back was to us as she opened the fridge door, pulled out a carton of orange juice, and poured it into a glass.

"Where's Aaron? Is he here?" I asked urgently as I rushed toward her. Startled, she let out a small shriek and dropped the glass. It smashed onto the tiled floor.

I heard a thump from above and footsteps growing louder, harder, and closer.

"Answer your phone, you fucking asshole!" I shouted angrily as Aaron hit the bottom step of the stairs. My eyes flooded with tears at the sight of him, looking dozy in pajama bottoms and sporting bed head.

Sera didn't say anything. She just ran to him, hooked her arms around his waist, and hugged him as hard as she could.

"What's going on?"

"You're a fucking asshole!" I shouted as I launched forward and hugged him myself.

Looking utterly confused, Aaron broke free of us. "What are you doing here? What's going on?"

"I think I ought to go," the girl said, embarrassed and awkward.

"Adam, Sera, this is... is...." Aaron looked like he instantly regretted his decision to introduce us.

"Julie," she said, looking rightly annoyed that he'd forgotten her name.

Trying to cover his tracks, he turned back to us as if our appearance had caused his memory lapse. "Adam, what's happened? Why are you here?"

"Sweetheart, go upstairs to your room," I said to Sera. Aaron had declared one of his two spare bedrooms as Sera's the day she came to live with me. "Give us a few minutes to have a chat."

Sera looked up at Julie, her face full of sadness as she released her uncle from her hug. She nodded and slowly walked upstairs while I switched on the television. I turned the volume down so it was just loud enough to hear. Aaron sank back into a chair as he watched in horror.

"I thought you might have been in one of them," I said to Aaron, but my words didn't register with him. His eyes fixed on the screen and his mouth gaped open.

Julie snatched her dress and shoes from the back of a chair and hurried into the kitchen. She emerged minutes later, dressed and frantically looking for her handbag and cell phone.

"Did you know anyone who worked there?" I asked as I pointed toward her handbag, the corner of which was just visible from under Aaron's backside. Julie said nothing. She nodded quickly before pulling her handbag by the straps. Her eyes were wide. She didn't wait to put on her shoes before rushing out. The slam of the front door brought Aaron back from his stupor.

I went into the kitchen, kicking the broken glass out of the way, and pulled a couple of juice boxes, an apple, and a box that held a half-eaten pizza from the fridge. I went up to Sera's bedroom and put the food on top of the dresser. Sera sat on her bed, looking upset.

"He's okay, sweetheart," I said as I joined her on the bed. "Uncle Aaron's fine."

Sera nodded.

"You okay?"

She nodded again, but I could see she was still upset.

"Scary, huh?"

"What's happening?"

"I don't know, sweetheart. I'm going to go back downstairs and find out." I opened her satchel. "Do you have any schoolwork you can do? Or do you have a book to read?"

It was a lame attempt to find some kind of normality in the day. I'd rather distract her than have her downstairs watching the news. She nodded again.

"I'll come back and check on you. If you need anything, just shout, okay?"

I gave her another hug and went back downstairs to find Aaron still staring at the screen.

"I took the morning off. I was meant to be in the south tower to run some software, but I rescheduled it for tomorrow," Aaron said in disbelief. He reached for his laptop and searched his e-mail. I watched his eyes dart from left to right as he read the memo from his company explaining that none of their contractors were in the towers at the time of impact. There had been one person in World Trade Center 7 that morning, but he'd been safely evacuated in time.

Though Aaron didn't have any colleagues in the buildings, he had clients, many of whom he considered friends.

The hours went by as we watched the news unfold. Aaron checked his laptop every sixty seconds as desperate e-mails to clients went unanswered. I checked on Sera every so often before rejoining Aaron in the living room. We shook our heads at the footage of aircraft slamming into the side of the buildings. The continuous replays from every angle were only interrupted by images of one side of the Pentagon blown out and a scorched field in Pennsylvania littered with aircraft debris.

Though we couldn't see the people in the planes or offices, it was stomach-churning to witness the deaths of thousands of victims over and over and over again.

Without taking his eyes off the screen, Aaron cleared his throat and said, "Michael."

"I know."

Nothing more was said. It was my brother's way of acknowledging that Michael had worked in the World Trade Center. If the aneurysm that ended his life eleven years before hadn't burst, or if it had been discovered and treated, he would have been in the tower as the jet fuel exploded. I shuddered at the thought.

"Aaron, there's a TV in Sera's room, right?"

"Yes, why?"

"I hope she isn't watching this. She's a sensitive kid. I'd better go check on her again."

I heard the muffled whimpers before I reached the door. Sera sat on the floor in front of the television with her knees against her chest, rocking back and forth. She shook so violently it looked like she was having a seizure. As I rushed to hold her, I glanced at the screen, which was on but had no sound. The news channel, different from the one we were watching downstairs, showed small dark shapes falling against a blur of lines. My first thought was the television wasn't tuned in or was suffering from static as the picture wobbled. But then a dark cloud of smoke came into the shot, and I could just make out that the blurred lines actually were windows. I assumed it was falling wreckage from the plane, or perhaps jagged lumps of steel or concrete from the impact of the aircraft. It wasn't until the camera changed to a different angle that I saw the cause of Sera's distress.

A long-lensed camera was trained on the highest floors of the World Trade Center. The dark smoke streamed out of the windows and the arms of people trapped by the fire were desperately trying to call attention to themselves. Three faces appeared through the smoke. The shot changed again. The camera slowly panned down as it followed the body of a man who had jumped. The figure fell like a rag doll, his limbs flailing and twisting as he plummeted toward the ground. Another figure emerged from the window and leaped. From the black smoke two floors above, another man appeared in the frame of the blown-out window. He held on as long as he could before letting go. I switched off the television before the fifth person trapped decided whether to burn alive or jump to their death.

"Why is he letting this happen?" Sera screamed at me through hysterical tears. "Why is he letting this happen?"

I knelt on the floor next to her and tried to hug her to calm her down. "I'm sorry, sweetheart. I should have checked on you again sooner."

But she pushed me away with as much force as an eleven-year-old could muster. "Why is this happening? Why isn't he stopping this?" she shouted.

"Who, sweetheart? Who are you talking about?"

"Why is he letting this happen? What's wrong with him? All those people have been killed. They're jumping! Why? *Why?*" She sobbed and gasped for breath. "I prayed for those people, but they still died. I prayed on the bridge that the other building wouldn't come down, but it did. I prayed to him and he still let it happen! Why isn't he listening to me?" she screamed, thrashing her arms in anger.

I moved in again to try to calm her, but she pushed me away. The crazed look in her swollen eyes unnerved me. Her fists swung, taking down everything on the shelves. She picked up a heavy snow globe Aaron had bought her and threw it into the mirror above a chest of drawers. The shattered glass fell between mementos and presents she had displayed on the chest over the years. She swept her bare arm across the top of it, taking every glass shard, figurine, music box, and picture frame with it. She started toward the television with a look of fury in her eyes, as if she was ready to topple it. I ran behind her and closed my arms around her like a straitjacket. She screamed, not at the sight of the blood now dripping down her arm and off her hand, but at the blue sky framed by the window.

"Where's Sophia? I can't see her! *Where is she?*"

Aaron burst through the door and looked alarmed as he watched me wrestle Sera into submission. I lifted my head and shot my eyes to the door. She was in enough of a state as it was without having an audience.

"Sera, this isn't God, sweetheart."

"He could have stopped it! I asked him to and he still let it happen. Why? I don't understand! Why didn't he hear me? He let those people die! Doesn't he care?"

Sera struggled with all her might to break free of me. "This isn't right. Where's Sophia? *Why did they make her leave?*"

I continued to rock her. It took a while, but she slowly began to calm down. It had been five years since I'd heard the name Sophia. Aaron came back through the door holding a small first aid kit. He tossed it in my direction and left the room.

A stream of blood poured from her hand and forearm but, thankfully, on closer inspection it was the accumulation of many small cuts rather than a large, deep gash. I stopped rocking her and opened the first aid kit. She didn't seem to register the sharp sting of the antiseptic wipes. Even when I removed the splinters of glass, there was no reaction to the pain. She just continued to look desperately around the room as if searching for something. I used every bandage in the kit to patch her up and held her again until she stopped shaking, thankful her injuries weren't worse on a day the hospitals were surely overrun with casualties.

She wept until she went limp with exhaustion. I laid her on the bed and sat with her until she finally closed her eyes.

As I watched her sleep, I worried about how she'd reacted. Maybe the overwhelming relief that her uncle was safe somehow manifested as anger after seeing what might have become of him. But she was still so young, and I had no idea how a child would react to witnessing such horrors. But in my gut, I knew something about her reaction felt wrong.

CHAPTER NINE

THE MONTHS after the terrorist attacks of 9/11 revealed a city I hadn't seen or experienced in my lifetime. As the mourning began, the collective anger of brash New Yorkers softened into a willingness to smile at one another in the streets. Even the meanest-looking laborers or members of high society cliques stopped and became noticeably more polite and civil as they silently shared their grief. There were small but significant gestures: holding the door for a stranger, giving someone else the taxi they'd hailed, or showing appreciation to tourists who continued to flock to the city despite the tragedy.

In the weeks immediately following the attacks, Sera and I saw people tiptoe along the sidewalks to avoid the melted candle wax that dripped from makeshift memorials. Hardcore New Yorkers crossed the street rather than disturb people reading walls of "missing" posters. The respect shown was heartening, the acts of kindness, no matter how small, big enough to suggest the city would survive, despite the scar that was etched so deeply into the earth in Battery Park.

But amid this newfound sense of community lay ugly pockets of people who showed their fear and unease at the presence of those they believed were to blame.

On Thanksgiving morning I took Sera across the street to Lei and Choi's store to pick up some bits and pieces I'd forgotten. Maggie and Maria were coming over to the apartment to celebrate. Miss Dee was spending the morning in Brooklyn with her daughters, as she did every holiday, but she always returned in the afternoon to be sure she could celebrate with Sera. Aaron was also coming and had told me about yet another new girl in his life. I wasn't sure if he planned to bring her with him, so I set an extra place.

Having arranged for her to spend the rest of the day in the company of adults, I wanted Sera to have some time with someone her own age. Although Lei and Choi's daughter Meena attended a different school than Sera, they'd become best friends and had grown up together. But in recent weeks, I hadn't seen them together as much. Sera had grown quieter and more withdrawn.

We'd talked a lot about the attacks and about jihad, the Taliban, and whatever else came out in the news, but with each explanation came further questions and demands for answers. I tried to talk things over with her, since I didn't want her believing everything she heard in the schoolyard or on television. Though she remained calm when we spoke, and she seemed to grasp more of what had happened, by November the news organizations had decimated any hope of getting the horrific images out of our heads. Instead they played them on a loop every day. If it was a conscious attempt to burn them into the nation's psyche, they were doing a spectacular job.

"Hey, Choi," I called over the long line of customers who'd forgotten essentials for their Thanksgiving meals. "Is Meena around?"

Choi showed a combination of aggravation that he hadn't had a break and pure joy he was selling so much in his store.

I walked around the side of the counter and spoke over the chewing gum. "You look like you're having a rough day. Do you want me to take Meena off your hands? She can come and spend Thanksgiving with us if she's under your feet. I'll bring her back when you close up."

"Could you? That would be big help, Adam. Thank you. Thank you," Choi said in his broken English before giving a slight bow in gratitude. He called out something in Mandarin, and Lei, who was desperately trying to restock shelves to keep up with demand, popped her head around the aisle. She looked just as relieved not to have the added stress of looking after an eleven-year-old.

As we left the store, I took hold of both girls' hands. Though Sera always insisted she didn't need help crossing the street, she didn't resist my automatic habit. Neither did Meena. As we reached the sidewalk on the other side, three young white men in their early twenties passed, with sneers on their faces.

"You filthy fuckin' raghead!" shouted the largest and most intimidating lad.

A few steps ahead of them, a young woman wearing a light yellow scarf around her head hunched her shoulders as if cowering. She was around the same age as the men behind her. She was walking alone and clearly scared.

"You people need to fuck off back where you come from," he continued shouting, his two friends nudging him in encouragement. "You're a bunch of fuckin' murdering sand niggers!"

Sera's palm slipped from my right hand. She headed toward the men. I started to go after her but was anchored by Meena, who stood rooted in fright, gripping hold of my left hand.

"Sera, get back here!" I shook Meena free and ran toward them. I saw the largest guy's chest begin to rise as he sucked in a guttural breath. Sera reached him just as he rounded in front of the young Muslim woman and spat into her face. The young woman screamed as the other two men grabbed hold of her wrists before she could run. A hand grabbed the scarf that covered the girl's dark black hair and ripped it down. Her head flipped back and she screamed in pain.

I barreled toward one of the men restraining her and knocked hard into him with my shoulder. He hit the ground, and I kicked him hard in the stomach. The man holding the girl's other wrist turned to look for backup from the leader, giving my adrenaline time to kick in and my fist the moment it needed to take advantage of his distraction. I simultaneously heard and felt his nose break as my knuckles crashed into his face. He released his grip on the girl's wrist to bring his hands up to stem the flow from his bloody nostrils.

I turned to go for the third, the largest of the men, and saw Sera standing in front of him. Her arms were straight out in front of her as she held his wrists. He wasn't struggling or attempting to swat her out of the way. The sneer and anger had gone from his face. He looked passively down at Sera as if hypnotized. Then his legs buckled and he fell to his knees.

"Go," Sera said clearly.

The man bowed his head and only moved when his two friends helped him to his feet. He walked backward, not taking his eyes off Sera as I stared the other two down.

"Sera!" I reached to hug her, but she pulled away from me and walked toward the Muslim girl, who had sunk down against the wall and was holding herself tight.

"You're okay now. There's no need to be frightened anymore," Sera said as she slid her thumb over the girl's cheek to wipe away the phlegm. The girl took Sera's hand and kissed it.

Meena, who had sensibly hidden in the entrance to our building, came running up, my small plastic bag of purchases swinging on her arm.

"Are you okay?" I asked her as I reached into the bag and pulled out a pack of paper napkins. She nodded as she looked around me, frightened the men would return.

"It's okay. They've gone," I said as I tore at the wrapping and pulled out a couple of sheets to hand to the girl, who was still clinging to Sera. I helped the young woman to her feet. She was unsteady at first but soon found her balance. "Listen, I'm going to take these girls upstairs, and then I'm going to walk you home. Okay?"

A sudden look of panic spread across her face. "No. No. Thank you for your help. I don't know what I would've done... if... if you hadn't been here," she said, as if she was suddenly aware of her surroundings. "I have to... to go now."

She began backing away from me. Sera stepped up with a look of confusion. "Why are you still frightened? This is my dad. You don't need to be frightened of him."

"She's not, sweetheart," I said, trying to defuse her confusion with a smile. "I want you to take Meena and go inside and wait."

"But—"

"Sera, don't argue with me, sweetheart. Go inside."

I waited until the two girls were out of sight. "Do you have enough money to get a taxi?"

The young woman shook her head.

I reached into my right pocket and winced; my sore hand pulled out a twenty-dollar bill and handed it to her. "Listen, get in a cab but stop a couple of blocks before you get home."

I walked out to the curb and flagged down a yellow taxi. I opened the door for her and stood to the side.

"Thank you so much."

"I'm sorry this happened to you. But I'm glad I was here at least to show you we're not all like those guys."

"Thanks for the offer to walk me home too, but if my father or brothers saw you—"

"It's okay. I understand."

She smiled bravely and got into the taxi, which drove off into the holiday traffic.

I opened the door to the building to find the two girls sitting on the bottom step of the stairs. Sera had her arm around Meena, who seemed to have calmed down.

"Meena, would you like to go back home?"

She shook her head.

"Okay. Up you go to our place. The door is open. We'll be up in a minute. I just have to have a quick chat with Sera."

Meena walked upstairs while I took her seat on the step next to Sera.

"What the hell were you thinking?"

"She needed our help, Dad. What was I supposed to do?"

"There are other ways of helping, Sera. Instead you put yourself and Meena in danger. We could've called the police. You and Meena could have come in here and let me deal with it. You had no idea how those men were going to react to you. What if they'd turned on you too? What if they'd hurt you? We've talked about this before, Sera, and if you don't get your head around it soon, we're going to have big problems."

Sera sat in silent contemplation for a moment. "I don't understand, Dad. The men were gone and the girl was safe. Why was she so scared of you taking her home after you helped her?"

I sighed as I tried to find the words, but, as so many times in the past few months, I was stuck trying to explain the lives of people on whom I was no expert. I didn't think she was quite ready to understand the complexities of the Muslim faith or culture. I wasn't sure I understood them myself.

"Maybe she wasn't scared. Maybe she just wanted to get home quickly and be with her dad. Wouldn't you want to come home to me as fast as you could if something like that happened to you?"

Sera nodded, but I knew my answer didn't convince her.

"I have to go and see Meena's mom and dad now to let them know what happened. So run upstairs and I'll be back soon."

Sera got up, turned, and took each step slowly.

"Don't think for a moment we're done with this conversation, young lady."

Sera took hold of the banister to steady herself as she turned. "I didn't like to see you like that, Dad. I didn't like seeing you hit those men."

"Do you understand why I did it, Sera?"

She nodded but looked sad.

WITH CHOI and Lei satisfied that Meena was safe and that it was still okay for her to stay with us for the day, I returned to the apartment to find Aaron had already arrived.

"You okay?" he said, jumping to his feet off the kitchen island. "Sera said you had trouble downstairs."

"I'm all right," I said, stretching out my injured hand. "What the hell makes three grown men start on a girl who's on her own?"

"Sera said she had a scarf around her head."

"Yeah, she was Muslim."

"And you took on all three guys?"

"Well, two of them. It was weird; the third didn't even try."

Aaron leaned back against the counter and crossed one ankle over the other. "Tempers are still running high out there. Especially against Muslims."

"That's no excuse. What if it was Sera being terrorized by three grown men?" I asked, more harshly than I intended.

"Hey, wait a minute. I didn't say it was okay."

"I know, I know. Sorry, I'm just wound up." Aaron dropped his hands from the palm-forward defensive position, and I poured myself a small glass of whiskey. "It's just bugging the hell out of me that parts of the media are insinuating that every Muslim in the world was in some way complicit in what happened. Like each one of them was somehow involved in the planning of the hijackings. It's like the media are giving license to go out and attack people."

"They're cowards, Adam. They don't need a license, they just need an excuse."

"True. I wonder whether those guys downstairs would've been so quick to start on a Muslim man."

"They're no better than the fucking cowards who hijacked those planes."

"Well, I don't think you can really compare the two."

"I can compare whoever I want," Aaron said sharply. He pulled the whiskey bottle from my hand and took a swig.

"Steady there, Aaron."

My brother raised his eyebrow as if to warn me off the subject of his drinking. I'd asked about it the week before, after he'd called me while drunk in SoHo. It was the third time he'd called in the early hours to talk about nothing—mundane conversations about what the weather would be like that weekend or whether I'd won a case. He didn't even know what cases I was working on.

"Is Sera in her bedroom? Is she okay?"

"Seems to be. Why?" His tone was softer, as if his attitude had switched again.

"She's never seen me act so aggressively before. I think I might've scared her."

"Nah, I'm sure she's fine. She's getting older. I'm sure she understands. But if you want, I can go and speak to her, you know, just to double-check."

I shook my head as I heard the front door open. Maria, Miss Dee, and Maggie filed in with big smiles and arms full of food. At once they knew something was amiss.

"Oh Lord, what have you done to yourself, child? Looks like you done battled the bees to get the honey," Miss Dee said, inspecting my swollen hand. She opened the kitchen drawer and pulled out a sandwich bag before making her way to the freezer. "Let's get some ice on that."

I downplayed the incident as much as I could. I didn't want any of the ladies to worry about their safety in our neighborhood.

"Did you see your daughters this morning? Did you wish them a Happy Thanksgiving from us?" I asked while Miss Dee chipped away at the ice cubes and filled the small clear bag. I'd never met her daughters, but I often gave her small holiday gifts to give to them. I always felt bad they had to share their mother's time with Sera, though Miss Dee never once said they complained when she came back early from her visits with them. But if they were half as kind as Miss Dee, I wouldn't have expected them to.

"I'm blessed. They are as beautiful as ever, and I thank the Lord they'll never change," she said with a wide smile.

I pulled my hand back as the shock of the cold hit my knuckles.

"You big wuss!" Aaron teased.

"Why are you here on your own, anyway? I thought you were bringing a date," I said, wincing as Miss Dee lowered the bag back onto my knuckles.

"You want me to bring a girl to meet my family? On Thanksgiving? Why don't you just propose for me and be done with it?"

"So the girl you told me about... it's not serious?"

"No. And if she finds out about the other two girls I'm seeing, I am in deep sh—" He stopped as he heard Buddy growl in his sleep. "Oh great, now even the dog is judging me." He pulled a beer from the fridge and sat on the sofa. The sounds of crowds and sports announcers filled the room as he switched on the game.

Maria sidled up to me while Miss Dee applied a little pressure on the bag of ice cubes. She spoke almost in a whisper. "Is your brother okay?"

"Yeah, as far as I know. Why?"

"I may be imagining it, but the last couple of times I've seen him, he seems to be a bit... up and down. And he talks about dating a lot of different girls."

This was true. In the past ten weeks, I hadn't seen as much of Aaron as usual. He blamed this on a constant flow of new women he'd met. He'd also hooked up again with one-night stands from the past. On the occasions we did see him, he seemed to go from a vibrant high to moping around with a face of impending doom.

"He's always had a penchant for the ladies."

"Does he talk much about his friends he lost in the World Trade Center?"

"No, hardly ever."

Maria looked like she was choosing her words carefully. "I might be wrong, and maybe it's because of all the people I've seen come through the doors at Amnesty, but I think it's worth keeping an eye on him."

"What do you mean?"

She pulled in her lips and looked to the side as if searching for the words. But I already knew what she was thinking.

"What, survivor's guilt? You think because he wasn't in the towers—"

"I don't know. All I'm saying is that you may want to watch him."

ONCE THE table was laid, we began our Thanksgiving meal the way we had ever since Sera came into my life. It was something I'd once scoffed at, but since I had my own family, I'd changed my opinion about the popular tradition.

"Okay, before we start, we'll go around and say what we're most thankful for."

"Oh God, do we have to?" Aaron whined.

"Yes," I said with a rebuke. "Who wants to go first?"

"I'm thankful to have such great neighbors and friends," Maria said, looking around the table with a big smile. Everyone returned her warmth except for Aaron, who looked like he wanted to get this part of the meal over with as soon as possible.

"I'm thankful for my two precious daughters," said Miss Dee.

"I'm thankful that I still get to teach, even though I'm retired now," Maggie said, winking at Sera.

"What about you, Meena?" I asked.

"I'm thankful I got an A on my math test. Dad would've been so mad at me if I didn't."

"Your dad is very proud of you," I said, smiling. "And what about you, Aaron?"

He'd turned his head and was watching the game on the TV, making it plain he wasn't interested in the round robin of gratitude.

"Aaron!"

"Okay, okay. I'm thankful that I'm so incredibly handsome and so damn charming that the ladies love me!" he said puffing out his chest. "Seriously," he added, looking around the table, "they adore me! And what's not to love? They're practically lining up to get them some Aaron!"

Maria's eyes darted to mine and then back to Aaron. I think Aaron expected people to laugh, but instead Sera, who sat on his right, broke the silence.

"I'm thankful Uncle Aaron wasn't in the towers when the planes hit," she said before she put her small hand on top of his and held it.

Aaron's free hand swept up as if he was trying to trap the air in his mouth from escaping. His shoulders began to shake and a couple of tears sprang from his eyes. He looked away from the table as he finally let out his breath.

"Christ, Sera, you really know how to get to your uncle, huh?" He rose and walked calmly to the bathroom to splash water over his face.

"What about you, Adam?" Maggie asked, trying to draw attention away from Aaron. "What are you most thankful for?"

She already knew. I'd given the same simple, one-word answer every year for the past eleven years.

"Sera."

CHAPTER TEN

BUDDY RAN to Oscar and nuzzled his shoulder as he sat on the steps of the church. The dog's hindquarters swayed as he whipped his tail from side to side at the excitement of seeing the homeless man, who scratched his ears and roughly petted him. Oscar leaned in and wrapped his arms around Buddy's neck, pulling him into a long hug. It was something he'd never done before. But in the chill of February, a cold man will try to find warmth any way he can.

"Good morning!" I called. Oscar held up his fingerless-gloved hand and waved to us. Sera dropped the brown paper bag of food on the step next to him as she did every morning. She smiled and waved back as I pulled Buddy away. The dog would have stayed there all day if he had the choice.

We stopped at the gates of the school. "Sweetheart, remember we're going to visit the man we talked about this evening."

Her face was expressionless as she stood on her toes to kiss my cheek. I watched her go through the doors with a heavy heart. The man we had an appointment with was a child therapist. I'd contacted Donna the week before and asked for a referral. Throughout the years she'd dealt with many kids with issues and recommended a therapist in Midtown named Dr. Arnold who had proven experience with problem kids.

Not that Sera was a problem kid. In all other ways, she was perfectly normal, apart from being alarmingly intelligent for someone her age. So it wasn't naïveté that made her too kind, generous, and compassionate. But since 9/11 and the attack on the girl outside the apartment, she'd developed what I considered an extreme interest in, if not obsession with, the Muslim world, and in particular Muslim women. Each evening, she bombarded me with questions: *Why do they wear scarves over their heads? Why aren't they allowed to drive? Why aren't they allowed to show their faces when the men can?"* I tried to answer the questions as best I could, but I simply didn't know enough. So we would look on the Internet together for explanations. This only made it worse and brought up more questions for which she wanted answers: *"Why aren't they allowed to go out in public without a man? Why aren't they allowed to pray with the men?"*

One evening I left Sera alone at the computer while I checked on our dinner. When I returned I saw she'd clicked on a link. There were images on the screen of boys with makeshift bombs strapped to their chests. A banner across the top of the screen read *"For Allah—a new generation of child suicide bombers."*

I switched off the computer at the plug.

Sera looked at me defiantly. "But they call God 'Allah.'"

"That's enough, sweetheart. I don't think we should look at this anymore."

"But it said they kill people for God. For their religion."

"A lot of people have died in the name of Christianity too," I said, instantly regretting my words.

"But—"

"That's enough, Sera. Those people are extremists. They don't all do that. There are millions of Muslims who don't buy into this. They live good, kind lives."

"But—"

"Sera, dinner's ready. We'll talk about it another day." I grabbed the remote control and switched on the TV, but I should have checked what channel was on before I walked back to the kitchen.

"These people want to kill Americans! These jihadists were promised they'd be given seventy-two virgin women in heaven. And for what? As a reward for murdering thousands of innocent people!"

I ran back to the television and switched the channel just as the animated news pundit hammered his fist on the round table.

"A reward?" Sera said looking confused. "They tell them they'll be given women if they kill people? What do they mean they are *given* women?"

I tried my hardest to explain, but so much of what I said didn't make sense to her. How do you explain that kind of thing to an eleven-year-old when it doesn't make any real sense to you as an adult? How do you explain people being brainwashed to the point that they are willing to become killers at the cost of their own lives.

AS WE sat in Dr. Arnold's waiting room that evening, I looked around at the décor. The office was laid out to appeal to kids of any age. Comic books and teen magazines were scattered on the table in the middle of the room, while a large plastic box holding Barbie dolls, G.I. Joes, and Lego pieces was pushed up against the back wall.

"What will we talk about?" Sera asked as she stared at Dr. Arnold's office door. "Will you come in with me?"

"No, you'll be talking to him alone. But don't worry." I put my arm around her shoulders and pulled her into a side hug. "I don't know exactly what you'll be talking about, sweetheart, but whatever he asks you, I want you to tell him the truth."

I'd already spoken to Dr. Arnold and told him my concerns. Long pauses in the conversation over the phone gave away that he was taking notes. His manner was quite blunt during our discussion. If I offered a theory for Sera's behavior, his dismissive tone became quite pointed, as if to say *"I'm the professional. I'll decide what's wrong with her."* But I was grateful to have even gotten an appointment with him. His schedule was full, and I suspected Donna had pulled a couple of strings for me to get Sera in faster. In this first meeting, he'd agreed to a ninety-minute session, hoping to arrive at some initial diagnosis on which he could work on in future sessions.

Dr. Arnold emerged from his office with a pale-looking boy around seven years old. The doctor patted his sullen young patient on the shoulder and directed him toward his mother, who looked embarrassed to be there.

"Sera?" he called as he took off his thick black-rimmed glasses and rubbed at his eyes.

It wasn't until Sera nervously stood that I saw how short Dr. Arnold was. They were practically the same height.

"In you come."

Sera walked into his office. She'd just sat down when he closed the door behind them.

Sera's appointment was the last of the day, so I was alone in the waiting room with nothing but the sound of the receptionist tapping away at her computer and the occasional shuffling of papers. As I sat in one of the plush high-backed chairs reserved for adults, I wondered whether I was doing the right thing. I wanted the best for Sera but was torn by the idea that my daughter was in that room alone with a man, telling him... what? Did she even have secrets? Were there things going on that I didn't know about? Was someone hurting her? Was she confessing something to a stranger that she hadn't felt comfortable telling me?

I looked around the room again and thought about all the terrible things the walls must have heard: sinister tales of abuse and the tragic stories that scared children were brought in to confess. But Sera and I had a great relationship. She never acted like she was scared or frightened to tell me anything. And if not me, surely she would have told Miss Dee, Maria, or Maggie. And they would have told me if it was something bad. Was I creating a problem by bringing her here?

When Sera came out of the room, she looked neither relaxed nor uncomfortable. In fact, her stoic demeanor hadn't changed from when she'd walked in.

"All done for today, Mr. Goodwin," Dr. Arnold called. "Sera has said it's okay to talk to you about our session, so if I could have a word?"

"Are you okay, sweetheart?"

She simply shrugged and picked up one of the teen magazines.

The therapist closed the thick wooden door behind me, and I took a seat on the leather sofa.

"Is there a problem? Is there something I don't know about?"

"Relax, Mr. Goodwin. By the sound of things, you know everything she has told me. But I think I may interpret it in a different way."

I was relieved there weren't going to be any major shocks coming my way.

"Sera is suffering from a kind of post-traumatic stress disorder. I've treated many, many children since 9/11, from those who lost parents in the attacks to those who are overly sensitive to the coverage and fear that they or their loved ones are in constant danger."

"But she's obsessed with Muslim culture now. Is that normal?"

He didn't address my question. Instead he looked over his notes. "Sera told me she's adopted."

"Yes, I've never kept that from her. She's known since the moment she could understand."

"Do you have any idea of her parentage? Her ethnic origins?"

"Maybe. I think her mother was Caucasian, but I can't be one hundred percent sure."

He laid down his pen and crossed his legs. I felt for a moment like I was the one being examined.

"It's natural for any adopted child who has no contact or knowledge of their parents to try and figure out where they came from—their history, their culture, their 'people,' if you will. I don't doubt the events of 9/11 were traumatic to her, as they were to many children. But I admit this is the first time I've seen it cause a child to immerse him or herself in the Muslim culture. From what I have seen, she's a very intelligent and well-balanced girl. She converses easily and isn't shy about putting her point across."

"So why the obsession?"

"I think she processed the events of 9/11 much the same way as any other child. It seems she'd started to move on, but I understand there was an incident that involved a young Muslim woman being attacked outside your apartment."

"Yes."

"I think that's the real cause of her post-traumatic distress. You see, Sera's skin color, hair, even her eye color, don't belong to any particular race. She's the proverbial melting pot. She has some Caucasian features— her nose and mouth—but her hair has a curl to it that may suggest Northern African descent. She has oval-shaped eyes with dark lashes that she may identify with Arab women, but her eyes aren't dark; they're a cross between Nordic blue and the Irish green, and yet her skin lacks the typical paleness of those races. Since she doesn't know where she's from, I think she identifies with all these women. And seeing the attack on the Muslim girl and the way the media has portrayed Muslim culture, perhaps there's a part of Sera that takes it personally."

"And what about Sophia?"

"You say she hadn't mentioned her for years before 9/11. I think she probably just had a one-off episode where her anger got the better of her, and she temporarily regressed to her younger self as a way of coping. The return of an imaginary friend would fit that theory."

"Did she talk to you about her?"

"No, but that could be for two reasons. She either was so distressed that she doesn't remember mentioning Sophia, or she is simply embarrassed that she did. She's of an age now when she wants to be regarded as a young adult, which is just another way of saying her teenage years are in sight and she wants to get there sooner rather than later. Mentioning an imaginary friend, however briefly, isn't going to help if she wants to be taken seriously. I will address it, but I didn't think it wise on the first session. As we proceed with sessions, she'll open up a little more as I gain her trust."

The doctor returned to his desk and took out a small pad on which he scribbled briefly.

"This is a prescription for clonazepam. It will calm her down if she begins to get overly distressed or you feel like she's getting herself too involved in something that might bring about another bout of stress. It will make her—" He paused, looking for the right words. "—a bit more placid for a while, but that's normal. It will pass."

"Wait.... You want me to medicate her?"

"I've prescribed this to dozens of children since 9/11 and have had good responses. If you feel she's getting overly anxious or obsessed about something, which it seems you do, I would suggest giving it a try."

"Is there something I'm doing wrong? Is there any other way I can help?"

"You're doing all you need to do, Mr. Goodwin. You've recognized there's a problem and you've sought professional help to address it. I think one session a week with Sera will help tremendously. I'll ask my receptionist to set it up."

I STOPPED at the pharmacy on the way home and dropped off the prescription while Sera wandered the aisles. She occasionally looked up at me, smiling, as if forgiving me for taking her to that place—a place where a stranger who examined each word that came out of her mouth silently judged her. When we arrived home, Buddy was in the hallway of the apartment, watching the door as always. But instead of bounding up to us as usual, he returned his head to the top of his paws and lay still, looking reproachful. Aaron was right: there were times when it felt Buddy was judgmental.

Sera headed to her bedroom to change out of her school uniform. I sat on the sofa and opened the paper bag; the small pills rattled inside the orange container as I rolled it in my hand reading the label.

SERA GOODWIN
Clonazepam 0.5mg
Take 1 pill as needed for anxiety
Qty 30

Buddy rose and slowly walked over to me. He nudged my hand with his wet nose, causing the pills to shake.

"Hey, Buddy, what do you think?"

He nudged my hand again as Sera came back into the room.

"Dad, will I have to go back to talk to that man again?" she asked as she sat next to me on the sofa and pulled Buddy's head away from me.

I looked once more at the bottle of pills. What was I thinking? How could I do this to her? Sera had always accepted me for who I was; she never once questioned me, only ever loved me. And here I was with a bottle of mind-altering drugs in my hand that I'd been encouraged to feed to her by a man who'd only known her for less than two hours.

"No, sweetheart, you'll never have to talk to him again."

I leaned over and kissed her cheek then walked to the bathroom, where I flushed the pills down the toilet.

CHAPTER ELEVEN

AT FOURTEEN years old, Sera had blossomed into a young woman who displayed a self-assurance I'd never seen in anyone of her age. She'd grown her thick auburn hair to below her shoulders; when wet it reached the middle of her back. Though her eyes remained the same startling blue, her long dark lashes emphasized the flecks of green in her irises. The freckles that had once given her an adorable little-girl look had begun to fade, but in the right light they were still visible. She spoke eloquently, well beyond her years, with the confidence and clarity of a college student, her arguments well thought-out and well-reasoned. Occasionally I almost believed she was older than she was, but then I'd see her in her school uniform and remember that she still needed to be protected.

It had been three years since I'd last heard mention of Sophia and had any real cause to feel troubled. Though she hadn't stopped investigating Muslim culture, African and Asian cultures fascinated her as well, and rather than an obsession, it seemed more like a healthy interest. She remained gregarious with adults and as popular as ever at school. I'd dreaded dealing with a teenager's attitude, but the tantrums and storming off and the slamming of doors never materialized, though that might have been because something else took precedence over hormonal hardships. Because this was around the time we lost Maria to breast cancer.

By the time she discovered it, it was too late for successful treatment. Since Maria was a childless widow, we were her caregivers, ensuring her last weeks were comfortable and filled with the love and support a family would have provided. In reality, we had become her family and, as caring and as giving as she was, she had become part of ours.

We'd all become closer than I ever could have imagined. The women also came to see Aaron as part of this nontraditional family, offering him the same motherly advice they gave to Sera and me. Miss Dee, the most qualified, nursed Maria in her apartment since she'd insisted that she didn't want to spend her final days in a hospice. Sera came home after school and sat reading to her, while Buddy kept guard at the foot of the adjustable bed I'd bought to keep her comfortable.

Miss Dee alerted us to the signs that Maria was nearing the end so we could gather around her and say our good-byes. Though Maria was hazy at times, in a moment of clarity she told the doctor she was ready to go and refused any more morphine, worried that our last memory of her would be of a doped-up, incoherent woman beaten by pain. She wanted to remain strong and brave to the end.

Aaron couldn't take it. He was the first to kiss her cheek and leave the room. I suspected it reminded him of our own mother's passing. He'd been just eighteen years old when we lost her.

Maggie stroked Maria's hand softly. They'd said everything they wanted to say to each other in the days that led up to this final good-bye. "Adios por ahora, mi querida amiga," Maggie said before she kissed Maria's cheek and followed Aaron from the room.

I kissed Maria's forehead and stroked her hair. "Thank you, Maria. I'll never have the words to express how much you mean to us. We love you and will miss you more than you could ever know."

The corner of her lips rose just enough to indicate a smile. "Thank you for letting me be a part of your lives."

I turned to Sera and indicated that now was the time to say whatever she wanted to, but Miss Dee spoke next. She put on a smile and gave the hearty chuckle she'd used when Sera was a little girl and had fallen or grazed her knee. It was the same comforting laughter that showed there was no need for tears and everything was going to be okay. "Oh Lord, I'mma miss you!" She leaned in and kissed Maria's cheek. "But not half as much as I bet your Carlos has. You go to him now. You go be together again with your husband and catch him up on everything that's happened since you two parted. Maggie and me will be along as soon as our work is done, so you get that gin rummy table ready, okay, darlin'?"

She cupped Maria's cheeks in her hands, leaned over, and softly kissed her lips before straightening a gray curl I'd disturbed.

"Hold them for me 'til I get there," Miss Dee whispered.

I imagined Maria sitting at an ethereal kitchen table, holding her cards, waiting until her friends arrived to resume their game.

As Miss Dee made her way to the door, she took hold of my hand and gave it a little tug to indicate we should leave Maria and Sera alone. Since Sera was the closest thing Maria had to a child, and Maria was one of the three women Sera looked upon as a mother, I followed her out to give them their privacy.

We sat in Maria's living room for two hours while they talked. Through the wood of the closed door, their words were muffled, though I could make out that Maria's voice did most of the talking as the tone and speech became more labored. But there was also soft laughter. What had they found to laugh about? Maybe a memory of Sera as a baby and Maria's first attempt to change a diaper, which had been as clumsy as my own. Maybe Sera as a toddler, learning how to run and Maria trying to keep up as she sped down the hallway in only a My Little Pony T-shirt and no shame. Whatever it was, it was heartwarming to hear. But then came near silence, as if they were speaking in whispers.

Miss Dee rose out of her chair and went through the bedroom door as Sera opened it. With a sad smile, Sera walked over to me and hugged me so hard I could feel my ribs bow. I kissed the top of her head as Miss Dee came back out of the bedroom and simply said, "She's with God now."

In the days following Maria's death, I expected Sera to go into a depression. The loss of Maria hit me harder than I expected, and I'd already experienced losing loved ones. I'd also had more time to prepare for it, as Maria came to me the day she was diagnosed and made me promise I wouldn't tell Sera until she was ready to tell her herself. I respected her wishes, but every day I imagined Sera walking in from one of her visits in tears after learning Maria's news.

When that day finally came, Sera came to me and cried for hours. So when Maria passed, I waited for the breakdown, the moment when it finally hit her that this was it: her beloved Maria was gone. But Sera, far from moping around the house, became even easier to talk to. The realization of Maria's passing seemed to energize her. Her outlook on life became more positive. She rejoiced in small things the way she had as a little girl, as if something had become clear to her and the world had come into focus.

By the age of fifteen, Sera had not only become her own person but someone I could have seen myself hanging around with when I was in high school. We'd banter together like friends, and she could make me laugh and disarm me with a few well-chosen words delivered with wit and humor. Wherever we went she was the fun and the light in the room. But then again, to me she always had been.

In honor of Maria, Sera offered to volunteer at Amnesty International. At first I refused. Though it had been years since 9/11, I was concerned that the harrowing stories Amnesty uncovered would be too much for her. I didn't want her involved with anything that could lead to another breakdown. But she argued so passionately that my continued refusal would have suggested a lack of trust, or confirmation that I believed there was a problem and didn't think she could mentally cope with the challenge. So I relented, but on the condition that she work only two Saturdays every month and that we reevaluate the arrangement after six months.

Nevertheless, I was still concerned. So when Amnesty contacted me and asked if I would consider joining her, I agreed immediately. Sera's schoolwork was taking up more of her attention, so it gave me an excuse to spend more time with her while supporting her desire to pay tribute to Maria.

I advised them on legal matters where appropriate and assisted with completing forms for desperate people seeking asylum in America, while at the same time chaperoning Sera. She took on light support work like filing and assembling information packs for the organization's donors.

Occasionally we contributed to Amnesty's letter campaigns, and I was able to explain many of the issues, such as the death penalty, equal rights and protections for the LGBT communities of the world, the plight of refugees, and asylum for transgender men and women at risk. I let Amnesty's staff explain other issues, if I felt they were appropriate or if I felt Sera was old enough to understand. She soaked up information, always wanting to understand how things worked. On occasion she surprised me with her knowledge of things about which even I wasn't aware. Between her bouts on the computer and the years of stories I suspect Maria had told her, she showed a better grasp of world affairs than I had at her age.

Though her commitment impressed me, I was a little concerned that she was loading too much onto herself. The problems of the world become apparent to us all eventually, whether we choose to acknowledge them or not, but she was just a teenager. So when Aaron walked through the door one day with a box wrapped in pink paper, I was thankful he was giving her a tool to interact with others her own age.

"Uncle Aaron!" Sera exclaimed as she tore off the paper. "Is this really for me?"

"It's about time you stopped using your dad's PC and got something of your own," Aaron said as he opened the cardboard box and pulled out the shiny new laptop from its polystyrene case. "I'll teach you how to set up your iPod, get your own iTunes account, and get Microsoft Messenger up and running so you can chat with your friends online. I also want to show you a new website that started a few months ago called Facebook."

Sera looked excited for a moment, but then her face fell. "I know about Facebook. A lot of my friends are on it, but Dad won't let me have a profile."

"That's because your dad's an old Luddite." Aaron winked at me.

"No, Aaron, it's because her dad doesn't want middle-aged perverts pretending to be teenage boys talking to his daughter."

"Here we go," Sera said rolling her eyes before she started her impression of me. "Sera, I'm not letting you go on Myspace because the next thing you know you'll be hitchhiking to Canada to meet a forty-year-old man living in the basement of his deaf mother's house, pretending to be a fifteen-year-old boy." She paused for effect. "It happens. I saw it on *Dateline!*"

"Who the hell still uses Myspace?" Aaron asked.

"Young lady, you're going about things the wrong way if you want my permission to go on this Facebook thing," I said. "Though I must admit, I've heard good things about it."

A brief look of hope appeared on Sera's face.

"Adam, let me set it up. The privacy settings are pretty strict, and I'll be one of her friends on her profile so I can keep an eye on it. I'll keep her updated if their privacy settings ever change."

Sera held her breath, waiting for my response. I knew I'd seemed overprotective in the past, but she wasn't even a teenager the last time she'd asked to go on Myspace. But now she was older and maintaining stellar grades and, with the commitment she'd made to Amnesty, she'd proven herself responsible.

"Okay," I sighed.

Sera screamed with joy but stopped when she saw my raised eyebrows.

"There will be rules. If I ever get concerned and ask for the password to your account, you will give it to me immediately. No arguments."

Sera nodded quickly.

"You must let your uncle be your friend on the site so he can make sure you're keeping safe."

She nodded frantically again.

"And finally, you can't go on Facebook unless all of your homework is finished. You're doing well at school, and I don't want to see your grades slip. If you're okay with all that, you can have a page."

"A profile," Aaron corrected me.

Sera was beside herself as Aaron sat us both down and explained the social networking site and how it worked. The first name she looked for was Meena, who she found almost straightaway. She sent a friend request and moments later, I heard a ping. A notification appeared on the page that it had been accepted. She pulled up Meena's full profile.

"You see? These are all the photos that Meena has added," Aaron said pointing to the screen. "You can create albums of pictures for different events or just photos you like. Then, if you want to, you can tag yourself or friends in the photos and they will be notified that you've added a photo that they're included in."

Most of Meena's photos were well posed and presented her as a respectable young lady, something I expect her parents insisted on before she was allowed to upload them. Since Lei and Choi were rather strict, it gave me some comfort that they trusted the website enough to let Meena on it.

"Then over here you can see some of the groups that Meena has joined and a list of what she likes." Aaron clicked on a button that revealed a list of pop stars, actors, and movies.

"What if they have a common name, like John Smith? There must be thousands of John Smiths in the world," I asked, becoming increasingly interested in the mechanics of the site.

"Well, at the moment Facebook is relatively new so you may have to search a few pages, but you can narrow down searches by geographical location. But for Sera, if she has a friend with a common name who also knows Meena, her name will be listed at the top since they have a friend in common."

"So do you have to know someone to add them as a friend?"

"No. In fact, a lot of people connect through friends of friends, or have a common interest like the *Harry Potter* books or maybe a local band."

Sera took particular interest in this. "So if I wanted to get to know someone in another country, I could become friends with her and we can just chat?"

"Yes. I've set your location as just 'New York—USA,' as I don't think your dad would want you to put any more information than that on there." Aaron turned as I nodded my approval.

"Why would you want to talk to someone in a different country?" I asked Sera.

"Why not? It would be fun to chat with someone in China or Australia. Don't you think?"

"So long as you're careful, Sera. You don't know what agenda strangers may have."

"I know. I'll be careful. Besides, with you looking over my shoulder, it's unlikely they'd get very far. You'd scare them away!"

"Damn right."

"You know, Dad, you should get a profile on here too so we can be friends."

"I'm not your friend. I'm your dad."

"Dad, you're my best friend."

Even after fifteen years, she could say something to fill my heart instantly, even when I knew I was about to be played.

"Okay, you're my best friend too, sweetheart," I said.

"Can I have a cell phone?"

"No."

"You're a terrible best friend."

WE LEFT Sera to search for school friends on her new laptop while we stood in the kitchen. I pulled a beer from the fridge and passed it to Aaron.

"Promise you'll keep an eye on her," I said as I cracked open my own can.

"Are you worried about boys?"

"She hasn't shown any interest in boys so far, thank God."

"None she's told you about."

"If there's a boy she has a crush on, I'd know about it. She'd have absolutely no problem talking to me about stuff like that," I said. "Anyway, what about you? You haven't brought a girl home for a while." By "home" I meant "to introduce to Sera and me." That was the only telltale sign he was even remotely interested in someone.

"No, still just having fun. But I well and truly messed up the other day. I arranged a date with a girl named Victoria who I'd met in a bar. She was a bit cold at first but agreed to go out for a meal with me. Anyway, we got to the restaurant, and over appetizers she told me that we'd dated before, two years ago! So for the next half an hour all I heard was 'Why didn't you call me? Why did you ignore my texts? I thought we had something special. What was wrong with me?' Blah, blah, blah."

"What did you do?"

"It was an ambush! What do you think I did? I got up and walked out. I had a good reason not to call her back."

"And that was?"

Aaron laughed. "I thought it was rude to text her while I was in bed with another girl!"

I shook my head. "You know, you're going to get too old for this soon. You're going to get burned, and it'll serve you right!"

He shrugged as if the prospect didn't bother him.

"Thanks again for Sera's laptop. She's thrilled."

"My pleasure. You know how much I love that girl."

"Just do me a favor and keep an eye on that profile of hers," I repeated.

"She'll be fine. Hey, it might be good for her to stay off your PC for a while. Perhaps you can start online dating?"

Aaron was keen to get me back out into the dating world. The excuse that I was too busy working and raising a kid was getting less and less sympathy, especially as Sera was no longer a kid.

"I prefer the old-fashioned way of dating."

"What, you mean paying for an expensive meal only to sit over it in silence for an hour because you have nothing in common? This is New York! You haven't got the time to sort the wheat from the chaff in this city. Get all that out of the way online beforehand."

"But I don't like the idea of this cyberdating thing. Knowing my luck, I'd be the one who finds the forty-year-old pervert who lives in his deaf mother's basement. It happens—I saw it on *Dateline*."

"Hey, you gotta start somewhere!"

CHAPTER TWELVE

IN THE following months, Sera kept her word, maintaining her grades at school while at the same time building her friend list on Facebook. The teachers at her high school regularly complimented me on her progress, and every day after school, she completed her homework in Maggie's apartment long before I arrived home from work.

I hadn't checked on her profile at all, other than on the odd occasion when she voluntarily turned the screen to show me a new photograph she'd posted. I bought her a digital camera for her birthday, and Miss Dee and Maggie encouraged her to post pictures of things in which she found beauty: a simple flower growing out of a rock wall, Buddy chasing birds through the park, the light that beamed behind the silhouette of the church in the late afternoon. One day she even tried to take a picture of Oscar's face, as she desperately wanted an image of him smiling. But the moment she produced the camera, he comically bolted like the cops were after him.

"He must have been a superstar in a previous life," Sera joked as we watched him limp rapidly around the corner. "Please, please, no pictures! I may be famous but I'm just a normal guy!"

"HELLO, MISS Popular!" Aaron said as he came through the door on one of his unannounced visits, hoping to nab himself dinner after a late evening at work. "You're doing well. I see your friend list is up to 1,100 people. Mine's only 500!"

"Don't you ever knock?" I asked him for the hundredth time. I turned to Sera. "You have more than a thousand friends on Facebook? But you don't know that many people."

I could understand Aaron having 500 Facebook connections. With high school and college classmates, old acquaintances, friends, and work colleagues from the past forty-two years, he could easily rack up that number. It would have reached 600 if he'd had the nerve to add ex-girlfriends to his tally.

"Actually it's 1,120!" Sera corrected him. "I get friend requests every day from people all around the country: Alaska, Florida, Ohio. Everywhere!"

"But why are they requesting you as a friend if they don't know you?" I asked, forgetting we'd already discussed this.

"They see I'm a fan of the same band they like, or that I posted about a movie, or commented on another friend's photo. It kind of grew from there, just like Uncle Aaron said it would. It's interesting to see how things are in other states. They have such different attitudes about things, especially people in California. I know 1,120 sounds like a lot, but there are people out there with thousands more than me."

"You know, there are ways to increase your number even faster," Aaron began. "If you see something that interests you on the Internet, you can link the article onto your page to share with your friends. That way your friends can share it with their friends too. When they share it, it'll come up as 'via Sera Goodwin' and their friends might friend you if they think you post interesting or funny stuff."

"All I heard was 'friend, friend, friend,'" I said.

"That's a good idea," Sera said. "There are a few websites I like that I bet some of my friends would love."

"Also, if there are any websites you like, you can offer to write a post for them. Say, for example, you like cupcakes—"

"I love cupcakes!"

"Well, you could find a website dedicated to cupcakes and maybe write an article on your favorite one, or offer a recipe, or where to get the best ones in the city. Then, at the end write 'you can follow Sera Goodwin on Facebook' and link it to your profile page. The more you do outside Facebook, the more people you'll attract who enjoy the same things you do."

Sera popped in her headphones and immediately set to work looking at the websites and blogs she followed. Aaron joined me in the kitchen, where I was stirring a pan of Bolognese sauce for dinner.

"Why are you encouraging her to get even more people on Facebook? Isn't over a thousand enough?"

"No, Adam. Sera lives in a different world from the one we grew up in. She's almost sixteen years old, and you have no idea what she wants to become in life. And really, neither does she. I know she keeps talking about how much she wants to travel, but as for a career, the world is her oyster. Networking and building a following now could help her a lot when she gets to an age when it could become useful."

"How so?"

"It's going to be the nature of business in the next few years. Sera just said she likes cupcakes, right? Just say, for example, she wanted to open up a cupcake store in New York. By the time she's in her twenties, she could have the potential to reach thousands upon thousands of customers on social media. She could sell them direct online and ship them all over the country, because she would already have a kind of captive audience who feel like they know her and trust her. Networking and advertising on social media is the future, Adam, trust me."

"But it increases the risk of more lunatics contacting her too."

"I understand why you're worried about that, but I promise I'll keep an eye on it. She's a smart kid, Adam. Stop worrying. If anything, building a following will occupy her time better. Wouldn't you prefer that to her spending hours talking to a boy, maybe one she hasn't actually met? This gives her a purpose and a goal."

There was some logic to what he said, and it put me at ease.

SERA'S NEW goal to increase her friend list didn't take the turn I expected. I thought she might take Aaron's advice and contact individual websites about things that interested her. But instead she turned to teen blogs that covered everything from popular culture to fashion styles and college choices. Sera confidently approached the bloggers and submitted articles she'd written that covered topics she knew were missing from these websites. In between the articles of the latest Jonas Brothers album and the endless threads discussing prom dresses and celebrity gossip, Sera slipped in serious issues, ones she knew affected people her age.

Though she was incredibly bright, I wouldn't have pegged my daughter as a writer. But somehow her words instantly connected with her peers. She researched the most popular blogs and submitted an article to each of them. All were accepted and went on to create long threads of comments that numbered into the hundreds, sometimes thousands.

Sera carefully researched each subject, checking and double-checking the facts and making her views as balanced as they could be.

Her first blog was directed at girls and dealt with body image. She argued that magazines dictated what was considered beautiful through immaculate images shot by professional photographers in artificial light. She included before-and-after pictures to show blemishes airbrushed out, stretch marks erased, and curves straightened with the touch of a digital pen. She also embedded a video from a relatively new website called YouTube that showed the process on film, exposing the lie these magazines were trying to sell.

She went on to write about both schoolyard and cyberbullying, the physical effects of prescription and narcotic drug abuse, the realistic consequences and dangers of sex, the health effects of anorexia and bulimia, as well as the health effects of obesity. She didn't hold back or dance around the subjects. She was brutally honest, and this honesty gave her credibility. Although they were billed as opinion pieces, she used the collective "we" when discussing solutions and responsibility.

Before she submitted each post, she ran it by Maggie. As a retired teacher, Maggie knew the best way to structure the article so, having introduced the problems, they could end on a positive note with the hope of a solution. Then I read each post as a second set of eyes before she submitted it. In every article she included phone numbers and website addresses that offered professional support for the issue. And she took her uncle's advice and included a link to her Facebook page. At first I was uncomfortable with her addressing issues like STDs, abuse, and suicide, but her mature and positive approach reassured me.

Over five months and twenty articles, Sera's profile continued to expand rapidly. The day after her first blog posted, I asked her to mute her laptop since the relentless pings of notifications of friend requests became unbearable to listen to hour after hour. It was like being trapped in a giant elevator whose doors constantly warned they were about to close.

She struck a chord with girls her age and younger, and older ones too. She posted links to other articles she'd found with a positive message. Those links were shared hundreds of times, and within sixteen weeks, Sera had more than 30,000 friends on Facebook.

She began to spend a lot of her free time answering messages from girls who told her their problems. There were nights she went to bed exhausted after desperately trying to answer as many as she could.

"You have to slow down and stop taking on all of these girls' problems. There are just too many of them, and it's beginning to affect you. I haven't seen a smile on your face for a month," I said to her as we walked Buddy through Central Park.

"I can't help it, Dad. It's heartbreaking to hear about overweight girls in poor areas living such sad lives because their parents can't afford to buy them healthy food."

"They can exercise, Sera."

"They can. But can they exercise when they have to go to a job straight after school until late at night to help their families afford to pay rent?" Sera took a deep breath. "Then there's the other side. Rail-thin girls eating cotton balls and drinking sips of water so they don't gain any weight at all. Or they binge eat and then throw it all up. And why? Because someone in their class or family keeps telling them they're fat. Their body image becomes so distorted that they honestly can't see how skinny they are. One girl told me two girls held her down in the cafeteria and forced food into her mouth while everyone chanted 'fat bitch' at her."

"I know, but—"

"I'm sorry, Dad, but you don't know. It's constant. Girls are being bullied because they've hooked up with a boy. Some never even had sex, just fooled around. But now they're shunned by girls and constantly bothered by boys who think they're going to put out for them. Some even get violent when the girls refuse. Their sense of self-worth is taken from them a little more every time someone calls them a whore or a slut. But the boys get hailed as heroes by their friends."

"I hate to say this, but that particular double standard has been around for an awfully long time."

"But that doesn't make it okay! It doesn't make it acceptable! I heard from a girl who's told on a daily basis that she's ugly. Imagine it, Dad—every single day someone tells you that you're ugly, you're gross, you're disgusting."

"High school is tough, Sera. A lot of people go through stuff like that. But then you leave high school, grow up, and find yourself."

Sera rounded on me. "It gets better? Is that what you're saying?"

"Hey, calm down. All I mean is that high school doesn't last forever. It's a few years out of your life, not an eternity."

"But for these girls each day feels like an eternity. Every hour, every day is lengthened by torture and constant fear. You may look back at high school and shrug that it was 'only four years,' but remember how long that felt like back then. You talk about your high school days when you felt like summers lasted forever. Imagine being bullied all the way through it, hoping the sun would never go down so you wouldn't have to face the next day."

"Sera, is there something you want to tell me?" I asked delicately. "Are you having problems at school?"

"No," Sera said with exasperation, as though I was missing the point completely. "Dad, I'm fine. But seeing what some of these girls go through is just terrible. There are gay girls being ridiculed and having boys expose themselves to them to 'straighten them out.' If someone did that here in Central Park they'd be arrested, but at school it's okay because 'they're just kids doing what kids do.'"

"A lot of people find their teenage years difficult. I know there was a time when I did."

"Yes, but people my age deal with different types of bullying than what you went through when you were at school. Everyone makes mistakes, but now those mistakes are plastered all over the Internet and social media for everyone to see. A girl the same age as me sent me a message yesterday. She said she was contemplating suicide because she'd let a boy take a picture of her breasts with his camera phone. When they split up, he posted the picture on an 'ex-revenge' website where people send embarrassing or naked pictures of their ex-girlfriends or ex-boyfriends. She was wearing makeup and looked older than eighteen, so the website posted it. The boy sent the link in an e-mail to her dad's work. Then, just to top off her humiliation, he photoshopped a picture of a pig's head onto her body and mass texted the image to everyone in her school. He just tore this poor girl down to the point that she wanted to end her life."

"Cowards always cause more destruction than the brave."

Sera gave me an odd look. "That's deep for you, Dad."

"I've seen a lot of cowards in my life," I said, thinking of my time at Legal Aid.

As we continued to walk, I thought about what Sera was saying. My experience of high school hadn't been so bad, but the thought of what it would have been like to have my own secrets exposed so publically at her age sent a cold chill down my spine.

"You're right," I said, "Things are very different now. I love that you're concerned about these girls because it shows how compassionate you are. But really, Sera, you are only one person. Letting all of these girls' problems get on top of you like this isn't going to end well. You can't solve all of their issues."

Sera called Buddy over and put on his leash. We walked in silence for a while before she spoke again.

"I think a lot of the time they just need someone to talk to. Some of them are so brave and go through so much. But they feel alone."

"The best way to unhinge someone's mind is to isolate them. Sometimes people just need to be heard or feel they're being listened to."

"That's pretty much what Oscar said."

I stopped. Sera was old enough to walk home after school on her own, but I still went with her in the mornings to give Buddy a walk before I headed to work. I hadn't seen Oscar on the steps of the church for a long time, so I assumed he'd moved on.

"You talk to him? Is he there in the afternoons now?"

"No, hardly ever. I occasionally see him on Sunday mornings if I go out to meet Meena. I think he expects to get more money sitting outside the church on Sundays, but more often than not people pass him by on their way in. He said they're much more generous on their way out. Not all of them, but some."

"What do you talk about?"

"He asks how school's going. He asks how you are. Just general chitchat, really. I told him about Facebook and what I'd written for the blogs. He seemed really interested. But I think he probably just feels a little lonely, so I spend a while chatting with him. He's a very smart guy. He observes a lot about people."

"He's had a lot of practice."

"He likes you. He thinks you're a good man."

"Well, that's nice to hear, but Sera—"

"I know, I know. Be careful."

CHAPTER THIRTEEN

IT WASN'T as much an intervention as a brainstorming session to find a way to help Sera scale back on the time she spent on social media. For six months I'd seen signs of her sinking back into the same withdrawn state she'd shown in the months after 9/11. She obsessed over the problems teenagers faced as though it was her personal responsibility to help, or at least respond to, everyone who contacted her. With her online friend list increasing at a staggering rate, it was an impossible task. Not all her messages were requests for advice, but even a small fraction was far too many for her to deal with on her own.

Aaron and I had talked it over the day before as we sat on the end of the Chelsea Piers. He was disappointed Sera hadn't joined us for lunch, but he perked up when I asked him to come over the following day to see her and offer advice. It was clear he missed his niece.

MISS DEE, Maggie, Aaron, and I met to discuss our approach before we sat down with Sera. It was the late summer of 2006, and she was preparing to enter her junior year of high school. Instead of the bright-eyed, vibrant teenager she'd been just a year before, she was walking around the apartment with dark circles under her eyes and her shoulders slouched as if the weight of the world rested upon them.

Miss Dee wasn't sure how she'd be able to help other than to back up anything we said with positive reinforcement. Maggie took a more academic approach by mapping out the numerical history of Sera's friend list and forecasting a figure if the trend continued.

"We all love what you're doing," Maggie said kindly as Sera sat at the table, eyeballing her closed laptop. We could all see that, although she tried to pretend patience, all she wanted was to get the gathering over with so she could get back online. "But you're getting to the point where you're not going to be able to help anyone soon. In the space of a year, you've accumulated a following of over 50,000 people. You're tired, Sera. You may be on summer break right now and can stay up later than usual, but what's going to happen when you go back to school and you have to concentrate on your classes? These last years of high school are vital to your future. What's going to happen if you try to keep up this pace for another year?"

Sera sighed. I think she knew she couldn't continue the way she was going, but her overwhelming desire to help these girls was too strong. As her dad, I could take her laptop away or simply demand that she delete her profile, but Maggie and Miss Dee insisted that would only make matters worse. She would still find a way to get online, all the while resenting me for standing in her way.

"But what can I do?" Sera asked. "Girls write and tell me things like they're being sexually abused by someone in their family."

"They should call the police. Or you should," Aaron said.

"It's not as simple as that. A lot of them aren't even using their real names. They tell me because they can't tell anyone else. They're frightened and can't find a way out. They say they want to commit suicide. How can I not respond?"

"But Sera, this is so much to take on, sweetheart," I said.

"What do you expect me to do? Just switch off my laptop, go to bed, and hope that by the time I write back the next morning, all refreshed and caught up on sleep, they're not hanging from the back of their door?"

Miss Dee silently raised her right hand to her forehead, then down to her chest and across to each shoulder.

"Groups, Sera," Aaron said. "I've worked out a way that will take a lot of the pressure off. I also think it's best to think about removing your name."

"Why?"

"If people are baring their souls to you, they could become obsessed. People might try to track you down if you don't—or can't— answer their messages on time. If they're as desperate as you say, you may be the only thing holding them back from killing themselves. If they can't get in contact with you, they might try to find you if you're their last hope."

"How can I possibly change my name? It's how people know to look for me."

"Okay, then why not just go by your first name? Like Prince or Madonna. There are new ways to use Facebook that can take your personal identity out of it. You've just said yourself that many don't use their real names. You're just omitting your last name. And your name is spelled uniquely enough that they could still find you."

I loved this idea. I was never happy with the fact that she used her full name, especially once the number of her online friends started growing out of control.

Aaron continued, "You can now set up private groups on Facebook. So, for example, you could have a group called 'I'm Being Bullied.' You can add people to this private group and be the moderator."

"How does that work?" I asked.

"Okay, say I was being bullied at school and I'm friends with Sera on Facebook. She could invite me to a private group called 'I'm Being Bullied,' where I'd be added to a list of others who are dealing with the same issue. I could then start a new conversation on that page where others could comment. That way I'd be able to see that I'm not the only one facing the issue, eliminating the sense of isolation, and I could offer or receive support from others going through the same thing."

"That makes sense. So they'd be a part of a group, or kind of create a 'tribe' of others just like themselves," Maggie said before turning to Sera. "You often say that with so many of these issues, like bullying, that these girls feel alone, and if they only knew they were in the majority, not the minority, they'd feel better."

"Exactly. And like I said, you could just be the moderator," Aaron continued. "You'd be able to see the discussion, and if anyone got out of line you could kick them out of the group, or if you felt someone needed an extra word you could contact them directly. So what it boils down to is instead of you taking it all on yourself, your friends could find help, advice, and support through one another."

Sera chewed on her lip as she considered Aaron's idea.

"Maybe you could get Meena to help you," Miss Dee chimed in. "That way there'd be two pairs of eyes."

Sera's face shifted from contemplation to exuberance at the suggestion. "I could ask a friend from school named Amy too!" she said enthusiastically.

I'd met Amy a number of times. She came from a wealthy family in the East Village and was what many might consider the "All-American girl." Her long blonde hair was always styled in the latest fashion, and she came across as polite and polished. But she also had a touch of the down-home girl, a tomboy willing to get messy, watch sports, and revel in pop culture.

"Can there be more than one moderator?" Sera asked.

"Yes, so you and your two friends can all keep an eye on it," Aaron said.

"This sounds great. Show me how!"

"Okay, but before I do, I want to tell you about another site called Twitter."

"No," I said firmly. "Facebook is enough. The idea of this little get-together was to allow Sera to have more free time, not to double the time she's spending on the computer with another social network."

"But Twitter is—"

"No!" I repeated. "I've heard of Twitter. I know what it is."

"Adam, will you listen to me? I'm trying to make things easier and more effective for Sera."

His first idea had made sense, so I grudgingly nodded. After all, he was the technical genius in the family.

"First, you set up a profile on Twitter. Then announce on your Facebook wall that you can now be followed on Twitter too. Then put the link to your Facebook profile in your Twitter description and a link to your Twitter profile on Facebook. That way you will direct traffic from Facebook to Twitter and vice versa. And when you write for more blogs you can link to both."

"Won't that just make things worse? You're increasing her time on the computer!"

"Let me finish, Adam," Aaron said. "YouTube is massive now. People post links from YouTube onto Twitter all the time. If Sera wants to continue helping these girls, all she needs to do is spend a few minutes each day finding some kind of inspirational story on YouTube, post the link, and it's done! If anything, it works even better. She'd increase her following, but the amount of actual work she'd have to put in is cut in half, since she's sharing stories instead of actually telling them. Does that make sense?"

"Um... I think so," I said uncertainly.

"Listen, Sera already has a massive following. She can now sit back and use what others have put on YouTube, Facebook, and Twitter to advance her point of view. If she sees a video posted anywhere of a girl who has overcome her problems, Sera can share that link as an inspiration to others. Instead of writing for hours on end, it's just a simple click. And if she has friends helping her, they each can collect just one story a day to post, giving her three stories of hope to share. Hell, you don't even need to look for them. You could just write a post that will be seen by thousands, asking them to send you links of things that inspire them."

"That makes sense," I said, finally following what he was saying.

"Let's face it," Aaron said enthusiastically, "from what Sera has said, this is all these girls need—a feeling of not being alone, belonging to a community or something bigger, and a sense of hope they don't have now. Plus they have the advantage of being part of a kind of hive-mind where they can offer advice and solutions."

"I think it's a great idea!" Sera said, smiling at Aaron.

Sera opened her laptop, and I watched as Aaron changed her Facebook profile name and showed her how to set up groups, moderate threads, share links, and set up her Twitter account. Maggie and Miss Dee stood behind them, watching with more interest than I expected. I'm quite sure they weren't following what was happening, but they seemed intrigued by this new way of connecting with people.

AARON'S ADVICE did everything he said it would. Sera already was the best friend, big sister, and confidante to thousands of girls around the country and soon, much like the ever-growing Facebook, her appeal stretched further than just America. Teenage girls from Canada, Australia, England, and just about every other English-speaking nation began joining her groups and adding Sera as a friend.

But even with Meena's and Amy's help, the constant demand for moderation or approval requests for these groups became too much. So Sera enlisted the help of another friend, Carla, who attended the same public school as Meena. Sera and Carla had known each other since they were around eight years old, when Meena first introduced them. Carla lived with her parents above their restaurant on the Lower East Side. Her father, a second-generation El Salvadoran immigrant, was a placid and easy-going guy. But Carla had inherited much of her Puerto Rican mother's feistiness. Even when she was a kid and came to the apartment, she was never shy about saying what was on her mind, and I liked her for it. Sera was thrilled at the prospect of Carla joining her work and was exuberant when she accepted. And to make a good situation even better, Carla could open up the groups to young Latinas in their own language and with their own cultural voice.

Nearly every evening the four girls sat at the kitchen table discussing the problems and issues they saw among the online threads. I had to impose a limit of an hour and a half every night, as I knew the other girls' parents would be on my case if the girls were away from their own homes for too long. Though they had this time reserved in the evenings, I knew they likely used their lunch breaks and free periods at school to jump online and check on their projects.

With no real input or direction from me or the other parents, they dedicated their time and resources. And though I was worried at first, I was able to see the difference they were making in the lives of these young women they'd never met, yet with whom they shared such a kinship. Sera validated their work by showing me heartfelt messages of appreciation or photos of young women holding up signs that simply read "Thank you."

The most remarkable part was watching Sera's focus and determination. She wasn't going to let anything get in her way. She continued to turn in her schoolwork on time and she received her usual excellent grades. I'd feared she might let her work slip because of her concentration on Facebook and Twitter, but she was so worried I might find a reason to stop her crusade that she worked hard to prove me wrong.

By the spring of 2007, Sera's friends, or "followers" as they were known on Twitter, exploded into a dizzying number I couldn't even start to comprehend. Between Facebook and Twitter, over 200,000 people followed her online. Her profile was an all-in-one source of information for teenage issues, funny pictures, inspirational quotes, popular memes, and guest blogs. One of Sera's longer blog posts about the effects of bullying was shared thousands of times. Somehow it caught the eye of one of the most popular female pop stars in the world. She was an entertainer known for her outrageous fashion, self-expression, catchy tunes, and rabidly devoted fans. Her own story of being bullied as a child was well documented and struck a chord with many of the 30 million people who followed her online. She was one of the first pop stars to utilize social media to keep a sense of personal contact with her fans, and it had worked remarkably well. Along with personal photos of her tours, behind-the-scenes glimpses of video shoots, candid selfies with dancers, and the occasional drawing of a costume design on the back of a napkin came words of vulnerability, self-doubt, and a longing to help others. She rose as the queen of music, encouraging her fans not to run from their titles of misfits, freaks, and outcasts. She empowered them by demanding they stand by their uniqueness and embrace what made them different. I don't know if she'd gone back and read any of Sera's previous blog posts, or whether the one about bullying was enough for her to investigate Sera's profile further. Either way, one evening an ear-piercing shriek came from the living room. I ran in to find Meena with her hands up to her mouth, staring wide-eyed at the screen.

"Piper Dawn is following you on Twitter and has just sent you a friend request!"

Sera, Carla, and Amy shot around to the back of Meena's chair.

"No way!" Sera shouted.

As soon as Sera accepted the friend request, there was another round of shrieks as Sera read aloud Piper Dawn's most recent Twitter post:

"Follow Sera on Twitter and Facebook. I'm a big fan. I love what she has 2 say."

The links to Sera's Facebook and Twitter accounts, as well as the bullying blog, were appended to the tweet.

Then the page on the laptop froze. Sera kept hitting the refresh button, but the screen didn't move. She tried logging out and then back in to her accounts, but once again the page was blank.

"What's happened?" Sera asked, looking frantic and confused.

"Sera, the biggest pop star in the world just endorsed you!" Amy said in disbelief. "There must be too many people trying to follow you at once. Your page must not be able to keep up with the number of requests!"

This single, simple tweet detonated an explosion in Sera's following. By morning two million people were following her. By the next evening, a further million and a half people had joined them.

CHAPTER FOURTEEN

"SHE LOOKED so beautiful!" Maggie said. Her cane shook as she tried to balance herself while we walked out of the auditorium following Sera's high school graduation. The ceremony was held across town, as the school's facilities were too small to hold all the graduates and their invited families and friends. I crooked my elbow to offer Maggie extra support, which she took gladly. Aaron and Miss Dee walked a few steps ahead. "Such a beautiful ceremony. And Sera was so brave, getting up and speaking in front of all of her classmates."

It was an immensely proud moment in my life. As valedictorian of the class of 2008, my daughter had given a stirring speech. She may have had over five million followers on Facebook and Twitter with whom she spoke everyday via computer, but when she was faced with the prospect of standing up and speaking in front a large group of people, I'd gotten the first glimpse that she wasn't quite as fearless as I'd originally thought.

Maggie, Aaron, and I had experience in public speaking, though it wasn't on the scale Sera faced. During her career as a teacher, Maggie had stood in front of classes full of adults at PTA meetings at the school, while I'd spoken many times in courts and boardrooms. Part of Aaron's job involved standing in front of scores of bank employees, training them on his new software. So we'd done our best to coach her through her upcoming speech at home. Miss Dee assisted by sitting in the back of the living room and calling out to Sera: "Child, speak up! It sounds like the wireless is on in another room but I can't tell what song's playing!"

The practice paid off. She no longer looked like she was going through an ordeal the way she had when she first practiced in our living room. Her first public speech was confident and inspiring. She spoke about the amazing potential their lives had and how they could make an impact in the lives of others if they were just willing to try.

"She did a great job," I said as we waited for a group of parents to move so Maggie could walk without being jostled.

"You've done a great job," she said kindly. "I was thinking about Maria the other day."

"Me too. It's such a shame she wasn't here to see this. I know she would have been proud of Sera."

"Oh, Maria saw it. She's up there just beaming, I'm sure."

I pushed open the door to the fresh early evening air and tugged Maggie's thin wrap a little closer around her shoulders as we waited outside for Sera. She was on a high and bounced around, saying good-bye to friends and collecting hugs from as many people as she could. Once the crowd began to disperse, Aaron walked to the curbside and tried to hail a cab, but an unofficial line had formed and we were at least twenty rides back.

"It would be quicker to walk," Aaron said impatiently. "It's about ten blocks."

"Let's wait." My eyes flashed to Maggie, hoping he would understand that, although we weren't too far from home, the journey would be difficult for her.

"Actually, I could do with the exercise, Adam," Maggie said, tugging at my arm. "And I'd like to have a little chat with you, if that's okay?"

"Sure, of course. If you're sure you can make it."

Sera, excited and a little hyper, stood between Miss Dee and Aaron and linked her arms in theirs so they could walk together. Maggie and I watched them ahead of us. It looked like Sera was preparing to skip down the yellow brick road with her friends from Oz.

"So what would you like to chat about, Maggie? Is everything okay?"

"Yes, dear. I just wanted to talk to you about Sera." She paused to pull her embroidered shawl over her thin shoulders. "Now, we all know she's a special girl who has developed an extraordinary talent for communicating with young people...."

"She sure has."

"Well, Miss Dee and I won't be around for too much longer, and—"

I gently squeezed her arm. "You know I hate it when you talk like that."

"No, no, let me finish," Maggie said. Like any schoolteacher, she hated being interrupted. "Sera will go on to do incredible things. And even though she's an adult now, you know she'll always need you to be there, especially when we're gone. It's imperative that you support her any way you can in whatever road she chooses to travel."

We walked a few steps in silence. I didn't know what to say. It felt like I'd been stung by an insult in the form of friendly advice. Maggie might have been in her eighties, but she was still sharp as a tack. She must have known I'd take exception to the suggestion that I'd do anything other than support Sera, because she continued before I could react. "I know you love her with all your heart, and I know you'll do what's right. Of course you will—you always have. But many parents whose hearts and intentions are in the right place believe they know what's best for their child. But sometimes being behind them one hundred percent in their choices, regardless of whether you believe they're the right ones, can lead to amazing success because the child has the support needed to achieve their own personal goals."

"Of course I'll support her. Why would you think otherwise?" I asked, still smarting a little.

Maggie stopped for a moment to catch her breath before we continued to walk slowly. "I don't. It's just that I saw so many children I taught grow up and argue with or become estranged from their parents because they felt they didn't have support for the way they wanted to live their lives. Sometimes parents are blind to their child's ambitions if they don't match or fit the vision the parents have in mind. It leads to feelings of being let down on both sides."

"Maggie—"

"I'm sorry, Adam. I didn't mean to offend. I'm just an old woman dispensing unsolicited advice because I can hear God calling me. In my old age I tend to say things because if I don't say them now, I may never have the chance."

"You've still got a lot of life left in you," I said, the sting of her words receding.

"Please understand. I'm scared of leaving Sera. What I'm saying gives me peace. I need to know you'll be there for her, always. No matter what."

I looked down at Maggie. She seemed so small and frail. How could I possibly be mad at her? She'd more than earned the right to express any concern she had. In her own way, she was battling the fears any parent would face knowing they soon could leave their child behind. I wondered what advice I would feel compelled to give if I was in the same position.

I stopped walking and turned to face her. I hooked her cane over my forearm and took both her hands to keep her steady.

"Maggie, I promise you I'll do everything I can to support Sera in whatever she chooses. She will always come first," I said, giving her hands a little squeeze to show my sincerity. "You have my word."

She shuffled forward to give me a hug. "Thank you," she said into my jacket. "God couldn't have chosen a better man to find her."

Just ahead, Aaron was walking backward with his arm in the street, hailing a cab. He'd clearly lost patience with walking. He finally flagged an empty taxi and pulled open the door.

"You go ahead with Aaron and Miss Dee," I said to Maggie, who now looked relieved she wouldn't have to walk much farther. "Sera and I can walk the rest of the way."

I winked at Aaron to acknowledge his finding a way to get back to the apartment and warn our guests that Sera was on her way home. We'd organized a surprise graduation party for her, as well as for Meena and Carla, who graduated the same day but at a different venue. Although several of the kids in our neighborhood went to different schools, they'd grown up together and we'd gotten to know the parents fairly well, so I agreed to hold a joint graduation party for them all.

As the taxi pulled away, Sera bounced with the excitement that high school was over and her speech had been a success. I waited for the conversation I knew was coming. I hoped she was so happy that she wouldn't be too let down at my refusal.

"Dad—"

"No, Sera. You're going to college and that's the end of it. You've just been named valedictorian, and you've been accepted into NYU. You should be thrilled!"

"I am. Of course I am. All I'm asking is to take a year off before college so I can travel. There's so much of the world I want to see! I want to meet new people, find out how they live, experience their cultures. I'm not saying forever. Just a year!"

"Sera, look at all the people following you online. They look up to you. What kind of message are you sending by saying you're not going to college? Don't you want to set a good example?"

"I will go to college. I just want to travel first!"

"No, Sera. First of all, you're only seventeen. I'm sorry, but you're simply not old enough to go gallivanting around the world. And I know you're going to hate me for saying this, but your readiness to abandon college just shows that you're not ready to go off on your own!"

"But I'll be eighteen in just a few months. And I'm not abandoning college, just putting it off. You're forever saying how sensible I am."

"You are sensible, sweetheart. But there are situations you've never been in or may not even recognize at your age."

"I could join the Peace Corps," Sera said, in what was meant to be a humorous threat.

"Sure, go ahead. You'll be old enough. Just remember that you have to commit yourself, and you certainly won't be able to travel as extensively and won't have complete control over where you're sent."

We walked a block in silence before she spoke again.

"Please!"

"Get an education under your belt first, and then I'll gladly help finance your trip."

Sera looked deflated. I hated being the one who made her look like that, especially on such a happy day. I know it made me a sucker, but I just couldn't stand seeing her so dejected.

"Okay, how about a compromise?" I said, "Spend the first two years at college, have a gap year to travel, and then complete your degree."

"Really?"

"Yes. In a way I think it may even do you some good. It might give you a new perspective on education, especially when you see how hard life can be without one."

"You promise?" A smile returned to her face.

"I promise. But as with everything else, there will be conditions. It's still a couple of years away, so we'll talk about it nearer the time."

Sera contained her happy squeak just long enough to release it in my ear as she squeezed me tightly.

WE WERE a couple of blocks from home when we saw a dark figure on the steps outside the church. As we approached, a man stood up from a nest of blankets. He wore a mismatched outfit of a secondhand navy blue suit jacket and black pants. The white shirt beneath his jacket looked yellowed, but that could have been because of the orange streetlight overhead. The brown paisley tie he wore around his neck was crooked and clumsily knotted. He hadn't removed his black fingerless gloves but, all in all, Oscar looked quite dapper for a homeless man.

He walked down the steps, unsteady on his feet, his face contorted like he was walking on hot coals. I looked down to see his spit-polished Goodwill shoes didn't match, and were both left footed.

"I thought I'd dress for the occasion," Oscar said awkwardly. It was the first time I'd ever heard him speak. His voice was deep and dry from years of battling the elements in the harsh New York seasons. He looked at me for approval before he approached Sera. The permission he requested and waited for wasn't needed, as Sera rushed forward and embraced him.

"You did this for me?" Sera asked, before stepping back again to show how much she admired his efforts.

Oscar faltered before he answered. I don't know whether it was a reaction to the dry dusty wind or a sign of emotion, but his eyes glassed over. The years had aged him, but the deep lines on his face that I had once worried showed aggression now amplified the kindness in his eyes. "It's a big day for you."

Sera leaned in and hugged him again. "Thank you so much," she whispered as she let him go.

"You have a big future in front of you, and a smart girl like you is capable of anything," he said, extending his gloved hand to take hers. "Don't let the world treat you the same way it treated me."

Until I saw him there, I hadn't I realized how much time had passed. Since Sera walked to school on her own or with a friend in recent years, I hadn't seen much of him, but for twelve years she must have seen him almost every morning. He'd been a fixture in her life, a constant. He'd been there for her all along, maybe more than I realized.

"Would you like to come up to the apartment?" I offered. "We're having a party for Sera's graduation."

"There's a party?" Sera asked with excitement.

I nodded and smiled. Giving up the surprise was worth it if Oscar would attend. "Will you come? Please?"

Oscar held his hand up and shook his head. "Thank you for the offer, but it's getting late and I have to get back to the shelter."

I took the opportunity to shake his hand. He winced and I released it, surprised that I could have hurt him so easily.

"You're welcome to stay with us tonight. We have a large sofa you can crash on," I said. I was still reeling a little from the guilt that I'd somehow allowed this kind man to escape even the periphery of my life.

"No, but thank you," he replied politely. "I really must be going now."

Bent at the waist and with a stiff back, Oscar slowly bowed to Sera. It was lower than the typical bow one would offer to excuse himself from a lady, so low that it resembled an aristocrat's bow to royalty. This show of gentlemanly respect didn't go unappreciated. Sera giggled and curtsied back. He threw his blankets over his shoulder and hobbled down the street, his shoes occasionally slipping on the smooth sidewalk.

"I'll save you some cake!" Sera shouted to him. But he didn't look back.

CHAPTER FIFTEEN

IN HER first year at NYU, where Sera decided to study communications, Aaron designed a website for her that she named "For My Sister." It was a portal for women to contact Sera and the girls, as well as a hub for the articles and blogs she continued to write, each of which was then linked to Facebook, Twitter, and other bloggers' sites. Sera's massive Internet following and the countless hits her website received every day hadn't gone unnoticed. Various companies tried to capitalize on her popularity by asking her to advertise or endorse their products. Sera's following had grown to over ten million people online, the vast majority of whom were in the lucrative eighteen-to-thirty-year-old female demographic. Makeup, clothing, and other cosmetics companies contacted her, all hoping to overtake their competitors. They tried to convince Sera to write articles that included their products. The new tech-savvy interns and junior executives in the advertising world knew that any endorsement from Sera would be successful, especially if it was included in a blog shared on Facebook and Twitter, sites that until recently hadn't succumbed to traditional commercial advertising.

Although she was offered money, often in large sums, Sera steadfastly declined each request. She knew endorsing the latest must-have products between articles and blog posts about teenage suicide and workplace sexual harassment would betray her following by diluting the message of unselfishly helping one another and drive people away.

Aaron, of course, thought it was a great idea and encouraged her to take the money, but Sera didn't want to risk it. Her argument was clear: those products only fueled the myths that girls needed them to be beautiful. She didn't want to increase their suffering by advertising things they couldn't afford or might be bullied for not having.

IN THE summer of 2009, a young journalist from the *New York Times* who was in his first year at the paper contacted Sera. Dalyn Taylor was looking for a piece with a new angle on the explosion of social media and blogs. The usual approach focused on the uglier sides of the online community: "trolls" who intentionally set out to create havoc by posting negative, racist, or downright cruel messages on comment threads, hoping to get a reaction from the originator of the post or fellow readers. Instead, Dalyn was looking for an angle that showed a more upbeat and positive aspect of the online world. That was how he discovered Sera's website and social media pages.

He'd scrolled as far back as he could and spent weeks researching before they finally met. I had my suspicions about journalists, so I wasn't too keen on the idea of him meeting Sera alone on the NYU campus as originally planned. Though the *New York Times* had a solid reputation, I was concerned he might have his own agenda. I couldn't see how he could write a negative exposé on Sera, but I wasn't a young journalist trying to make a name for myself any way I could. So I insisted that Sera invite him to the apartment, where I sat at my desk and pretended to work while surreptitiously listening in on the interview.

Dalyn was a smartly dressed, handsome young man with wavy, dark blond hair trimmed short on the back and sides and longer on top. He was three years older than Sera, but they talked like equals. During the interview Sera asked as many questions as he did, which he happily answered. He described his determination to become a journalist at a young age, his passion for stories, and his desire to expose the truth. Though he was new at the paper and had only been given small assignments, he spoke freely of his ambitions and the kind of hard-hitting journalism he wanted to pursue.

My initial thought was that he didn't have the "killer" instinct journalists need to pursue a story beyond the point where it became intrusive. But as their discussion continued, I began to wonder whether he might actually have it but had been smart enough to leave it at the door. The conversation seemed relaxed and casual, and at times they seemed to be having fun. Dalyn occasionally appeared bashful, which only added to his charm, and I noticed that Sera studied him in a way she'd never done with a boy before. She didn't flirt but responded to his smile with a playful one of her own. It was cute watching the two of them interact and to witness Sera's pleasure in discovering someone who shared the same kind of passion.

My initial worries were proven unfounded when the edition of the *New York Times* with Dalyn's article was published the following Saturday. I found it under the headline "Social Media with a Message." It was well thought out, and I was impressed at the space his editors had allowed him in such a prestigious paper. I poured a fresh cup of coffee and sat down to read the article carefully.

A nineteen year-old girl known only as "Sera" has spent the past four years cultivating an online presence, including an eponymous blog that brings girls and women together in a positive way to provide support to one another during difficult times. With over ten million followers, her database of friends—which she truly considers each of them to be—has grown into a massive network of young women sharing stories through her main profile and a large number of private groups, many of which are moderated by Sera and three close friends. They are collectively referred to as the "For My Sister" pages.

After covering the growing popularity of Facebook and Twitter as a platform for the young, the article went on:

Employers complain that sites like Facebook and Twitter cost them thousands of paid hours and reduce their employees' productivity. Parents worry that they prevent their children from getting fresh air and exercise. But there are those who have used these sites to connect to the world in a way that changes lives for the better.

As Sera explains: "Young girls who are being bullied can join our online groups and find support. Many of them have spent so long feeling isolated and alone that when they are able to interact with others who are going through the same thing, they build lasting friendships and start to regain their strength."

The groups cover serious issues like anorexia, bulimia, obesity, sexual abuse, schoolyard and cyberbullying, teen pregnancy, prescription narcotics abuse, family breakups and divorce, and self-harm. But they also discuss more common teenage issues like living with acne. The network of participants extends across all major cities in the US, as well as thousands of small towns, so girls have an immediate community with which they can identify.

Sera and her cadre of friends select and allocate moderators who have enough experience to help others overcome their problems. The local sites provide listings for professionals dealing with specific issues, free help lines, and emergency services, ensuring access to professional help when needed.

Statistics show that female teen suicide has risen steadily in the past decade, and Sera's social media outlets provide a means for young women to connect, dealing with the root causes. "They need someone who can identify and empathize because they're going through the same things themselves. They need to be listened to and have someone with whom, maybe for the first time in their lives, they can connect, and who is completely on their side. Listening to someone who doesn't feel like they're being heard can be the single most powerful thing in the world."

As Sera's sites have expanded, so has the range of topics discussed. "As I've gotten older, so have the girls who follow the profiles. Their circumstances, trials, and tribulations change, and so have the website and blogs. We are setting up new support groups for single mothers, female workers in typically male-dominated careers, wives of young veterans whose husbands who have been deployed overseas, college girls under academic performance pressures, and mothers coping with disabled children. As the problems and issues of our followers grow and expand, so must we to give them the support they need."

Though largely run by Sera, the subject of most posts on the For My Sister site is "we." Sera does not claim individual ownership over the network. "I don't need the recognition," Sera explains. "I'm no more important than any other member of a group or follower or reader of the site."

Sera's message of empowerment is the hallmark of the For My Sister collective. "I'm very proud of my friends, each of whom contributes to our work in their own way. I'm especially proud of those who have overcome their problems and are now giving their time and energy back to others who are in the same positions in which they once found themselves. Each group has become a kind of sorority. They are sisters dedicated to helping one another."

Sera and the For My Sister followers are a movement. Their efforts have reshaped the visions of social media innovators, to reach out, communicate, and connect. Sera has given weight and evidence to the idea that the global community is at our fingertips. "All we need to do to help is simply click a button."

I put the article down and took a deep breath. Everything in the article was true, though I'd never really stepped back to survey the real, everyday impact Sera was making. Seeing it in black and white—and in the *Times*, no less—really drove home just how much Sera's work meant. And it truly was work, not just the hobby I'd always thought it was. She was on a mission, and she was determined to see it through.

CHAPTER SIXTEEN

AS SERA approached the end of her sophomore year of college, the agreement we had that she could take a year out of her studies to travel was swept away by the news that Miss Dee had been diagnosed with pancreatic cancer.

The initial prognosis was optimistic. The cancer had been caught early and, with the help of chemotherapy and radiation treatments, the odds were in her favor; after the first round of treatment, the cancer seemed to recede. But her remission was short-lived. Just a year after being given the all clear, the cancer returned, but this time it was deemed terminal. Like Maria, Miss Dee wanted to spend her last weeks at home. As a retired nurse, she knew what awaited if she was admitted to a hospital. The clinical atmosphere was too much to bear for a homebody who relished her own comfort, space, and loved ones.

Maggie wanted to help, though she was fragile and unable to do much in the way of care. But the comfort and company she provided her old friend was better than any medication. Sera, too, spent as much time as possible with Miss Dee in her final months. The patient delighted in trying new wigs, and Sera styled the hairpieces and took photos to show Miss Dee, who laughed at the daily reinvention of herself. Between dispensing advice and retelling stories that ended with old southern sayings, Miss Dee sat back in her chair, attached to an oxygen bottle, and patiently instructed Sera in how to cook the comfort food we'd all grown to love. At Miss Dee's urging, Sera packaged the food in her old Tupperware containers to give to Aaron whenever he arrived for a visit. She would have given it to Oscar, but he'd disappeared and we hadn't seen him since the night of Sera's graduation.

I helped where I could, but Miss Dee often shooed me away.

"Don't you worry 'bout me! You gotta work and bring up this child!" Miss Dee would say if I ever expressed worry that she needed to rest. She seemed almost happy, like her impending death was something she was preparing for with excitement, but she never spoke of how fast her health was deteriorating, and if she ever felt the conversation going in that direction, she would quickly pat her newly styled wig. "How d'ya like my hair, honey? Miss Etta James and Miss Diana Ross ain't got nothin' on me!"

THE DAY Miss Dee died, I wept like a child. A powerful mix of emotions washed over me: grief that my friend was gone, overwhelming gratitude for the help and wise advice she'd given me over the years, and deep sadness that I'd never be able to repay her for everything she'd done for Sera. In a moment of selfishness, I was scared that she was no longer there to help or guide me.

Maggie came to me the following day and told me Miss Dee didn't want a fuss. No funeral or big church service, just a private cremation. I was surprised, especially after all the years I'd known her to attend her gospel church in Harlem. I waited for some kind of contact from Miss Dee's daughters to ask if we could attend some memorial to pay our respects, but we heard nothing.

In a way, I was almost pleased not to get their phone call. I felt nothing but anger toward them both. In all the time I'd known Miss Dee, neither of her daughters had ever come to visit her. And worse, they'd never even bothered to make the journey the whole time she was sick. I'd pleaded with Miss Dee to let me call them, but she insisted she didn't want to be a bother. Instead, drained and weak, she climbed into a taxi that took her to Brooklyn to visit them. I thought their selfishness might be the reason she'd taken to Sera so much; that she'd received the love and respect from Sera that her own daughters denied her. I couldn't understand how they could show such disrespect to their mother, a woman who'd proven to be a phenomenal mother figure in my own daughter's life.

I was concerned about Sera, as I had been when Maria passed. I wondered whether the stress might revive Sophia or trigger something worse. But Sera, though brokenhearted that Miss Dee was gone, gave no cause for worry. Perhaps it was because both women had been ill for months before they died, and she'd had time to prepare for it. It wasn't a sudden trauma the way 9/11 had been. We'd expected it and dealt with it as well as we could. I was proud of the way she held it together in the days after, while comforting Maggie, whose slight frame shook when she cried.

Within a month, Miss Dee's apartment was listed by a realtor, put on the market, and sold. I missed the echo of her booming laughter that always brought the building alive. After her death it was like one of the lights had permanently gone out in the communal hallway. Things were never quite as bright.

SINCE SERA didn't have the break in her education she'd planned, it gave Meena a chance to work in her parents' store and save up the money to join Sera on her travels. Amy's parents had promised her the trip as a graduation present, and Carla had spent three years working as many shifts as her time allowed at her parents' restaurant. Between her salary and tips, she'd saved enough to join the other three girls traveling. I especially admired the commitment shown by Meena and Carla, since they were working, studying, and still contributing to the website and social media pages.

While Sera, Meena, and Carla tried to keep up with the ever-growing popularity of the For My Sister sites, Amy made the travel plans. She listed the countries and cities they were interested in visiting, researched the recommended vaccinations, applied for visas, and began to assemble a yearlong itinerary. It wasn't easy to plan, so Aaron and I helped where we could.

Sera lived at home with me while she was in college, so this would be our first time apart. Though I was concerned for her safety, I was relieved she was going to be with the other girls. In the past her naïveté could've landed her in dangerous situations, so I was happy she'd be with friends who were a little more street-smart.

Amy had sourced an "open world" ticket that was valid for a year and allowed them to fly to almost any destination serviced by the chosen airline or its alliance partners, so long as there was space on the flights. The ticket was expensive but cheaper and more flexible than buying separate tickets.

They planned to make their way across Europe before travelling to Asia, Africa, and some of the more liberal areas of the Middle East. Sera wanted to backpack across the countries, staying in hostels and cheap bed and breakfasts, but I insisted if they were going on the trip they had to stay in reputable hotel chains, which they accepted without much fuss since Aaron agreed to pay the difference—a small price to pay for my peace of mind.

"Sera, swear to me you'll be careful," I said for what felt like the millionth time since her college graduation the month before. We were at JFK's international departures terminal, and the other girls' parents and I were seeing them off. "If there's anything you need, or if you get into any trouble, you call me right away."

"Dad, I'll be fine. I promise." She kissed my cheek and gave me a hug. "Look after Maggie."

"Of course I will," I said as she released me. "Your uncle is sorry he wasn't here to say good-bye, but he wanted me to give you this." I pulled a thick envelope from my pocket. "He wants you to have a good time and says if there is anything you need, all you have to do is call." Sera gasped as she opened the envelope full of cash. Aaron had been exceptionally generous.

She joined her friends at the security gate. I stood to one side and waited until they neared the head of the line to have their passports checked and their carry-on luggage scanned. They looked so excited. Sera turned to see me, the last parent standing there.

"I'll miss you," I mouthed, looking rather pathetic.

She returned a look somewhere between sadness and exasperation. "I'll miss you more," she mouthed back.

I gave her a big smile and wink to let her know—or make her think—I was joking and turned to leave. But I stayed at the airport until their plane bound for London took off.

APART FROM the occasional times when Sera had a sleepover at Meena's, it was my first night alone in the apartment in more than twenty years. I lay in bed and looked at the photo of Michael on the dresser. The glow from the streetlamp outside cast just enough light to see it clearly.

"This wouldn't be nearly as difficult if you were here to share the worry," I said out loud. "I wish you could've known her. The two of you are so similar, both headstrong and ambitious. It's incredible how, even though you never met, you share the exact same sense of humor.

If you'd both been around at the same time, we'd never have stopped laughing. You would have adored each other."

My thoughts wandered to memories of settling into bed at night when Sera was a toddler. Though I'd tucked her into bed hours before, I'd hear her little bare feet slapping on the wood floor as she walked from her bedroom to mine. She'd appear in the doorway in her pajamas, her tired eyes looking through her bed-head locks. I'd pretend to be asleep, keeping my eyes open just enough to watch her through my lashes. I could see the creases on her face from her pillow as she climbed up onto the bed, her stuffed lamb held tight in her hand. Then she'd snuggle up next to me. Sometimes I imagined her lying between me and Michael: a family of three.

"Dream of me, Mikey," I whispered in the dark. It felt strange saying the words after so many years, but I found comfort in them.

AARON STROLLED through the door the following Sunday afternoon, ready to watch the Giants play the Patriots. He carried a six-pack of fancy imported beer.

"Will you ever knock?"

"Where's Buddy?" he asked, expecting the old dog to jump up at him the way he always did.

"He's standing guard outside Sera's bedroom door. He's been there for days. He sleeps there too. He howled the first couple of nights, once he realized she wasn't coming home."

"How are you doing without Pipsqueak around?" he asked, joining me on the sofa.

"I miss her."

"You should get out there and date. Now's the time! You have the apartment to yourself, and you don't have to worry about Sera walking in on you."

"No, I just have to worry about you. *Because you never knock!*"

"Well?"

"I know you mean well, but no one could ever replace Michael. I think I've known that since the day he died."

"Of course no one could replace him. That's not what I'm suggesting. I know he's gone, but that doesn't mean you should spend the rest of your days on your own. It doesn't mean someone else couldn't bring something different into your life."

The problem was, even after all these years, I didn't want anyone other than Michael.

"But I've never felt like I was alone. Besides, now isn't the time to date. I've got a lot of work ahead of me in the next six months."

"How come? Big case?" Aaron asked.

"No, they're finally making me a partner at the firm," I said, glad to have changed the subject.

Aaron jumped up. "Congratulations! It's about damn time!"

"Thanks. I can't blame them for waiting so long. I didn't put in the same hours as the other guys because I had Sera."

"You mean you didn't have a wife at home looking after the kid while you stayed in the office every hour God sent like all those other guys did."

"It was worth it."

"So what are you going to do? You've been able to afford to move out of this place for years. Now you could find a place somewhere on the Upper East Side or maybe come over to Brooklyn."

"I couldn't do that. This is our home. I mean, could you imagine coming over and watching the game anywhere else?"

"Good point." He raised his can of beer. "Here's to partnership. May it bring you everything you want!"

I tapped his can with my own, though I wondered whether his toast was a sly last-ditch attempt to make me think about dating again.

WITH SERA away on her travels, I had more time on my hands on the weekends. Without the distraction of my daughter and the time she occupied in my day, I began to feel my age. Her company had kept me feeling young and vibrant, but now with her gone, I started to feel old and lethargic. When Sera was younger, I had tried to keep up my running. But as she grew into a teenager and things at work ramped up, opportunities to get away became few and far between. I hadn't run on a Sunday morning for years but decided to add it to my routine again.

As I walked into Central Park, the first thing that hit me was the familiar smell of the frost on the trees and the dead leaves on the ground. Late fall was Michael's favorite time of year to run. Even on the Sunday mornings of our late twenties, after we'd spent the night before drinking in the bars in Chelsea, he would pull me out of bed at 6:00 a.m. and force me into my sneakers, ignoring my complaints. But once I was there, and my hangover was suspended in the frigid air, I'd watch Michael bounce on his feet, grinning at me as he warmed up. He knew I'd eventually break through my moans and enjoy it. On those cold early mornings as we ran through the empty trails, it felt like we were the only two people in New York City.

Often we'd have to stop so I could massage a stitch out of my ribs. It was rarely from exhaustion, but because Michael said things that would leave me laughing until I was gasping for breath. He insisted I was only laughing as an excuse to stop, that nothing he said could be that funny, but he was wrong. Michael could keep pace for hours if he wanted to. He was a seasoned New York marathon runner and possessed the dedication to keep up his training in all types of weather. His fitness level, strength, and endurance were incredible, which is why the news of his aneurysm seemed even more shocking. In the hospital bed, where he lay unconscious in his last hours, I imagined him silently fighting desperately to survive. His athlete's body looked wrong and out of place hooked up to monitors and a ventilator. He was strong, but ultimately the undetected brain aneurysm that tore him away from life and from me was stronger.

As I began to run alone through the park, I tried to push the sad memory of Michael's death and saying good-bye to one side and concentrate on the good times we'd had together. The only small consolation was to think of my suffering as a gift to him. That I'd been left behind to miss him, and not the other way around.

But focusing on happy memories often brought me to tears. I'd excused the redness of my eyes as allergies to Sera so many times when she was a girl that she'd stopped asking about it, assuming that it was just a normal part of running for me. But in those years, each time I ran alone, something would set me off. A song randomly played on my iPod brought back a memory, or I'd be lost in a runner's high and turn to say something to him and realize he wasn't there—and never would be again.

I'D PROMISED to give Sera space and not constantly hassle her and, in return, she promised to call me once a week. I checked on her progress and travels through Facebook and Twitter, each day seeing her with a new monument, palace, castle, or other historical European landmark. The girls looked happy and obviously were enjoying themselves. Waiting in train and bus stations, airport terminals, and ferry ports afforded them the time to manage and maintain their online presence and upload short video clips to YouTube. They'd also started posting pictures on a photo-sharing site called Instagram and documenting their travels on Tumblr. My worries subsided and my fears eased a little with each post, especially as I noticed one person in particular commenting on the posts, linking her to her home in New York.

Throughout Sera's college days, she'd kept in contact with Dalyn, the young journalist at the *New York Times*. When Sera was younger, I hadn't even wanted to think about her dating. The idea made me worry I'd turn into an old man chasing boys off the farm with a shotgun. But the line of schoolgirl crushes and first broken heart never happened, as Sera's world revolved around her social media activity.

Dalyn's first contact with Sera had been professional, but it had become clear that he'd developed a crush on her. He'd come to the apartment on his days off, ostensibly to talk to Sera and the girls about their work, but I could see from the way he looked at Sera that she was more than just a story. While Amy animatedly discussed a new group or another follower milestone, he couldn't keep his attention from wandering to Sera's face. It was obvious he was smitten.

Dalyn and the girls had become friends, and they invited him to join them on their trip, but such a long time away was impossible for a young man with ambition at the start of his career. Amy seemed especially disappointed. He made a point of commenting on new photos or posts while they were travelling, though most of his comments were directed at Sera. Her responses, while never flirtatious, were warm and positive.

And at least once a month, Dalyn showed up at my door. He always insisted he was just passing, but it was clear Sera had asked him to check on me to make sure I was doing okay. It was sweet of her, but unnecessary, though I continued to let him visit anyway, hoping it would help him curry favor with my daughter. It also gave me a chance to get to know him better, and over these visits, I grew to appreciate what a hardworking, down-to-earth young man he was.

AS SUMMER came, Sera's phone calls became less frequent and her once solid travel plans began to change. She called to say they'd changed their tickets and were planning to travel to Cambodia, India, Dubai, and Ethiopia. I tried to convince her to travel to more traditional gap-year destinations, but she refused. I even contacted the other girls' parents, hoping they could convince their daughters to change their travel plans, but they, too, were unsuccessful.

As the weeks went by, I noticed Sera seemed down and unwilling to talk about her travels the way she had at the start of her trip. She no longer expressed the joy of seeing so many places and seemed reluctant to talk about the things they'd done and the experiences they were having. Then the calls became shorter. It felt like I was being kept out of the loop. She listened to my rants and raves, warnings and worries, but I knew none of it was really getting through to her. All I got was the usual "Dad, don't worry. I'm fine."

After eleven months of being away, she called while I was in a meeting and left a voice mail telling me they'd arrived in Jordan, a destination I didn't even know she'd planned to visit. Something was wrong; it wasn't like her to be so secretive. I tried reaching her for days without success. She hadn't updated her Facebook and Twitter pages in days, which in itself was cause for alarm. And it had been weeks since she'd posted a photo of herself and the girls.

The next time she called, I told her to stay where she was. I was getting on the next flight to Amman, no matter what she said. She insisted she was okay and told me to stay at home, but I was already on the Internet booking my ticket.

But that evening everything changed as I packed my bags.

CHAPTER SEVENTEEN

I LEFT my suitcase by the front door and called Buddy from Sera's room. I collected his leash, bowl, and a bag of dog food and let him lead the way down the hall. I only planned to be away for a few days, just long enough to check that Sera and the girls were all right, so Maggie had agreed to keep Buddy overnight until Aaron could pick him up the following morning.

I knocked on Maggie's door and waited. It sometimes took her a while, as she was old and the arthritis in her knees slowed her pace. When it took longer than usual for her to answer, I knocked again. She was expecting me, and I could hear the muffled sounds of her television, so I knew she was at home. I knocked once more, then slowly turned the handle, calling her name as I cracked open the door.

I found her unconscious on the tiled kitchen floor, her body twisted and her head bleeding from her fall. I called for an ambulance and tried to rouse her. She came to and her eyes moved, but when she tried to speak, only a trail of saliva came from her bottom lip. She was so pale. When the ambulance arrived, I watched as they put her on the gurney. She regained a little strength, but only in her left arm and leg. The whole right side of her body drooped like a ragdoll.

"It's okay, Maggie, we're going to get you to a hospital. I'll be right here with you," I said as I held her unresponsive hand. She was so disoriented she couldn't even acknowledge I was speaking to her.

SINCE I didn't know any other way to get hold of Sera, I sent her a Facebook message telling her to call. Just as we reached the hospital and Maggie was being transferred from the ambulance, my cell phone rang.

"It's Maggie, isn't it?" Sera said the moment I answered.

There was no point in sugarcoating it. "Yes. I'm sorry, sweetheart. She's in a bad way."

"I'm coming home."

IT TOOK Sera and the girls two days to get back to New York, as poor
flight connections forced a layover in London. I stayed at Maggie's
bedside all day and night, only taking a brief break when Aaron came
to the hospital after going to the apartment to check on Buddy and
bring me a change of clothes.

"How is she?" Aaron asked, entering the hospital room as quietly
as he could.

"She has no control on the right side of her body," I whispered.
"The doctors don't hold out much hope. They said it's more than likely
she'll suffer another massive stroke before she goes."

Just then Maggie began to stir.

Her left eye opened and she looked around until she saw my face.
I took hold of her hand.

"Hey," I said softly as I watched the left side of her brow furrow.
"You're in the hospital. I'm here and so is Aaron."

Her brow furrowed a little deeper as she tried to figure out how
she got there.

"You've had a stroke, Maggie. But the doctors are here, and
we're going to get you better as soon as we can." I smiled at her in the
hope she'd believe me.

The side of Maggie's mouth opened like a bad ventriloquist as
she slurred, "Seh-rah."

"She's on her way. Her plane has landed, and she's coming
straight here to see you."

Her brow relaxed. She caught my eye again. "Ta-mas Ba-la."

"Don't try to talk. You need to keep your strength."

"Ta-mas Ba-la. La-ta inda draah," she gasped.

Then she slipped back into unconsciousness.

"What do you think she was trying to say?" Aaron asked.

"I don't know, but I hope Sera makes it here in time."

I looked at Maggie. She seemed so small. I couldn't reconcile the
fragile old woman in the hospital bed with the memory of the woman
who had the energy to chase after Sera when she was a toddler.

SERA ARRIVED just before midnight. The moment I saw her, my heart sank. Not only because I knew she was about to face the death of her last mother figure, but because she looked like she was close to death herself. If it hadn't been for her long auburn locks and the green flecks in her blue eyes, I wouldn't have recognized the painfully thin girl who opened the hospital room door. The gold bracelet she wore hung off her thin wrist as loosely as it had on her tenth birthday when Maggie had given it to her.

Aaron looked at me, obviously as alarmed as I was at her appearance. I got up and rushed over to her. Before I had the chance to speak, she threw her arms around me. For a moment I was scared of hugging her back, as though returning her embrace might snap her bones.

"Sera," I said, plainly showing on my face all the fear coursing through me.

"I'm okay," she said softly before walking around to the side of Maggie's hospital bed and taking her right hand.

In the light of Maggie's bedside lamp, I could see that Sera's face was washed out and drawn. I'd never seen her looking so unwell.

Maggie woke at her touch and saw her face smiling down at her. "Sera, sweet Sera."

"I'm here, Maggie."

Maggie's tongue ran over her dry lips, and she stretched her jaw.

"Look after them," Maggie said, as if the paralysis from the stroke had suddenly lifted enough to allow her to form clear, coherent words.

"She's confused," I whispered to Sera. "She's still heavily sedated. Go gentle with her."

Sera nodded and returned her eyes to Maggie.

"You understand," Maggie said. It was less a question than a statement. "Your father loves you, Sera. He's always been there and will never abandon you. He will protect you. Accept the guidance and always remember what we taught you."

"I will," Sera said as she gently moved Maggie forward, just enough to wrap her in an embrace. My throat closed in emotion at the sight of them, not just saying good-bye, but as they hugged, I could see that Sera's frame was as thin and frail as Maggie's. Sera slowly eased Maggie back onto the pillow. "I love you."

A ghost of a smile crossed Maggie's face before her heartbeat flatlined on the monitor. I stood to one side to make room for the doctor and two nurses who rushed into the room. Aaron took hold of Sera's hand and led her into the hallway. I stayed in the room as they attempted to resuscitate Maggie. But she was gone.

WHEN WE finally returned to the apartment, I poured Aaron and myself a whiskey. I held up the bottle to ask if Sera wanted a nip, but she shook her head. I wasn't surprised. She only drank white wine on special occasions and never touched spirits.

The taxi ride home had been silent as we all registered the fact that Maggie was gone.

"Sera, we need to talk," I said.

"We will, but can I go to bed first? Today has taken a lot out of me."

"Has... has something happened?" I asked as delicately as I could. "I mean, besides Maggie. You've lost so much weight."

"I know. It's nothing to worry about. I promise we'll talk tomorrow." Sera turned and hugged her uncle, who looked just as worried as I was.

We waited until she was in her bedroom before we spoke.

"Drugs?" Aaron whispered. "I mean, I can't believe I'm saying this, but she looks like she's been on heroin. I looked at her arms. There aren't any track marks."

"What? Sera? Of course not."

"Cocaine?"

I sighed heavily and shook my head. "I just... I just can't believe it of her. She isn't that kind of girl."

"What about the girls she was with? Could any of them be a bad influence on her?"

"No, I know them all. And so do you. None of them would get into drugs. Apart from the fact their parents would go crazy— especially Meena's—these girls have spent so much time researching the dangers of drugs to help teenagers on social media, they probably know more than many professionals."

"Maybe they thought they would try them so they could understand better," Aaron guessed, grasping at straws.

I shook my head. "One of them experimenting I might be able to understand. But I don't believe that at least one of them wouldn't have returned home if they saw the others getting into drugs. No, it's something else. Hopefully she'll talk about it in the morning."

"Okay, I have to get home, but I'll come over tomorrow evening once you guys have had a chance to speak. I've missed her too, so I want to spend some time with her."

"Sure. Thanks for staying with me at the hospital."

Aaron gave me a hug and started for the door. "Hey, what do you think Maggie was talking about before Sera got there?"

"I have no idea."

I SAT on the sofa in the silence. Buddy nudged my hand for attention. I was restless and assumed Sera was sound asleep in her room, so I decided to take him for a late-night walk around the block. His excitement hadn't calmed since Sera stepped through the door.

As we walked past Maggie's apartment, I checked the handle, since I couldn't remember whether I'd locked the door when we left for the hospital. It opened. I found the keys on the kitchen counter and was about to leave when I saw a photo of Maggie, Miss Dee, Maria, and Sera on the shelf of Maggie's upright bureau. It was from a day trip they'd taken to the Natural History Museum when Sera was a kid. They stood in front of the skeleton of a giant dinosaur.

Just as I turned from the bureau, it suddenly came to me. In the hospital, Maggie was trying to say "Letter in the drawer."

It didn't feel right. It was like I was going through her home without her permission. I opened the drawer of the bureau slowly, expecting to find the clutter of an old woman—elastic bands, pens, notebooks, and tins of peppermints. But it was empty, apart from a solitary envelope simply marked "Adam."

I opened the letter.

"Adam, in the event of my death, please contact Thomas Baylor—917-555-4853."

THE FOLLOWING morning, with Sera still in her room, I called the
number, unsure whether I was about to break the news of Maggie's
passing to an unknown relative.

"Fellows, White, and Associates. How may I direct your call?" a
polite voice answered.

I recognized the name. It was a law firm in Midtown.

"Hi, is it possible to speak to Thomas Baylor?"

"May I ask who's calling and what it's regarding?"

"Adam Goodwin. It's regarding Maggie O'Dowd."

I drummed my fingers on the desk while I waited for him to answer.
I didn't know what to expect. Had she left instructions for her funeral?

"Mr. Goodwin?" asked a deep voice.

"Yes, hello. I'm a friend of Maggie O'Dowd," I said tentatively. I
wondered whether there was still a chance he was a relative. I didn't
just want to blurt it out. "I have a letter from Maggie that asks me to….
Well, I don't know how you know Maggie, but—"

"It's okay, Mr. Goodwin. I gather from your call that Maggie has
sadly passed."

"Yes. Yes, I'm afraid she has."

"I'm sorry to hear that. She was a lovely lady," he said genuinely.
"I'm Maggie's attorney. She said to expect a call from you should… well,
anything happen. She left me in charge of executing her last will and
testament, as well as tying up any loose ends in the event of her death."

"I see. Well, she died last night at St. Mary's Hospital. I'm not
aware of any family she had outside of Ireland, so if there's anything I
can do to help with the arrangement of the funeral, please let me know.
You can contact me at—"

"I have your details, Mr. Goodwin," he said before I could finish.
"I'll need you to come into the office for the reading of the will." He
paused for a moment as if looking over paperwork. "Also your
daughter, Sera. She's a beneficiary of Maggie's estate, so we have
many things to discuss."

SERA EMERGED from her room around six in the evening. After
taking a long shower, she dressed and joined me in the living room. Her

once comfortable jersey pajamas looked baggy on her thin frame. She still looked tired.

"Sleep well?"

"No, I didn't sleep at all. But it's nice to be back home and in my own bed."

"Why couldn't you sleep?"

"I've had problems with that recently," she said without even a hint that she was going to explain.

"Do you need to go to the doctor?"

Sera shook her head. I was about to insist, but she cut me off. "Dad, I'm okay, I promise."

"Where are your suitcases?"

"I didn't bring them home. There was nothing to bring back."

"What do you mean? Where are your clothes?" I started to panic. "What happened? Were you girls robbed? Are you okay?"

Sera let out a long sigh.

"I gave it all away. The clothes, the toiletries—everything."

"To whom?"

"Anyone who needed it."

"Sera—"

"Dad, please give me a chance to explain," she said softly. "Though to be honest, I'm not entirely sure where to start."

"Were you hurt?" I asked, a feeling of dread washing over me. I was terrified something had happened and she was trying to protect me by not telling me. "Sera, you have to tell me."

Sera leaned across the table and took my hands in hers. They felt smaller than I remembered them, perhaps because of the weight loss.

"Listen to me, Dad. I wasn't hurt. Nothing happened to me or any of the girls. I know I look different, but the trip took its toll on me."

"Swear to me, Sera."

She tightened her grip on my hands. "I swear. I won't lie to you, there were times I could've been hurt or was in danger, but nothing happened. If there was anything, anything at all, I would tell you."

She released my hands as relief swept over me.

"Your uncle will be here any minute. He's picking up the biggest pizza he could find."

This brought a smile, but it was short-lived. The moment her smile died, her eyes started brimming with tears.

"Dad, I've missed you so much. I always knew I was lucky to have you, but—" She stopped long enough to wipe the tears that streamed down her cheeks. "I never knew exactly how lucky I was."

"I'm the lucky one."

"I've got so much to tell you. I know you'll be mad at me, but hopefully you'll understand when I'm through."

There was a bumping at the front door. The handle turned and Aaron burst through, balancing a huge pizza box, a bag of sodas, and a six-pack of beer in his hands. He must have used his elbow to press the door handle down. I was too disturbed to make my usual protest about his failure to knock.

Sera wiped her cheeks again and rushed over to hug him. Aaron noticed her damp, red eyes.

"She okay?" he mouthed over her shoulder.

I nodded. I knew he was thinking they were tears over Maggie, but Sera hadn't mentioned her since she'd gone to bed.

"Should I go?" he mouthed. I shook my head and indicated for him to take a chair.

We sat around the table, and Aaron opened the pizza box. "Dig in, Pipsqueak. You need to put some of that weight back on," he said as he wriggled into his chair to show he was settling in for the long haul. "So tell us about your trip! We want to hear all the stories of what you got up to." He smiled.

It was the last smile of the night.

CHAPTER EIGHTEEN

"WE STARTED with a few days in London and then traveled by train down to Paris," Sera began. "We took a flight to Madrid, then a train to Rome, and then across to Berlin. We chatted with girls we met in the street, at tourist areas, on the train, everywhere, really. Some of them were a bit wary at first. They weren't used to four American girls just casually approaching them without a hint of embarrassment, but they soon opened up. We explained about the website and that we were trying to find out how girls lived in other countries and cultures. We wanted to see if American girls dealt with the same issues as European girls, and if not, why not. They became interested in what we were doing, so they began feeling comfortable talking to us. Among the four of us, we had enough language skills to understand what they were saying and to translate their stories. The whole experience in Europe kind of showed that, for the most part, girls have the same problems all over. That's why the profiles and website became so popular over there. I mean, same problems, different language, right? Don't get me wrong, we had some great times and we saw some incredible things. We saw everything we'd dreamed of, but we all knew that we weren't really learning anything new, if that makes sense. Then we flew to Cambodia and everything changed."

Sera put down the slice of pizza she'd been holding but hadn't taken a bite from. She looked numb. "We traveled to the capital, Phnom Penh, and only planned to stay for a few days before we made our way to Bangkok. After we settled into the hotel, we visited one of the dozens of night markets off the main strip in the city. It was kind of what we expected: knockoff DVDs, T-shirts, spices, handbags, that kind of thing. But it was still exciting because we'd never been anywhere like it before.

"As we headed back to the hotel, we passed a long row of open-faced bars, which were obviously tourist hotspots. Most of the men inside or at the tables outside were western. Then Amy pointed out that most of the men appeared to be alone and had young Cambodian girls sitting on their laps as they sat back, drinking and smoking cigars. The girls were obviously prostitutes trying to pick up a john for the evening. The bar owners didn't look twice at what was going on. If anything, they seemed to be encouraging it."

"They were probably getting a cut or at least an amount per night from the girls to let them work the bar," Aaron said.

Sera nodded. "It's not that I'm naïve. I know it goes on, but these men were so blatant with their public displays of, well, you couldn't call it affection. They leaned back on their chairs like they were kings, like they were the most desirable men in the world and women were flocking to them and falling to their knees to be near them. And they just sat back with big smiles on their faces or giving thumbs-up to the other Western men surrounded by girls."

"There's a seedy side to every city. Men who pay for sex also pay for the feeling they're being worshipped. And if they can have an audience, that's even better," Aaron said.

I gave my brother a look.

"What?" he said. "I've been to bachelor parties in strip joints here in the city. I know what she's talking about. Dirty old men with fists full of dollars leering at the girls. They creep me out."

Sera closed her eyes and slowly shook her head. "What we saw later was different."

"Go on," I said, pushing the pizza box toward her to encourage her to eat.

"These bars were on the main strip. Just off the main road, there were dark narrow streets not much bigger than alleyways. There were a few neon lights on the front of dilapidated buildings that shone with just enough light to reveal lines of girls standing in front of them. It was clear as we walked by that they were brothels." Sera shook her head again. "The girls couldn't have been any older than sixteen or seventeen, and they were dressed in next to nothing. They smiled at the men walking past, laughing and reaching out to take their hands to try to pull them toward whatever brothel they were working in. The men who owned the brothels watched them like hawks, and if one of the girls wasn't actively trying to get a customer, they would whisper in her ear. Though they started to smile, you could see they were scared.

"About halfway down I saw a girl. Dad, she looked like she was twelve years old. As we passed, she smiled at one of the men walking in front of us, desperately trying to make him follow her. It made me feel sick. I just couldn't understand what was happening. She was just a kid. I reached out to talk to her, but she turned and looked at the brothel owner, who started to walk toward us with a metal bar in his hand."

"Sera!" I exclaimed instinctively.

"Dad, we weren't hurt. Please, let me finish."

"How could you put yourself and your friends in that kind of danger? What were you thinking?"

"What did you expect me to do? Just walk away from a child who was begging a middle-aged man to go into a brothel with her?"

"But—"

"Dad, I know you worried about us, and I understand why. But when I tell you we weren't hurt in any way, you have to believe me. I want to tell you what happened and what we saw. I need to tell you. But I can't keep repeating the same thing over and over again. We were all okay. Nothing happened to us. None of us were hurt. I'm not lying to you."

I took a deep breath. She was in her twenties, but I still saw the little girl who needed my protection. "Okay, go ahead."

"So we were in this narrow street with the brothels, and the guy was coming toward us with a metal bar. Meena grabbed hold of Carla and me, and we started to run. Amy was already in front of us, so we ran out of the street and back onto the strip. When we looked back, we saw the brothel owner shout at the girl and then return to the door. We didn't know what to do. We looked around and saw the narrow street opposite the one we'd just come from had another row of girls standing outside even more brothels.

"There was a middle-aged Thai woman outside one of them holding a plastic bag and talking to one of the girls. She looked nervous and kept checking over her shoulder. She reached into her bag and pulled out a handful of condoms, which she shoved in the girl's hand just as the brothel owner saw her. He chased her through the alley and back onto the strip. She looked frightened but at the same time a little defiant. She was headed in the same direction as our hotel, so we walked behind her for a while until she stopped and sat outside a small restaurant. We stopped, too, and spoke to her. She spoke broken English, but it was enough for us to understand.

"Her name was Kanya. She was such an incredible, amazing, and brave woman. She worked as a cleaner at one of the hotels during the day and spent her evenings trying to help the street girls out of prostitution. She went out every night with a bag of condoms that she had bought with her own small wage and leaflets that she'd photocopied about sexually transmitted diseases and pregnancy, to give to any girl she could. She had to do it without any of the brothel owners knowing. She'd been threatened with death, beaten, and raped twice by these men in the past, yet she still continued to try to help.

"We told her about the young girl we'd seen, and she immediately knew who we meant. She told us that one night the brothel owner had three drunken customers who turned violent and he was trying to get them out of the brothel. There was a lot of shouting and scuffling, which gave Kanya enough time to speak to the young girl.

"Her name was Champai and she was fourteen years old and had worked at the brothel for about eight weeks, but Kanya suspected she'd been working in the sex industry for much longer. The owner of the brothel where she worked was notorious not only for being the most violent in the city but also for offering underage girls to customers. Kanya tried several times to get Champai away, but the brothel owner kept a close eye on her, since she'd become one of his higher earners.

"A couple of days later, we met a group of young American guys. They'd just finished college too and were backpacking their way across the Far East. I managed to talk one of them, a really nice guy named James, into approaching the brothel owner to ask about taking Champai for the entire night. James offered him a hundred dollars, which was four times more than the going rate, but only on the condition that he could take her back to his hotel. The owner refused, so James kind of shrugged and began walking toward the next brothel.

"The owner called him back, and said he would give him Champai for the night for $125, but only on the condition that they go to a hotel just a couple of streets away. James agreed. When he brought Champai back to the hotel, the brothel owner's son stood watch outside all night to make sure she didn't try to run away in the morning. Meena, Amy, Carla, Kanya, and I were in the room when they arrived. Champai freaked out at first. She didn't know what was happening and was terrified that the brothel owner would find out. We sat her down, and Kanya translated her story for us.

"She'd been born in a village not far from Bangkok. She hadn't attended school. Instead she helped raise her younger brother and sisters, who were still very young. When she was ten years old, a friend of her father's said he'd heard of a job in the city for a young girl to clean and wash dishes in a restaurant. She would work for a good family with other children and live in the apartment above the restaurant. The extra money could be sent home to help feed the family, so her father agreed to let her go. The man then took Champai, not to Bangkok, but to Pattaya, where he sold her to a brothel owner for the equivalent of a hundred dollars. She was terrified, so she kicked and punched the man. He slapped her and locked her in a room. That night, he, his brother, and his son raped her."

Sera stopped talking for a few moments when she saw our horrified faces.

"Can you even imagine? Ten years old. Kidnapped, sold, and gang raped in one day," she said her eyes brimming with tears. "Can you see now why we had to help her?"

"Of course," I said calmly, though I was anything but calm inside.

Sera wiped her tears away but continued. "The next day she was in a lot of pain, but the brothel owner and his brother forced her to take customers. There were other girls the same age as Champai at the brothel, and some just a few years older. They were all kept naked so they couldn't run away and hide or keep the occasional tips a man might leave them. They were barely fed to keep them thin.

"One night one of the older girls in the brothel tried to run. She tied a sheet around herself like a dress and ran out the door when the brothel owner was distracted. They found her within ten minutes, running through the streets. They dragged her back and made all the girls watch as they made an example of her. One by one, each of them raped her while the other two punched her face. They urinated on her before one took a knife and carved out one of her eyes."

I gasped. Sera looked hypnotized. She spoke with deliberate clarity, as if it was the only thing that would help her get the next words out.

"Then they tied the end of the sheet she had escaped in around her neck. They put the other end over a door and hanged her until she was dead."

Aaron and I looked at each other, stunned and disgusted. But Sera wasn't finished.

"Champai was there for three years." Sera shook her head. "You know, people try to scare others with the idea of an imaginary hell as if it's a threat or warning of what their punishment will be if they misbehave. But the truth is, if they really wanted to scare people, I mean really terrify them, they'd show them the reality of hell here on earth. And then tell them that this hell is being suffered by children who did nothing to deserve it...."

"So what happened to Champai?" I asked.

"Every day was torture for her. She was only thirteen years old when she figured she would rather die than carry on living like that. But before she tried to kill herself, she decided she would try to escape first. She thought she would be killed if she was caught, and she knew it would be a slow death, so as to make an example of her, but she knew that it eventually would be over and she wouldn't have to suffer anymore. But if there was a chance she could get away, get back to her family, she was going to take it.

"One night the brothel owner and his brother went into the city and left the son in charge. Champai took a bottle and slammed it over his head. She grabbed a sheet and ran to the police station. She told them what was happening, and a policeman calmed her down. He was kind to her. He said that he would send police to the brothel to arrest the men and free the girls. He said she could stay at his home, and he'd take her back to her village the following day. He took her to his apartment to keep her safe and returned hours later and told her the men were in custody. She was so happy and so relieved that she offered him sex as a payment—she didn't have or know any other way to show her gratitude—but he refused.

"As planned, they left the following morning and drove out of the city. She trusted him because he hadn't taken advantage of her. She was excited to see her family and would've gladly stayed in the car for days to reach them. So she was surprised when they stopped after just a couple of hours. The journey was much shorter than the one from Bangkok to Pattaya."

Aaron slammed his cupped hand against his mouth in shock. "The policeman sold her to a trafficker," he said slowly through his fingers.

Sera nodded. "Champai was sold for thirty thousand baht, about ninety-five dollars, on the southern Thailand-Cambodian border. That's all she was worth, ninety-five dollars. The man she thought was there to protect her gave her up like she was a sack of grain. She was forced into a van and taken to the brothel in Phnom Penh."

I felt sick listening to the story. I'd read some horrendous stories working for Legal Aid. But this was truly the worst thing I'd ever heard.

"We talked to her all night. We told her we were going to help her escape and get her back to her family. It was a promise she'd heard before, but you could tell she believed us. We managed to smuggle her out of the hotel's side entrance without the brothel owner's son seeing us. It was in the early hours of the morning, and we managed to get her back to the hotel where we were staying. It took a couple of days to figure out the logistics of how to get her back to her village. She had no passport or documentation, since she'd been smuggled across the border by the trafficker.

"Kanya wanted to go to the police, but she knew that was no use. Many of the local police were regulars at the brothels. They often took girls as payment to turn a blind eye. And after Champai's last experience, there was no way she was going to trust them. Kanya came with me to the Thai Embassy to try to get information on how we could get her back into the country legally. We never told them her name or where she was. We just said we were asking questions for research. We couldn't just arrive at the embassy with Champai and hope for the best. We had to make sure there was a procedure in place that was reliable enough to get her home, and without risking her being caught by the brothel owner. Kanya agreed that if we could arrange it, she would fly with Champai and make sure she got back to her village okay.

"We all had our own rooms in the hotel in Phnom Penh. Usually we doubled up to save money, but the hotel was so cheap we could afford it. Champai was still so scared that Amy said she'd share her room to keep an eye on her. On the second night, Amy said Champai started to act strange. She'd started babbling and shaking. Kanya was at work, since she'd swapped shifts to come with me to the embassy, so we didn't have anyone to translate. Amy said she seemed uptight and nervous and wouldn't stop pacing around. When I went to her room, she was shaking and starting to sweat through her T-shirt. We thought that, after everything she'd gone through, she was beginning to panic that something was going to go wrong, or that the longer we stayed in the city, the greater the chance the brothel owner would have of finding her. I sat with her and held her hand and she began to calm down. By the time I had left to go back to my own room, she seemed fine. But the next morning Amy came to my room hysterical. When she'd woken up, Champai was gone."

"Gone? What happened?" Aaron asked.

"Carla stayed at the hotel in case she came back, while the rest of us went out to look for her. We searched the streets. She hadn't taken any of Amy's money, so we knew she couldn't have gone too far. We looked for two days, but she'd disappeared. A couple of nights before we were due to leave, we went back down by the strip. It was the last place in the city we hadn't searched. We found Kanya, slumped against the wall in tears. She said she'd just spoken to one of the girls in the line. Champai had gone back to the brothel."

"What? She went back?!" I exclaimed in disbelief.

"The girl told Kanya that when Champai first arrived at the brothel, eight weeks before, she'd caused a lot of trouble and was disobedient. The owner was mad because he'd paid a lot of money for her, so he started injecting her with heroin to keep her spaced out and in line. She became addicted in just a few weeks. The shakes, the weird behavior, and the strange babbling at the hotel were heroin withdrawal. She needed a fix, and the only place she knew for certain to get one was at the brothel. So she went back. The brothel owner was angry with her. Champai became hysterical, begging for the drug. He finally agreed, but he said he wouldn't inject her. She was fourteen years old and didn't know what she was doing. He stood by and watched as she overdosed."

"Did she die?" Aaron asked.

Sera closed her eyes and nodded, unable to say the words.

She pulled her laptop around and clicked on a file that brought up a photo of Amy, Carla, Meena, and Sera. Sera had her arm around a pretty young Thai girl. Everyone was smiling.

"This is Champai."

I looked at the photo again and tried to imagine the life this young girl had lived. The only thing I could think was that she was no longer suffering.

"This was taken in the hotel room on the second night. It was one of the first times we ever saw her smile."

"That poor girl," Aaron whispered.

"But it's not just one girl. There are hundreds of thousands of girls and women in Thailand and Cambodia going through the same thing every day. They call them prostitutes, but that title almost implies that they're doing it of their own free will. They're not prostitutes, they are slaves. They're considered property, only there to generate money. Each day these girls go through hell. And what makes it worse is they're forced to smile. Forced to smile as they're being raped. Forced to smile as they hope they're not picked out of the line of girls. Forced to smile as the men who believe they own them stare at them with an iron bar in their hand. Forced to smile each night as they're threatened with injury or disease. Forced to smile as another man violently erodes away another piece of their soul, while shame consumes them and they face whether this might be the night they're killed, or whether it might get so bad they'll take their own life."

"Sera, I don't know what to say. It's truly terrible what they go through. The Far East hasn't got the best reputation for the way they treat women," I said.

"Dad, it's everywhere."

"But it's particularly bad there," Aaron said.

"Yes and no. It was bad everywhere, but for different reasons. This was just the beginning." Sera closed her eyes and shuddered. "If only people knew. If only people could see."

CHAPTER NINETEEN

"HE'S GETTING so old," Sera said as we slowed our pace to let Buddy catch up with us. She bent down to the old chocolate Labrador and ruffled his collar. His tail couldn't wag as fast as it once had, but it still showed his love for her.

We walked past Sheep Meadow in Central Park and noticed that the green of the mall was beginning to swarm with people. All around us women walked briskly, dressed in pink tutus and leg warmers. Some shook pink pom-poms while others held up signs. Each wore a pink T-shirt that read, "Walk for Breast Cancer 2011." The stream of women headed toward a tall arc of large pink balloons that marked the end of their journey.

"Still no sleep?" I asked Sera as we weaved our way through the crowd. The heavy bags under her eyes hadn't lightened at all. After the story she'd told us, I could only imagine what images played through her mind, keeping her awake. I'd heard her get up during the night and pace around the apartment for half an hour. Just as I was getting up to check on her, I heard her bedroom door close again.

"I can't sleep at the moment, Dad."

"Why not? You look exhausted. Do you want me to dig out the lavender pillow Maria gave you when you were a kid? It always soothed you when you were little. I think it's in a cupboard somewhere."

Sera didn't answer. Instead she walked toward a park bench to avoid being a rock in the ever-growing stream of women rushing around us. I took a seat next to her as she took Buddy's dog bowl from her rucksack and filled it from a bottle of water. We sat for a moment while Buddy lapped his fill and then lay on the pathway in front of us.

"What's going on, sweetheart? I know there's something wrong, and it's killing me that you won't tell me."

"I want to tell you, but you're going to think I'm crazy."

"No, I'm not. I just need to know what's happening with you. I'm worried."

A large tear ran down Sera's face. Her bottom lip started to tremble.

"Sera, please, what is it?"

"Dad, I want to tell you, but more than that, I really need you to believe me. If you don't believe me, you won't be able to help me." Her voice quivered. "And I think I'm really going to need your help."

"What happened out there?"

She wiped away her tears, but they were quickly replaced with more.

"Sera, I'll help any way I can. You know that. Whatever it is, we can get through it together."

"Promise?"

"I promise."

Sera took a deep breath.

"Everything was fine when we traveled across Europe. The girls and I had a great time. But then we traveled to Cambodia and I started to have trouble sleeping. I would drift off easily enough, but then I'd hear a voice calling my name so clearly it woke me up. It happened twice the first week we were there, but I just dismissed it as a dream. With everything that was going on with Champai, I thought maybe my mind wasn't switching off."

She choked back tears.

"I spent the day at the embassy with Kanya and came back to the hotel exhausted. My mind was racing, trying to figure out how we were going to get Champai back to her village. The man we'd spoken to hadn't been a great deal of help, which was understandable because he didn't know the full story. That night I heard my name being called again. The voice sounded so familiar, but I just couldn't place it. Instead of just calling my name as it had before it said 'Save them.' I woke up to Amy banging at my door and, well, you know what happened next."

I took hold of Sera's hand and covered it with my own.

"Then we traveled to Thailand, India, Africa, and the Middle East, and the voice started to come to me almost every night. Sometimes even when I wasn't sleeping. I'd be awake with my eyes wide open and I could still hear it. It started saying 'This is why you are here. Save them.'"

I tried not to show the alarm that triggered in my head. I needed to know exactly what was happening with her, so I sat still and listened.

"I thought I was going crazy, and it scared me. I mean, it *really* scared me. I started to think I might have picked up some kind of bug or infection that was causing me to hear things. But the strange thing was that I was absolutely fine during the day. It only ever happened at night. At the time I wondered whether it was a side effect of the antimalaria pills, so I switched to another kind. But the voice kept coming. I'd read that malaria can make you delirious, so when we got to Mumbai, I had myself tested just in case the pills hadn't worked. But the results came back negative. After that the voice became louder and louder."

Sera stopped as if afraid to tell me the rest of the story.

"Go on, what happened?" I asked as reassuringly as I could.

Sera let out a sob she'd been holding in. "I can't. You're going to think I've lost it!"

"Sera, please. Tell me what happened."

Hesitantly Sera went on. "One night in Bangladesh, the voice woke me again. I don't know why, but that night I finally recognized it. And the moment I did, she appeared in front of me."

Sera stopped again. She shook her head as though she couldn't bring herself to say it.

"Who was it?"

"Dad, it was Sophia."

"Your imaginary friend from when you were little?"

Sera nodded but didn't look at me. I think she was worried about my reaction. She didn't know I'd been concerned about the reappearance of Sophia in the past.

"You know, I never thought she was imaginary," Sera said, her eyes wandering back toward the crowd of women in pink. "I could never understand why you couldn't see or hear her when I was a kid. She was clear as day to me. Well, until she left. I remember being so mad at Miss Dee, Maggie, and Maria for making her disappear."

I didn't feel it was the right time to tell her that it had been at my insistence the ladies had banished Sophia.

"So… what did she look like? What did you see?"

Sera faltered. "Her face had changed. She was older, probably about the same age as I am now. It was like we'd both grown up. It was so dark in the room, but I could see her so clearly—just like I could when we were kids and she would sit on the end of my bed and talk to me at night."

I thought back to the painting Sister Rose had shown me when Sera was a child—of Sophia drawn as a bird.

"So.... Sophia is an angel?"

"She didn't describe herself as an angel, but I guess that's what she is."

"So what did she say?"

"She told me that she'd always been with me, to guide me."

"What do you mean?"

"She said I was sent here for a reason, something that I was destined to do since I was born. Something I already knew myself to be true."

"And what do you think that is?" I asked warily.

"To save the women of the world."

I had to choose my words carefully.

"Sera, the stories you told us last night... they were... horrific. You've seen things that would traumatize anyone. And I know it's been difficult, especially having just lost Maggie. But to say that.... Maybe you're exhausted and not thinking straight? You need to sleep."

Sera turned to face me again. "The night before you were going to fly to Jordan to see us, I saw her again. She said, 'It's time to go home and say good-bye before she returns. It's time to begin.' I can't explain how I knew she was talking about Maggie, but the moment I heard your voice, I knew what you were going to say."

I let go of her hand and leaned forward, my elbows resting on my knees, my head in my hands. Was this it? Was this the psychotic break I'd seen hints of in the past? What was I meant to do or say to comfort her? Not only was she hearing voices and hallucinating, now she was convincing herself that her premonitions came true.

My thoughts instantly turned to psychotherapists. I would get her the best. But what would they say? It's a life-long condition with little hope of recovery? My heart sank as I realized the chances of Sera having a family of her own would be set with impossible obstacles. I blamed myself for not getting her help sooner.

Sera put her hand on my back. "Dad...."

"Yes, sweetheart."

"I know it's a lot to take in," she said as she began patting my shoulder blade. "It took me a while, but I have accepted it as the truth. Hopefully in time you will too, because I need you now more than ever."

As so many times before, her touch calmed me. Or maybe it gave me the sense that I needed to be strong for her. Either way, my next thoughts came more easily and I felt less helpless.

Maybe this was just an episode we had to get through, a short blip that could be overcome with the right therapist and medication. It had been over ten years since she'd last exhibited signs of a real breakdown. Maybe the trauma of what had happened to Champai and the other women they'd met had set her off.

But from what she said, it had been going on for months, not just a few hours. How long had she concealed her problem, never saying it out loud? Why confess it now? Was it because she was exhausted and had just suffered the loss of yet another mother figure? I needed to keep her life as trauma-free as possible, so these episodes wouldn't flare up again. We could work this out, but I would need help.

We sat in silence and listened to the din of the crowd gathering around the arc of pink balloons as more and more women arrived.

I considered my options. I could go to Donna and get the name of an adult specialist. I would have to do it quietly, though. If Sera was officially diagnosed with a mental illness, it would affect the rest of her life and destroy any chance of a good career. And for what—a momentary lapse in sanity? This could be fixed. Perhaps, through my contacts and with Donna's help, I could get her a job as a social worker specializing in women's issues. Would that be enough to fulfill her ambition? Maybe there was a chance this wasn't as bad as it seemed.

After a while Sera finally spoke. "Beautiful, isn't it?"

"What is?" I asked, pulled from my racing thoughts.

Sera gave an upward nod to the thousands of women now flooding into the park. Though she was tired and her face was pale and drawn, the sunlight shone through the wisps of her auburn hair, the embers still aflame.

I turned my eyes to the crowd. Women hugged one another in congratulation. Old friends stood exchanging numbers with new ones they'd met on the charity walk. Shorthaired women pinned pink ribbons on T-shirts and held banners that read "Survivor." Volunteers high-fived strangers as they walked the final few steps across the finish line.

"Women helping women." Sera smiled. "Look at their faces. Look at the pride it brings them to be part of something so much bigger, yet also so incredibly personal. The unselfish joy it brings to them to have accomplished their mission to help. They walked for the ones they love, the ones they've lost, and the ones they'll never know." She spoke with moving eloquence, transfixed by the crowd.

We watched as the women smiled, laughed, wept, and embraced one another.

"So Sophia told you that you're an angel too?"

Sera turned to face me. "No, Dad. She told me I'm the Daughter of God."

CHAPTER TWENTY

AARON AND I sat over lunch the following day outside Luigi's restaurant in Little Italy. I hadn't slept all night and was feeling a little punch-drunk. My voice sounded flat, almost as though I didn't care.

"She can't honestly believe it."

"She does, Aaron."

"No," he said, shaking his head. "She's far too levelheaded and too smart to believe what she's saying is true. Where is this coming from? And why the hell do you seem okay about this?"

"Of course I'm not okay with this!" I blurted, finally with some emotion in my voice. "But at the moment I'm tiptoeing around her. We didn't discuss it at all after she told me. I know we have to, but I have to get my thoughts in order and come up with a plan first."

"But you seem resigned to the idea that she thinks she's...," he began before looking baffled, "....God's daughter!"

"Will you keep your damn voice down!" I looked around at the other diners. Whatever their conversations were about, I was sure they'd stop immediately to listen to ours. "I'm not resigned to the idea of anything," I said in a harsh whisper. "I'm trying to remain calm. What good am I going to be if I start losing it?"

"So this vision.... Do you think she was on drugs? Was this just a bad trip?"

"I told you before, Sera has never touched drugs."

"As far as you know."

"Do you honestly think, after what happened to the girl she met who overdosed, that she'd take up drugs?"

"Maybe not heroin. But it wouldn't be too farfetched to think she may have tried Ecstasy."

"We've already been through this. You just said yourself that she's too smart to do something like that."

"Yeah, but everyone experiments."

I took a deep breath. "Aaron, listen. This isn't the first time she's said this."

Aaron looked confused.

"When she was a kid, she got things mixed up at school when they spoke about God being her father."

"Yeah, but she was only a kid!"

I nodded and raised my eyebrows to show I agreed.

"Do you think she needs help? You know, professional help," he asked.

I looked at Aaron guiltily. He'd been such a big part of Sera's life growing up and had always taken an active role, and yet I'd kept this from him.

"I took her to a therapist when she was eleven years old, a few months after 9/11. You remember how she freaked out that night?"

Aaron nodded.

"The therapist said he thought that she'd temporarily regressed to being a small child after the towers came down and after that Muslim girl was attacked outside our building. Basically she couldn't cope with the violence, so she went back to a time when she thought she'd decided who she was. So he thought that meant when she was five years old, believing God was her father. That was also the same time Sophia was around. He gave me medication, but I never gave it to her."

I thought Aaron might be upset that I'd kept this from him. Instead he remained focused on the problem at hand.

"So you think she did the same thing while she was travelling? She couldn't cope with what she saw? Not that I can blame her. I've been thinking about Champai ever since I left your apartment."

I took another deep confessional breath. "Do you remember, just before I adopted Sera, a girl came forward saying that she may have been her birth mother?"

"Yes. What's that got to do with it?"

"Aaron, I still don't know whether or not she was Sera's mom. The DNA test was never done. But that girl was a drug addict and had mental health issues. Before I was given custody of Sera, the social workers said she wouldn't stop crying. What if the girl was her mother and had been using drugs before she gave birth, and the reason Sera was crying was because she was having withdrawals? What if Sera was already addicted before she was born?"

"But—"

"And if the girl gave birth to her somewhere without medical assistance, it would explain a difficult birth and Sera's Erb's Palsy," I continued. "Aaron, I have to face facts. There's a good chance that the girl was Sera's mother. And if she was, maybe she inherited some form of mental illness from her. They say these kinds of issues usually begin to show in the late teens or early twenties."

"But Sera isn't crazy. She's not whacked-out screaming at people on the street or hurting anyone."

"Exactly, which is why I never gave her the pills the therapist prescribed her." I shook my head. "This seems to come and go every few years. I mean, look what she's accomplished with school and the whole social media thing. She's a brilliant, articulate, caring girl. She'd never hurt anyone. But what do I do now? She's an adult. I can't make her do anything. I can't make her see a doctor and I can't force her to take medication. Unless she's a danger to herself or others, there's nothing I can do."

"So do you have some sort of plan?"

"I'm not sure yet."

"Well, you have to get her help."

"I know, but it's not as easy as that. I'm scared, Aaron."

"Of what?"

"Years ago, when I was a Legal Aid attorney, I spent time up at Bellevue when I was representing patients or their families."

"The mental hospital on East Twenty-Sixth?"

I nodded. "I had to work with the doctors and social workers when someone was committed. That place was my idea of a nightmare. Men and women wandered around the halls either screaming at the voices they were hearing or walking like zombies because they were so heavily medicated. I was there once when two women became violent toward each other. It took four male nurses to restrain them, but they'd already torn out clumps of hair, scratched each other's faces, and punched the hell out of each other. Then they were sedated and locked away. I can't have Sera living like that. There's no way I would put her through it."

"Aren't you getting a little ahead of yourself?"

"Sera has always been a good kid. And maybe I'm looking at the worst-case scenario, but I have to consider every possibility. Since the last time she had an episode, she's been distracted with school and her social media following. Maybe keeping her distracted with something positive is the key to keeping the episodes at bay. She wants to come up with a plan of action that will help millions of women across the world. She's way out of her depth, but if the distraction keeps her sane for a while and calms her down the way her social media work did, then I'm going to do everything I can to make it happen. Hopefully she'll grow out of whatever this is or have enough time to learn how to deal with it."

"So you're hopeful this is just a phase?"

"It has been in the past. Let's hope it is again."

I indicated to the waiter that we were ready for the bill. "I have to go. I'm meeting Sera outside the attorney's office in fifteen minutes."

"What for?"

"Maggie left something for Sera in her will." I sighed. "Thank God the ladies aren't around to see this. It would've worried them to death."

"Listen, if there is anything I can do, make sure you let me know."

"I will. And remember, this is just between us."

AS I walked up to the entrance of Fellows, White, and Associates, I saw Sera leaning against the wall tapping on the screen of her iPhone.

"Still freaked out, huh?" she said with the smile she always gave me when she was trying to lighten the subject.

I gave her a casual shrug and returned her smile. I wasn't ready to say I believed her, but I also didn't want to say I didn't for fear it could make matters worse.

"It'll take some time to get your head around, but we'll talk more later. I'll help you understand." She gave me a hug, and we made our way into the attorney's offices.

We were shown into a small conference room where Thomas Baylor, a rotund man with a happy face, met us.

"Ah, you must be Sera," he said as he shook her hand. "It's wonderful to finally meet the young lady I've heard so much about!"

We sat down as he took out a large file and began sorting through papers. "I know this looks terribly complicated, but it all boils down to something quite simple."

He settled back on his chair and began to read from Maggie's will.

"I, Margret Siobhan O'Dowd, hereby leave my property and all cash assets to Miss Sera Goodwin."

The attorney placed the will down and opened another file he'd carried into the room.

"She's left Sera everything?"

"Yes, Mr. Goodwin. Sera will now be the owner of Maggie's apartment, as well as a substantial amount of money." He pulled an envelope from his file and handed it to Sera.

"What do you mean 'a substantial amount'? Maggie was a retired schoolteacher."

"Yes, but her estate also included all the proceeds from the estates of Miss Della Walker and Mrs. Maria Fuentes."

"Wait, I don't understand," I said, utterly confused.

"It's okay. It was meant to be confidential and only brought to light when the time was right. The three ladies had an agreement. Each of them left their cash and property to the surviving others. The lady who passed away last was to give the entire lump sum to Sera."

"But that can't be right."

"I assure you it is. I arranged the three ladies' wills myself."

"But Miss Dee had two daughters of her own. Surely she left the apartment to them."

Mr. Baylor sat back in his chair and momentarily looked confused. "She did have two daughters, Mr. Goodwin. But they didn't survive her."

"Yes, they did. They live in Brooklyn. She used to visit them all the time."

"I'm sorry to tell you this, but Miss Dee's two daughters died when they were four and six years old."

"But... that doesn't make any sense," I said.

"Miss Dee's daughters were caught in the crossfire of a drive-by shooting in 1972. They were buried in Brooklyn. She often travelled there, but only to visit their graves."

I remembered the last words Miss Dee had whispered to Maria before she died. "Hold them 'til I get there." I turned to Sera, whose face was tight with anguish. She handed me the letter that Mr. Baylor had given her. I immediately recognized Maggie's schoolteacher handwriting.

Our Dearest Sera,
You brought so much love and joy into our world.
You will bring the same to so many more. Remember what
we taught you.
    With all our love,
    Maggie, Miss Dee, and Maria.

"Of course it's entirely up to you what you do with the property," Mr. Baylor said, addressing Sera. "But Maggie indicated that all three women hoped you would keep and move into the last apartment so you could remain close to your dad. I think they just wanted to leave knowing he would keep you safe."

Sera's sad smile mirrored my own.

"I did ask whether they wanted me to advise you on investments," the attorney continued, "what with it being such a large amount. But Maggie said she wanted you to carry on with your work. She assured me you would know what to do with the money when the time came. Hopefully you understand what she meant, since she didn't elaborate."

Carry on with your work. The words brought me out of my state of confusion and surprise. Sera's recent "revelation" could be more difficult to manage if she had access to substantial funds. "Mr. Baylor, do you happen to have statements of how much cash Sera's been left?"

"Of course. The assets of each estate were left in the name of a trust, granted and settled by Maggie, with Sera as the sole beneficiary. She named me as trustee but instructed that I should transfer trusteeship to you, Mr. Goodwin, upon her passing. I have drawn up the necessary documents to transfer authority over the trust to you." He passed me the document to review and turned to Sera to explain. "I asked Ms. O'Dowd why she didn't want to liquidate the trust and have the funds and assets transferred directly to you upon her death. She said that she had great faith in your future, and that you shouldn't be burdened with such mundane details as asset and investment management. There is a clause in the document your father is reading that gives you authority to direct disbursements and investments. But the day-to-day management of the accounts will be left to him."

Sera nodded her understanding. The document appeared to be in order to me, and Mr. Baylor left the room briefly and returned with two of his colleagues, one to witness the signatures and another to notarize them. Once the document was fully executed, he pulled out a thick, expandable folder and passed it over to me.

"Congratulations, Mr. Goodwin, you are now the custodian of these detailed account statements related to the trust."

"Thank you, Mr. Baylor." I opened the folder and glanced at the top sheet, which appeared to be a recent statement of the trust's assets. "Do you mind if I have a quick look at these documents, just in case I have any initial questions?"

"Of course not," he replied.

"Sera, do you mind? It'll only take a few minutes."

Sera smiled at me. "Of course, Dad. Go ahead. Mr. Baylor, is there a ladies' room nearby where I can get some tissues?"

"Certainly, I'll show you," he said as he got up from the table and led Sera out of the conference room.

I pulled out the bank statement and reviewed the entries, which appeared in order, but with much higher balances than I would have expected from three women of modest means. I thumbed through the rest of the folder and pulled out an old statement, which was in Miss Dee's name. It showed consistent weekly deposits in amounts I instantly recognized. They were exactly the amounts I'd paid her for looking after Sera during the week when she was young. I found identical bank statements in the names of Maria and Maggie showing the same history of deposits. The three women had put every cent I'd paid them for taking care of Sera into the bank. Over the years, that had grown into rather large amounts. Combined with the proceeds of their life savings and the sale of Maria's and Miss Dee's apartments, it was indeed a substantial sum. So much, in fact, that Sera wouldn't have to worry about income for a long time, provided I kept up the conservative investments with consistent returns Mr. Baylor had prudently made.

The trust structure gave me even more comfort that any property would be held in the name of the trust and not by Sera individually. As trustee, I could take care of maintenance and taxes, but Sera would be able to use it as she saw fit. Plus, with so many online followers, I was relieved that the trust would give Sera an added layer of privacy.

Sera returned with Mr. Baylor just as I put the statements back into the folder. "Everything in order?" he asked.

"Yes, thank you. I don't think I have any questions right now. But I may want to take you up on that offer of investment advice. You've done a fine job with the trust assets."

"Of course. Feel free to contact me any time. Ms. O'Dowd drove a hard bargain and insisted that I set up my trustee agreement so I would be on retainer based on a lump sum payment, so there aren't any worries about hourly rates," Mr. Baylor said.

Maggie had thought of everything.

When we got up to leave, Mr. Baylor stood and reached across the table to shake Sera's hand.

"It really is a pleasure to meet you, Sera. Whatever your plans are for the future, I can tell you the three ladies had every faith you would achieve your goal."

WHEN WE got outside the law offices, I turned to Sera.

"Well? Do you want to keep and live in Maggie's apartment so I can keep an eye on you?" I asked, playfully nudging her until she began to topple.

The rib-crushing hug I received was all the answer I could hope for.

"But can I stay living with you, Dad? I've missed you so much. I know it's only next door, but I don't think I'm ready to leave just yet."

"Of course! It will always be your home."

"Maybe I can use Maggie's apartment as somewhere to work from."

"Sounds like a plan." I smiled.

CHAPTER TWENTY-ONE

WE MANAGED to avoid further discussion of Sera's divine parentage for the next four weeks. She told me she appreciated that I needed time to come to terms with her belief, which made things even more confusing, since that in itself was the act of a sane person. So instead of awkward conversations, we spent our time renovating Maggie's apartment and shopping for furniture for what was to become the base of operations for her mission.

We spent the month laughing and joking, reminiscing, and arguing over wallpaper and paint. As we fell back into our old banter and teased each other the way we always had, the possibility that the issue might be mentioned was always there, but it never came up. I was always on the watch for signs of mental health problems, but I didn't really know what I was looking for. She didn't talk to herself and seemed the fun-loving Sera I'd always known. Things became so normal that I sometimes forgot the conversation we'd had in the park, but then Sera would bring up another story of her travels, and its shadow would come rolling back.

On the whole, though, it was a month of happiness and I treasured every moment. My upbeat mood was further bolstered when I learned that Amy, Carla, and Meena had all arranged to take another year off before starting their careers. They'd each spoken to their parents, who had agreed they could continue living at home rent-free, while Sera could afford to pay them a small wage to help support them.

The girls had resisted at first, but Sera insisted they would be more effective if financial issues weren't on their minds. But even after Meena and Carla agreed, Amy continued to argue. Coming from an affluent family, she insisted she didn't need it. But something in her tone suggested to me that she didn't like the idea of Sera being her employer and, therefore, her boss.

"IT DOESN'T feel right, does it?" Sera said as she rolled another strip of paint onto the living room wall. "It kind of feels like we're erasing a part of Maggie."

"Do you want paisley walls and a floral sofa?"

Sera laughed. "If I wasn't going to use this place as a base of operations, I'd have no problem keeping it the same. I spent so much of my childhood here, it feels like a second home."

"Yeah, I guess it was. But eventually it'll be your own first home, so you should have it the way you want it, sweetheart. It's what Maggie would have wanted," I said as I assembled another piece of IKEA furniture Sera had picked out. I looked up and smiled. She'd regained some weight and looked much healthier. "Did you sleep again last night?"

"Yep. All the way through! The lavender pillow did the trick. I could've slept all morning if you hadn't woken me up."

"Sorry, but if you want to get this done, we have to do it on my days off."

Sera rolled another half dozen strips of paint on the wall before she spoke again. She gave me a cheeky smile. "So, any questions?"

My first instinct was to ignore the opening, hoping for a few more days of ignorant bliss. But she clearly thought it was time to address the angelic elephant in the room. I started asking my questions in an offhand manner while I hunted for screws and looked over instructions. Her tone of voice indicated she wanted this talk to be light and casual, and I was more than happy with that.

"Have you heard from Sophia?"

"No. She tells me I'm the female Messiah and then just disappears! No call, no text, no e-mail. Nothing." Sera swung her roller around and pointed at me, a large smile on her face. "You know what I think that is? I think that's rude!"

I laughed. I knew she was trying to make it easier for me. I waited for her real answer.

"No, I haven't seen or heard her since the night she told me about Maggie." Sera dipped her roller onto the tray and saturated it with paint. "Next?"

"Are you prepared for the reaction when you tell your millions of followers on Facebook and Twitter?"

"I haven't told anyone apart from you so far. In time I may confide in Amy, Carla, and Meena. But for now I think revealing myself will only work against me."

"So when?"

"When I can address the injustices against women." Sera looked back at me. "I know why you're worried. I promise I won't announce anything until they can see the proof I put before them. And that proof will be our success."

There was a shift in the room. I felt a palpable sense of relief at her assurance she wasn't about to declare herself divine and open herself up to ridicule. I began to laugh as if I'd just been granted a reprieve.

"What?" Sera asked, a quizzical smile spreading across her face.

"I don't know. You just seem so... I don't know... so reasonable about the whole thing."

"I've had more time to get used to it. Don't get me wrong, I was confused for a long time. The sense of responsibility and not having any idea of a solution made me sick with worry. But now ideas are forming in my head on how to effect change. I can see now that I've been building toward this for years without knowing it. I have the tools at my disposal. I just have to figure out where to start."

I slid a large flat-packed box across the carpet and sat cross-legged as I opened it.

"What questions do you want me to ask?" I offered. I really wasn't sure what the protocol was here.

"Honestly? I don't know. It's not because I don't want you to ask them. I just don't feel like I have the right answers for you yet."

"How so?"

"I can't explain the meaning of life, and I can't perform miracles. I don't know why there's evil in the world or why good people suffer. I can't give you the reason why God doesn't talk to me or why He remains silent to the world. I'm just as confused and lost to the mysteries as everyone else. But I think that's the point. Maybe God wants us to figure these things out for ourselves."

"I think what I find the hardest to understand is that you've never been a particularly religious girl. I mean, you went to a Catholic school, but you were never one to pray."

"That's because they taught the Bible, a book that contradicts so many things I know to be true. If it ever was the word of God, it's been twisted, manipulated, edited, lost in translation, and used as a weapon. I can't rely on something that isn't true in its entirety. The only thing I can accept to be true in those words is what I have seen evidence of."

"Like?"

"When Jesus spoke He gave a template for a life worth living, one of goodness and kindness. His words made sense. But then there are the parts of the Bible that make no sense at all. How am I supposed to believe that Noah crammed millions of species of animals onto one boat while God drowned every other living thing on earth? And after everything I've seen, how can I possibly accept that slavery is okay because the Bible says so? And let's face it, women didn't exactly get a good deal in that book. And what makes matters worse is they're still suffering for its words thousands of years later."

"Mary Magdalene?"

Sera's face turned sad for a moment as the history of that name hung in the air. She shook it off. "Among others. But the first was Eve. A woman blamed for pretty much everything. A woman who apparently spoke to snakes and had the audacity to eat an apple."

"Yeah, that's pretty messed up."

Sera stepped back from the wall for a moment as if to see where the paint was thin. "Let a woman learn in silence with all submissiveness. I permit no woman to teach or have authority over men; she is to keep silent. For Adam was formed first, then Eve; and Adam was not deceived, but the woman was deceived and became a transgressor. Yet woman will be saved through bearing children, if she continues in faith and love and holiness, with modesty."

The quote unnerved me for a moment. I was reminded of the Christian fundamentalists on TV. But unlike those who spoke with absolute conviction, Sera said it matter-of-factly, like the words were so ridiculous they didn't warrant any emotion.

"Wives, submit to your own husbands, as to the Lord. For the husband is the head of the wife even as Christ is the head of the church, his body, and is himself its Savior. Now as the church submits to Christ, so also wives should submit in everything to their husbands."

"You've been studying the Bible?"

"I have to try and make sense of the origin of the idea that women are second-class citizens," Sera said before quoting again. "Women should keep silent in the churches. For they are not permitted to speak, but should be in submission, as the Law also says. If there is anything they desire to learn, let them ask their husbands at home. For it is shameful for a woman to speak in church."

I woefully nodded, agreeing how ridiculous it sounded.

"Some of the things written in the Bible are not only ludicrous, but dangerous for people to believe. There are so many examples where it's acceptable to sell, enslave, or stone women. There are translations that say if a man rapes a woman, he must pay her father fifty shekels and then marry her. The list goes on and on. I refuse to accept that those are the words of God. It just doesn't make sense. A man wrote or translated those words for his own ends."

I wondered whether this was the time to confess. Since we were being open, I felt like lying to her could do more harm than good if she was to find out later. "Don't be mad with me, but I've told your Uncle Aaron about, well, what you believe."

Sera slowly replaced her paint roller in the tray. I could tell she was anxious to learn what his response was. "Oh? And what did he say?"

"He's both worried and proud of you. You admit yourself that what you're saying sounds pretty out there, so you can't blame him for thinking the same." Sera nodded. "But he's also very proud that you are dedicating yourself to helping women. After hearing your stories, he even made a donation to a women's rights organization."

Sera didn't say anything, but I got the feeling she wanted to.

There was a double knock at the door.

"Well, I know it's not your uncle since he never knocks," I said.

"Can you get it?" Sera asked, holding up her paint-spattered hands.

I opened the door to find Dalyn, smartly dressed in dark chinos and a white polo shirt. He held flowers in his hand—a proper bouquet, not a bunch you'd find in a bucket outside a bodega. He looked embarrassed to see me.

"You have a visitor!" I called as I showed him in.

"These are, um, a housewarming present," Dalyn said, offering the bouquet to Sera.

"Thank you so much!" She stopped just short of hugging him for fear of wiping paint on his shirt.

Dalyn looked unsure. His head wobbled before he leaned forward and pecked Sera on the cheek. I expected Sera to blush, but it was Dalyn who reddened. To give him time to recover, I asked him to help move the four desks I'd just assembled. Sera and I had knocked down the wall separating the two bedrooms, making one large room that Sera had designated as a workspace and office.

"This place looks great!" he said as Sera followed behind us.

Hundreds of 8x10 photo prints of faces, each one of them a woman Sera and the girls had met on their travels, covered every inch of the walls. Sera randomly pointed out faces on the wall and told brief stories of how and where they'd met.

"Sera, if there is anything I can do, if I can offer you any kind of exposure for your work, let me know, okay? Human rights stories are big with the *Times*, though I dare say you have more followers now than even we have readers."

"Thanks. As soon as I've come up with a plan of action, I'll let you know. Anything that creates awareness will help."

"Well, it's great to see you. Hopefully I'll get a chance to see you again soon." He turned to leave. "I know this sounds stupid, but it's almost sad that you're back. I'm going to miss receiving your letters and postcards."

"I'll e-mail you, I promise," Sera said kindly.

A second awkward pause passed as Dalyn seemed to consider going for another kiss on the cheek but apparently chickened out.

After he left I opened yet another flat-pack box that held the large dining table Sera had bought to put in the living room. It was large enough for all the girls to eat or work at should they want a change of scenery.

"Do you think I should get a couple of sofa beds? The girls have been working quite late at night, updating the online groups and getting in touch with the group moderators. If they carry on like that, it might be nice to have somewhere for them to crash if they stay here late. Nothing fancy, just basic enough to sit and sleep on."

"You know that boy likes you, don't you?"

"Huh?"

"Don't play innocent with me, young lady!" I laughed. "Flowers? The blushing? He obviously has a crush on you."

"No, no," she said, trying to brush it off. "We're just friends. That's all. And like he said, the flowers were a housewarming present."

"He likes you. And as more than just a friend."

Sera guffawed as though the idea was absurd. "No, he's just interested in what we're doing. That's all, honestly!"

"The letters you wrote obviously meant a lot to him."

"I was just updating him on where we were and what we were doing!"

"And he couldn't have read that on your thousands of Facebook or Twitter updates? Which I know he did, because he was forever commenting on them!"

"You've got it all wrong, Dad. He's genuinely interested in what we're trying to achieve. I think he wants to be involved in some way. Besides, I'm not interested in being in a relationship."

"Uh-huh," I teased. "You keep fooling yourself, but I'm telling you, I could hear that boy's heart beating quicker every time you spoke."

Sera put one hand on her hip, pointed the paint roller at me, and jerked her head to one side, the way she used to do to make Miss Dee laugh. "Child, don't you make me come over there and smack you upside the head. I told ya, I ain't got no time for no romantic gestures. I got stuff I gotta do! Now hush with that nonsense, ya hear?"

"Okay, okay," I said, laughing and letting it go—for the time being. I rotated the paper diagram of the unassembled table again. "Say what you will about Noah, but I bet God's instructions were better than IKEA's."

CHAPTER TWENTY-TWO

WITH THREE walls of paint drying in Maggie's old apartment, Sera invited Amy, Carla, and Meena over to our place to start preparation for their mission. They sat around the dining room table while I finished up some work at my desk.

"We have to start this week. I can't go another day without actively doing something to help these women," Sera said, underlining the word "Ideas" on her pad for the tenth time.

"We all agree with you, but if we don't plan this out, what are we giving people? All we're doing is telling forty million women terrible stories without giving them any way of helping," Amy said.

"She's right," said Carla, "but the first thing we need to do is create awareness. None of us knew how bad it is out there for women, so you can be sure we aren't the only ones."

The front door of the apartment opened and Aaron strolled in, closely followed by an attractive middle-aged brunette, who looked shy at seeing such a crowd.

"Really, there's no need to knock!" I called sarcastically as I turned from my desk.

"Just a flying visit," he said before extending his arm toward his date. "This is Nina."

I got up from my desk to shake her hand. "Lovely to meet you, Nina."

"We have a dinner reservation in Chinatown," Aaron said, leaving her standing alone while he walked toward the kitchen, "but I got the time wrong, so we have an hour to kill."

He pulled a bottle of wine from the rack on the counter and turned. "Do you mind?"

"Of course not, help yourself." I turned to Nina. "Would you like a glass?"

Nina smiled and nodded. I think the idea of a little Dutch courage appealed to her after she'd been so suddenly introduced to her date's family.

"This is Meena, Carla, Amy, and my daughter, Sera," I said pointing to each of the girls that Aaron hadn't bothered to introduce. They gave a quick wave back.

Nina looked at the pictures of various women scattered across the table.

"What lovely photos!" she said as she meekly walked toward them and extended her hand to each in turn. "Are you working on a project?" She glanced at Amy's open laptop. "My daughter reads For My Sister all the time!" she said. "And I encourage her. It's such an amazing website, don't you think?"

There was a collective grin at the table.

"She's forever telling me about it," Nina said, glad she'd found common ground almost instantly with the strangers she'd just met.

"They don't just read it. They run it," Aaron said, putting the bottle of wine down after filling their glasses.

"You mean Sera's your niece? *The* Sera?"

Aaron nodded proudly. Amy looked a little irked.

"Oh my God, my daughter is going to be so thrilled that I've met you!" Nina exclaimed, turning back to Sera. "She talks about you all the time!"

"That's great!" Sera said. "If she ever wants to stop by or get in contact, just let me know. What's your cell number? Perhaps we can set something up next week?"

"Really?" Nina gushed as she wrote down her number on a piece of paper Meena slid across the table.

While Nina and the girls chatted, Aaron and I remained across the room in the kitchen area. Aaron caught me up on his work. He'd been promoted yet again and was pretty much running the company in the owner's absence. Aaron's boss moored a yacht in the marina and had a penchant for golf, so he left management of the company to his most valued employee.

"It's easy enough. But I must admit I'm getting a little bored. Business is booming, which is great, but I miss being part of the team. I miss the technical aspect of designing new software and staying busy promoting and training people to use it. Now all I'm doing is overseeing everything that's going on with the tech guys."

"But the money's good?"

"It's incredible. At this rate, I should be able to retire sooner rather than later."

"But you're only forty-nine years old!"

"I know. Good, right?" Aaron looked over at the table. "What are the girls up to?"

"Brainstorming."

"Good luck to them," Aaron said, taking another sip of wine.

Nina excused herself from the table. "Could I use your restroom?" she asked.

"Sure, it's just around the corner, second door on the left."

"How's work going with you?" Aaron asked as Nina walked away.

"It's okay, I guess. Life as a partner is a lot busier than I thought it would be. I'm expected to do a lot of schmoozing outside work to get new business, and I'm no good at that."

"Let me know if I can help out. A lot of big companies are clients of ours. I can always put feelers out and get your name out there. Drum up a bit of business for you. Do you have a LinkedIn profile?"

"Huh?"

"It's a business networking site. I'll set you up a profile."

"Is that how you met Nina?"

"No. LinkedIn is specifically designed to talk about your work experience, your professional specialty, and a list of the companies you've worked for. It's essentially an online resume that a lot of professionals rely on to stay in the loop."

"So where did you meet Nina? She seems to be a sweetheart."

Aaron turned back to the kitchen counter and poured another glass of wine. "She works downtown. Divorced with one kid, but I'm not going to find anyone at my age without baggage. She served us at a client development meeting last week. She's got a beautiful pair of tits and a damn near perfect ass. She's a waitress, so probably dumb as a box of rocks, but after a few more glasses of wine, it should be a good night!"

The disapproving look I gave my brother lasted longer than usual as we both froze, suddenly aware of the complete silence in the apartment. I didn't want to look away from him but was forced to when Meena cleared her throat. The girls, who'd heard the last part of our conversation, were looking at Aaron as though they'd just witnessed him strangle a kitten. But the true reason for their silence was revealed when Sera glanced toward the hallway. I slowly turned and saw Nina standing behind me. She'd returned from the bathroom and heard every word Aaron had said.

The longer the silence lasted, the more Nina's humiliation showed on her face. Aaron's words still hung in the air. She turned and started to walk toward the door with as much dignity as she could muster, her quickening footsteps almost breaking into a run.

"Wait!" Sera called getting up from the table. Nina stopped.

Sera rounded on her uncle. "That's the way you describe women? Their only positive attributes are their bodies? Their profession dictates their intelligence? Get them drunk and they'll give you a good time? After everything I've told you, how could you still be this way?"

Nina took another step toward the front door.

"Hang on!" Sera demanded. "He needs to hear this. Tell him what you think and how that made you feel!"

Aaron's head turned from Sera to Nina. I couldn't tell whether he was upset with himself or with Sera for forcing him to confront the consequences of his words.

"I'm angry," Nina said, turning to face Aaron again.

"Go on," Sera encouraged her.

"Yes, I may *only* be a waitress, but I work damn hard. It's a job that allows me to work in the evening while I go to school during the day. Do you have any idea how hard it is to go back to school at my age? But I'm doing it to get a better job so I can afford to send my daughter to college when she's ready."

Nina's voice slowly began to rise as the initial humiliation faded, replaced by building rage.

"I'd work every hour God sent if it meant giving my daughter, or as you so nicely put it, my *baggage*, a better shot at life."

"I really didn't mean—"

"And you know what? I'm proud of myself! That's right, I'm proud of myself. Can you say the same? Seriously, do you think you're something special? You're in your late forties, never been married, and not in a relationship. I think it's safe to assume your opinion of women is the reason why!"

"It's not like that! I was only kidding around with—" Aaron began.

"You're an asshole!" Nina shouted before she stormed out, slamming the door behind her.

Sera wasn't finished with Aaron. "You've been this way since I was a kid. You never knew how much it upset me. But even now it's like you think I don't notice how you treat women," she said sternly.

"Look, Sera, I'm sorry. You know I didn't—"

"Sorry? Why are you saying it to me? Don't you think you should be chasing after her, apologizing and asking her to forgive you?"

"You're right," Aaron said as he walked toward the door like a chastised child.

He looked back once more. And in an act of righteous indignation I'd never have expected from Sera, she turned her head away as though she couldn't bear to look at him anymore. An awkward silence lingered that acknowledged the embarrassment in the room as Aaron walked out.

I set my wine down on the kitchen island, the clink of the glass getting the girls' attention. "Sera, I know what Aaron said was wrong and out of line, but so were you. You're going to call your uncle in the morning and apologize for the way you just spoke to him."

"I will not," she said defiantly. "It's about time he realized that how he treats women is wrong."

"Sera, Nina overhearing what Aaron said hurt her. I know it was incredibly disrespectful, but you and I both know he didn't really mean it, and he certainly didn't say it out loud with the intention that she or anyone other than I hear it."

"Then why say it at all? Of all people, why act all macho in front of you? It's not as though you're going to be jealous or impressed or consider him some sort of hero."

"Your uncle talks to me the same way he talks to his buddies. He may joke, brag, and boast, but that's just his way. Do you honestly think he's intentionally malicious or a bad person?"

"It doesn't matter if he meant it. The fact that he said it at all—" Sera began.

"He said it and he got caught. You should have left it to him to deal with. Making that woman pour her heart out in front of strangers on your command didn't help matters."

"But I bet she left feeling more empowered—"

"This isn't one of your horrific stories, Sera. Pick your battles! You made your uncle feel even worse than he probably already did just to prove a point. I know you're feeling frustrated at the pace of your efforts at the moment, but taking it out on Aaron isn't going to make things go any faster."

"But—"

"Tell me the truth, all of you," I said, looking to all the girls at the table. "Aaron helped you start up your presence on social media. He came to you with solutions when you wanted to expand. He even helped you financially when you wanted to travel to investigate how other women in the world lived and what problems they experienced." I turned directly to Sera. "And he has never once shown you anything but love. Now tell me, do you honestly think he is truly a misogynist? Do you seriously believe that he's in the same category as the other men you've told us about?"

"No, but it doesn't make it okay to say that sort of thing," Sera said.

"He'll make it right with Nina. I know he will. He'll admit he was wrong and apologize. He'll grovel if he needs to. Not at your request, but because he knew it was the right thing to do even before you berated him. He knew he'd embarrassed her, and trust me—I know my brother—he was mortified. I know you're frustrated, but you should focus that energy on the people it should be directed at."

Sera nodded slowly. Aaron may have talked big, but when it came down to it, Sera knew as well as I did that he was quite sensitive. Though he was a grown man full of charm when he wanted to be, sometimes his actions reminded me of a schoolboy being mean to the girl in the playground to cover how much he secretly liked her.

"Don't you see that he's lonely? Why do you think he spends so much time here? He doesn't have someone in his life! Being with his family is important to him."

Sera looked at the girls. Each one either seemed to be chewing the inside of her cheeks or holding her bottom lip between her teeth. I couldn't tell whether it was because they agreed with Sera or perhaps thought she'd overreacted.

Sera surrendered. "Okay, I'll call him tomorrow. But he'd better have learned his lesson and made it up to her."

ONCE THE girls left, Sera and I settled in for the evening.

"I'm telling you," Bill Maher said to his panel of guests, "there's always a problem in male-dominated institutions where women are either absent or have little to no power. The church, the military, even governments."

"He's got that right," Sera said.

"You know he's an antitheist, right?"

"I know. But he still has a good point."

I turned the volume down.

"Are you okay? You know, about what happened earlier?"

Sera pulled one of the throw pillows to her mouth and let out a muffled scream. "I'm just so frustrated. We've been back for a month, and we haven't even begun to get started. Every day I think of those women and the hell they're going through. I have this overwhelming sense of guilt that I'm here, roof over my head, food in my stomach, and the freedom to come and go as I please."

"But surely you don't expect things to change overnight, do you?"

"Of course not, but every day lost is another day those women live in nightmares."

"You're not losing days, you've been preparing. How far did you get in your plans?"

"We've decided the first thing we have to do is bring the issues to people's attention. So every week I'm going to write a blog about a woman we've met. I'll write it in English, Carla will translate it into Spanish, Meena into Mandarin, and Amy into French and German. Then we'll post them on the website, Twitter, Pinterest, Tumblr, and Google +. Then we'll send them to each of the moderators of the groups on Facebook and ask that they encourage conversation on the story. In the meantime we're going to come up with a plan for how we can do something effective."

"So kind of stirring up the troops before going into battle?"

"Exactly."

"There's no point in sugarcoating or exaggerating it," I warned. "Your delivery method is short. Be blunt and tell them the truth."

"Is that how the gay rights movement did it?"

"We had no choice. We had to fight back against the police brutality at Stonewall. We were the voices for those silenced by an unknown disease killing our community. We demonstrated against those who desperately tried to deny us our equal rights and protection. And still, to this day, we continue to fight for marriage equality, because if we don't, it will never, ever change."

Sera nodded slowly in understanding. "The reality of what these women are going through is pretty harsh."

"Then show them."

"I'll do my best."

"In the meantime, don't forget to call your uncle tomorrow."

"I will. I promise." Sera sighed and slouched in her seat.

"You know I still call you and your friends 'girls.' I know you're all women now. It's just that old habits die hard."

"Don't worry, Dad, I know you're not that way. You can call us whatever you want, take your pick. We are girls. We are women. We are all-powerful queens!"

"Easy, there."

Sera dramatically raised her arms into the air and flourished her hands before exclaiming, "We are goddesses!"

We both caught each other's eyes. It should have been an awkward moment. Instead we laughed until our stomachs were sore and our throats were dry.

CHAPTER TWENTY-THREE

"SO THIS is the first blog?" I asked as I made myself comfortable.

"Yes." Sera turned the screen of her laptop toward me and pulled up a chair. "I tried to call Uncle Aaron again today, but he still hasn't called me back. Do you think he's mad at me?"

"I think he's probably too ashamed. He managed to clear things up with Nina and said they were on good terms, but they're not dating anymore. I think he's genuinely upset about that. Despite what he said, I got the feeling that he really liked her," I said, recalling how low Aaron sounded on the phone. "Don't worry, he'll call you when he's ready."

Sera gave a hopeful nod before clicking on the webpage. It was headed by a photo of a young black girl smiling in front of a village hut that obscured most of the desolate landscape behind her. I began to read.

This is twelve-year-old Bebi. As one of three female members of her family, Bebi is charged with the responsibility of collecting water for the household. Every day she walks with other girls and women of the village to collect water from a hand-dug well two miles away.

On the way to the well, flies pester her as she travels in the blistering heat of the Ethiopian sun. Bebi considers this the easy part of her day as the five-gallon plastic container on her back is yet to be filled. While her brothers sit in a classroom learning to read and write, she complains that her back hurts from the weight of the water and that her ankles are sore from tripping over the uneven mud path she walks along barefooted. Her father says it will strengthen her back and make her strong. A desirable wife. But Bebi is already convinced that her spine is damaged.

Bebi lives a life of labor that many of us couldn't even begin to imagine. At such a young age, she is responsible for fetching the untreated water that her mother will use for cooking and washing, but most importantly, to quench the thirst of her family. Bebi worries that one day she will bring home a container of water that carries a bacteria or illness that will harm her family or possibly lead to their deaths.

"Oh," I said, a little surprised.

"What?" Sera asked. "What is it?"

"I don't know. I mean, it's short, and it ends a bit abruptly and doesn't really tell me anything I didn't already know. And it's—"

"Dad, you need to scroll the page down. Don't you use a computer at work?"

"Okay, okay. Jeez, sorry."

For a moment I'd thought she'd played it safe, but as I continued to read, I was quickly disabused of that notion.

But this story isn't about Bebi. This is the story of the girl who walks beside her to the well each day. It's about her sister, Damisi.

Damisi is fifteen years old.

We met Damisi in Senbata Lencho, a rural village in southern Ethiopia. Our guide, Hafsa, with whom we had traveled from Addis Ababa, introduced us to her. Hafsa is one of the leaders of the Free Womanhood Foundation, an organization combating the widespread practice of female genital mutilation in Ethiopia.

When we were first introduced to Damisi, it was obvious from her large round belly that she was heavily pregnant and perhaps just days away from giving birth. Not that this stopped her from making the journey to the well several times a day with her twelve-year-old sister Bebi, carrying five gallon containers of filthy, untreated water for cooking, washing, and bathing....

There was no excitement in Damisi's eyes as she felt the baby move. The only look in her eyes when the baby kicked was that of sheer terror.

When Damisi was nine years old, an older woman she hadn't seen before arrived in her village. Damisi overheard the whispers about the women. They called the stranger "the cutter." One day, soon after the stranger's arrival, the parents of the village gathered their young daughters into one hut where they were told that the time had come for them to be prepared for womanhood. The girls' ages ranged from six to twelve years old.

The village elders explained that being "cut" was for their own good. It was to ensure they were sexually desensitized; therefore there was less chance of them becoming promiscuous. It promoted chastity and fidelity. The girls obviously didn't understand what that meant, so didn't know whether it was a good or bad thing. They were told their future husbands and their families would pay large dowries of cows and goats to each girl's parents for a virginal bride. This in return would help their parents pay to send their sons to school where they could receive an education.

Damisi waited for her turn as she heard the screams of each of the girls who went before her. When it was her time, she struggled as she was taken to the back of the hut where the girls had been gathered. Her hands were tied to the base of a small tree and her dress was pulled up to her stomach. Two women from the village forced her legs apart and held her down as "the cutter" removed Damisi's clitoris, labia minora, and labia majora with a knife. The cut edges of her labia majora were then brought together and stitched with a straight needle and thread, leaving a hole just large enough for her to urinate out of and allow blood to pass when she came of menstruating age. The women who had held her down then bound her legs together with thin rope and ordered she remain in the hut until the wound had healed. After just a quick wipe of the blade with a dirty cloth, the cutter then used the same knife on each of the waiting girls, creating further risk of infection or the transmission of the HIV virus that was prevalent in the surrounding villages.

As the binding would hinder their ability to evacuate their bowels, the girls were barely fed and were given just sips of water for five weeks until they had healed. During the second night of their recovery in the hut, one of Damisi's friends hemorrhaged and died. From that night on, each girl worried she wouldn't wake up.

When Damisi was fourteen, a suitor in his early twenties offered a dowry to her parents for her hand in marriage. On her wedding night, it was clear that Damisi's husband, a fully grown man at least twice her size, was not going to be able to "perform his sexual duties" due to the small hole that had been left by the stitches after the cutting. This meant his reputation was at risk, since custom and tradition dictated they consummate their marriage on the same day as the ceremony. Like countless men before him who had found themselves in a similar situation, her husband took a knife and "opened" her.

I could tell Sera was watching my reaction as I turned away from the screen for a moment. The image was too horrific to imagine.

Ten months later, after her new wound had gone through a slow healing process due to her husband's persistent demands for sex, and various infections, Damisi discovered she was pregnant. Like many of the other girls in the village, she feared giving birth, as she knew her life would be in danger. The knitted scar tissue around her vagina was now tough and had no elasticity. She knew she would not be able to give birth without once again being cut open.

Our guide, Hafsa, explained it is common practice in the village to have a razor blade at hand when a woman gives birth, as the baby's arrival will be hampered and complicated by skin that simply isn't able to naturally stretch. Coupled with the fact that these girls are so young and many of their pelvises are not yet wide enough to carry a pregnancy full term without complication, many babies and their mothers die in childbirth.

If this doesn't happen, the mother is often disabled by rectovaginal fistulas that leave them unable to control urine or feces leaking from their vagina. The woman is then shunned by the community, who find her condition unbearable to be around.

Beneath this paragraph was a series of photos. Once again, Sera hadn't held back. The images included a group of crying girls as they sat in a pool of blood, the blunt and rusty razors and knives often used in the cutting, and a photo of a scarred vagina.

Female genital mutilation, or as it's sometimes known, "female circumcision" or "female cutting," is practiced in alarming numbers across Africa and other parts of the world. Some procedures will cut only the woman's clitoris away, while others will cut the clitoris and labia majora. In many parts of Africa, they practice full genital cutting, such as Damisi's experience. The practice always harms and often leads to infection. This is particularly deadly since medical assistance is so scarce in such rural areas.

UNICEF has reported that more than 125 million women alive today have undergone some form of genital mutilation, and a further thirty million are at risk in just the next ten years.

Whether it is cultural, tribal, traditional, or an act of gender inequality designed to lessen the importance of a woman's role in society, thousands of girls are cut every day. Their families and communities may not be armed with the education or awareness of the dangers, but they all live with the consequences: the loss of or disablement of a wife, a daughter, a sister, or a mother.

We must help girls like Damisi. We must end this practice before her sister Bebi is called into a hut when the old woman returns to the village.

We are an army.

Stand by.

I was shocked. The content of the blog and its accompanying photos were graphic. I'd heard of female circumcision but was unaware of the actual procedure. Though I wondered how Sera's followers would react to the descriptions, there was no doubt the blog would leave a painful, indelible memory. If I, as a Western man, was troubled by the pure brutality of the ceremony, I could only imagine how Western women would feel.

Sera had definitely hit her mark.

CHAPTER TWENTY-FOUR

THE RESPONSE to Sera's blog was stronger than anyone expected. We sat at the table over dinner while she clicked on the comment feed of just a few of the larger groups to which it had been sent. *"View previous 10,602 comments."*

"Well, you certainly have them talking," I said.

"This is just the beginning. I haven't added them up yet, but the comments from all of the other groups will go into hundreds of thousands. And that's just on Facebook."

"Have any of the moderators gotten back to you?"

"Yes. They've told us the discussion is still going on days later."

"I'm sure it is. The images in the photos alone aren't easily forgotten."

Sera dropped her fork on her plate. "Oh, I forgot to show you something!" she exclaimed as she clicked on another folder that held just some of the thousands of photos from her trip.

I continued to eat until she finally found the image she was looking for. She turned the laptop toward me again and smiled.

The photo was of a middle-aged Indian man with graying hair covered in street dust. His month-old stubble looked pure white against the brown of his skin. A dirty tunic covered his legs and feet as he sat cross-legged on the ground. Bandaged hands held a tin cup to collect the odd coin thrown the beggar's way. There was something familiar, but I couldn't put my finger on it until Sera clicked onto the next picture, which showed him smiling at a passer-by, unaware his photo was being taken.

"It's an Indian Oscar!"

"I know," Sera grinned. "I couldn't believe it when I saw how similar they looked. And just like Oscar, he hated having his photo taken. It was strange. Everywhere I traveled I caught a glimpse of someone who kind of looked like him."

"I guess he has one of those kind of faces."

"Have you seen him since I left?"

"No. Sorry, sweetheart. I think it's probably safe to say he's gone."

"I hope he's at peace wherever he is," Sera said sadly. "I miss seeing him."

"So what is the next story you're going to tell in your blog?" I asked, changing the subject. I didn't want her to dwell on what might have become of Oscar. I didn't want to think about it myself, either.

"Actually it's about a woman we met in Mumbai a couple of days after this photo was taken."

THE FOLLOWING week I was sitting in my office when I got a text from Sera asking me to look at her website. I clicked on the link on my work PC. Once again, a photo of a young woman greeted me, this time a teenage Indian girl, her head slightly turned to face the camera, posed like the glamour shots I'd seen outside studios in the mall. Incredibly dark irises were set in the brilliant whites of her eyes. She wore a small gold ring through her nose that added to the decoration of her features. A small, jeweled bindi lay between her perfectly sculpted eyebrows and a bright, colorful headscarf adorned with tiny ornaments along the fringe framed her almond-shaped face. Bright and happy, she threw a stunning smile to the camera.

I started to read.

This is a two-year-old photo of our new friend, Neetu. We first met Neetu and her mother, Klinda, aboard a long-delayed train that would take us from Mumbai to Bangladesh.

By chance, Neetu and her mother shared a small old-fashioned carriage with Amy, Carla, Meena, and me. They sat directly opposite us. Unlike the bright and colorful material she wears so proudly in the photo above, Neetu was wearing a gray sari that completely covered her head and face. Only a small gap was open, just large enough for an eye to peer out from. She sat with her head bowed, staring at the floor. Neetu's mother looked tired and sad.

About an hour into the journey, Amy pulled some fruit from her bag and offered some to Klinda, who gratefully accepted an orange and began to peel it. She meticulously cleaned away the pith and rolled a segment of the orange between her finger and thumb before handing it to her daughter, who withdrew her hand from the folds of her sari to take it.

Klinda noticed we had seen her daughter's badly burned hand as she accepted the fruit. "More easy for her. More juice, less chewing," she said sadly in broken English.

Carla reached over and squeezed Klinda's hand as a tear rolled down her cheek. The train hit a rough stretch of track, causing the carriage to jolt and rumble. An agonized cry came from beneath the scarf that covered Neetu's face. Klinda reached down and began stroking her daughter's ankle as she spoke to her in Hindi in an obvious attempt to soothe her.

You could be forgiven for thinking that the ankle is an odd place to touch someone in an attempt to comfort them. But it isn't odd when it's one of the only places on your body that doesn't feel pain. The train jolted again, and Neetu let out another sound, this time sharper and louder.

"Sorry," Klinda said, waving her hands to apologize, as if Neetu's cries were disturbing us. "My daughter—it is paining her."

We were helpless to do anything other than nod sympathetically. We didn't want to intrude on a person who looked like she was doing all she could to conceal herself.

"It's okay, we understand," Meena said.

But it was clear from Klinda's face that we didn't understand. She took a deep breath as if to compose herself, then turned to speak to Neetu, who responded by nodding. It was her way of giving her mother permission to tell us her story.

Neetu had married a man on her seventeenth birthday. She loved him very much, and the day of their wedding was the happiest of her life. They were excited to begin their life together and to start a family. But Neetu wanted to continue with her studies before they began to have children. She was training to be a nurse in Mumbai and still had two years left of her education. Her husband, a good man who loved her, supported the decision.

Just ten days after their wedding, when Neetu was returning to school, she was confronted by a boy whose proposal of marriage she'd refused the year before. He was from a wealthy family and was used to getting what he wanted. The boy persisted throughout Neetu's engagement, attempting to bribe her parents with the promise of money and property in return for their daughter's hand, but her parents saw how happy Neetu was and were convinced she would become a modern Indian woman with her own career, able to support herself without the help of a man.

When the boy discovered Neetu had married, he was furious. He waited outside the gates of Neetu's school for her arrival. As she parked her bike, he walked toward her and called her name. When she turned to face him, he threw a large open container of liquid over her face and body and screamed, "Whore!"

There had been a recent spate of bride burning in Mumbai, so for a moment Neetu thought she had been doused in kerosene. She felt her clothes cling to her body and her back as if soaked. Terrified, she tried to run before he lit the match. But pain knocked her to the ground. He stood over her and laughed while he tipped the last drops from the container over her.

She could smell her skin, her hair, and her clothes burning but saw no flames. She wiped the liquid from her eyes and her fingers started to burn.

The boy had thrown acid over her.

By the time she reached the hospital, she was unconscious from the pain and had suffered burns to 70 percent of her body. In parts the acid burns were so severe her flesh was corroded down to the bone. Her nose, ears, and lips burned away to nothing but holes. She was already blind in one eye, and the acid had caused so much damage the doctors had to remove it. Thankfully they managed to save the sight in the other, but much of her eyelid had burned away, so her remaining eye is constantly open.

Neetu stayed in the hospital for six months, battling infection, undergoing skin grafts and attempts to improve her respiratory system, which had also been badly damaged in the attack. Her husband stayed by her side throughout.

"He is a good man. His family told him that he must leave Neetu. She cannot give him children now. They say she look like a rakshas... a monster. But he refused. We live all together with my mother in a small house now. My husband sold our house to pay for medicine. But now money is all gone. And the boy who did this—his family rich. The police, they do not care."

Neetu pulled a pen and a piece of paper from her mother's cloth bag. We saw her hand shake in pain as she wrote. Klinda explained that writing was Neetu's main form of communication since the attack, *as the acid had burned away her lips and much of her tongue, rendering her unable to speak. Neetu slowly tore the sheet of paper from the pad and handed it to us. It read: "I am loved."*

We spent the rest of the long journey talking, and Neetu became more involved in the conversation as she became more comfortable. This was mostly done by nodding to her mother to give her permission to speak for her.

"Neetu is not going to let this end her life. She has much more to give to the world. She will return a stronger woman."

Klinda explained that the reason they were on the train, making such a long and painful journey, was to reach a free clinic in Bangladesh that treated women who were victims of acid attacks. The clinic wasn't funded by the government but by charitable contributions.

After we told Neetu about our work in America, about the website and you, our Twitter and Facebook friends, she reached for the paper again. Once again we watched her hand tremble, but she believed the note she gave us was worth the pain.

"Tell them my story."

As the train approached Bangladesh, I reached into my bag for my phone to get Neetu's address so we could stay in contact with her. Seeing my camera, she pointed to it and painfully motioned an imaginary click of the button to indicate she wanted to take a photo with us. She then pointed to her mother. We arranged ourselves in the carriage, conscious we were unable to hug her for the group shot, although we all so desperately wanted to. At the last moment, just before Klinda snapped the picture, Neetu removed her scarf.

The photo beneath was gut-wrenching. I saw my daughter and her friends, carefree and whole, standing next to a horrifically disfigured young woman. The pigmentation of her beautiful brown skin had been stripped and now showed patches of white. Her head and neck looked as though it had once been made of polished wax but had been held too close to a fire. A horrible comparison came to mind for which I instantly felt guilty, but her face resembled the well-preserved remains of an Egyptian mummy. My heart wept for her. I lingered on the tragic image for a moment before I continued reading.

This is the face of bravery. This is the face of courage. This is the face of determination.

There are 1,500 acid attacks every year. The vast majority of these hideous acts are aimed at women and frequently include a successful attempt on their infant children who cling to them. Most incidents are the result of jealousy, revenge, fending off sexual advances, family disputes, or land ownership (though it's rarely the woman who owns the land at issue, she will still be the target). Acid attacks are a cheap, cruel, and effective way to destroy a life.

The act itself isn't designed to kill the woman, but to disfigure her so badly that she will remove herself from society. It also ensures that the perpetrator is never charged with the higher crime of murder. But on so many occasions, the attack effectively will have the same outcome. Many victims of acid attacks commit suicide to avoid being shunned by their community or in a desperate attempt to escape the unbearable pain. This, of course, means that on the rare occasion when the authorities don't turn a blind eye and do push forward with an investigation, the main witness—the victim of the attack—is not alive to face or testify against her accuser. The case is dismissed for lack of evidence and the man walks free.

We must help people like Neetu.

We are an army.

Stand by.

I closed the blog and sat back. I was infuriated that the perpetrators were never brought to justice; that the victims' suffering was silenced, as though it was acceptable not to speak openly about these heinous acts—or worse, as though they were somehow considered acceptable.

But a nagging part of me wondered whether some of that anger should be directed at myself. In America these crimes would never go ignored. The men would be arrested and face their day in court. I thought back to my time as a Legal Aid attorney and the violent men I'd defended whose victims had been women. At the time I'd rationalized that it was my sworn duty to give them the best defense I could. Though I'd never represented a man involved in an acid attack, there had been other crimes and occasions when I'd attacked a victim's credibility while suspecting in my heart of hearts that my client was guilty. Had those women viewed me as another attacker? Did my search for ways to excuse their attacker's behavior only add to their pain? How much anguish had I caused them as I stood in the courtroom picking apart their characters?

I'd always thought these moments were balanced by all the good I'd done in those years. After all, I'd also defended the vulnerable and helpless. But looking back, especially looking at the world through Sera's eyes—or maybe through my own eyes now that Sera had opened them—those acts of good didn't make up for the damage I must have inflicted.

As usual, Sera's words had hit their mark. I didn't know what she was building up to, but if she managed to affect me so deeply—someone who'd dealt with some truly horrific things in the past—I knew she'd be able to reach and change so many more people.

Chapter Twenty-Five

On the anniversary of Miss Dee's death, I agreed to mark the occasion by accompanying Sera to the church Miss Dee had taken her to so many times when she was a kid. I'd never attended a gospel service before, and I immediately was taken with the sense of community and fellowship. I felt entirely out of place when we first entered the church, certain the eyes following us knew I wasn't a believer. But as we made our way down the aisle, congregants reached across to Sera and grasped at her hands or touched her shoulder. The smiles of recognition and welcome were heartwarming. They all said the same thing. "We've missed you, child." I couldn't help being reminded of Miss Dee's voice.

The pastor's energy was absorbed and returned threefold by the congregation. Unlike the Catholic church Aaron and I had attended occasionally as kids, where pronouncements of praise were fixed phrases delivered at preset times, here the animated man conducting the service welcomed hollers and claps as signs of affirmation.

Cheers and exaltations resounded after words of love and unity. A young black woman in her late teens, draped in a deep purple satin choir robe, took the microphone and slowly nodded to the pianist. She turned to face the congregation, looking slightly nervous, but a brave smile showed she was overcoming her fear. After just a couple of notes were played, Sera turned to me with a wide smile of recognition.

"This was Miss Dee's and my favorite. This is perfect!"

The young woman began to sing as the rest of the church choir looked on proudly at one of its youngest members. A slight hint of nerves quavered her voice as she eased into the slow-paced first lines that built her vocals up to the powerful last lines of her solo.

"Am I blind to those who bleed?
Deaf to the slaves in need?
Might got no sight in my eyes,

And my ears hear no cries,
But I know the Lord's callin' to me."

The young girl held a robust final note as the twenty men and women of the choir sitting behind her rose and joined in the up-tempo chorus. Their voices sent a chill through me as they began to sing louder, supporting the young soloist. At first their collective harmony and rhythmic claps drowned out her riff, but that only seemed to empower her with more confidence. The choir exclaimed their pleas, and the soloist raised her voice in exuberant affirmation.

"Save your sisters!"
"Yes, I will."
"Tell them Misters!"
"Oh yes, I will!
I'll let my heart feel joy
'Cause I know the Lord's callin' to me."

Sera nudged me and laughed as she tried to encourage me to join in with a song I'd never heard before. The congregation began singing along with the choir, and soon the walls vibrated with the echoes of their voices. I watched Sera as she closed her eyes and, without even a hint of embarrassment or self-consciousness, immersed herself in the rising energy of the room. Peace and serenity appeared on her face as she swayed and clapped to the music.

"Save your sisters!"
"Yes, I will."
"Tell them Misters!"
"Oh yes, I will!
I'll let my heart feel joy
'Cause I know the Lord's callin' to me."

This uplifting music was a far cry from the monotonous hymns of the Catholic services I remembered. Miss Dee used to say to me that she never felt closer to God than when she and her congregation were singing to Him. She found it impossible to believe that God wouldn't be able to hear such joy. Now that I was submerged in their voices, I understood the euphoria emanating from Miss Dee and Sera each time they returned from church.

Midway through the song, Sera opened her eyes and looked at me as I stood stiffly beside her. I was the only one in the room not moving, and I was growing quite self-conscious.

"Oh Lord! This white boy ain't got no rhythm!" shrieked an older lady in a violet suit and matching hat in the pew behind us. I turned to see her laughing with her two friends, who were also dressed in their Sunday best. "You gotta feel it, child. Feel it—here," she said, patting her heart. She leaned over and took both of my hands. "You let Miss Mabel show you, honey. Keep up now!"

Miss Mabel dipped her shoulder from side to side and signaled for me to do the same. I felt the heat rise in my face as those around us started to encourage me. I followed her lead, and once I was in rhythm, she began clapping my hands together. I could hear Sera laughing beside me, but I was determined to show her I was trying to get into the spirit of things. Miss Mabel slowly released my hands. She looked like a mother letting go of her wobbling baby for its first steps, keeping her hands close in case I fell.

"That's it, honey! Feel it!"

"Go for it, Dad!" Sera shouted over the voices.

I must have looked so awkward, moving from standing stiffly to flailing about as though I was possessed. Sera nudged me and took a step to the side, brought her feet together, then took a sidestep back to teach me the moves that accompanied the song. It was worth going along with just to hear her laugh so hard. I closed my eyes and focused on the movement of my feet, trying to get the steps right and in time with my clapping hands.

While Sera and the church regulars knew the last note was coming, I of course had no clue. A full five seconds passed before I realized that the sound of music had been replaced by uproarious laughter. I'd carried on dancing while everyone else had taken their seats. Sera doubled over in hysterics. A thunderous applause rose as I tried to sit, but Sera blocked me with her arm.

"Take a bow!" she cried out.

I stood up, my face flushed, and bowed my head in appreciation for their good-natured attempt to make me feel better. "You're wicked," I said, nudging Sera's ribs as I sat down.

"You loved it!"

"Just you wait until I do a 'dad dance' somewhere that will embarrass you. Then we'll see who's laughing."

"That'll never happen. I love you too much to ever be embarrassed by you." Our elbows battled to block nudges. We must have looked like two schoolkids in class. "But Miss Mabel is right—you ain't got no rhythm!"

SERA SAID her good-byes as we left the church, and I shook the preacher's hand. The service had ended with a prayer for Miss Dee. I didn't know if it had been planned or whether Sera's reappearance had jogged the pastor's memory. Either way, the kind words he spoke summed up the woman we still missed.

On the subway ride home, Sera let out occasional snorts of laughter just to remind me of my embarrassment.

"It's great to see you laugh," I said once she composed herself for the fourth time. "Writing those blogs and reliving those experiences must be hard on you."

"It'll all be worth it." Sera sat quietly for a moment. "Do you think they knew?"

"Who? Knew what?"

"Maggie, Maria, and Miss Dee. Do you think they knew about me? You know, that I'm the—" Sera looked over her shoulder to make sure no one was listening.

"Well, if they did, they never mentioned it to me."

"They always seemed to know how to answer a question or explain things to me in just the right way. Like everything was a lesson."

"They were remarkable women."

Sera looked out into the dark tunnel. In the reflection of the window, I saw her pull in her bottom lip and then release it. It was a habit she had when there was a question she wanted to ask but was unsure whether she should.

"There was a time when I was a kid when I thought I heard you crying. It was my tenth birthday. You were acting a bit strange that morning, but you seemed happy enough. You had told me to go and see Maggie because she had a special birthday present for me. When I got home, I thought I heard crying from your bedroom. It was the first time I'd ever heard you cry and it really worried me, so I went back to Maggie's. She said you were probably upset that I was growing up and that it wasn't anything to worry about. But she told me not to say anything because fathers don't want their daughters to see them cry. It was the only time I ever felt that any of them had lied to me or withheld the truth."

Sera was a grown woman now, and her remark about telling the truth had clearly been added for a reason. She was waiting for a response.

I sighed. "Occasionally, I had attacks of guilt that you didn't have a mother. When I found you, there must have been thousands of couples in New York who would have killed for the opportunity to adopt you. You could have had a mom and a dad. You meant more than anything in the world to me and, although I adopted you for all the right reasons, I sometimes worried that I'd been selfish by denying you the chance to have a mother."

Sera looked at me like it was the most absurd thing she'd ever heard. "You have no idea, do you? I had you, Dad. That's more than millions of others. I couldn't have asked or wished for any more than you gave me." It was only when she released my hand that I even knew she'd taken hold of it. "So was that the reason you were crying that day?"

The vibrations of the train rumbled through my feet, just as they had on the platform all those years ago. I shook my head.

"No."

"Then why?"

I took a deep breath and hoped a short sniff would keep my emotions at bay. "I'd been working all week and though I'd bought your birthday present, I hadn't had the chance to wrap it. So I sent you along to Maggie's so you wouldn't see me do it. She had a special present that she'd wanted to give to you for a long time."

Sera smiled as she looked down and tugged at the gold bracelet Maggie had given her that day. It hung nicely off her wrist again now that she had regained her normal weight.

"Anyway, I went into my bedroom in case you came back early and put it on the top of my chest of drawers to get a flat surface. As I wrapped it, I turned the roll of paper and knocked over a framed photo of Michael. The glass broke."

Sera looked at me. She knew there was more to it.

"Michael and I had made a promise to one another. We said wherever life took us, the other would follow. But then—" I bowed my head and closed my eyes. It was the first time I'd ever admitted our pact out loud. "I had visions of Michael waiting for me somewhere, all alone. Waiting for me for ten years. Waiting for me to follow."

"But you couldn't, Dad," Sera said softly. "Like you said, it was wherever *life* took you. I'm sure neither of you meant—" She stopped herself. Realization swept across her face. "You didn't think about—" She couldn't bring herself to say the word.

"Suicide?" I suggested, as if shocked. I'd suddenly come to my senses. Discussing suicidal thoughts with Sera, knowing she was having mental health issues, would have been a horrible idea. I had to lie. "Of course not. That's never the answer, no matter what the situation."

I don't think Sera was entirely convinced. She reached down and gently took hold of my hand again. It pushed out the thoughts of the glass in the frame, as shattered as my promise to Michael.

CHAPTER TWENTY-SIX

AS THE weeks went on, and Sera told more stories, the response from her followers increased. Many were frustrated by not knowing what they could do to help. But others came forward with ideas.

"So is that the plan? The more people who put forward ideas, the more they're involved and, therefore, the more likely they are to act?" Dalyn asked while sitting at the table with Sera one evening after the others left for the day. He somehow managed to plan his visits when the other girls weren't around, bolstering my theory that he was interested in a relationship with her. And it didn't hurt that the timing also helped avoid Amy's attentions, which had become more obvious.

"Yes and no. It's fantastic that we're already getting such a reaction to the blogs, but we do need to come up with solutions. There are people trying to help, and many of them have been successful. But what we need is a global effort, one that steals the spotlight long enough to create a change that matters—a tidal wave of opinion."

I looked on as they returned to their laptops. Dalyn had become invaluable when it came to collecting statistics to be included in later blogs. Every so often I'd catch him stealing a look at Sera as she twirled one of her curls around her fingers.

I was of two minds about Sera and Dalyn as a couple. Although I sometimes teased her about his crush on her and even encouraged her to embrace it, it was only because I wanted her to have that giddy feeling I'd once felt with Michael. She deserved love. But at other times, the idea of them being a couple scared me. What if Dalyn broke her heart? Would it have such an emotional impact that her condition—whatever that was— might get worse? But then I'd see him look at her, and I couldn't believe he'd hurt her, which brought me back to the idea that I should encourage it.

SERA HADN'T seen or heard from Aaron since his shame-fueled exit from our apartment. I knew he was still smarting from Sera's anger, but the longer he left it before speaking to her, the more awkward the situation would become. Sera had texted him and tried calling him several times, but he hadn't responded.

One day at work, I'd spent my lunchtime preparing to see a client. With fifteen minutes to spare before my meeting, I started to read Sera's latest blog entry.

You'll recognize four of the women in this photo. It's Meena, Amy, Carla, and me. The young woman who smiles as she tries to hug all of us at once is Chevaya. Consider her a new friend.

We met Chevaya in Bangkok. She was calling out "Veema!" as we passed her on the street. Every few feet she would call out "Veema!" again and then stop while her eyes searched the surrounding area.

Chevaya is a beautiful name for a beautiful and remarkable woman. She is twenty-four-years-old and grew up in a small village outside Chiang Mai with her younger brother and sister, whom she calls her "best friends." When Chevaya was eight years old, she took on the responsibility of looking after her two siblings and kept house, as her parents worked long hours in the rice fields to earn a wage.

When Chevaya was twelve years old, her uncle came to the village to visit her family. He said he knew of young girls around his niece's age who were being hired by a new hotel and restaurant in Bangkok. A cleaner or kitchen staff could earn a wage that would never be available to her in her small village. Chevaya would share housing with other young girls her own age who also worked at the hotel.

My heart sank. Having heard the story of Champai, I thought I knew what was coming.

"My parents didn't want me to go. But they knew it could bring the family out of the poverty we lived in. I was excited. I had never been to a city. I was also proud I could help my family. It would mean enough money to send my little brother and sister to the school in the nearest town. But I was also very afraid. I had never been out of my village, and I knew I would miss my family very much."

Her father reluctantly agreed to let her go.

I braced myself and continued reading the story. Chevaya's uncle had sold her to a brothel. She fought and resisted, enduring beatings and even having cigarettes stubbed out on her feet. And the story grew even more harrowing from there.

"One night Wife Boss came to me. She put her arm around me and started to stroke my hair. It was the softest I had ever known her to be. She said that Big Boss wasn't angry anymore and he was sorry. She handed me a doll and said it was a present. It wasn't in a box, and it wasn't new, but I was grateful for any kindness. Then she handed me a glass of wine and told me to drink it."

Chevaya woke the following morning sore and bleeding. The wine had been drugged. She can't remember the name or the face of the man who raped her. But she knew he must have smoked, as she could smell it in her hair.

"I was no longer pure. I was no longer a virgin."

Chevaya felt overwhelming guilt. She cried because she felt she had brought shame onto her family. She cried because the money she had promised, the money the family was depending on, was never going to reach them. She cried because she believed her family by then must have thought she had abandoned them and left them to continue to live in poverty while she selfishly lived a better life.

Sera told the story with delicacy and care that conveyed the terror Chevaya endured. For the next two years, she was forced to sleep with up to fifteen men each day and finally became pregnant. When her baby girl was born, who she named Veema, she was taken from Chevaya immediately. The brothel owner's wife raised the child, but Chevaya sneaked into the kitchen to spend time with her daughter as often as she could. Eventually she realized the only way she could prevent her child from sharing her own fate was to escape and seek help.

"One night I managed to escape when Big Boss had been drinking. I ran to the police station and told them they had my baby. When the police arrived, Big Boss's brother told them that he was Veema's father. He said the baby was safer with him because I was a whore, I had no money, and I was homeless. The police believed him. Big Boss caught me when I came out of the police station and took me back to the brothel. He beat me so bad it was three months before I could see another customer."

Chevaya finally managed to escape when she was twenty by hacking off her hair, disguising herself as a boy, and walking out as if she was a customer.

When she finally returned to her village, her family was overjoyed to see her. Her uncle had died and had taken his secret to the grave with him. With no others in the village except for her parents knowing her "shame," she tried to settle back into life. She met a respectable and successful man named Bao who was kindhearted and showed affection for her. She fell in love but rejected his repeated proposals of marriage. He was heartbroken. She didn't want to hurt him, but the truth would be the only thing he would understand, so she confided her secret to him. Chevaya was convinced he would abandon his attempts to pursue her, that he would never want to be involved with a girl with her history. Instead he continued to tell her that he loved her and that he would help her get her daughter back, regardless of the stigma her illegitimate child would bring to their relationship.

"Veema was seven years old when I married Bao. I knew it was only a matter of time before they made her take customers. I had to save her."

Chevaya and her new husband traveled back to Bangkok, and Bao, along with a small security team he had hired for the day, confronted Big Boss, who sneered at them. "You think I wanted a girl that looked like her mother around me? She was a constant reminder of a bad investment. I sold Veema months ago."

They searched the brothel, but Veema was gone, and the brothel owner claimed he didn't know the man he'd sold her to or where he'd taken her.

Chevaya now spends any free time she has traveling to red light districts in Thailand. She calls out her daughter's name outside the brothels hoping that one day a young girl who looks like her will run into her arms.

"Sometimes I worry Big Boss lied to us. I worry he killed Veema when I wasn't there to be punished. I worry Veema was beaten because I escaped. But I mustn't think like that. Veema was—is—a beautiful girl. I think Big Boss knew this and considered his greed for money. I think that's why he let me give birth to her. I hope he saw the idea of a profit outweighed the satisfaction of punishing me. But if she is dead, she will never suffer like I suffered."

My attention was pulled away from the screen when my phone beeped. It was a text message from Sera asking me to pick up food on the way home from work, as she was busy writing another blog. While I had the phone in my hand, I decided to try Aaron again. After reading about how heartless Chevaya's uncle had been, I was reminded how lucky Sera was to have an uncle who adored her. The two of them needed to reconcile, but he hadn't answered my recent calls when I'd tried to contact him. But to my surprise, this time he answered.

"What's going on?"

"Adam, I'm a bit busy at the moment. Can I call you back?"

"Only if you promise to call Sera first."

It took a moment before he replied. "Not yet. I'm working on something to make up for what I said."

"Aaron, you can fix it by calling her. Things got entirely out of hand. You guys need to sort things out. She's as unhappy about this as you are."

"I doubt that," Aaron said. "What she said was true. And I'm doing everything I can to make it up to her—which is why I'm busy and have to get off the phone."

"Have you been reading her blogs?"

"Yes. I saw the one about the girl named Chevaya this morning. It's hard-hitting stuff."

"I'm reading it now."

"Really, Adam, I have to go. I have a big meeting in a few minutes. Tell Sera I'll be in touch soon. I promise." Aaron hung up.

I returned to the screen and read the last few lines of Sera's blog.

Chevaya's story, while heartbreaking, is also a testament to her determination. After years of living in a structured hell, she was still able to show bravery and will to live.

I wish I could tell you that her story is unique. But it isn't.

The US State Department estimates that between 600,000 and 800,000 people are trafficked across international borders each year. 80% of those trafficked are women and girls, mostly for sexual exploitation. This figure reaches an estimated three million when you take into account women and girls who, like Chevaya, are trafficked within their own borders.

We must help these women.

We are an army.

Stand by.

The story tapped into every fear I had as a parent. The idea of my own daughter going missing and my never knowing what had happened to her—whether she was dead or alive, safe or in pain, sheltered or in danger—would be too much to bear. It was almost unimaginable to have such a horrific nightmare fall on a person who'd lived such a life of torment herself. But there it was on the screen, the true story of a woman who had the courage and the bravery to continue.

Once my client arrived, I found it hard to concentrate in the meeting. I wasn't as animated as usual and it must have been noticeable, as one of my clients asked if I was okay in the middle of a discussion about her case. I reassured her, but the vision of that young girl calling out for her daughter haunted me. When the meeting was over, I hurried back to my desk and called Sera immediately.

"Just calling to say I was thinking of you," I said. "I've just read your last blog and needed to say it. Do you think she'll ever find her daughter?"

"The odds are stacked against her. But she's a determined woman. If Veema's still alive, Chevaya won't give up until she finds her."

I hoped Sera was right.

CHAPTER TWENTY-SEVEN

THE DAY after the blog about Chevaya was posted, Sera came home and collapsed into the dining chair, looking tired and irritable, but her face changed as she raised her nose in the air.

"Bolognese!" She smiled as I began to dish the pasta out onto plates.

"I was contacted by a lady named Amanda East today," Sera said as I set the plate down in front of her.

"Who's that?"

"She's a kind of liaison between police and social workers. She's been in the job for twenty years, mostly dealing with sex workers, but she's moved on to working with authorities helping rehabilitate girls who are victims of human trafficking within New York City. A girl she works with suggested she read our blog, and now she wants to meet with us tomorrow evening."

"Why?"

"I'm not sure. I guess she wants me to write about and bring awareness of sex trafficking in America. Someone with so much experience would be great to talk to."

"Is that something you want to get involved in?"

"Trafficking anywhere in the world needs to be addressed. Would you like to come and meet her too?"

I knew these issues spanned the globe and that New York certainly wasn't immune to them, but I was wary of Sera's work coming to our own doorstep. I needed to watch her carefully and be prepared to intervene if it became too much for her.

"Sure," I said. "I think it would be really informative." I only hoped it stayed as information. I didn't like the idea of her putting herself in the same kind of danger she'd faced on her travels here in New York.

I arrived at the apartment the following night later than I intended, to find Amanda, a middle-aged woman who somehow pulled off her slightly hippie hairstyle with a business suit, already engrossed in conversation with Sera, Carla, Meena, and Amy. I introduced myself and quietly took a seat.

We listened as Amanda explained how New York had become a central hub for the sex trafficking of young girls. In the 1980s and 1990s, back when crime was rampant and Manhattan had a reputation as a dangerous and sleazy city, it wasn't uncommon to see prostitutes on the street, brazenly propositioning customers while their pimps stood by. However, since the previous mayor had enforced new laws to clean up both the streets and reputation of the city, the sex industry had been forced underground. With so many girls forced off the street by the risk of jail or prosecution, trafficking had become widespread in the city.

"Where are these girls coming from?" asked Carla.

"Most of them are from Eastern Europe and speak little or no English," Amanda said as she passed over lists of statistics. "The traffickers usually approach the poorer communities and often prey on sisters. They encourage the siblings to leave for America with the promise of an exciting new life in New York. For young Croatian or Polish girls from impoverished rural towns, it's an attractive offer. They're promised work, language classes, and high salaries. They're young and naïve so of course they believe what they're told. It all seems legitimate, especially when the traffickers offer to arrange tickets and pay for their airfare. But when they get to New York, they're immediately separated from their sisters and forced into prostitution. They are told they will be released once they have worked to pay off their travel expenses. If they try to flee, they're told their sisters will be harmed or even murdered."

"So what can we do to help?" Carla asked, ever the practical one.

"I know much of your work has concentrated on girls in other countries, but what many people don't realize is that it's happening in major cities in America too. There are instances when sex trafficking in certain cities is rife, especially if that city is the home to the Super Bowl that year. Thousands of men travel alone or with male friends to the host city. They are away from home, want to get drunk, and 'have a good time' away from their families. The traffickers know that the demand will be high, so they traffic more girls into the city. You have such a huge following. I was hoping you'd consider writing a blog about the problems we're facing here, particularly in New York."

"Of course we can," Meena said, speaking for the girls. Carla and Amy nodded, but Sera remained silent. She was staring off into the distance as if she was listening to something. Amanda seemed disappointed by her lack of enthusiasm and seemed ready to plead her case when Sera snapped back into the conversation.

"We'll do everything we can to help," she said with a sense of urgency. "Let's get to work."

IT WAS midmorning on Saturday, just a couple of days after Amanda's visit. I was making my first cup of coffee after sleeping in, though I'd woken briefly at eight to the sound of Sera and the girls shouting to one another in the hallway. Thankfully I'd managed to get another couple of hours of sleep before dragging myself out of bed.

Just as I retrieved my cup from the coffee machine, there was a knock at the door.

"Sorry, Mr. Goodwin," Carla said, averting her eyes and looking embarrassed that I stood before her in just a pair of pajama bottoms. "Sera forgot her phone. Is it okay if I grab it from her room?"

"Of course you can." I stood to one side to let her in.

I threw on one of Michael's old T-shirts, and as I walked out of my bedroom, I saw Carla heading for the door.

"What are you girls up to today?" I called casually as I grabbed my coffee cup.

Carla stopped and glanced in my direction. She hesitated. "Mr. Goodwin, we're holding the demonstration today outside the mayor's office."

"What?"

"The demonstration. It's this afternoon."

"What demonstration? What are you talking about?"

She looked uncertain. "You mean…. Sera didn't tell you?"

"No, she didn't! What are you girls up to?"

Carla slowly closed the front door and walked over to the kitchen island. She pulled out one of the stools and took a seat.

"Sera decided that we should hold a demonstration outside the mayor's office at City Hall this afternoon. The idea is to demand that he set up a special task force dedicated to combating sex traffickers in the city."

"When was all this planned? And why the hell didn't she tell me?" I slammed my cup down onto the island. Carla jumped. I turned toward my bedroom. "I have to get down there. What on earth were you girls thinking?"

"Wait," Carla said. "I don't think you have anything to worry about."

"Why?"

She took a slow deep breath. "This was only decided last night. We tried to talk Sera out of it.... We said it was too soon and too impulsive, but she disagreed. She's put a call out to all our followers to join us this afternoon at City Hall. To be honest, I don't think anyone will turn up."

"You don't?"

She looked awkward. "We have so many followers, and I know their hearts are in the right place, but we've never asked them to actually go out and do something. I mean, actually *do* something. It's one thing to show your support by sharing a blog link or 'liking' a post. I mean, that's all great, and it does the job of raising awareness. But when it comes to physically taking a stand, traveling to a demonstration, and making signs to hold at a rally...." She shook her head slowly. "And all without any notice...."

"You think no one will show up?"

I could tell Carla was uncomfortable admitting to me that she doubted Sera's judgment.

"I think we could have drawn a crowd if we'd spent more time organizing it, but Sera didn't want to wait. She's frustrated that we're not doing more now. So last night, when she came up with the idea of the demonstration, she posted a message asking all our followers in Manhattan, the Bronx, Staten Island, Brooklyn, and Queens to join us at City Hall this afternoon. She's absolutely positive people will turn up. There's no question in her mind. She even went so far as to ask a follower who's in an all-girl rock band if we could borrow their microphone, speakers, and stage equipment so she could be heard." Carla looked away as if ashamed. "I hate to say it, but I think she's going to be badly let down."

My phone beeped on the kitchen island. I reached over and picked it up. The screen showed Aaron's name. I hadn't spoken to him in some time.

"I'll let you answer that, Mr. Goodwin. I'll get her to call you," Carla said, tucking Sera's phone in her jeans pocket as she got off the stool. "Don't worry, we'll probably be done by around one o'clock."

She waved good-bye as I answered Aaron's call. "Hang on, Aaron. Carla, wait!" But she had already closed the door behind her. I returned the phone to my ear.

"Have you eaten yet?" Aaron asked. "I'm in Chinatown. You wanna meet for breakfast?"

"Now isn't really a good time, Aaron. I have to get down to City Hall."

"Speak up, I can't hear you!"

"I have to go to City Hall! Sera's down there."

"I still can't hear you. I'm just around the corner. I'll pick us up something to eat and come over," he said before hanging up.

I threw on some clothes and as I searched for my sneakers, I heard the front door close. I rushed out, hoping it was Sera.

"Bagels!" Aaron said, holding up the white paper bag like he'd won a prize.

"Aaron, I'm sorry, but I haven't really got time to stop. Sera and the girls are planning a demonstration down at City Hall," I said as I stamped my foot into a sneaker.

"Hold up. What are you talking about?"

I explained what was happening as Aaron took the stool Carla had left minutes before.

"Oh, I was hoping to see her." I could tell he was disappointed. It must have taken courage to face her after so many weeks of avoiding her. "So what are you worried about?"

"What if no one shows up to this demonstration? She's going to be so disappointed, Aaron. I'm worried that she'll get depressed or it might bring on an episode."

Aaron slowly nodded. "Okay, but noon is an hour and a half away. If you go storming down there now and cause a scene, she won't thank you for it."

"But—"

"Adam, if this is what she needs to see, let her see it. I totally understand where you're coming from and why you're worried. But doesn't it make more sense to arrive under the guise of help? She'll take what you're saying better if she thinks you're there to support her rather than lecture her."

He was right, but I still felt panicked.

AFTER EATING, we started to walk briskly in the direction of City Hall. As we got closer, the sidewalks started to fill with more and more people. I turned to Aaron, who seemed just as surprised as I did. "You don't think—?"

"I don't know. It's not a holiday weekend, is it?"

A feeling of optimism began to swell in me, but I was still worried we might be reading the steady flow of people wrong. Was there some other event—a sale, maybe?—creating this sudden throng? But instead of the shopping bags I'd expect to see, people were carrying long rolls of paper. The crowds hampered our speed as we made our way toward the grounds of City Hall. Above us a helicopter hovered, blocking the sun, creating a black silhouette. We stopped to wait for the crosswalk light to change so we could cross at Bowery, not that there was any real need since the traffic was at a standstill. Aaron tapped my shoulder.

I turned to see him looking dumbfounded. "What?"

He took hold of my arm and walked me back from the curb to the electronics store behind us. In the window, playing on a large flat-screen TV, I read the headline "Breaking News: Thousands March on Mayor's Office in Sex Trafficking Protest."

The screen changed from the blonde anchorwoman to an aerial compilation shot. It must have been coming from the helicopters above us. It showed thousands of people swarming out of subway stations, exiting buses, walking off the Brooklyn Bridge, coming out of the Staten Island Ferry Terminal, and a steady march of people along the streets of lower Manhattan. Car traffic on every street had come to a standstill, and the only vehicles moving were a steady stream of police cars attempting to get to the mayor's office. They had obviously been caught off guard and unprepared.

We battled our way through the crowds, who were unrolling their signs of support and holding them above their heads. They were packed in as tight as at a music festival. I suddenly heard Sera's voice. It was amplified with a slight echo.

"...through the use of force, coercion, or other means for the purpose of exploiting them."

"I can hear her, but I can't see her," Aaron said, scanning the area. "Can you believe this?"

"Over there!" Above the heads in the distance, I could see Sera standing on a box perched on the small wall that enclosed the City Hall Park Fountain. She was wearing a pair of jeans and a simple white T-shirt and holding a microphone. Her hair was down, a loose lock of auburn hair bouncing off her cheek as she became more animated. "We have to get closer."

"It is everyone's concern. It endangers public health and fuels violence and organized crime in the city in which you raise your children."

We managed to get closer, perhaps a hundred yards away. Sera ramped up her voice.

"...lured by the false promise of a better life in a city watched over by Lady Liberty. We can change this. We can change this today! Raise your voice to the man you elected to protect us."

The sound of the crowd was deafening, and she was still too far away for us to get her attention. I came to an abrupt stop as I finally took in what was happening. I looked at Sera, standing alone on that box, speaking with such clarity and conviction. It was a far cry from the girl who'd been so nervous about her high school graduation speech. Was it her belief in her divine parentage that gave her the confidence or her passion to make a difference? Whatever the reason, she commanded the crowd's attention. Her voice carried across the grounds of City Hall, each word given just the right amount of emphasis and weight, edged with hope and anger. I looked back in awe at the ever-growing crowd. The women were transfixed by her every word, while men, some with their young daughters on their shoulders, stood next to them in solidarity. They were looking at my daughter, my little girl.

"Free them!" Sera shouted to the crowd. Amy stepped up and joined her on the box, pounding her fist in the air as if she was conducting the rhythm. I tried to call Sera's name but the chanting drowned out my voice.

"Free them! Free them! Free them!" The crowd chanted as they balled their fists and punched the air. "Free them! Free them! Free them!"

Sera surveyed the crowd. Her face showed the same serenity it had at the gospel church as they sang to the heavens.

"There are four cops heading toward her," Aaron shouted above the din, giving my shoulder a slight push to get me moving again.

"She hasn't got a permit," I called back over my shoulder as I started to weave through the crowd again. We were still about a hundred yards away when I saw Sera turn and lean down as the cops spoke to her.

"Have they arrested her? What the hell is going on?" I shouted to Aaron, who lagged behind me.

The crowd started to grow angry as they saw men in uniform escorting Sera away. I tried to think where the nearest police station was. I signaled to Aaron to turn back around so we could get down there for her booking as Amy took the microphone and waved her hand to try to quiet the crowd.

"Thank you all for your support. As you've seen, Sera has left with the police."

The crowd began to boo again, causing Amy to appeal for calm.

"Wait, wait. She hasn't been arrested. She's being escorted to City Hall. The mayor has requested to meet with her to discuss our demands for a special task force to wipe out human trafficking in New York City!"

Meena and Carla, who stood on either side of Amy, raised their hands and began to clap, which encouraged applause to run through the crowd.

"Look at what we have done! All of us, together. Our voices have been heard!"

There was increased enthusiasm in the shouts and applause of the crowd.

"We *will* free them!" Amy cried.

The crowd's roar of agreement was deafening.

We finally were able to make our way through the mass of people. Each person we passed wore a proud look of achievement. I thought that perhaps the crowd would begin to disperse, but it was clear that no one intended to move until they had news of Sera.

WE STOOD to one side while Amy gave an interview to a news camera and Carla answered questions from a group of reporters, while more and more journalists and camera teams poured in. Even after two hours with no word from Sera, the crowds remained. Suddenly Meena pulled her phone from her ear and ran to Amy. A smile spread across her face while she whispered in her ear. Amy turned back to the camera with a look of triumph. We approached them just as Amy made her announcement.

"We are proud to report that Sera has met with the mayor, and he has agreed to pilot a special task force to tackle human trafficking in our city." Her eyes darted toward the camera trained on her. "We would like to take this opportunity to thank all of the incredible people who made this happen today. And, of course, we thank the mayor for listening to the concerns of the citizens of New York. We're hopeful that, by working together, we will eradicate sex trafficking of young girls and women in our great city."

"She did it," Aaron said, amazed. "She actually did it!"

Amy made her way to the box to announce the news to the crowd. It was met with thunderous applause and cheers.

"And you were worried people wouldn't turn up!" Aaron shouted over the noise. He stopped laughing when he saw my face.

"I'm so proud of her, don't get me wrong. But I'm worried that this is just going to make things worse," I said as I watched the crowd begin to disperse, blissfully unaware of their mass contribution to my daughter's delusion. "These people are following her. I mean, *really* following her. And they're just a tiny fraction. I just hope she doesn't take this as confirmation that she's the Daughter of God. They're following her for a different reason, and I hope she understands that."

A look of understanding washed over Aaron's face.

"Let's go find her. She'd love to see you," I said to him.

"I wanted to see her too. But no, not yet. Give me a while. I promise I'll be back in touch." He started to walk away.

"Come back!" I shouted after him. "You guys have got to sort this out."

He turned. "Not until I can help." With that, he melted into the crowds headed for the subway.

CHAPTER TWENTY-EIGHT

I SAT with Sera and Dalyn in the vet's waiting room. It was the first time I'd seen my daughter hold someone's hand other than mine. It had been a week since the demonstration, an event that had revitalized her and her mission. But not even the support of thousands of voices could make her feel any better about what we were facing.

"I've seen too much death in the past few years," Sera said. Her knuckles whitened as she squeezed Dalyn's hand tighter. "I know it's a part of life, but saying good-bye is always so hard."

"Especially when it's family," I said, wiping a tear from my eye. Sera reached her other hand across and took hold of mine. I was grateful I wasn't getting the "He's going to a better place—he'll be with God" speech. I couldn't have coped with it. I don't know why she wasn't headed for that conversational minefield. Maybe because she knew it wouldn't make me feel any better, or maybe the sudden religious outpouring would have come as a shock to Dalyn, who insisted on accompanying us.

A door opened and a man in a white coat came out and called my name. I gathered Buddy into my arms and carried him to the vet's table.

"Seventeen years old," the vet marveled. "That's old for a Labrador. You must've taken good care of him," he added kindly.

"I can't do it." I slid my hands under Buddy and picked him up. "This isn't the way he should go."

"Mr. Goodwin, I assure you he has very little time left. And he will experience some pain as his organs begin to shut down."

I looked over at Sera, who stood leaning against Dalyn, her head resting on his shoulder. "You were right, sweetheart. We should let him die at home, in his basket, with us around him." I turned back to the vet. "Can you give him some painkillers to make him more comfortable?"

The vet hesitated, then nodded and took a small bottle and syringe from his stores. He took the loose piece of skin from behind Buddy's collar while I ruffled his ear. I hoped it would distract him from any pain caused by the injection.

When we got home, Sera and I sat on the sofa with Buddy laid across us. Dalyn folded the removable cushion from the bottom of Buddy's basket and put it in the tumble dryer on high heat for a few minutes.

"Thanks, Dad," Sera said. "I know you think it would have been better for him to be put to sleep, but this way he's still at home."

I watched as Dalyn replaced the cushion in Buddy's basket to give it some warmth. I turned back to Sera and returned her brave smile before she reached across and stroked the length of the old dog's back.

I didn't expect it to happen so soon. I thought maybe we had another day with him, but I felt the weight of Buddy's head relax completely into my lap, the way it did when we watched television after our long walks.

He was gone.

BUDDY'S DEATH seemed to compound the feeling of loss and the reduction of our family as much as Maggie's had. Our circle had become so much smaller, and it made me even more determined to make sure Sera always knew she had my support.

It took some time to get out of the early morning ritual of taking Buddy for his walk. When he was still with us, I would playfully curse him for dragging me out in cold downpours, but now I would have gladly jumped out of my warm bed and tackled an Arctic blizzard to see his head rise and snap at the snowflakes.

A COUPLE of weeks later, the girls sat around the dining table. They were in good spirits, as they'd continued to get a fantastic response to the blogs and their success at the rally. Their following was increasing by a staggering amount every day, and their blogs were being relinked by thousands of other bloggers around the world. The For My Sister website had been called a "juggernaut for change" by two of the biggest online newspapers in the world. But with the success came a question: what exactly were they going to do to help? Sera's blog posts showed the war, and her followers had become a mass battalion of soldiers clawing at an invisible chain link fence, desperate to get into the fight.

It was surreal that such an incredible number of people were following a girl and her three friends in an apartment in downtown New York. And not just any girl. My daughter.

"Is Dalyn coming over today?" Amy asked.

"No, he's meeting with his editor," Sera said. "They've offered him the chance to write and report on stories overseas. It's a great chance for him to see some of the world, especially since he wasn't able to come along with us when we traveled."

"Oh, that'll be nice for him!" Amy's tone was enthusiastic, but I could see the disappointment in her eyes.

"Would you read the blog for us, Mr. Goodwin?" Meena asked. "Tell us what you think before we send it out?"

I took a seat next to Meena, who turned the laptop in my direction, and braced myself for another heartbreaking tale. I had a sense of guilt that I found these stories so difficult to read. If I wasn't Sera's father, I wondered whether I would have turned away. But what Sera had said was true. How could I understand if I didn't allow myself to be informed?

The following story is true, but we have changed the names to protect the women involved.

On our trip to Bangladesh, we met an elderly widow named Kalaa. She is an unpaid community support officer, volunteering her time to help girls in Dhaka's low-income areas. She spends her days speaking to families who do not allow their daughters to attend school, trying to convince them to let the girls receive an education. It's a struggle Kalaa has never given up on. Many do not consider paying to educate a girl a good investment, especially when girls can work instead and provide income for the family. Despite Kalaa's many successes showing that girls with an education can raise the family out of poverty if they are only given a chance, it is still a hard sell.

Kalaa has become somewhat of a role model for the young women, and they often seek her advice. After many conversations with us, Kalaa became interested in our mission and suggested we investigate something she'd seen many times in her youth. Many considered the subject taboo, and she told us we would have trouble getting anyone to speak openly and honestly about it.

Honor killings.

Kalaa told us of a woman named Shori. They'd met many years before during a regional women's conference and had remained good friends through regular correspondence. While Kalaa has remained in Bangladesh concentrating on education of girls, Shori runs a safe house in Jordan for women at risk of honor killings at the hands of their own families.

The women come from the surrounding countries and are all still in danger, so secrecy is paramount. After many phone calls and promises, Kalaa finally convinced her friend to meet with us. We arranged travel to Jordan. A young Pakistani man named Farooq, whom Shori sent to escort us, met us at the airport. He drove for half an hour until we arrived at a large white building on the outskirts of the city.

On the sidewalk, apparently awaiting our arrival, was Shori, a five-foot-five Jordanian woman with a stern face and a no-nonsense attitude. She questioned us on the street for an hour about our intentions, travels, and website. We allowed her to search our bags and suitcases and remove money, phones, cameras, and laptops. She then insisted on holding our passports in return for entry into the safe house, informing us that she would make copies of the pages with our photos and names. Shori then made us swear that we would keep the location of the safe house confidential and sternly threatened us with her "friends" should we fail to keep our word.

She told us that her "friends" worked in the local government offices, at the hotel where we were staying, and at the airport where our outbound flights would depart. If we revealed anything about the location of her operation, or if we were not who we said we were, she made it clear that we would pay—one way or another. It would be impossible to leave Jordan easily. Once we agreed, her mood and attitude toward us lightened. We had passed her rigorous test.

She asked us to get back into the van, and she took the front seat next to Farooq. Our original destination had been a decoy. We drove another half an hour before the van stopped at a large compound. Two armed security guards opened tall iron gates, which were hastily locked behind us.

I turned to Sera. "What the hell were you girls thinking? Let me get this straight.... You got into a car with a guy you didn't know, were taken to a place you had no idea of the location of, and then were threatened by a woman you'd never met? And after all that, you got back in the car? And all the while not telling *anyone* where you were or what you were doing?"

"I trusted Kalaa."

"And that's your problem. You trust people too much, Sera."

"Dad, we can talk about this another time. Can you just finish the blog?"

I let out a breath of frustration and started to read again.

The safe house was bigger than we expected. It was attached to a large, working textile factory. As we walked through the workshop, thirty women worked on large looms, at screen presses, or at rows of sewing machines. Many of the women proudly held up their work and smiled as we passed by. A radio played music across the factory floor and the women sang and eyed their work for perfection.

Shori built the textile factory, but ownership records, tax documentation, and all other official paperwork are in her brother's name. He is the front man who deals with customers, authorities, government, and police officers. Shori, who actually runs the day-to-day business and completes all the paperwork, is officially little more than an employee. The reason for her brother being the face of the business is simple. "He is a man. If he is the owner, there is less suspicion of the workers and less investigation—much less than if a single woman like me was running such a successful company. Men would not take me seriously, and I would be open to extortion. But more dangerously, they would see my workers, the women I am trying to protect."

Shori showed us up iron steps to her surprisingly modern office, which is elevated to overlook the factory floor. We sat down on firm upholstered chairs, and Shori handed us each a pad of paper and pencil to keep notes. Her sternness returned as she warned us that she would look over them before we left to ensure no description of the building was included.

The textiles business is a front to help women escape from families who want to kill them in the name of honor. She pointed out a small window to another large building that houses the women when they're not working.

"When the women arrive, many have no skills, so they are immediately trained and set to work. It is very expensive to provide housing, food, and hire security for the women, so they work in the factory. Much of the profit goes to run the safe house. This way they are kept safe and protected while they are here but also develop valuable skills. Should they wish to leave, or if they feel strong enough to become independent, these skills will help them acquire work elsewhere. Any profit left is used to assist women who need to get here. Many have fled their homes fearing for their lives and leave with nothing. They have no money or provisions, only the clothes that they wear when they escape. We must pay people to help smuggle them across the borders from places like Pakistan and Iraq and then into Jordan. They come so far because they want as much distance between them and their families as possible. They know if they are tracked down, they will be killed."

And what crimes are these women guilty of that would make their own families—fathers who once held them as babies, or brothers who grew up playing with them—turn so violent and attempt to murder them?

"Honor killings happen for many reasons. A girl may refuse to enter into an arranged marriage. Her family will see this as disrespectful and disobedient, and they will be embarrassed that she has shamed them.

"If a girl has sexual relations outside marriage, or even so much as shows a boy affection or attention in public, she will be labeled 'loose and easy' and will bring dishonor to her family. Killing her is an acceptable way to cleanse a family name of shame."

One by one, Shori pointed to the women in view and told us their stories, each more horrifying than the last. One was attacked, beaten, and raped in an alleyway, but her family said she had shamed the family by having sex outside marriage, and they planned to kill her to restore the family honor. Another was trying to shoo away a young man who'd sneaked into her house to see her when her father found them alone. Even though she'd done nothing wrong at all, her father said she'd brought dishonor to their name and he vowed to kill her, just as her uncle had murdered her cousin who refused to marry the suitor chosen for her by the family.

As Shori told the last story, Farooq began to weep in the corner of the room. He got up and walked out. Moments later we heard the lower iron door slam shut.

"Is he okay?" I asked.

"Farooq is not a hired guard like the other men. He came to me three years ago and begged me to let him help these women. He patrols the grounds at night, drives for us, and accompanies the girls to doctor's appointments when I am unavailable to chaperone. He also helps with inventory and whatever else needs to be done. He asks for nothing in return. He has a story, but it is not mine to tell," Shori explained.

We stayed with the women in the safe house for four days and listened to their stories. We marveled at their bravery and their will. The women ran the safe house efficiently, and they each seemed to thrive on having a position or chore in the home that was their own responsibility. It gave them a sense of independence they'd never felt before. Despite the crowded space, we heard no arguments, frustration, or crying. Only laughter. Each evening after work in the factory, they voluntarily took lessons from Shori to learn the languages of the other women.

On our last afternoon, after days of building Shori's trust in us, she showed us the many small hidden spaces concealed behind wooden panels of the safe house walls. These were panic rooms, to be used if the authorities raided the building for illegal workers or if one of the women's families tracked her down. Thankfully neither had occurred so far.

We gave Shori our heartfelt thanks when we left. As Farooq drove us back to the airport, he was very quiet. We hadn't seen him since he walked out of Shori's office. When we arrived at the airport terminal, he asked to speak to me alone. The other girls waited on the sidewalk. He'd wanted to speak to us from the moment he heard we were coming, but recounting his story was too painful in front of so many. He thought he might break down.

But now, bravely, he told me of his own family.

Farooq had spent many years as a taxi driver in his home city of Islamabad. He met a young girl named Sabika and they fell in love. But Sabika's family disapproved of the match and thought Farooq, a simple taxi driver, was beneath their daughter and an embarrassment to their family. Her father, in particular, was furious. But Sabika remained true to her love for Farooq, despite threats from her family. The couple married without the blessing of Sabika's parents and lived in a small apartment in the city, where they were blessed with two small children,

Omar and Saba. Though they didn't have a great deal of money and the family lived in just two rooms, they were happy. Sabika's family remained angry and severed ties. On the odd occasion when they would run into one another on the street, Sabika's father spat at her and her young children if she was alone without Farooq.

One day while Farooq was working, Sabika received a panicked phone call from her brother, who told her that her mother was desperately sick and on the verge of death. Sabika rushed to her family home with her children to say good-bye to her estranged mother. But it had been a trap. Her father, brother, and uncle kidnapped Sabika and took her to an abandoned warehouse on a wasteland outside the city. Her father and brother bound her and held her head. They made her watch as her uncle threw her four-year old son and eighteen month-old daughter from the top of the twelve-story building onto the concrete below. Then they dragged the corpses of her children and buried them in a small shallow grave in the wasteland. They dug a larger hole next to it.

When the bodies were later uncovered, dirt was found in Sabika's lungs and esophagus, confirming they had buried her alive.

Farooq was sick with worry at his family's disappearance, so when the police arrived he was anxious for news. But instead they arrested him. They also arrested his two brothers, who they held in cells for a month. Each day the police tried to beat a confession out of the men and demanded that Farooq tell them what had happened to Sabika. Then one day, during a particularly harsh beating, they told Farooq that Sabika's family had led them to the bodies and they were now charging him and his brothers with murder. The authorities used a wooden baton to beat Farroq as they told him his wife and children were dead.

Without evidence or a confession, the judge ordered that Farooq and his brothers be released. They were met outside the jail by his father-in-law and a large group of men who were obviously there for his protection. He happily told Farooq that he'd been the one who murdered Sabika and her children. Farooq reported what he knew to the police and continued to press them to investigate Sabika's family. But it became clear from their constant refusals, brush-offs, and thinly veiled threats that the authorities had been bribed. There would be no investigation and no justice for his family. The head of the police department told Farooq to leave the city since his life and the lives of his brothers were in danger if he continued to "make trouble."

"You must tell everyone you can about what happens. How the families get away with it. How there is no justice and how the system is corrupt. I will get justice for my family one day, but I cannot do that if I am dead. For now I must help protect others."

Honor killings claim the lives of thousands of women every year. They are often tortured, maimed, beaten, or burned before they are actually killed. The people who commit these crimes are rarely charged, as society seems to condone or turn a blind eye to such brutality.

But perhaps one of the cruelest elements to their stories is that the victim often has no one fighting for justice on their behalf after they have been murdered. In the Western world, the badgering of police and medical coroners for investigations, autopsies, trials, and justice would ordinarily be led by the victims' families. But here, and in so many places, the family has colluded, schemed, and plotted to carry out the crime. Since the victim is "only a woman," they can simply say she has gone away to stay with family in another area. Without anyone reporting her missing, who wouldn't believe the family's word?

Such horrific killings are hard to imagine or comprehend. But to truly understand the problem, you must see the results of such violent acts. An archaic method of honor killing still exists in the world today that is particularly horrific: stoning.

The link below shows a video of the stoning of a seventeen-year-old girl named Ariya Barzani in the town of Bashiqa in northern Iraq. Ariya was an Iraqi Kurd who was accused of converting to Islam, as she intended to marry her Sunni Muslim boyfriend—though there was never any evidence of either. One night Ariya failed to return home and was accused of having sex with the young Sunni boy. The following morning she was forcibly taken from her home. The video is upsetting to watch and it is incredibly graphic, but it shows the true result of honor killings.

I clicked on the link. The footage was shaky and a little grainy, but it was clear enough to show what was happening. It had obviously been filmed by one of the spectators in the crowd who thought it was okay to capture the torture, humiliation, and death of this young girl.

The recording began with a chanting mob of twenty men gathered outside a simple Iraqi home. Men in uniform, the local security forces, stood by and watched as two men dragged a young girl wearing an orange shirt and long dark dress in a headlock from her home and into the public square. When the two men let go of her, the crowd pushed her from side to side. She was trapped, surrounded, and had nowhere to escape to. She was thrown to the ground as the swell of hundreds of men moved closer to watch. Her dress was ripped away, exposing her. In a particularly sickening moment, the video panned around to show dozens of other phones held up to record her punishment. A circle formed around the young girl crying out for help. But no one came forward.

Men farther back in the growing crowd stood on their toes to catch a glimpse of the seventeen-year-old as large rocks and pieces of concrete were hurled at the young girl's head. The cheering and jeers grew louder as she tried to get up. A man burst from the circle, ran at her, and kicked her hard in her back, knocking her back to the ground. The security forces continued to look on but did nothing. Larger rocks were thrown and brick-sized concrete blocks slammed into her head. The blood covering her face obscured her horrific injuries. Amid the chaotic cheers and shouts, the young girl's twisted and battered body became still. Another man walked forward and threw his jacket over her exposed legs, as if seeing her flesh in public was now indecent. He then stepped back to allow the hoard of men to continue throwing stones. It was clear she was dead, but her head continued to move as more and more rocks ricocheted off her skull. Another cheer rang out from the crowd before the video shut off.

The blog continued.

After her murder, Ariya was tied to the back of a car and her body was dragged through the streets. The local men buried her with the remains of a dog in an effort to show they believed her to be "just as worthless." Days later, Ariya's body was exhumed and sent to the coroner's office, where he performed tests to see if her hymen was still intact. He confirmed she had died a virgin.

We have to help the girls and women like those who have sought refuge in Shori's safe house. We must help Sabika and Ariya and countless other girls who have suffered such brutal deaths to receive justice, so their murderers cannot harm again.

We are an army.

Stand by.

IT HAD never occurred to me that Sera would go so far as to offer up the footage of someone's death to make her point. But hadn't I encouraged it? I'd told her not to sugarcoat the truth. While Sera's stories were hard-hitting and blunt, they were real tales of very real women who had been through the horrors of living in a society that didn't respect them.

But was including the footage too much? There would be hundreds of thousands, if not millions who'd see the video on her blog. Would they be traumatized? Was that a good or bad thing? With such a graphic display of human brutality, would they turn their backs so as not to be subjected to more? Or would it kick them in the gut like it had me and give them a sharp shock that, in the real world, such terrible acts of violence existed? Would the image of that girl, lying battered on the ground, stay in their minds as long as I knew it would stay in mine?

I couldn't imagine a more tragic death, the final moments of Ariya's young life filled with fear as a torrent of violence was directed at her. She must have felt so alone and struggled to understand why no one was helping her, why no one protected her. The last memory she'd had was being the object of hatred and disgust before her life was finally extinguished.

I was emotionally exhausted as I turned away from the screen. "It's powerful," I whispered to the girls. "Really powerful."

Sera could see how the video had affected me. "Are you okay?"

"Yeah.... I just.... As a dad I can't imagine seeing my daughter treated like that. It would just kill me."

"It's even worse when you consider that her father was probably in the house that they pulled her from and stood by and did nothing."

I sat for a moment, baffled by how these men could subject their daughters to such brutality.

"Are you sure you want to include this video, Sera?" I asked. It was horrific, but that horror was amplified by the depravity of the people callously standing aside recording it so it could be replayed over and over again. Would Sera inadvertently perpetuate that by including the link?

"People need to see it. It shows the truth,"

"I know, but...." My voice trailed away as the chilling images played in my head.

"Statistics are not enough. If they were, maybe something would have been done about this by now."

"How many more blogs do you have to write?"

"I still have to write about maternal mortality rates, gendercide, girls being sold into the black market organ trade, and worldwide domestic abuse. Then we'll start thinking about putting our plans into action."

"How are they coming along?"

"Good, I think. But we're still missing something, something that will enable both men and women to help easily. I'm not naïve. I know that I can't expect people just to drop their lives and fly to other countries and save women. There has to be a way that we can push forward and make a difference."

The solution Sera was searching for came in the form of an act of contrition from her uncle.

CHAPTER TWENTY-NINE

THE DOOR handle flipped and flipped again. I could see why Aaron couldn't get a good hold on it as he finally toppled, unannounced as usual, through the front door balancing files, a whiteboard, and a flip chart in his arms. It was Sunday but he was dressed in a business suit.

"Where are the girls?" he asked without a greeting, looking around the living room.

"Next door. Why?"

Aaron dropped everything he had in his hands onto the sofa. "Do you think they'll mind if I go and talk to them?"

"Of course not. Sera will be happy to see you at last. But you shouldn't have left it so long. She's tried to call you a dozen times. It's been weeks."

"I know…. I was embarrassed."

"You've only made things more awkward by avoiding her."

"I know, I know. But I didn't want to speak to her until I had concrete help to offer." Aaron shook his head. "I don't ever want her to look at me that way again. It broke my heart."

"I think ignoring her calls hurt her more. Especially after losing Buddy."

"How is she? I mean, have you had any more… episodes? Has she said anything else?"

"No, she hasn't mentioned it, and I'm not going to bring it up. She'll talk to me about it when she wants to."

"I've been reading her blogs," he said in a serious tone.

"They seem to have been effective. She's been getting offers of help from all over the country and even abroad."

"That's good, that's good." Aaron nodded to himself. "Can you give me a hand carrying all this gear next door?"

"What's going on?"

"You'll see."

AARON KNOCKED on Sera's door. When she answered and saw who it was, she threw her arms around him, causing him to drop everything he was holding. "What's all this?" she asked, pulling herself from the hug to collect the files from the ground.

"Are you ready for a presentation?" Whatever awkward discussion they were going to have didn't seem necessary at that moment. They were both just glad to be in the same room together again.

With the whiteboard and flip chart set up behind him, Aaron stood as if he was pitching to the board of directors of an international company while the girls sat around the table watching. His suit showed he took this seriously.

"Before I begin, of the forty-five million followers you have, how many would you say log on to social media from a smartphone, tablet, or laptop?"

"Pretty much all of them will use one or the other," Amy said. "Why?"

"I want you to remember that as I begin." Aaron smiled.

The girls looked at one another, not knowing what to expect.

"With Generation Z coming of age, they are soon to join, if they haven't already, the Millennials in their fascination with the smartphone. Instruments like the iPhone are becoming less of a luxury and more of a necessity in the world today as we embrace the age of instant information."

Aaron paused to make sure his audience was following. Reassured they were, he continued, "Perhaps the greatest addition to this tool is the invention of the app. There are already thousands available to download, but today I want to introduce to you one of my own design."

The girls listened to Aaron, rapt with attention and intrigued by where he was going with this. Sera's eyes darted toward me. I shrugged.

"I introduce to you the For My Sister app that will soon be available for your millions of followers to take an active part in your efforts to help women around the world."

Adam began turning sheets of diagrams on the flip chart as he explained. The pages showed a mock-up of the app. It had a sleek design and modern font and veered away from the old-fashioned look adopted by many charitable organizations.

"The app is already in production and will be available to download free of charge from any app store."

"How does it work?" asked Carla.

"Once the user has registered and confirmed their bank details, they are able to donate securely to the charity or cause of their choice by selecting one of the preexisting amounts: one, five, ten, twenty, or fifty dollars. Or they can input the amount they wish to donate in an empty text box. With one simple touch of a button, the transaction will be complete."

"But won't the bank charge for the—" I began, but Aaron cut me off.

"As you know, one of our biggest clients is Global Capital Bank. I've met with them for the past two weeks, and they've agreed to host all bank transactions, which will be handled and processed free of charge."

An audible gasp rose from the girls.

"The app has been tested and is ready for use, and the banking system has been arranged. However, what we need to do—and this is where you ladies come in—is have a comprehensive list of charities and organizations that will benefit. The charity must register with you, as the 'owner' of the app, in order for funds to be deposited. So say you know of a local charity, organization, or even a person working on their own in Cambodia," Aaron said, looking at Sera directly as if to acknowledge Champai's story. "All they need to do is write a short bio about themselves, pass on their bank details, and the money that is donated from the user will go straight to them. In some instances they may have to register as a charity for tax purposes, but that's a small task for attaining the help they need."

"So even local support workers, the ones who do their work off their own backs, will have access to donations?" asked Meena.

"If they've applied, been screened, and registered with you, yes."

"So as long as they're on our list, they'll be able to collect money or even have it allocated to them?" Meena clearly grasped the app's significance.

"Yes. That way it's the user who decides where the money goes. There's no central charity. There's no central account. It's up to the individual donor to read the profiles and decide who benefits from the donation."

"That's amazing," Meena said excitedly. "Do you have any idea how big an impact this will have?"

"That's the idea."

Sera looked deep in thought. "Uncle Aaron, is there any way to divide or create several different apps?"

Aaron considered this for a moment. "I don't see why not, so long as there is a central banking unit that it runs through, and they're registered with the app store as one company."

"Which company?" Sera asked.

"It's registered—with the approval of my boss, who really didn't have much choice in the matter since I'm running his business—by the company I work for."

"So we could have more than one app, right?"

"Yes. Why do you ask?"

"I have an idea."

FOR THE next three months, Sera continued to write blog posts for the website. Meanwhile Amy, Carla, and Meena researched charities across the world dedicated to the advancement of women. They contacted the women they met on their travels and, through them, got further contacts of charities they'd worked with or knew. For those who found it difficult, the girls helped them streamline their profile and translated it into English or Spanish. On occasion an Amnesty International volunteer Sera had kept in contact with came to the apartment and provided further details of charities and updated their existing lists of contacts.

Dalyn continued to visit in the evenings after work and between his short trips away. Together he and Sera would run through the archives of *Times* articles reporting on women's rights issues that mentioned charity names and funds that the girls could research the following day. They worked late into the night, and Sera often didn't return home until past midnight. Though she may have been tired, the evenings spent with Dalyn seemed to lighten her mood. Her life might have revolved around her mission, but having the young journalist around to talk about other news of the day gave her the break she needed to stay on track without burning out.

"ARE WE ready?" Sera said to the girls. The time had come for her to upload her last blog post before implementing the ideas they'd agreed would effect change.

The girls nodded. They'd worked hard for the past few months and knew this last post would be an important step in what was to come. It was a Sunday afternoon, the ideal time to get the best exposure for the blog.

"I think you should do it," Sera said to Meena.

Meena looked honored as she clicked the button.

"We want you to be the first to read it, Dalyn," Sera said as she handed him the laptop. Dalyn had been traveling and so had been unable to contribute as much in recent weeks. I think Sera wanted to reassure him that he was still very much involved.

He read the statement out loud, allowing them to hear their own words back.

"Every person on earth should be afforded the basic human right of a life free from persecution, enforced slavery, and oppression. But every year alarming statistics show that women routinely are denied these rights on a scale that is hard to comprehend.

"It is 2011 and women's rights are still discussed, deliberated, and voted on by men without a woman even being present to contribute an opinion or attempt to address the imbalance. From small village councils to major national governments, women's voices are dismissed, excluded, nullified, and silenced as laws and policies that violate and impair their rights to fundamental freedoms are debated and implemented. Governments continue to make inadequate efforts to protect the rights and lives of the mothers to whom they were born, sisters with whom they were raised, and wives with whom they have made a home. Even the daughters born to them cannot escape the oppression they bring down on the women in society.

"Throughout the world tens of millions of girls are denied access to school, as they are considered unworthy of education. They are expected to remain illiterate with little, if any, chance to escape a life that often has already been decided for them, a life dedicated to the service of men in which they will remain unequal within their own homes and communities.

"Each year over a million pregnancies are terminated for the sole reason that the tiny heartbeat that echoes on legal (and illegal) ultrasound machines belongs to that of a baby girl. Their lives are written off before they have even taken their first breath. This is endemic in cultures that, even in this modern age, believe that a son promises wealth and security, while a daughter is an expense that promises nothing.

"In parts of the world, a girl's virginity can be auctioned and taken against her will by a stranger for as little as twenty dollars. In other parts of the world, virginity is factored in dowry negotiations of a marriage in which the girl had no choice. And once that virginity is taken, she often is no longer seen as pure, as if a woman's body and chastity dictates her worth. If it is proved—or even suspected—that she had sex outside marriage, she can be shunned and driven away from her community and family.

"Laws meant to protect are being overlooked and ignored as gay women are subjected to electric shock treatment or 'corrective rape' just for daring to express their love for someone of the same gender.

"Every year hundreds of thousands of women and girls are kidnapped from their homes and trafficked across borders and into the sex industry or forced labor. Here they will live each day with the threat of physical, sexual, and psychological abuse. They are considered nothing more than property. They are 'owned' chattels who can be bought and sold with impunity. This injustice is facilitated by police and other authorities who turn a blind eye or even partake in these girls' horrific ordeals for sexual gratification or financial gain. The countless crimes against these stolen girls go ignored and are rarely punished.

"Violence against women is not confined to a specific culture, region, country, caste, religion, or economic state. The roots of violence lie in persistent discrimination against women and girls and how they are seen or regarded by society.

"Like us, you are outraged and angry. And you should be. There is no doubt you believe things must change. Women suffer in ways that can break the mind, body, and spirit. But somehow they remain brave as they face their captors and tormentors. They hold tight to their dreams of being released from their shackles. They hold strong in their belief that someone, someday, will extend a hand that will pull them out of their nightmare and into a better life. They cleave to their faith that someone will step forward and help give them safe passage to freedom and that an army they can trust will win the war and end their agony.

"You are that person.

"We are that army.

"Stand by."

When Dalyn finished reading aloud, it was clear that Sera would get a tremendous response. The build-up was remarkable. And now they were poised for the next phase.

Chapter Thirty

THE GIRLS posted nothing on social media for a full two weeks. It gave their last post time to reverberate across the world. Sera insisted that she and the girls take time off to prepare for what they hoped was to come. During their cybersilence, every follower had a chance to read the blog and comment. They shared, "liked," and relinked the blog post hundreds of thousands of times. Thousands of bloggers who followed Sera on their "blogroll," a list of blogs promoted on their own sites, sounded the battle cry. Within days it was impossible to count or track how far and wide their message had traveled.

At the end of the hiatus the girls got together again and read over Sera's draft of their first salvo in a new mission. They'd created the awareness they wanted, and now they were prepared to go into action. They gave it to me to have one more pair of eyes look over it.

We are an army. And the time for standing by is over.

Your overwhelming messages of support tell us that you, too, are ready to fight for the rights of women all over the world. The ingenious, practical, and solid ideas you have provided have been collected and now are ready to be put into action.

Below is a list of viable solutions that can effect immediate change for the women we so desperately need to protect, as well as working plans for the future.

The list included many of the ideas that had come from their supporters: using online petitions that would trigger government action when they reached a certain figure; ideas for fundraisers to support various women's charities; and educational and business mentoring offered by members to other women. Finally, the post explained the apps Aaron had designed for them, each with an explanation of its aims and processes.

The "For My Sister's Education" app would fund schoolbooks and uniforms for young girls. The "For My Sister's Rights" app supported women fighting legal battles, whether personal or human rights causes. The "For My Sister's Protection" app would help build safe houses and refuges for women in danger. The "For My Sister's Health" app raised funds to train midwives and provide medical fees to those in need. The "For My Sister's Independence" app set up microloans for women wishing to start their own small business. And the "For My Sister's Support" app established a fund to cover the expenses of volunteer engineers, counselors, farmers, and health workers to travel to where their help was needed, through donations of cash or air miles. Collectively, the apps covered a remarkably broad spectrum of women's issues.

The blog ended, not with its usual "Stand by" sign off, but a deliberate call to arms.

Please download the apps, register to mentor, and sign the online petitions now.

We are an army, and we must defend one another.

Sera hit the Send button. Nothing could have prepared them for what happened next.

Chapter Thirty-One

WITHIN AN hour of posting the blog, the iTunes App Store servers crashed from the overwhelming traffic. Within twelve hours, two FBI agents arrived at the apartment, investigating a claim that the whitehouse.gov website might have been compromised due to hacking. They couldn't understand the twenty-two million signatures that came all at once, causing the site to freeze. Within a day, tens of millions of dollars were being distributed around the world. Within a week, the link to the blog had been shared on social media by forty million of Sera's followers to a further 200 million users. And within a month, every major news network and countless local news outlets had covered the For My Sister movement as people came forward to tell stories of how they intended to raise funds and awareness.

Over the next twelve months, foreign and domestic news channels interviewed Meena, Carla and Amy, and they often disappeared into the spare room for the silence needed for countless radio interviews. A media consultant who followed Sera online and also grew up in New York offered her services, providing the girls with full media training free of charge. She worked with the girls for days to ensure they managed to get the name of the app and the organization crowbarred into just about every response they gave during interviews. They concentrated on sound bites that would stick with listeners and viewers—ones that would ensure the audience would open their laptops or PCs to get more information.

Watching the momentum of their work over the year was incredible and, at times, almost unbelievable to witness. Every time I opened my computer to read online news or blogs, I saw the name and a link to the For My Sister website. It was everywhere. Bloggers across the Internet made room in their advertising to dedicate space for the For My Sister website at no charge.

While Amy, Carla, and Meena rose to the challenge of being spokeswomen of their movement, Sera was media shy and refused to give any interviews. She insisted that no one be seen as the sole "face" of For My Sister, but inevitably she was the one who was profiled the most, which, understandably, seemed to rile Amy since she performed the majority of the television interviews. Sera said that, should she ever give another interview, it would be to Dalyn, the man who had supported her quest from day one. And even then she swore it would only be once she had something significant to share. There had already been many happy stories of success, but Sera was waiting for some great, monumental change before she would grant him an interview.

In the meantime Dalyn interviewed Amy, Carla, and Meena for a series in the *New York Times* Sunday supplement magazine. They were informal Q&A sessions, short enough to link to other online blogs and social media. In the interviews they spoke of their success in empowering women around the world. The first major issue covered was their work fighting sex trafficking. Millions of followers had petitioned the United Nations to pressure the countries with the worst reputations for human and sex trafficking violations. Under the increased scrutiny, richer governments added conditions to foreign aid packages. In order to qualify for assistance, the offending countries dramatically overhauled their legal regimes, imposing stricter penalties for trafficking, and showed robust enforcement of the law. They worked swiftly to increase their conviction rates and crack down on border controls, rescuing thousands of girls and closing hundreds of illegal brothels. To show absolute compliance, the governments had gone a step further and offered tax breaks to businesses and industries to employ the girls rescued, giving them an opportunity for training and to work a legitimate job.

Donations to the For My Sister's Health app had funded the Free Womanhood Organization to employ more women to travel to hundreds of villages to give communities education on the health risks and dangers of genital cutting. The organization also convinced villages to adopt a "coming of age" ceremony, eradicating the practice of cutting across Ethiopia and other African countries.

Thousands of Sera's followers petitioned and demonstrated outside Indian embassies all over the world demanding restrictions of acid available to the public, demanding it only be sold in diluted form.

Shamed by the media attention, the government caved, and the number of acid attacks had been dramatically reduced.

But perhaps their biggest achievement had been the increasing education of women. Through the financial aid of the apps, the mentoring of followers, and increased media attention of successful female scholars, entrepreneurs, and farmers, there had been a tremendous increase in the education of girls and the training of women. Many other governments finally invested in what they saw to be true—that women were the largest untapped resource of talent and progressive thinking in their nations.

IN THE summer of 2012, I returned from a long day at work. Just as I collapsed onto the sofa and opened a beer, I heard screams that carried through the wall of the apartment. I dropped the can on the table and ran next door.

The girls gathered around a single laptop on the dining room table. Meena was wide-eyed and teary, Amy jumped up and down as though she couldn't contain herself, and Carla was still screaming. Meanwhile Sera sat with her eyes fixed on the screen of the laptop, a simple smile on her face that spoke of happiness and relief.

"What the hell's happened?"

Sera turned the laptop to face me. On the screen was a photo of an Asian woman who looked vaguely familiar. She was hugging a young girl with similar features. She was smiling but holding the girl tight, as if her life depended on it.

"Is that...?"

"Chevaya found her daughter," Sera said.

"One of the street social workers in Phnom Penh who we help support through the app rescued her when the brothel was raided," Amy said excitedly.

I was thrilled they'd found one another, but at the same time I was sad the young girl had met the same fate as her mother. Sera must have seen the bittersweet look on my face.

"Dad, when the brothel was raided, they found Veema working in the kitchen. She hadn't been forced to take customers yet. Though by what Chevaya has told us in her e-mail, they'd already started grooming her for it. Thankfully she was saved before it ever went that far."

"I know I've said this a thousand times before, but what you are doing is just amazing!"

"We have to celebrate!" Meena said.

"Not yet. There's too much to do."

"For heaven's sake, Sera, give them their victory," I said. Though they had many stories of success, this one was personal. "They deserve it and so do you! It's too late to go anywhere tonight, but I promise I'll take you out to dinner tomorrow evening."

Sera nodded but seemed almost relieved she could carry on with whatever she was doing.

THE FOLLOWING day I arrived home early from work. I heard the girls leave the apartment next door to go home and get ready for our celebratory dinner. I was glad Sera had agreed, as I hadn't seen her eat a meal for days. Though she wasn't as thin as she had become on her travels, I'd noticed she had lost some weight.

As I passed the coffee table, I saw an envelope addressed to her. I instantly recognized the patriotic logo I'd seen repeatedly on the side of campaign buses on the news. It was the brand of Dehlia Evesmith, a female senator running for her party's nomination in the next presidential election. She was from a conservative state, and her campaign was still in its infancy. I was surprised to see Sera had been picked from a database to solicit donations, especially since she'd only recently registered to vote and hadn't declared a party affiliation.

Sera waved her last good-bye down the hall as she came through the front door.

"Dehlia Evesmith, huh?"

Sera slapped her hand against her head. "Damn, I forgot all about that!"

"Don't worry about it. I'm sure it's just asking for a donation to her campaign," I said offhandedly.

I didn't want to discuss my personal dislike for this candidate because I was aware she was the only woman running. But I was sure Sera would share my views. In the days leading up to her announcing her candidacy, the once obscure senator had appeared on the news at every given chance. If there was a camera in front of her, she twisted the conversation into defending the Second Amendment or supporting drilling in the northwest of America, despite the environmental damage it would cause. In the recent months she'd also suddenly become an expert in climate change, denying its existence while disregarding the opinions of scientists qualified to comment on the effects of global warming. Other candidates seemed to use these arguments to pander to their base, but Dehlia Evesmith was different. There was something in her eyes, blank and unfeeling. Looking at her, I could see she believed everything she said and that she would be more than happy to stand by and watch the world go up in flames if it meant she could be in power.

Sera shook her head. "No, it's not asking for money. Go ahead and read it."

I turned the envelope in my hand and saw it had already been opened. Instead of stickers, donation slips, or leaflets on how Dehlia Evesmith was the best the choice for the presidency, there was an official-looking letter with her campaign logo in the top right hand corner.

> *Dear Miss Goodwin,*
>
> *Senator Dehlia Evesmith will be in New York City this week and has requested to meet with you to discuss her presidential candidacy. As you can imagine, her schedule is hectic, but a time has been cleared to meet with you at 6:00 p.m. on June 6. It will be a private audience at your home, if you are agreeable.*
>
> *Please contact the phone number below to confirm.*
>
> *Yours faithfully,*
>
> *Thomas Edder*
>
> *Senior Campaign Manager*

I flipped the envelope over and looked at the postmark. "Sera, when did you get this?"

"A couple of days ago. I meant to tell you about it, but you got in late from work the day it arrived and after all the excitement yesterday over Chevaya, it slipped my mind."

"I take it you've already told them you're not interested? I mean, you didn't actually consider—"

"No, of course not. I'll call them tomorrow and let them know."

"Sera, today is the sixth!" I looked at the clock as two loud knocks came at the door. It was 6:00 p.m.

"Don't answer it!"

"It's okay. I'll just tell them I'm not interested in speaking to her," Sera said as she walked toward the door.

"No, no, Sera, no!" I whispered urgently.

She opened it to reveal two men in suits wearing dark sunglasses and communication headpieces like they were Secret Service agents designated to protect the future president. In fact, they were just hired security guards.

"Sera Goodwin?" one of them asked as he put his head around the doorframe and peered around the living room and kitchen.

"Yes, but—"

"All clear," the other suited man said sharply. They parted as a middle-aged woman walked between them like they were sliding doors on a late-night show.

I bristled at the sight of her. She looked just as she did on television. Her dark brown, shoulder-length hair was professionally styled and lacquered to make her look no-nonsense and businesslike, but with just enough bounce to remain feminine. Her wide eyes blinked unnaturally slowly, like she was challenging everyone she looked at to a staring contest. She walked into the apartment wearing a crimson dress suit with shoulder pads any leading lady from an eighties soap opera would have killed for.

"So lovely to meet you!" the senator exclaimed, forgoing the usual ritual of shaking hands. She turned her attention to me. "And this must be… your dad?"

"Yes, it is. Listen, thank you for the letter, but—" Sera began.

"You must be incredibly proud of your daughter!" she said, cutting Sera off. "She's doing such wonderful work!"

I tried to remain polite for my daughter's sake. "Yes, very proud." I smiled at Sera. It was hard to keep that smile on my face as I turned back to our visitor. "I don't mean to seem rude, but may I ask how you got our address? There's no surname or address given on Sera's profile or website. How were you able to get in contact with us?"

The senator looked surprised and then feigned confusion. "Well, I'm not too sure, to be honest. I leave those things up to my campaign manager. Maybe he has your details on our list of supporters? Have you ever made a donation to my campaign?"

"No." I said bluntly. "And even if I had, it wouldn't explain how you'd know that Sera is my daughter."

Sera looked at me disapprovingly.

"I'm sure my campaign manager can explain. Unfortunately he's at the next stop organizing an event. But I'll be sure to let you know."

She swept past me and took a seat at the dining table, beckoning Sera to sit. Sera looked at me and gave a small shrug of resignation. I was about to join them when she turned to me and mouthed, "Let me deal with this."

I gave a quick nod and remained standing, leaning on the edge of the kitchen island.

"Now don't be nervous, Sera, I know it may feel a little overwhelming that I'm here," the senator said in a patronizing tone that made my hackles rise. "Just think of it as two women having a little chat." She leaned over the table and put her hand over Sera's, giving it a little shake like she was reassuring her.

Something changed in Sera's eyes, and she snatched back her hand as though she'd received an electric shock.

"What do you want?" she asked coldly, her bluntness a 180-degree turn from her silent disapproval of my lack of manners.

As with most politicians, Dehlia Evesmith seemed to live her life on a four-second delay that gave her the chance to consider any question she'd been asked.

"Well, I've taken a special interest in your work, Sera, and I must say I'm incredibly impressed with your fight to gain equality for women all over the world." Another four-second delay. "As a woman in politics and a potential candidate for president, I find a kinship between us. We are both pioneers in the effort to bring women's equality, aren't we?"

Sera didn't answer or give any acknowledgement of either her comparison or the compliment.

"Now, I understand you have quite the following on social media sites like 'the Facebook.'"

Sera seemed to be studying the politician as she spoke.

Senator Evesmith didn't wait for a response before speaking again. "It really is wonderful how you started your little movement in just the past few years and it has grown to such a massive number. It's a testament to your dedication. I'm sure all of those millions of followers are just as concerned about the advancement of women as we are. Am I right?"

Sera gave nothing away. It was a ridiculous question to ask someone whose entire work was dedicated to the cause.

"I've also seen that you've involved a great many churches in your efforts, which proves that you are a good Christian," the senator said as though she was talking to a child. "Am I right?"

Sera's eyes darted to mine before returning to the politician's. Dehlia Evesmith tipped her head to the side in what looked like an attempt to show empathy.

"It's okay, Sera," she said softly. "You can trust me. I mean, you know who I am, right?"

"Oh yes, I know who you are," Sera said stonily.

"I propose that we work together—" Dehlia Evesmith began.

"Work with each other? Do you think we are of the same mind or purpose?" Sera asked incredulously.

"We could be."

Sera looked the senator over like she was a puzzle, an anagram she was trying to decipher. "I'll never agree with what you believe."

"And which of my beliefs are you having the most trouble with?"

"Where do I begin? Your agenda is what it has always been. It's designed and executed to harm others."

Always been? I didn't know where Sera was going with this, but I was surprised she had challenged the senator so quickly and that she seemed to know so much about her.

"Harm people? Me?" the senator asked, her false innocence fooling no one. "Who do I harm?"

"I expected more from you," Sera said as if she already knew this woman and the conversation they were having had always been inevitable. "Okay, let's start with the most obvious one, shall we? Why do you continue to fight to deny gay Americans their rights?"

I knew what she was doing. She was a lawyer's daughter. I could tell she was setting the senator up with open-ended questions she would have to answer. Then she'd turn those words against her.

The four-second delay increased to six. "Well, I turn to the word of God when I consider the lives of homosexuals. The Bible is very clear in that respect."

I was confused. The room was uncomfortable enough as it was. Had the senator really not done her research? She must have gone to some effort to find Sera, but had her team not investigated far enough to find out Sera's dad was gay? Or worse, and probably more believable from what I knew of her, was she aware of it but still addressed it as if I wasn't in the room?

"The word of God?" Sera said as if amused.

I tensed. Nothing good was going to come out of talking about the figure who Sera believed to be her father.

"Well, didn't God say it was a sin?" The senator flashed a fake smile.

Sera glanced over at me. I waited for her to begin the debate, well versed in her argument and knowledge.

"Is it really that important to you?" the senator asked.

"You know it is," Sera said in an even tone that didn't disguise her anger.

The corner of the senator's mouth twitched into the briefest of smiles. I had seen the same look on countless prosecutors' faces when a defense witness had given them what they needed to win the case because they'd pressed the right buttons. However, to my surprise, Dehlia Evesmith didn't pursue it.

"Now," the senator said, as if abandoning the subject, "if I win this election to become president, I will be in the position to help your cause."

"Cut the bullshit," Sera said firmly. "I'm not going to join you in this little dance."

I was shocked. I had never heard Sera speak to someone in that manner. The senator's sweet façade broke almost immediately.

"Fine," she said, becoming businesslike and prepared for hard negotiations. "I'll just lay it all out for you, shall I? If you support me in my campaign, I'll fight for an enforced equal wage for women and will work to ensure the renewal of the Violence Against Women Act."

"You'll do this 'if' I support you?"

"I can't do it if I don't win," she said icily. "But with your—"

"My endorsement?" Sera exclaimed. "We're both well aware that millions of my followers are female American citizens who've followed me since they were in their midteens. You're also well aware they're now of voting age and easily could swing the vote your way and secure your candidacy. And then even the election."

"Yes." There was no point in denying it. "And if I win, I'll be in a position to appoint you as an ambassador for women's issues."

"So what you're asking me to do is help you become President of the United States, therefore the most powerful woman on earth."

"Yes. And think of what that will mean. Think of what we can achieve together," the senator said persuasively.

"I assume in order for me to do that I'd have to be seen to agree with all of your policies? I mean, like your continued efforts to deny gay Americans their rights. You wouldn't want someone to endorse you who believes in equal rights for gay people when you've gone out of your way to block them... that wouldn't make sense now, would it?"

"For the greater good, yes, I'd ask that your opinions publicly align with my own to achieve maximum—"

"Let me be clear. That will *never* happen," Sera said emphatically.

"We all have to make sacrifices to get what we want. You should know that better than anyone."

What the hell did she mean by that?

"Do you honestly expect me to believe your lies? That the promises you make aren't worthless? You must take me for a fool. You're trying to tempt me with power, but I see through you." Sera looked intently into the senator's eyes. "I know *what and who you are, and what you're really asking me to do.*" The legs of the chair Sera was sitting on scraped loudly on the wooden floor as Sera stood and pointed at the door. "Get out!"

The senator relaxed back in her chair. She gave yet another smile, but there was no mistaking the malice behind it. "Hmmm, you're not quite the wholesome girl you make yourself out to be, are you? You're full of courage now because you believe you have support. But the people *will* turn on you. You know it's happened before. What will happen when your *other* unspoken truths are exposed and people find out who you *really* are? Will you be so brave then?" She leaned forward. "I'm giving you the chance to have real power, and all you have to do is—"

"I will never deny who my father is!" Sera screamed.

The senator looked at Sera, her eyes wide and unblinking. Sera leaned forward, her face red with anger. She slammed her palm on the table, leaning right into the senator's face. *"Get out,"* she screamed. *"Now!"*

I rushed forward and grabbed Sera by her shoulders, sure she was about to swing at the woman, who was now being shuffled out by the two security guards as if an attempt had been made on her life. "She's not worth it!"

As the door slammed, I held Sera tight. She was shaking in anger. As her fury subsided, she turned and rested her head on my shoulder and hugged me tight until I could no longer feel her trembling. I couldn't ask her the question I wanted to for fear of the offense it could cause. Who was she not going to deny? Was she pre-empting the question she knew would inevitably be asked if she told the world her secret? Was she saying she wouldn't ever deny that she believed God was her father, or that her dad was gay? Or was it both?

CHAPTER THIRTY-TWO

"DALYN!" SERA shouted as the young journalist walked through the door. Carla and Meena rushed to hug him while Amy waited her turn.

He'd been away on assignment for the newspaper in Iran and Afghanistan for five months, but his high spirits at being back in New York swept away any hint of exhaustion.

Sera waited patiently for Amy to release him and then threw her arms around him. He held her tight, adjusting his arms under the guise of finding a more comfortable position, but it was obviously just an excuse to hold her longer. He rested his chin on Sera's shoulder, closed his eyes, and inhaled the scent of her hair, then let out a long sigh as if finally able to breathe.

Before Dalyn had left for his assignment, he'd begun spending more and more time at the apartment. I knew he really was there to see Sera, though she continued to maintain that their relationship was a friendship and nothing more and that he was helping them organize groups, research statistics, and vet charities for funding. With the girls' work exploding, it had become almost impossible for him to see Sera alone. Their time spent together always involved the company of Amy, Carla, and Meena. Amy was as attentive as ever, offering cold drinks or spending hours researching anything he'd put forward as an idea.

Since the senator's visit, Sera had become even more determined to get her message out. She refused to discuss the incident with me, clamming up at the mere mention of it. Although she hadn't become quite as angry as she had that evening, there were moments when her temper flared. With any other woman her age, I wouldn't have thought twice about it. People get angry from time to time and their emotions get the better of them. But Sera had never been that way. So when she became uncharacteristically frustrated or raised her voice, my mind instantly leapt to *Is this an episode?* Although her outbursts were few and far between, I couldn't help but jump to the conclusion that they were symptoms of something more.

So I was particularly concerned when, late one night, as I was closing the last curtain in the apartment, I saw Dalyn standing with Sera on the sidewalk below in what looked like the middle of an argument. Dalyn's hands were rigidly gesturing in what appeared to be frustration at Sera, who was angrily shaking her head. His voice was raised, though I couldn't hear his words through the window. But it was obvious from his tone that he was pleading with her. Sera walked toward him with her palms out as if trying to pacify him, but Dalyn turned and walked away, a look of anger on his face.

I didn't want to pry into her business for fear she'd think I was meddling, so I waited for her to come to me to explain what had happened, but she went straight back to work. I found her sleeping on the sofa in her office the following morning. Her computer was still on, so I left her sleeping, assuming she'd worked through the night.

The following evening when I knocked on her door, I found her and the girls tapping furiously away at their laptops. Dalyn was sitting next to Sera on his phone on what sounded like a work call. He smiled and waved courteously, as he always did, and then returned to his conversation. Whatever their argument was, it must have been resolved.

"How are things going?" I asked.

None of the girls answered. Maybe I was being paranoid, but I got the feeling they were tapping quicker and studying their screens even more intently as an excuse for ignoring my question. Amid the pings of messages and general noise of a small busy office, the atmosphere was thick with tension that, for whatever reason, had to do with my presence.

I didn't know what I'd done to get such a reaction, so that evening I asked Sera about it. She brushed it off, saying it was nothing and that I was being hypersensitive. But every day for the next two weeks, if I was in the room, the girls, and Dalyn when he was there, continued to act differently toward me. If I asked a question, I was given a one-word answer, and these responses were usually prefaced by a brief look to Sera.

Finally, after giving up on getting Sera to give me the reason why everyone was acting so weird, I walked across the road to Lei and Choi's store to speak to Meena. She pretended ignorance, while Lei and

Choi stood by and scowled at her, as if she was being rude by not giving me an explanation.

As I walked back through the hall to my apartment, I heard a man's loud voice behind Sera's door. I stopped. It was Dalyn, but this time he sounded like he was shouting, almost screaming at her. "For fuck's sake, Sera, this isn't a game! You can't keep ignoring me. You have to do something about it—"

I stormed through the door to find Sera sitting at her computer ignoring Dalyn, who stopped shouting at my appearance.

"What the hell is going on?"

Dalyn stared at Sera. I saw her shoulders tense.

"Mr. Goodwin—"

"Don't you ever, ever raise your voice to her like that again. Do you understand me? Who the hell do you think you are?"

Far from backing down, Dalyn met me in the middle of the room. "Who am I? I'm the one trying to talk some sense into your daughter." He turned back to her. "Well? Are you going to tell him or am I?"

Sera looked alarmed. "You promised, Dalyn."

"Then do it yourself."

"Do what? Someone had better start explaining now or neither of you is leaving this room."

After a couple of seconds, Dalyn spoke again, this time more quietly. "Please, Sera. Tell him."

CHAPTER THIRTY-THREE

DALYN, SERA, and I sat in front of Aaron's desk at his office in Battery Park.

He was reading aloud a sample of the threats Sera had received over the previous year, documenting the dates and the times. Although I'd read them myself earlier, hearing them again made my blood run cold.

"Kill yourself, bitch!"

"Some girls love to be raped. I bet you're one of them. See you real soon."

"I will bring justice for my brother."

"Infidel whore. I will remove your head so you can no longer speak of things that do not concern you."

Aaron wrote down the source of each threat, whether it was from Facebook, e-mail, or a message left on the For My Sister website. Most were short one-sentence statements, blunt, and often in broken English.

"We will teach you your place. We will find you, rape you, and kill you."

"You make my wife leave me. I have gun. After I find her, I come for you."

The list continued, each threat as chilling as the last. Some e-mails consisted only of photographs of dead women, the kind easily found on Internet crime scene websites. They were attached to e-mails with subject lines that read "This will be you" or "You're next."

"Do we go to the police? The FBI?" I asked my brother as he tapped away at a laptop that looked like it came from a NASA laboratory.

"For what it's worth," he said in an attempt to reassure me, "I think you could probably disregard ninety-nine percent of these threats. They're obviously designed as scare tactics."

"And the other one percent?" Dalyn chimed in, obviously rattled that Aaron was downplaying the situation. My anger toward

Dalyn had vanished the moment I found out about the threats and how shouting at Sera had been a desperate attempt to make her see she needed to protect herself.

"With the kind of work Sera is doing, there's bound to be some kind of backlash. Things may have started to change for the better, but that leaves a lot of people who now consider themselves victims of her work: husbands in Africa who can't control their wives as easily or whose wives have left them altogether, pimps in Asia who've had their brothels closed down and lost their main source of income, families of Indian men who've been prosecuted for battery and sent to jail and can no longer support their extended families," Aaron said, still tapping away. It was extraordinary that he was able to hold a conversation as his quick fingers commanded the computer. "There, I've found the first three."

"You found them? How?" I asked.

"I've traced their IP address. It gives me a location and the Internet service provider."

"Are they here in New York?"

"No. Cambodia, Pakistan, and India. And by the looks of things, they're all sent from servers that had more than five live connections."

"Internet cafes?" Dalyn asked.

Aaron nodded. "The fourth, fifth, and sixth ones look to be the same."

"Do you think we should be worried?" I asked.

Aaron leaned back in his chair. "I'll check every one of them this evening. If they're all coming from places outside America, I wouldn't worry about it too much. The thing is, so far the messages are coming from poorer countries where Sera's work has had an impact. I very much doubt they're going to Internet cafes because they don't want to get caught. They simply can't afford to have the Internet in their own home. And if that's the case, they certainly can't afford to fly to the United States and stay in a hotel in New York City while they try to track Sera down. An e-mail is pretty much free and can impose terror. And that's want they want—some small form of revenge."

Aaron's analysis made sense and, for a moment, I felt a slight sense of relief. "Do you think we should go to the police?"

"Yes. Absolutely. They should document each one to be on the safe side."

"You see?" Sera said turning to me. "This is why I didn't tell you. They were idle threats, that's all. But this is one of the reasons I have to continue with this work. There are thousands of women who face these threats every day, from within their own homes or from people who've enslaved them."

Aaron studied Sera from his chair for a moment before he got up and walked around to sit on the front of his desk.

"Look, I'm not a police officer, and I don't want to frighten you," he said, "but it would be foolish not to be cautious. A lot of your work has focused on sex trafficking."

"So?"

"Sex trafficking is one of the largest sources of illegal income in the world, second only to drug trafficking. It has an annual profit of thirty-two billion dollars. It stretches across every continent and has an effect on every major city. As you know, here in New York we have a big problem with sex traffickers bringing in girls from Asia and Eastern Europe and supplying them to illegal brothels. And your work has brought a lot of attention to it. Your demonstration and petitions forced the mayor to take action. And so far the task force has been incredibly successful. The arrest and prosecution statistics are triple what they were a year ago. While you should be proud, you should also be aware that this has cost a lot of hardened criminals and members of organized crime their livelihoods. If anyone would seriously think that taking you out of the picture would make their lives easier and more profitable, it's them."

We all sat slightly stunned at my brother's knowledge of the subject.

"What?" Aaron said defensively. "I've been paying attention and reading up on what's going on! Isn't that what you wanted?"

"Yes, Uncle Aaron. And I appreciate it."

"But if you can get their IP address, location, and provider, doesn't that work the other way around?" Dalyn asked, clearly still worried. "Could they track Sera down the same way?"

"Yes, and that's an issue. But the good news is that one of my guys used to be a forensic computer tech for the NYPD. I'll ask him to come with me to Sera's apartment this evening and do some cyberwizardry. I'm sure we'll be able to bounce the server signal around so the IP address is untraceable."

"Is it that easy?" I asked.

"It is for someone who knows what they're doing."

I turned to Sera. "Do you think that's how the senator tracked down our address? I mean, they couldn't know your surname from the website or social media. Do you think they went through the computer?"

Sera didn't respond, but Dalyn nodded.

"What can we do in the meantime?" I asked.

"Come stay with me tonight!" Aaron said enthusiastically. I appreciated that he was trying to put our minds at ease, which was hard after his speech about the sex traffickers. "It's been ages since you've been over. You guys can relax and watch a movie while we work to sort out all of your computers. Just make sure you have Amy, Carla, and Meena's laptops. And be sure to leave your own out too."

AFTER REPORTING the matter to the police, Sera and I returned to Aaron's house. The wait was excruciating. The idea that some of the threats could have come from within New York was terrifying. Sera seemed less concerned.

"Dad, I've had threats from people on Facebook for the past couple of years," she said casually. "At first it troubled me, but then I looked at other things on the Internet and saw it was common."

"Common?"

"Sure. You can look at any message board and see insults and threats run through the comments sections. When it comes to race, religion, sexual orientation, or anything else some people might take issue with, they're not shy of sharing their opinions. People hurl anti-Semitic, anti-gay, anti-immigrant, and anti-woman slurs without a second thought. Horrible comments and name-calling are everywhere, mostly done by cowards hiding behind keyboards," she said in a slightly exasperated tone, as if I should already know this.

"I didn't realize there was so much hate on the Internet," I said sheepishly.

"And cats." She smiled. "Lots and lots of cats."

When Aaron returned he gave us the all clear. The threats had all come from outside the country. This wasn't to say that the thousands of others Sera had already deleted didn't come from closer to home. But I felt more at ease that, should anyone try to locate her now, they wouldn't be able to do it through her IP address.

AS THE year went on, success stories replaced many of the blogs and discussions about the cruel realities women face. There were photos of smiling girls sitting at their school desks, ready to start their education. Proud women showed off their new businesses, whether simple market stalls or large-scale training centers put together by groups of entrepreneurs. One by one, Sera's movement was changing women's lives.

The success of Sera's mission hadn't gone unappreciated. She'd been contacted via e-mail to receive various humanitarian awards, to have foreign hospital and treatment centers bear her name, and to give interviews to the biggest names in media, all of which she politely declined. Sera didn't want to be a spokeswoman for her cause. She wanted the cause to speak for itself.

LATE ONE Sunday afternoon, I heard Sera talking to herself in her bedroom. This wasn't particularly strange, as I'd often seen her trying to solve a problem by talking out loud, but on this occasion I heard her repeating herself over and over again.

"We must move on. We must move on."

She eventually came out from her room, still in her pajamas, and took a seat on the sofa beside me as I watched an old black-and-white movie. She looked like a big kid.

"You okay?"

"I didn't get much sleep last night."

"What kept you up?"

"I had a dream."

"A nightmare?"

"Yes, to me it was. I was in a child's room. It was pink and had flowers painted on the wall. Then Miss Dee came in and sat on the bed. She doubled over and started sobbing. She was holding what must have been one of her daughter's dolls." Sera sat silently for a moment. "Ever since we found out about Miss Dee's daughters being killed, it's stayed on my mind. Not a day goes by when I don't think about it."

"Me too," I said, thinking about the many times Miss Dee had spoken about her girls.

"I think it may be time."

"For what?"

"For the next step. They're ready."

I didn't know what or whom she meant. But I wasn't sure *I* was ready.

CHAPTER THIRTY-FOUR

"OF COURSE I agree with you," said Dalyn. "I'm more than aware of the damage they cause. But going up against the gun lobby to ban the sale of handguns is a fight you're not going to win. You're jeopardizing your reputation as an organization that can get things done."

"I agree with Dalyn," Amy said, predictably. "Besides, a lot of women carry handguns. What message are we sending to them? That they aren't allowed to protect themselves now?"

Aaron and I watched from the kitchen as the debate continued. "So, this Dalyn likes my niece, huh?" he whispered to me.

"Yeah, he's been sweet on her for a long time."

"He had better be good to her. I'd hate to see Sera get burned."

"I don't think there's much fear of that. If anyone's going to get burned, it's going to be him. Sera doesn't seem interested in him other than as a friend."

"I don't think Amy thinks of him that way."

"You've picked up on that too, huh?"

"To be honest, I thought they were already seeing each other. Amy seems to be quite demanding of his attention."

Meena raised her voice to join the debate. "Why not try? Why not give it a shot?"

Carla groaned at Meena's unintended pun but then agreed that nothing could be lost by trying.

Amy wasn't giving an inch. "What's this got to do with women's rights, Sera? You're suggesting that we fight something that we just can't win," she said, repeating Dalyn's argument. "It's in the damn Constitution! This has been tried a thousand times before, and they haven't even come close to getting them banned. Are you out of your mind?"

I could tell Amy's resistance surprised Sera. "After everything we've done, after everything you've seen, Amy, you don't have the faith that we could win this?"

"You're pulling focus away from what we set out to do! This has nothing to do with women's rights."

"Well," Carla said slowly, "you can't deny that thousands of mothers bury their kids every year because of gun violence. Isn't it a woman's right to be able to raise her children in a society without the threat of guns? I mean, look at how many kids have been killed in their classrooms or playgrounds."

"Or caught in a crossfire," Sera said, looking over at me.

"What's next, Sera? Are we going to go after power companies because they're polluting the atmosphere and kids breathe in dirty air?"

"Actually, Meena has already suggested that we do that in the future. Maybe not every power company in the world at first—perhaps start with just the ones here in the US."

Amy stared in disbelief at Meena, who refused to meet her glare by looking down at the table. She then turned to Carla for support, who just shrugged as if confirming that it wasn't such a bad idea. Amy gave a short laugh. "Okay, and exactly how do you propose we go about going up against multibillion-dollar gun and power industries who lobby the government every day?"

"The same way we brought women's rights to people's attention—by telling the truth of what's really happening out there." Sera said flatly.

I walked over to the table and rested my hands on Sera's shoulders. "Listen, sweetheart. After the threats that came out recently, are you sure this is wise?"

"I can't live in fear!"

"Sera, you're the face of the organization," Amy pleaded. "The press will crucify you if this doesn't work."

"Then I guess I'll be crucified," Sera said, refusing to meet my eyes.

IT WAS three months before the press got wind of their plans, though no one could explain how. Newspapers contacted Sera asking her to respond to reports that she would go up against the gun lobby. She replied that she had no comment on the matter. This, of course, was taken as confirmation of their plans by reporters, who immediately ran with the story.

"I see Sera's getting herself into trouble again," Aaron said as he walked through the door.

"No, please, there's no need to knock," I said as usual, without moving my eyes from the TV screen. I'd been watching a news report on one of the more liberal media outlets. As expected, they had immediately taken Sera's side. Though they were skeptical of whether she could achieve a massive feat like taking on powerful industries or the NRA, they admired her gumption.

Aaron helped himself to a beer and joined me on the sofa as I switched to a conservative news channel. The host had dark brown lacquered hair and wide eyes that didn't blink at the normal rate. After suffering a humiliating defeat during the primaries, Dehlia Evesmith had bounced back with her own show. She was summing up at the end of a panel discussion that included a Republican senator, a conservative radio pundit, and an outspoken, well-known gun rights activist. I couldn't imagine there had been much of a discussion, as it was clear they all agreed with one another.

Dehlia Evesmith found her camera and took a deep breath before concluding the show with her "final thoughts." She raised her head and looked earnestly at the camera before starting.

"I am a proud American citizen, and I worked for many years as a public servant for the good people of this great country. I exercise my right to vote, I pay my taxes, and now I have the privilege of being welcomed into your homes to deliver you the truth about important issues in America. I am also a proud gun owner."

"Of course you are," Aaron quipped as the former politician cocked her head and offered her loyal viewers a fake smile.

"Sera Goodwin may come across simply as a sweet girl whose heart is in the right place. But I've met Sera, and let me tell you, in person she's a power-hungry, master manipulator. Just look at what she has achieved. She's managed to convince millions of young, impressionable girls and women to follow her and embrace her leftist feminist crusade. Believe me, she's no angel."

Her words jarred me, the last hitting a little too close to home. I also hated the fact that she was using Sera's full name.

"It would be foolish to underestimate a young lady who leads what many have described as one of the largest, most well-organized cults in the world. So, without sugarcoating the issue, let me be clear. Sera Goodwin is the single biggest threat to the Second Amendment America has ever seen."

She paused for effect to let the pronouncement sink in.

"The God-given liberties that our founding fathers enshrined in the Constitution through the Bill of Rights are at risk. Her efforts will prevent ordinary American citizens from protecting their families against intruders and criminals who want to do them harm.

"And if this happens, who will protect our children from those who don't obey the law? Who'll stop the bad guys who still hold the guns when the good guys' hands are empty? Now, I'm sure Sera Goodwin intends to spout statistics about the thousands of gun crimes that occur in America every year. But I'm sure she'll also omit that there are millions of crimes prevented each year because criminals know their potential victims could be armed and willing to defend themselves."

Another pause. The background graphics behind her faded to a gently waving, slightly-out-of-focus, American flag.

"So there it is. Are we, as private American citizens, willing to risk being just another statistic in a brutal murder, home invasion, or robbery? Especially when we know it can be prevented if we are able to defend ourselves? If we allow this one individual to wield her power and influence and weaponize the Internet to restrict our constitutional liberties, we are all at risk of losing a fundamental freedom that allows us to protect ourselves. I say we organize a counterattack against Sera Goodwin's mission to strip us of our rights. Because if we don't, there's just no telling what freedom she'll try to take away from us next."

"Bitch," Aaron spat as I muted the television.

"Don't let Sera catch you using that word," I warned.

"How did they even find out about this?"

"I have no idea. Maybe someone they've contacted to get statistics from has gone to the press. You've protected all of their computers so they couldn't have been hacked."

"I'll go through them all again just to be sure," Aaron said before returning his attention to the screen. "She's nothing but a scaremonger. All she does is play up to the gun totin' nutcases already out there."

"Of course she does, and that's what worries me."

Chapter Thirty-Five

I TRIED to offer Sera different ideas of projects she could concentrate on that didn't involve guns or going after titans of industry. She still hadn't published her blogs outlining her arguments or telling stories of those affected by gun violence, and it had been a mistake to wait, as the media had already started building their own narrative. But Sera refused to confirm their intentions until she'd drawn up a definite plan of how to tackle the problems. They'd been successful in the past due to meticulous planning, and she worried that rushing the project would lead to ineffective action.

Aaron suggested we all go out for a family dinner, something we hadn't done in a long time since Sera was working all hours of the day and night. Sera countered that instead of going out to an expensive restaurant, we should eat at home, and Aaron could donate the money he would have spent through the For My Sister app. It took a while to convince her that it was something her uncle wanted to do, and I had to guilt-trip her by reminding her of all he had done to help her cause, but eventually she relented.

Aaron and I agreed on our agenda: to persuade Sera to stick to women's rights issues. But the conversation was aborted even before the menus were handed to us. Despite her gratitude to Aaron, she made it clear in a kind tone that she wasn't going to debate the subject with him; she'd made up her mind and that was the end of it. To keep the peace, we let it go, hoping we could change her mind when she was more open to discussing it. Once that was decided, we ended up having a nice evening full of laughter as we reminisced.

We bade Aaron good night and began strolling toward the multilevel garage where I'd parked the car. I'd avoided getting a car for a long time, but at Aaron's urging I had finally given in and bought one.

"I had fun tonight," Sera said. "Thanks for getting me out. I know things have become a little intense recently, so it was great to be able to laugh."

"I miss seeing you away from your work," I said as I retrieved my credit card from the ticket payment machine. I hooked my arm around her shoulders as we got into the elevator to take us to the third floor. "But I'm so proud of you. You know that, right? I wonder whether I tell you that enough, but I spend so much of my time worrying about you, I sometimes forget to look at everything you've accomplished. I know you're a grown woman, but I still see you as that tiny baby who stole my heart."

The elevator door opened, and I had to squint to see where I'd left the car, as half of the lighting on the level was out. Once I was properly oriented, we began walking toward the car. The doors closed behind us and the empty elevator went to another level.

"Thanks, Dad. I have a lot of work left to do, but I'm not too sure how much time I have left to do it."

"What do you mean?"

A loud bang echoed as the heavy exit door on the far right-hand corner of the level slammed shut. Sera's nails dug into my waist as we saw three men dressed in black jeans and bomber jackets start toward us. Each wore a black ski mask and gloves.

My first thought was they were going to rob us or maybe try to steal the car. But then one called out. It was a crazed, demented voice, like he was trying to imitate the Joker from *Batman*.

"Who's been a bad, bad girl? Is it you?" he said as he pushed his hand into his jacket pocket. "Oh Seh-rah! It's about time you were taught a lesson."

The moment I saw the knife, I pushed Sera back toward the elevator, where she furiously punched the call button. The men walked slowly toward us, like they had all the time in the world.

The man to the left of the one holding the knife reached around to the back of the waistband of his jeans and pulled. He swung the gun around and pointed it at the floor as they continued to stroll casually toward us.

The whir of the moving elevator seemed distant, perhaps on a much higher floor. We had no time to wait for it to return. I grabbed Sera's hand, and we ran behind a cluster of cars for cover. On the far left corner of the level, I saw another exit, opposite the one the men had entered through. "Come out, come out, wherever you are!" one of the men called as they changed direction.

I raised myself high enough to look through the windows of the car we crouched behind.

"Yeah, we got something real special for you, Sera," called another, grabbing his crotch.

The three men laughed like sinister clowns, then fell silent to let us hear the sound of the knife scraping across the side of a car.

"Just sharpening it for you, baby," one called.

I pulled Sera close and whispered urgently, "Get to the other exit. I'll hold them off the best I can. Get outside and onto the street."

My hands shook like they were attached to an industrial drill. It wasn't because I was scared they'd kill me; I'd have gladly sacrificed my life for Sera. What made my hands shake was pure fear of leaving her alone. Who would look after her when I was gone? Who would understand her and protect her if her condition worsened?

As if she could read my mind, Sera's hand reached out to take mine. I don't know whether it was her touch or the realization that I could always depend on Aaron if anything happened to me, but in that moment, I became focused with the calmness and clarity I needed to get Sera out of danger.

I pulled my keys out of my pocket, checking that my car was now behind the three men as they came closer.

"When I say—" I started.

Sera cut me off. "I'm not leaving you!"

"Don't argue. Just go. Do you understand?"

Reluctantly she nodded. I think she knew I wouldn't run if she didn't, so in her way she was protecting me.

I punched the alarm button on the key fob, and immediately the garage was plunged into chaos. The deafening sound of the blaring horn and the flashing lights caught the men off guard. While they were distracted, Sera took off. I ran after her, keeping far enough back to run interference against the three men who were sprinting after her from my right.

I headed straight for the man with the gun. He was running awkwardly with the gun still pointed to the ground. He looked unsure, like a kid who knew he shouldn't be running with a pair of scissors.

The ski mask must have obscured his vision as he didn't appear to see me. I knocked him down and kicked the gun out of his hand with such force it spun like a pinwheel under a bank of cars. I stamped hard down on his throat with my foot to disable him long enough for me to catch up with the other two, who were gaining on Sera.

Just as she reached the exit, I managed to lunge forward and pull down the second man. As we struggled, I pulled his mask down over his face to block his eyes and kicked him hard in the groin. I turned to see the third man catch up with Sera and slam the exit door closed before she could get through it. She was backed into a corner against the wall, and he held the knife pointed at her throat as if daring her to move.

As I slowly approached, he looked around. His head darted wildly from me to Sera and back to me. He swung his arm around, brandishing the knife in my direction, and then back to Sera, like he was trapped and didn't know what to do. I saw his eyes flash to the two men on the ground, one doubled over holding his groin, the other on his knees, holding his throat and gasping for air. There was fear in his eyes now that he was on his own. There was no question in my mind what needed to be done. I had to be the one he attacked in order to give Sera a chance to get away. It had to be done now. I couldn't give him the time to figure out he could use her as a hostage.

With the blare of the car alarm and my quickened heartbeat pounding in my ears, I didn't hear the fourth man's approach. It was as if he just materialized next to me. He wore black suit pants with a cord tied around the waist, and an old Knicks T-shirt under a long, filthy tan raincoat, and mismatched sneakers. His hair and stubble were longer and whiter than the last time I'd seen him, but his face was unmistakable.

It was Oscar.

The man in the ski mask, now cornered, turned quickly and held the knife to the side of Sera's neck again. It creased her skin so deeply that any more pressure would cause the blade to split her skin. The knife trembled in his hand, but as Oscar got closer, the man seemed to become hypnotized. Oscar raised his arms, placed his palms on the knifeman's chest, and silently walked him backward until he was pinned against the wall. The knife fell from his nerveless fingers.

I grabbed Sera's arm and pulled her toward the exit. As I pushed the bar to release the door, I turned and saw Oscar saying something to the man, but I couldn't hear over the alarm. His palms rested against the man's chest, but there was no indication he was using any force. In the red light of the exit sign, I could see that the backs of his hands, gloveless for the first time I could remember, were badly scarred.

"Go!" he said in a calm but loud voice.

I pulled Sera through the door, and we ran down the six short flights of stairs and out of the garage. Music poured from a crowded Irish bar opposite, the patrons spilling out onto the street.

"Go to the bar and call the police. I've got to go back and help Oscar," I said, holding the exit door open.

Sera nodded and ran across the street, barely missing a car whose brakes screeched as it swerved to avoid her. My heart pounded as I took the stairs two at a time to get back to the third level where we'd left Oscar. But as I crashed through the door, my adrenaline pumping so fast I was ready for anything, I found the floor empty. The men who'd threatened us were gone, and Oscar was nowhere to be seen.

WE SAT behind the desk of Sergeant Marino. It had been over twenty years since I'd seen him in the courtroom when Judge Adesso asked for his account of what happened the day I'd found Sera. His years in service had transformed him from a naïve beat cop into a seasoned veteran who exuded authority. It was four in the morning, and we'd waited for the police to collect and view the camera footage from the parking garage.

"Something has to be done about this now!" I insisted.

"There are only four CCTV cameras in the building, Mr. Goodwin. Two of the cameras are trained on the car entrance and exit, and the third is on the side exit where you came out. But the camera on the fourth exit apparently hasn't been operational for weeks. We have security footage from the bodega opposite that shows the three men entering, but they were already wearing masks. As you know, they were also wearing gloves. Dusting for prints will come up with nothing."

"What about Oscar?" Sera asked hopefully. "Is there any footage showing he got out? That he got away?"

"No. In fact, there's no footage of him even entering the garage. But like I said, the fourth exit wasn't caught on film. If he's a homeless guy, he could've been sleeping in there for days. The homeless are usually the ones who bust these cameras so they won't get caught on private property and be forced to move along. This Oscar guy may have heard this garage was a safe place to shelter. By the sounds of things, you were lucky to have him there."

"I can't bear the thought of him being hurt," I said. "If it hadn't been for him, God knows what would have happened."

"We will, of course, investigate this threat to you and your daughter," Sergeant Marino said before turning to Sera. "I understand you're looking to take on the gun lobby with your influence on the Internet."

"Not anymore," I said, answering for her.

Sera ignored me. "Yes, we'll probably begin in the next few weeks."

"You can't be serious," I said incredulously. "These people have more money than you could possibly fathom. If they want to get rid of a problem, they will."

The sergeant leaned forward into a businesslike posture. He laced his fingers together and seemed to mull over my words.

"There's a good chance these men were hired just to scare you. It's unlikely they were there to do you any serious injury."

"One of them held a knife to her throat! One was carrying a gun! They were there to kill her!"

"But they didn't use their weapons, and from what you've described, the one with the knife only pulled it on Sera when he found himself cornered. That isn't the action of a hardened criminal. He would've done anything necessary to get out of there." The sergeant took a deep breath. "There were three of them, all tall men, one with a knife and one with a gun. If they wanted to kill you, they would have. They had every opportunity to shoot you. If you're suggesting they were assassins of some type, they wouldn't have played with you beforehand. They wouldn't have shouted or mocked. One person would've done the job, and you probably wouldn't have known it was coming. No, I think it's more likely this was a warning, a threat to get you to back off. It's more an intimidation tactic, usually used by organized crime."

"So what are you suggesting? It's not the gun lobby? It's the sex traffickers in the city?"

The sergeant nodded. "We've been cracking down on them hard. With the continued pressure the mayor is under from Sera and her followers, he had to do something. He was facing immense criticism in the press. We were surprised by how fast he took action, but then again, he's due for reelection soon and the bad publicity wasn't doing him any favors. I don't know whether you've read the statistics, but they've come down on the illegal sex industry with an iron fist. So of course the traffickers and the pimps aren't happy. They're losing money and customers and being arrested left, right, and center."

"So you're sure it's not the gun lobby?"

"Well, we can't rule out any of them completely. That's why it's going to take some time to investigate. I'll have units patrolling your area every day for the next few weeks until we come up with something."

"That's it? You're going to patrol the area?" I asked, dumbfounded at such a pitiful response.

"Mr. Goodwin, I appreciate how worried you are and how scary this situation must be to you. But we don't have the resources to guard Sera 24-7 for an indefinite period of time." The sergeant thought for a moment. "I'll tell you what I'll do. I'll have a unit outside your apartment for the next three days and station an officer outside your door. Hopefully that'll give us time to catch whoever did this and give you the chance to get some rest. You both look tired."

"Thank you," Sera said, getting up from her chair. "Could I ask you to do me a favor?"

"Of course." Sergeant Marino nodded.

"Can you put out a description of Oscar for us? Maybe the clothes he was wearing and what area he was in. If any of your officers spot him, can you let me know?"

"Sure." The sergeant smiled kindly. "Do you know Oscar's surname?"

Sera and I looked at each other. I felt ashamed. "No. In fact, Oscar isn't even his real Christian name. It's just the nickname we've used for twenty years. But he knows we call him Oscar, so I imagine he'd respond to it."

"Okay, hopefully the description will be enough," the sergeant said as he stood and showed us toward the door.

WHEN WE arrived home, I made Sera wait outside while I checked the apartment.

"Dad, I'm sure he's right. They were probably just trying to scare us."

"They did a damn good job of it, then."

A knock at the door startled us both. I peered through the keyhole and saw a uniform. I opened the door and two police officers introduced themselves. They assured me we were safe, which made me feel only slightly more at ease. The officers told us they would be just outside the door if we needed them and then excused themselves.

I pulled Sera into a tight hug, thankful that the events of the night hadn't robbed me of the chance to kiss her good night.

"I can't stop what I've started. You know that, right, Dad?" she said sadly, like she was disappointing me.

"We'll discuss it in the morning." Neither of us was in any state to make decisions.

Chapter Thirty-Six

"WHERE HAVE you been?" Sera asked as I walked through the door at lunchtime the following day. "The cops outside said you left early."

"I didn't want to wake you. I called in sick and then met your uncle in Midtown."

"Why?"

"We were looking for an office for you girls to work out of, one on a higher floor, with security guards at the door. I think we've found one near Washington Square Park. The rent is pretty steep, but it's a new building trying to fill its occupancy, so they're offering the first couple of months free. I'll cover it for another couple of months after that. Then we'll have to talk to your uncle Aaron and see if we can start using proceeds from an app to fund the cost of the rent."

"Dad—" she said, almost hopelessly.

"I'm not arguing with you over this, Sera. You're putting yourself in danger. And if you can't see that for yourself, you ought to think about the girls. How would you feel if Meena, Amy, or Carla were attacked? This is for their safety as well as yours. We have to think about the girls' parents too. I know they support what you're all trying to accomplish, but at the end of the day they've paid a fortune in college tuition for their daughters to live at home and work for less than minimum wage."

"Dad—"

"I know what you're going to say. It's their choice, and you can't put a price on the good you girls have done. But as your dad, I have a responsibility to the parents of those girls, and I can't have them at risk because you're too—"

"Dad, can we talk?"

I sat down at the table and watched her try to find her words, the same way she did when she was a kid.

"Sophia came to me last night."

It didn't come as a complete shock. The trauma of the previous night's events was bound to have had some kind of effect on her. I'd silently hoped it wouldn't come as another vision.

"What did she say?" I asked gently.

Sera gathered herself. "She told me it was time to reveal myself to my companions."

It was my worst fear: she was going to tell the girls. How would they react? I couldn't see any way they could accept this.

Sera continued, "Then she said something I didn't really understand. She said 'It's time to save the heart that beats but does not live, and release the one not held whose crying has not been heard.'"

I was stunned, unable to say anything. Her words were no puzzle to me. She was clearly talking about abortion. So why was she acting like she didn't understand?

"Sera—"

"There was another message. A message for you."

I steeled myself. "And what was that?"

Sera shook her head as if trying to rattle bizarre-shaped thoughts into the correct holes in her mind. "I'm sorry, Dad, I don't know. The moment the words were said, they vanished from my head. I asked for it to be said again but was told I'd recall the message when the time was right and you were ready."

"You can't tell the girls," I said, glad her hallucination's message had been forgotten. I was focusing on the more pressing concern.

"I have to. And before we move forward."

"They're not going to believe you, Sera."

"How could they," Sera said sadly, "when even you don't believe me."

"Sera, I do," I said without conviction.

A tear spilled from Sera's eye. "You're lying. I know you don't believe what I'm saying."

I stopped, unable to deny it because, out of everyone in the world, Sera knew me best. It hurt to acknowledge that her accusation was the truth.

"I believe that *you* believe what you're saying is true," I said, trying to avoid a rift that couldn't be mended. Or maybe Sera had avoided it by not confronting me.

"Dad," she said calmly, "whatever will be, will be. I can't stop it."

AFTER BEING told about the incident in the parking garage, it wasn't difficult to convince Amy, Meena, and Carla that they should move their work to an office with security. Amy was particularly happy, as it gave her a space and opportunity to be somewhere Sera wasn't living, and therefore perhaps a chance to be with Dalyn alone if he dropped by.

It was less than a week before the media somehow discovered they were working out of an office, and though most of them ignored this small change, one person took the change of premises as an opportunity to attack Sera using new information.

Dehlia Evesmith's wide eyes and sneering grin appeared on the television.

"Not content with going after the rights of citizens to protect their families and arm themselves, Sera Goodwin is now also going after big business. In a move that could potentially force the loss of thousands of jobs, Sera Goodwin has turned her attention to power companies who she claims are polluting the environment. And where is she doing this from?"

My teeth clenched.

"Manhattan. In her charitable wisdom, Sera Goodwin has leased office space on Washington Square, one of the most expensive areas in the entire country. So the question must be asked: are the donations that are meant to be going toward women's rights now funding plush new offices in New York? Will she be sitting in luxury while she attempts to take away your rights as an American citizen, or looking over a beautiful view of the city as thousands fret about the loss of their jobs and the incomes that provide for their families? And one of those power companies, PowerCo, is based in New York! She's actively attacking an industry based in her home state!

"And while we're investigating this, we wonder why there seems to be no record of any tax being paid by Sera Goodwin. Is this because she goes under a different name, or is she simply taking a cash wage from the donations of millions of hard-working American women?"

My phone rang.

"You have to set this straight! And she keeps using Sera's full name!" Aaron shouted. I could hear the repeated echo of Dehlia Evesmith's voice in my ear as my brother's TV relayed the same words coming from his set. "You've supported her all the way through this, and you're paying for the rent until we come up with an alternative. And we both know that nothing is in Sera's name because of the trust!"

"Do you honestly think she's going to report that? She's clearly out to sabotage Sera's work."

"Then go to the liberal media. Or tell Sera to take a direct route to her followers and announce on her website how she's funded."

"She won't do that. She won't give the impression she's some little rich girl who can afford to go on a crusade because 'Daddy' supports her. She'll lose credibility with her followers. Half of her appeal is that they can relate to her."

"You haven't always been a partner in a successful law firm, Adam."

"I know that and so do you, but do you think the masses will consider that when they judge her?"

"What about Dalyn? Can he write an article explaining that the money and donations don't even go through Sera?"

"I could ask. But the people who watch Dehlia Evesmith aren't exactly subscribers to the *New York Times*. She knows that, and she knows that even if she gets called out on what she says, it won't get back to her viewers. She's riling up her audience and fan base."

"Let me speak to Sera. Maybe I can talk some sense into her. Together we can come up with an idea to discredit Dehlia Evesmith's view of her."

I sat in silence, trying to devise a plan.

"Adam. You still there?"

"Yes. Look, I think she's going through one of her episodes. She's talking about being the Daughter of God again, but this time she's coming up with stuff that doesn't sound like before."

"What do you mean?"

"When she repeats what Sophia says to her, it sounds like she's reciting words from a book or a poem. Like what she's saying has some kind of cryptic message. But it's hardly difficult to decipher. I'm worried she's getting into even more dangerous territory. I'm afraid the negative attention and lies spread by Dehlia Evesmith are going to cause her to have a complete breakdown."

"Do you think you should have her evaluated? You know, professionally?"

"I'm holding out hope this is just another one-off episode and she comes back around. There seems to be a pattern to it."

"How so?"

"Sophia only appears when something terrible happens without any warning. When she thought she'd killed Buddy when he was a puppy, when the attacks happened on 9/11, when she was away on her travels and Champai overdosed and died. And now this time, right after she had a knife held to her throat in the parking garage. I think it's some kind of coping mechanism. She has these visions to help her get through."

"That sounds reasonable," Aaron said without thinking.

"Reasonable?"

"Well, not reasonable. I mean, it's a reasonable explanation for why she's acting like this. If what you're saying is right, all we have to do is keep her out of situations like that."

"And how are we supposed to do that? Look what she's doing with her life."

"We'll find a way," Aaron said, but this time I wasn't sure even he believed it.

SERA LEFT for the office the following morning while I worked from home. I was antsy all day and had called her several times, only to get her voice mail. I checked her website and social media sites, but none had been updated. I eventually got hold of Meena, who said everything was okay, but she never could tell a convincing lie. I asked her to pass the phone over to Sera but was told she was on another call. Considering how small the office was, I knew it was impossible not to hear her voice in the background. There was, however, a muffled noise of some kind of chanting.

"Meena, I want you and the girls to come over for dinner tonight," I said. "Make sure you bring Carla and Amy."

"Sure, Mr. Goodwin," she agreed quickly, as if she couldn't get off the phone fast enough.

Since our attempts to convince Sera to back off the anti-gun project had failed, I thought I could try to persuade the girls to help me. I already knew Amy would side with me.

When they arrived they nervously looked at the policeman, who was spending his last night at our door. Dalyn, who I wasn't expecting, shut the door behind them.

I tried casual conversation as I prepared to put dinner on the table, but Dalyn, Sera, and the girls seemed distracted and anxious about something. I assumed it was because of the continued need for the cop. The NYPD had agreed that, since there was adequate security at the office, they would pull back their resources and only stand guard in the evening. I tried to lighten the atmosphere by making a plate of spaghetti Bolognese for the officer, who ate it happily as he sat outside the door.

Once everyone was served, I sat down. "I asked you all over tonight as I was hoping you'd consider putting some of your plans on hold for a while. You girls have been working nonstop for a long time, and I think it's about time you had a break. A decent break. Not just days off but a real chance to get away."

"Dad—" Sera began to object.

"Hang on, hear me out." I was trying to keep my tone casual. "Don't you think you would be more effective if you had some time off? Not go too far, maybe just spend a couple of weeks in a cabin upstate."

"That might not be such a bad idea," Dalyn said. "Clear your heads and have some fun."

I was grateful for his support.

Meena and Carla continued chewing their food. Amy leaned forward and said, "You could come too, Dalyn! We could find somewhere big enough for us all—"

Sera dropped her fork onto her plate. The sound drew everyone's attention. She looked down at her food, and her chest rose higher with each breath.

"Sera, now isn't the time," I said, worried about what might come out of her mouth.

"There will never be a good time," Sera said as her eyes danced across each of the people around the table.

"Good time for what?" Carla asked.

"It's time you knew."

CHAPTER THIRTY-SEVEN

"PLEASE, SERA," I begged.

Sera looked at the girls and said in a strong, confident voice, "When we were travelling, I was visited by an angel. She told me I was the Daughter of God."

There was a silence. Then Carla began to laugh. "Yeah, and I'm the Queen of Sheba!"

"Carla, *stop!*" I slammed my palm on the table.

Everyone jumped.

I instantly regretted snapping at her. It was the way any sane, skeptical person would react to hearing such an outrageous statement. I was shocked by the way Sera had just blurted it out without warning or any buildup. There were none of the pleas for understanding she'd given me. And my reaction had given weight to what Sera had said— underlined it wasn't a joke. I'd made things worse before giving Sera a chance to backpedal if she wanted to. But Carla's laugh had gotten under my skin. She was the first person to mock Sera, and I knew she wouldn't be the last.

Carla's smile faded as she realized something was wrong.

"What are you talking about?" Amy asked, looking confused.

Sera looked at me with a plea for help in her eyes. I didn't know what I could do or say that would make it any easier for her. I couldn't just dismiss it; my actions had seen to that. I couldn't say I believed her, nor could show them that I wasn't supportive. I had to set them an example and hope they would follow.

"Tell them what you need to, sweetheart," I said softly. "It's better they hear it from you than from anyone else." I turned to the girls. "Just hear her out. We'll discuss it afterward. But for the time being, give her a chance to talk."

Sera explained about Sophia and how she'd been with her when she was a kid, then returned to give messages on their travels. She told them about her visions and how it was her mission from God to save the women of the world. She spoke with utter conviction in her beliefs and described the dream and how she'd been told it was time to reveal herself to her companions.

As she was speaking, I noticed the way Dalyn watched her, listening intently and respectfully, as though to someone he was interviewing. There was no shock and no disbelief, just his undivided attention. A sadness passed through me, a kind of grief when I looked at him and realized the chance of him marrying my daughter or becoming the father of my grandchildren was probably slipping away with every word Sera spoke. Now that he knew the truth.

I looked at Carla. She was utterly bewildered. A strange expression appeared on her face, like she was an instant away from laughing again. Her eyes flashed to mine to see if I was stifling a smile or giving any other indication that this was all about to be revealed as a big prank.

"She's not joking, Carla," I said, interrupting Sera, who was explaining how their work had been influenced by God to create a better world in which women would be equal. Carla's poised-to-laugh expression disappeared, and her face relaxed as she paid more attention to what Sera was saying.

Meena was listening attentively too, nodding her head occasionally, like a therapist who empathized with every word coming from her patient's mouth. I imagined it was the way she'd looked as she'd listened to the stories of all those desperate women.

And then there was Amy. When Sera started to speak, she'd looked confused, but as Sera went on, a smug expression crept across her face. Her attention was divided between Sera and Dalyn. Unlike Carla, Amy didn't consider it a joke. She realized this revelation was going to change the dynamics of the group, but it also meant that her designs on Dalyn would soon have one less obstacle—the biggest obstacle of all.

When Sera finished, she looked hopefully at her friends. "I know how it sounds. And I know it's a lot to take in. I'm just asking you to give me some time and have faith in me."

Carla released the edge of her bottom lip from between her teeth. "Sera, you're obviously going through something—"

"It's not something, it's—" Sera began defensively.

"Hang on," Carla said, putting her hand up. "We've listened to what you've had to say. Shouldn't you now listen to what we have to say?"

Sera nodded.

"We've been through so much together, and we've *all* felt the stress. What we've seen, learned, and heard firsthand would mess with anyone's mind. And we've each dealt with it in our own way. I don't know what's going on with you, but I want you to know that I'll always be one of your best friends. Whatever you want or need, I'll be there for you. The same way you've always been there for me when I've needed you," Carla said kindly.

Sera smiled.

"However," Carla continued, this time with a note of seriousness, "you must realize that telling people what you're telling us could do untold damage. Followers would abandon us and donations would stop. With that in mind, please understand that if we express concern that you're about to do something we don't agree with, you must listen to us."

I felt a sudden rush of affection for Carla.

"I'm not planning on telling anyone else. I can't let anything distract from the work we're doing. I think things have happened for a reason, and that reason was to show that people had to help each other and not just rely on prayer. I recognize that and I think that's why we've been so successful. But there will come a day when I will have to reveal myself more publicly, and on that day, I promise, all of your doubts will be put at rest."

"I believe you," Meena said abruptly.

"What?" Amy said in astonishment.

"You didn't know Sera the way I did when we were kids. If I was ever scared or worried about anything, she would always make me feel better." Meena turned back to Sera. "I always knew there was something special about you. I remember the way you stood up to that man attacking the Muslim girl. You were so brave. You didn't have to do anything, and the man just backed down. All the time we were traveling, I saw the way women were with you. You just—" She seemed to struggle for the right words. "—had a knack. It was just incredible. I always wondered how you did it. Now I know."

I knew Meena didn't believe a word of what Sera was saying. After all, apart from me, she was the only one in the room who could remember Sophia as an imaginary friend. But of all the girls, Meena was the most devoted to Sera. They'd grown up together, and I knew she would have followed my daughter to the ends of the earth to prove how much her friendship meant. At that moment Meena decided she needed to show Sera someone was on her side, and that someone—anyone—believed her without question. She showed her love for Sera by being that person.

Amy remained silent while Carla asked, "So what was this thing about saving the heart that isn't held?"

"No," Sera said. "It was 'It's time to save the heart that beats but does not live, and release the one not held whose crying has not been heard.'"

"And you think that whatever that means is what we should be concentrating on next?"

"I think so, but I don't understand what she meant."

A sudden flash of realization appeared on Amy's face accompanied by a look of genuine concern. Not about Sera's mental health but about something else. But she still didn't speak. Had she figured out what Sera was talking about as quickly as I had?

Sera shook her head slowly. "I just wish God would talk to me. I just don't understand what He wants me to do."

I silently hoped it would stay that way.

"It's okay," Dalyn said, moving his seat closer to Sera's. He put his arm around her and pulled her in close. "We'll work it out, together, I promise." Then he kissed her on the cheek. "I'll always be here. You know that, right?"

My heart flooded at the gesture, but the enlarging whites of Amy's eyes distracted me as she looked wildly at Dalyn.

"You can't be serious. You've got to be kidding me!" she shouted. "Surely you can't still like her. After that?"

"Amy!" Carla cried as Amy stood up violently, knocking her chair backward so hard it slid across the floor.

"She's out of her fucking mind! She's crazy! Am I the only one who just heard her say she thinks she's the Daughter of God?" She rounded on Dalyn. "And you're still interested?"

She turned her attention to Sera. "Are you happy now? You don't want him, but you don't want anyone else to have him either, huh? That's right, make him feel all the pity in the world for you so he sticks around. Christ, Sera, not only are you crazy, but you're damn selfish with it."

Sera looked stoic, as though she expected Amy's reaction. Not getting the desired rise out of her, Amy turned back to Dalyn.

"I've done everything she's done. I've given up my time and any chance of a career so I can help women. I'm just as important in what we're doing. What about me, huh? What's wrong with me?" she asked, slamming her palms on his chest. "What does it take for you to love me? This mental case has led you on for the past two years! Two fucking years!" She stopped shouting and began pleading. "You must know how I feel about you, Dalyn. You must have known for a long time. Why not be with me? Please, be with me!"

"Control yourself!" Dalyn shot back as he stood to face her. "The only one acting crazy right now is you, Amy."

"Please, Dalyn, I just want you to love me the way I love you."

"And you think the way you're behaving now makes you attractive? Look at yourself. Look how you're acting when your friend reaches out to you for support."

"How I'm acting? It's not bad enough that we have angry protestors outside the office, now you expect me to deal with a madwoman inside it too? She's crazy, Dalyn!"

"Protestors?" I asked Meena, suddenly remembering the chants in the background of our phone call. But she was too distracted by what was happening to respond.

"Stop saying she's crazy!" Dalyn shouted. "How can you say that when she's sitting in front of you, you spiteful—"

"Spiteful what?" Amy demanded, her mood turning sharply. "Bitch? Go on, say it!" she dared. "Let's see how much that endears you to your precious Sera."

"I wouldn't give you the satisfaction," Dalyn shot back.

Amy turned back on Sera. "This is punishment for Champai, isn't it? You still blame me. You think she wouldn't be dead if I'd kept a closer eye on her."

This was the first thing to get a reaction from Sera. "Of course I don't blame you, Amy. If anything, I blame myself. I should've seen the signs."

"You're a liar," Amy hissed. "You think she'd still be alive if I'd stayed awake and stopped her from leaving."

"I don't blame you, Amy!"

"Yes, you do. You've put all our lives in danger, and now you're determined to make sure Dalyn and I don't have a chance, you selfish bitch," Amy shouted before she spun back to Dalyn. "Why was I so stupid to think I even had a chance with you? I mean, Sera is perfect, isn't she? Hell, you already thought she walked on water even before she told you she thinks she's the Daughter of God." She laughed with derision.

Dalyn's jaw clenched. "You didn't stand a chance with me because I see the way you really are. You've changed, Amy. For the past year, it's been clear that all you want is the recognition, the praise, and the applause for helping people. But who really cares about that, so long as people are benefiting from your efforts, no matter how self-serving they are? The real truth is you didn't stand a chance with me because you're not half the woman Sera is. And you never will be."

Amy pulled her hand back so far it gave everyone, including Dalyn, a chance to see what was coming. Yet he stood his ground as she slapped him across the face with as much force as she could muster.

There was a knock at the apartment door. "Is everything okay in there?" called the patrolman in the hallway.

Amy turned on her heels and stormed out of the apartment. "That's it, I'm done!" she shouted in fury. "*You can all go to hell!*"

I rushed over to the door. Though I was furious with her, there was still someone out there threatening the girls; I couldn't just leave her to walk the streets alone. But my daughter needed me, so I asked the police officer outside the door to go after her and make sure she got home, or at least into a cab, okay.

AN HOUR later I walked Meena across the road and put Carla safely into a taxi. I thanked them for their attempts to comfort Sera after Amy walked out. Both were concerned about her, not just about what she'd said, but also because they knew that Amy's accusations about Sera blaming her for Champai would have stung Sera to the core.

As I walked back into the lobby, Dalyn came slowly down the stairs and without prompting, took a seat on the second to bottom step.

"First things first," I said as I joined him. "What the hell is this about protestors?"

"Amy called me this afternoon. She said when they arrived at their office this morning there were a few protestors outside, but as the day went on, more and more showed up. She asked if I could take her home, since she was nervous about going outside. I agreed because I knew it would give me a chance to speak to her alone about something that has been bothering me. But then you called Meena and arranged the dinner. I'm sorry, I know I wasn't invited, but I wanted to make sure the girls got here safely, and Sera insisted that I stay."

"Dalyn, you're welcome here any time. It didn't occur to me to invite you because, as you now know, I set the dinner up to try to talk them into going away for a couple of weeks while things cooled down."

He gave me an understanding nod.

"Tell me more about the protestors."

"It was peaceful from what I could see. There were a few signs in support of Second Amendment rights. They had the typical signs quoting the Constitution. Meena said there were quite a few power company workers protesting this morning holding 'Hands Off Our Jobs' signs, but then the number seemed to double at lunchtime. I don't know for sure, but I imagine PowerCo has hired stand-ins to bolster the numbers. There were a few other men, but I wasn't sure whether they were protesting or just milling around to see what all the fuss was about. By the time we left, the sidewalk was full. They shouted after us as we left, but they didn't follow."

"Were the security guards there?"

"Yeah, I wouldn't worry about that. No one is getting into that building. Not past those guys. They're massive. I got interrogated before I went up to the office. I had to show ID, too, as well as have Carla come down to escort me and sign me in."

I breathed a sigh of relief. The security team was the biggest factor in keeping the girls safe. It was good to know they were doing their job.

My thoughts returned to the scene upstairs. "Things got out of hand tonight. I've never seen Amy act like that before. Let's hope she calms down overnight."

Dalyn cocked an eyebrow. "You think she will? She was pretty pissed."

"You were pretty harsh with her."

"Please don't tell Sera I told you this, but Amy said to me that when their intention to go against the gun lobby was somehow leaked to the press, she thought it was a good thing. She believed that it gave them a chance to gauge their followers' reactions, and if it was negative, they could back out, since they hadn't actually confirmed anything. But they seem to have had a good response. While Sera, Meena, and Carla were pleased about that, Amy still insisted that it was foolish to take the focus from women's rights. Then the details about going after the power lobby miraculously appeared on the news."

"Are you suggesting it was Amy who leaked that to the press?"

"I'm almost sure it was. She and Sera have been locking horns recently. I wanted to confront Amy about it tonight when I took her home, but of course we ended up having dinner here instead."

"I just can't believe it of her. I know she's headstrong—but to betray Sera like that?"

"Like I said, I don't know for sure."

"Well, whether it's true or not, it was good to see you stick up for my daughter that way. You really like her, huh?"

"Like? I'm pretty sure you know I've been hopelessly in love with that girl since the moment I met her." He smiled awkwardly. "She's all I ever think about. Sometimes I look at her and she's just an ordinary girl who I can laugh and talk openly with. And I'm totally comfortable, and that's fantastic...."

"But...?"

"But then there are times when I see her or I'm near her... and I just turn into a wreck. A good wreck, if that makes sense. It's like she's just so... I don't know how to describe it. She's just so magnificent I can barely breathe."

I couldn't help but smile. Only a journalist, a young wordsmith smitten by love, could use a word like "magnificent" without sounding ridiculous.

"When Sera was away with the girls," Dalyn continued, "she used to send me letters about their travels. They were all so... I mean... who the hell gets handwritten letters anymore?" He smiled. "I checked my mailbox every day and looked for her handwriting on an envelope or postcard. Every time I saw a foreign stamp, I would just get so damn excited. I read them over and over again. I'd spend my evenings trying to find words to write back to her, but each time it sounded lovesick or overly sentimental, and I knew that wasn't what she wanted. So I'd have to start again. But once I found the words, I never had an address to send them to, because they were changing hotels or destinations so often that they'd have left by the time my letter arrived. So I e-mailed Sera what I'd written instead. I kept all of the handwritten ones, complete with postage stamps, and gave them to her when she returned, just so she could see I wanted to return the effort she'd put in for me." Dalyn gave me a golly-gee-shucks kind of look. "Stupid, huh?"

"No, not at all."

We sat in silence for a moment.

"How do you feel now? You know, about what she said."

"It took me by surprise at first, and it took a long time to get my head around it. But then she—"

"Wait, you knew?"

Dalyn nodded. "One night, about a week after you finished turning Maggie's apartment into an office, Sera called me and asked if I wanted to meet for dinner at a restaurant. You wouldn't believe how excited I was. I arrived in a suit and tie, holding half a dozen roses and the stack of letters, thinking we were going on our first date. But she soon made it clear, in a very kind way, that I had it wrong." Dalyn shook his head and smiled with embarrassment as he recalled the misunderstanding. Anyway, we sat and talked for hours and hours, and that's when she told me. She said she didn't want me to tell you I knew since you'd warned her about other people finding out. She didn't want to upset you or stress you out by finding out she'd told me."

I thought back to that day in the apartment when he gave her flowers. It was over two years ago, and I'd seen Dalyn countless times since. It said a lot about his character that he'd never betrayed a hint of knowing the truth.

"It would have stressed me out. But if I'd known then how you'd continue to support her, I wouldn't have been so worried."

"She was different back then. She'd lost a lot of weight, seen some terrible things on her journey, and Maggie had just died. It was the first and only time since I'd met her that she showed any self-doubt or insecurities."

"Doubt?"

"She didn't understand why she was who she thought she was."

"I don't understand."

"She talked about having a condition as a child. It was some kind of disability?"

"Erb's Palsy."

"Yeah, that was it. But she overcame it, didn't she?"

"With a lot of hard work, yes, she did. The symptoms haven't bothered her for years, but even now, she still rubs chamomile lotion onto her arm to relax when she's tired. I think it's a comfort thing."

"During the hours we talked about it, she was almost one hundred percent certain that what she was saying was the truth. The only time she expressed any doubt was when she talked about her Erb's Palsy. She couldn't understand why, as the Daughter of God, she wasn't perfect. That she'd been born with a flaw."

"Do you still talk about it now? I mean, does she talk about being the Daughter of God with you?"

"No. I was surprised at what she said tonight, because after that night in the restaurant, I got the feeling she didn't want to discuss it again. Like I said, at the time I thought she was just overwhelmed and she hadn't slept in days. I've never given up hope that she might someday look at me as more than just a friend. So I've never pushed her to talk about what she'd said."

A moment of what-could-have-been passed.

"I'm worried about her," I said.

"Me too," Dalyn replied. "But right now I'm more worried about what Amy's going to do."

Chapter Thirty-Eight

Sera was adamant about going to the office the following day, so I insisted on driving her there. I was worried about her state of mind, but at the same time I thought being around her two supportive friends and in a work mindset would keep a sense of normalcy around her. When I dropped her off, I saw a smattering of protesters had already arrived. I followed a few steps behind her, and once my identity had been screened, I escorted her up to the office. When I walked back onto the pavement, I spent a couple of minutes wandering around the area. Some demonstrators attempted to get me to join them and convince me of the importance of their protest. I nodded as if I understood their concerns, asked questions, and tried to act like their causes were of genuine interest to me. The pretense provided cover to gauge the atmosphere.

Many of the protestors seemed intelligent, well-informed, and reasonable. The ones who gave me pause were those who didn't hold signs and didn't seem to be supporting any particular cause. Before I left, I asked the security guards to pay particular attention to them. They agreed reluctantly; the office building hadn't been open long and, understandably, they seemed annoyed at the prospect of facing confrontation so soon.

I had to get to a work meeting, but I promised Sera I would stop by at lunchtime to bring them food to avoid them going outside or having something delivered by a stranger. Dalyn had already agreed to accompany Sera and Meena home and put Carla safely in a cab.

When Sera arrived home with Dalyn, she was in a good mood and seemed more optimistic than she had in days. The first draft of the blog with her solutions to gun crime was ready, and she was excited to show me what she'd come up with. As she opened her laptop, her phone beeped with a text alert. The laptop fired up and Sera pulled up the file. As she prepared to read the blog aloud, her phone rang.

"It's okay, it's probably Meena. I'll call her back in a minute." She turned back to the screen, cleared her throat, and began to read, "America has changed dramatically since—"

Dalyn's phone rang inside his suit jacket.

"Ignore it. It'll stop in a few seconds," he said, indicating to Sera to continue. Within a couple of seconds of Dalyn's phone falling silent, mine began to chime. I laughed. "It's probably work. It'll go to voice mail after a couple of rings. Go ahead."

Before Sera had a chance to draw breath, Aaron barged through the door, grasping his phone so tight in his hand his knuckles were white.

"For the love of God, Aaron, will you ever knock?"

He rushed over behind Sera and hugged her shoulders. "It's okay, we'll come up with something," he said, finally letting her go. "Just don't worry about it, okay? She's only one person. Just deny it. You know you have the support of—"

"What are you talking about?" Sera asked, looking as confused as Dalyn and me.

"You haven't seen it?" he asked, looking quickly at each of us in turn. "Amy just released a statement."

He motioned to Sera to move off her seat. He closed the file she was reading and connected to a web browser. We gathered behind him as he brought up the *New York Post* website. There was a furious knock at the door. Dalyn opened it to find Meena out of breath. She'd obviously heard the news and had run from across the street when none of us answered our phones. She stood with us as Aaron read the headline running in bold font across the top of the screen.

Breaking News: Sera—"I Am the Daughter of God."

Sera Goodwin, the popular feminist activist mostly known by her first name on social media and the For My Sister website, believes she is the Daughter of God, according to one of the foundation's key workers, Amy Jones. In a verified e-mail to the New York Post, *Jones explained that Sera Goodwin announced her belief last night over what was meant to be a meeting about gun control.*

Sera also announced to Meena Yun, Carla Ramirez, and Amy Jones, the main directors of the foundation, that she intends to pursue the overturning of Roe v. Wade, *the 1973 Supreme Court case that legalized abortion. In a statement, Amy Jones wrote:*

"It has become impossible for me to continue my work with the For My Sister foundation. This is not only due to Sera Goodwin's deeply disturbing mental health problems, but also because I believe an attempt to outlaw abortion goes against everything the foundation has worked to attain and all that it stands for."

Should this revelation of Sera Goodwin's intent to ban abortion in all fifty states prove to be true, it will shock the millions of followers of the foundation, which has been the vanguard for advancement of women's rights.

"What the hell is she doing?" Meena exclaimed. "You didn't say anything about abortion last night!"

Sera looked stunned.

"Right. Everyone, I need to speak to my daughter alone," I said firmly, walking toward the door. They all filed out and headed next door to Sera's apartment, thankfully without argument. When they were gone, I turned cautiously to Sera.

"Okay, first things first...." I began to pace around the living room. "Aaron's right. You can just deny it. I'm sure Meena and Carla will back you up. We'll write a statement and put it out tonight, as soon as possible. Then I'll contact Amy myself, but it'll have to be in person and not over the phone. I don't trust her anymore. She'll probably record everything I say. I'll distract her while you issue a longer article on your website that discredits her."

"But—"

"Sera, now isn't the time to consider Amy's feelings. She's already started to do harm to your cause. Who knows what else she'll say or where she'll stop. If you don't start with damage control now, everything you've worked for could be turned on its head."

"Maybe Amy's not lying," Sera said, her eyes dancing in all directions as she thought. They finally came to a stop as she met mine. "Did she figure it out? Is that what Sophia meant?"

"What?"

"'It's time to save the heart that beats but does not live, and release the one not held whose crying has not been heard.' Is this what God wants?"

Things were worse than I thought. After all, the vision was in her head, so she must have been the one to come up with the words. Why still pretend she didn't know what they meant? Had she gone past the point of no return and convinced herself that the meaning of her own cryptic message had escaped her? The moment she'd said the words the first time, I had tried to banish them from my mind, hoping this topic wouldn't be addressed.

"I don't understand." She looked genuinely confused, which only added to my worry. "It doesn't make any sense. Why did God lead me to save these women, only to expect me to turn my back on them?"

"You're right, Sera. It doesn't make any sense. Maybe Sophia meant something else." It was a long shot that she could make the words mean anything else. But I was desperate.

"When I think of all the women... the ones held down and cut as children. Their lives at risk when they get pregnant since they can't carry the child without risking death...." She shook her head. "What about the women in abusive relationships, beaten and tortured by their husbands? What if they don't want to bring a child into that environment to suffer the same way or allow a court to make the child a tether to that man? And the girls who've been trafficked and sold into the sex industry... how can I possibly say they should carry the babies of the strangers who violently raped them over and over again?"

"You can't, Sera."

"But I believe every life is precious. I mean, isn't that the point? That's always been the thing that's driven me. Why go to such great lengths if I didn't think every woman's life is precious and should be protected?"

"Sera, the two things—"

"How can I blame the innocent for the acts of the parents? Why shouldn't they get a chance at life because the circumstances of their creation were beyond their control? Don't they deserve to be protected too?"

"But it's not a man who has to carry that child. Or risk his life giving birth. It should be the woman's decision to have the child. It's her body."

"I know you're pro-choice, Dad. But how can I, as the Daughter of God, even consider that an option? How can I advocate for abortion?"

"Sera, I don't think anyone likes the idea of abortion and actively wants it to happen. No one is really *pro*-abortion. The opposite of pro-life isn't 'anti-life,' it's pro-*choice*. It's the woman's body and it's her right—"

"Even if God has blessed her with the child?"

"Blessed? Do you honestly think God would bless a woman with a baby by having her repeatedly beaten and raped?"

"But it's not the baby's fault. Doesn't that baby have rights?"

"And what about the child who has been gang raped and forced, at twelve or thirteen years old, to have a baby that could kill her? What about her rights? She's practically a baby herself. Who protects her life?"

Millions had debated Sera's argument, and it was something many still struggled with—myself included. After all, what if Sera's mother had decided to abort her? She would never have come into my life and brought all the joy she had.

"Surely you must have considered this, Sera. Abortion is one of the biggest women's rights issues in the world. You must have discussed it with the girls before now."

Sera paced the room.

"I thought I had more time," Sera said in frustration. "I wanted women to have full access to contraception so they were in control. I wanted the penalty for rape to be so harsh no man would dare attempt it. I wanted to eradicate trafficking around the world so babies weren't born into such terrible circumstances, destined for the same hellish life that led to their conception. I wanted to banish the practice of cutting so childbirth didn't pose such a danger. I wanted to show the world that women have the same potential as men and end gender-selective abortion."

Sera stopped and turned before pacing again. "It hasn't happened yet. I haven't had enough time. I was working toward a time when women rose to power, when they achieved full and unopposed equality with men. Women were to be the answer. They would be able to dictate laws and advocate for contraception, giving women the choice of when they had a family."

Sera's fists balled in fury, and her nails drew blood that seeped out of her palms. She looked to the ceiling and shook, tears of anger trembling in her eyes.

"Talk to me! Why haven't you given me enough time?"

CHAPTER THIRTY-NINE

IT WAS 3:00 a.m. and I couldn't sleep. I was at my wits' end over the idea of Sera wrecking everything she'd achieved and being ridiculed and harassed by the media. My anxiety was only made worse by the fact that I'd played a role in it all. I'd indulged her with the tools to do her work, no matter how delusional she'd been. I'd sacrificed her sanity to keep her happy. My head was never in the sand, but it was close enough to smell the grains.

I heard Sera's bare feet slap lightly on the wooden floor as she walked around the apartment. I got out of bed to check on her. She was walking as if in a trance, her eyes fixed on the floor as she circled the living room. When she spoke she didn't look at me. I wondered if she was even aware I was there or if she was sleepwalking.

"I won't be here much longer," she whispered quietly, as if not to wake anyone. "I must do the right thing."

As she turned I caught a glimpse between the locks that covered her face. Her eyes were now closed and a tear was suspended on her cheek. "But Dad, I'm so scared."

I walked forward, my arms out to comfort her, but she spun on her heel and began walking the length of the living room away from me.

"It's okay," she responded as if I'd answered her. "I'll come back. And when I do, I'll bring the true word of my father and brother. The word of my own. The word will be clear, so it can't be misinterpreted, mistranslated, or warped into a weapon of war or fear. I'll tell them that every person is equal. I'll tell them that God loves them, but they control their own destinies. Only they can save themselves. Man will save man. Woman will save woman. Man will save woman. Woman will save man."

She turned again and started walking directly toward me. She still didn't raise her head and continued to stare at the floor.

"When I return I'll give them the proof they so desperately need to believe. They not only need faith in God, but in one another. When I return they'll no longer question. When I return they'll know the truth. When I return they'll finally understand: they are the miracle. They are the miracle they need to witness."

I worried that I could make things worse by waking her or somehow cause psychological damage by interrupting whatever episode she was having. I wasn't equipped for this, but I couldn't bear seeing her like this either. I raised my arms again to comfort her, but she turned and headed back to her bedroom. "I'm so scared, Dad," she said as she reached the doorway to her room. "I'm scared."

IT WAS 10:00 a.m. when Carla called me. Either Sera wasn't awake or she hadn't ventured out of her room.

"Mr. Goodwin, I think it's better if Sera doesn't come into the office today. Things have gotten a little crazy here."

"What do you mean?"

"When we arrived this morning, there were a lot of protestors outside, a hell of a lot more than yesterday. The PowerCo workers are still picketing with the Second Amendment protestors. But now we've got feminist groups screaming outside about the abortion issue, and the East District Baptist Church wingnuts are here too, with signs saying Sera's going to burn in hell for declaring herself the Daughter of God."

"How many people are there?"

"I'd say at least two hundred and fifty. There seem to be a lot of foreign-looking men here too, as well as some shady-looking characters. There are counter protests too. The pro-choice, anti-gun, and pro-environmental activists turned up this morning with signs."

"Okay, I'll keep Sera away. Make sure you and Meena stay safe. If you start to worry about your safety, get the security people to escort you into a taxi, or I'll have a car come and pick you up."

"The owners of the building came this morning. They're not happy. There's been a lot of complaints from the workers in the other offices."

"I'll deal with them. But in the meantime, if you can, try and make it clear that Sera isn't there. I dare say a lot of the protestors have phones. Maybe put something out on the website?"

"I don't think that'll make much difference. The press is outside too. All of the protestors are trying to make their voices heard."

WHEN SERA came out of her room, she looked tired. Her eyes were bloodshot and she slouched as she walked.

"Want something to eat?"

"I haven't got time. I have to get into the office."

"Why don't you take the day off and give yourself a chance to think about what you're going to do? I'm not going to work today, so we can sit and talk about it as much as you want. Don't be too hasty in what you're going to say."

"I'll have to say something soon, Dad. I've just woken up to over six thousand e-mails. I haven't even looked at the social media sites yet. I can only imagine how many messages are on there."

"Even more reason to take the day off so you can figure out how you're going to respond." I paused for a moment as she considered it. "I don't ask a lot from you, Sera. Please, for me, don't make any rash decisions. Just take the day off to think. You're tired."

SHE RELUCTANTLY agreed and returned to her room. She hadn't mentioned what she'd said during the night, and I didn't want to talk about it for fear of reminding her.

In her absence I had the chance to research what I needed to do before I took action. It wasn't an easy decision to make. It tore at my heart and racked me with guilt. I'd done all I could to keep her out of this situation, but Amy had started a series of events that couldn't be stopped.

I couldn't risk Sera exposing herself to the ridicule. I was sure the pressure of it would send her over an edge from which I couldn't pull her back. In life it's hard enough to cope with one person turning their back on you. The idea of sixty million people turning their collective backs on you all at once would be enough to overwhelm even the sanest of people. If I could just buy her some time, get her some treatment before she publicly confirmed anything, there was a chance.

It would have to be a private facility, one that would guarantee her anonymity. If they could just diagnose her, or offer her some medication, maybe she would see sense. Maybe she would have the clarity to see that delving into the abortion argument now would be bad timing.

My plan went against everything I'd thought before, but this time was different. She was talking about dying and returning. I couldn't risk that her mental state might drive her to suicide just to prove her point. I had to make sure it didn't become a self-fulfilling prophecy at her own hands. In my heart I didn't think she would do it, but even if there was a tiny chance, it was still too big a risk.

I found a facility in New Jersey that assured me her treatment would remain confidential. They would assess her over a week and provide guidance on how to proceed. Since Sera wasn't being legally committed, she'd have to arrive of her own free will. The facility's beds were full, but they were due to have a patient leave that evening. That would give me enough time to stage some kind of intervention that would allow Aaron, Dalyn, Carla, Meena, and me the chance to express our concern and make a last-ditch attempt to reason with her. If we could convince her to go of her own volition, it would be a triumph and bring renewed hope that things hadn't gone past the point of no return. If she knew she would retain our support, perhaps she'd agree to humor us. I had to think of a way to bargain with her.

Sera spent the rest of the evening in her room, occasionally coming into the living room as if out of concern for me. My mind was tired from lack of sleep the night before, and I struggled to come up with an idea to which Sera might agree. Just before midnight Sera came into the living room and pulled a blanket over me as I lay on the sofa in the dark.

"I love you, Dad," she said as she leaned over and kissed me on the forehead. "I hate that I'm making you worry."

"I love you, too, sweetheart. Go get some sleep."

It was 5:00 a.m. when I last looked at the clock on the mantel. The next time I looked it read 9:00 a.m.

I rushed to Sera's bedroom, terrified she might have done something foolish. But she was dressed and alert, sitting on her bed with her laptop open, clicking away at the keys. She gave me a quick smile and returned her eyes to whatever she was doing.

I WAS due to meet the director of the facility downtown at 1:00 p.m., where we would discuss the process of a successful intervention. He would then accompany me back home and be a part of that intervention, along with Meena, Carla, Aaron, and Dalyn, whom I hadn't yet contacted. There was no question they would agree. The only one who might refuse was Meena, since she'd shown Sera the most support. But things had changed so dramatically since that evening. I was sure even she would know it was the right thing to do.

I laid out my clothes and got in the shower. It was going to be a long day. My muscles ached from sleeping on the sofa, so I turned the temperature of the water up. The heat only made me feel more lethargic. So, holding my breath, I turned the dial on the shower until freezing water pelted me. After the heat, it felt as though icy needles pierced my skin with every drop. It woke me up instantly and returned me to my wits. I stepped out and dried off, letting hot water run in the bathroom sink. I soaked my face before gliding a razor across my cheeks. It had been days since I'd shaved.

I changed into a suit. I'm not sure why. I think it was because I didn't want the director of the facility to think Sera hadn't come from a good home. I wanted to make a good impression for her so he would help her. I knew how ridiculous it was, but it helped pass the minutes before I explained to Sera that I'd be leaving her for a couple of hours.

I sat on the end of my bed and considered for the hundredth time whether I was doing the right thing. How much would Sera resent me? Would she ever forgive me? But there was nothing else I could do. I had to do it for her own safety.

Dressed and ready, I went into the kitchen. I called to Sera as casually as I could, asking if she wanted some breakfast. I didn't want to give her any indication that something was afoot. When she didn't answer, I called again. But there was no response. That's when I noticed the note on the table.

> *I know what I need to do.*
> *I love you, Dad.*
> *Sera.*

I dropped the note and instantly ran out the door, down the stairs, and onto the street. There was no sign of her. My heart raced as I began to panic. The car was in a private garage a few blocks away, so I raised my hand to flag down a taxi. One pulled over and I jumped in, and I urgently told the driver the address. I had no idea when she'd left. Was it five minutes ago? Half an hour? Was she already at the office, and if so, had she been met by security and escorted past the protestors?

I don't know what the taxi driver was saying. He may have been talking about the weather or his last fare. I heard his voice but nothing registered.

"Please," I said, "just get us there as fast as you can. Take Bowery."

He spoke again, but the ringing of my phone in my pocket distracted me. If it was the director of the facility, I would tell him to meet me at the office and stage the intervention there before Sera put out any statement. But the name on the screen showed the call was from the office building's management. In the thick of car horns sounding, road works, and general Manhattan traffic, it was difficult to hear the automated voice. I asked the driver to wind up his window, and I put a finger in my other ear so I could hear more clearly.

"—to evacuate the building immediately. Once again, this is not a drill—" The call cut off.

My shaking hands fumbled with the phone. I tried to call Sera, but after three rings it went to voice mail. I called Carla, who picked up almost instantly. A blaring siren rang into my ear. "Carla! What's happened?"

"There's been a bomb threat!" she shouted over the siren. "The alarms are going off, and we have to get out of the building!"

We were still four blocks away. I yanked open the handle of the taxi door and ran up the street toward Sera's office. The taxi driver shouted after me, but I ignored him and kept running.

As I got closer, I heard the faint sounds of police sirens in the distance. As I crossed Washington Square Park, I wove between the demonstrators. I shouted, *"Leave her alone!"* But their cacophonous chants drowned out my voice.

I pushed past one man holding a Second Amendment sign, clipping his shoulder as I tried to reach the entrance of the building. He pulled me by the back of my shirt in anger. He held on so tightly that I started dragging him through the crowd with me. I pushed past a woman holding a pro-choice sign. She, too, took hold of me. With all my strength, I tried to barrel forward, but in my attempt I just kept knocking people out of the way, and suddenly an angry mob surrounded me. Two more hands reached for me, either to block me getting to the entrance or out of anger for knocking into them.

"It's her. She's coming out!" a man from the East District Baptist Church suddenly yelled. I turned to the man still holding my shirt and swung my elbow into his nose. The two others who'd grabbed me instantly let go, their bravery slipping as they watched the bloodied man hit the ground. Over the top of the protestors' heads, between the signs and the balled fists, I saw a flash of curly auburn hair. I raced forward again, but the crowd started to move, blocking my way. Some of them I recognized as anti-gun and pro-environment protestors, who obviously believed it was my intention to harm the one they came to support.

"*Sera! Get out of here!*" I yelled as I shunted people with my elbows and knocked down the signs that blocked my view.

I could see Meena and Carla on either side of Sera, pushing back the people who were screaming in their faces as they tried to get out onto the street. While Meena looked scared, Carla had a look of determination and anger on her face and broke away, her arms wide, to drive back the crowd. The protestors and the counterprotestors began to turn on one another. There was a palpable shift in the crowd, like a spark had been ignited. We were on the verge of a riot, and the police were still blocks away.

I saw it before I heard it. At first glance it looked as though a rogue breeze had caught the side of Sera's face, slowly whipping a couple of curls of hair behind her, separating the strands so the fiery embers shimmered in the wisps. But it wasn't a breeze. The force of a bullet had flipped a lock of Sera's hair, narrowly missing her head.

The crowd collapsed into chaos. Some instinctively ducked and dropped to their knees; others scattered. People screamed and yelled as they tripped over one another to get out of the way. I rushed forward as I saw Meena and Carla push Sera to the pavement to keep her out of the line of fire.

But the sound of a second gunshot had already rent the air.

By the time I reached them, Meena and Carla had thrown themselves over Sera to protect her. But it was too late.

"*No, Sera. Please, God, no!*"

Meena helped me pull Sera across my lap. Her head rested in the crook of my elbow as I cradled her. The patch of blood on her chest grew wider by the second, soaking her shirt, clinging the material to her skin. Her eyes were closed, but she was still breathing.

"Sera, please. Please, sweetheart, please don't go," I whispered, gently rocking her the same way I had when I tried to wake her as a child. "Please, please, don't leave me."

Sera's eyes opened as if stirring from sleep. She looked up at me as the panicked sound of the crowd and Carla's cries dissolved into a mere muffled noise.

"Sophia."

"Don't talk, sweetheart," I urged as I heard the once distant sound of sirens growing louder. I held my hand to her chest to try to stem the blood. "The ambulance is coming."

"The message… from Sophia," she said, using what little strength she had left to turn her head so her dimming blue eyes met mine. "I remember now…. It was Michael." She took a breath that bubbled in her throat. Her hand gripped and twisted my shirt. "He said… he still doesn't dream, because he's still here with you. He still runs beside you."

"Sera, they're almost here. Please, baby, hold on."

A smile shone through the agony of her pain. "I see now. Amy was wrong. It was Michael. It's his heart that beats but doesn't live. And you… you're the one who has not been held and whose crying has not been heard." Sera's voice became weaker as her face began to pale. "You've never been apart."

"The ambulance is almost here. Stay with me."

"I'll come back. I promise."

My tears dripped onto her face, wetting her cheeks. I wiped them away with my thumb. I stroked her hair, kissed her forehead, and whispered, "I love you so much. Don't leave me."

"What I've done, it was just the beginning…. Please believe me. I'm here to save them."

The tears stung my eyes. "You saved me."

I knew it would be the last time I held Sera in my arms. I swallowed the crushing fear and sadness and stifled the scream that rose inside me long enough to smile at her. It was my greatest honor to repay the comfort she'd given me ever since the first time I'd held her in my arms.

"I'll come back, Daddy."

"I believe you, sweetheart," I whispered.

The sound of Sera's last breath was stolen from me as clicks and beeps filled the air. I pulled Sera's body closer to me and looked up at the crowd. Outstretched arms held camera phones trained on us, capturing and recording Sera's death. A line of women joined Meena and Carla as they stood in front of us to shield and protect Sera from the lenses. But it was too late. Within seconds I heard the familiar tones that confirmed photographs had been successfully uploaded and posted onto social media sites. The image of my daughter's dead body was spreading across the Internet.

EPILOGUE

HOW IMMEDIATELY and easily the dark thoughts returned. But unlike twenty-four years before, I couldn't contemplate acting on them. Not until the person who took Sera's life was found.

I sat in Sergeant Marino's office two days later. The voice in my head was screaming at him. Why hadn't he arrested the person responsible? Why hadn't he deployed every police officer in New York City to investigate? Why wasn't a worldwide manhunt underway to find the person who'd murdered my daughter?

Instead I sat numbly. Despite my anger and desperate need for justice, I didn't want to be there. I wanted to be at the morgue, holding Sera's hand. I didn't want her to be alone.

"We're taking witness statements and going through every second of CCTV footage in the area. We know the perpetrator must have been to Sera's right due to the bullet's trajectory—"

I held up a hand to stop him. I couldn't hear it again.

"Mr. Goodwin, I hope you understand why we have to be cautious going forward and ensure that we arrest the right person. There were members of staunch feminist groups that had major issues with Sera's alleged views on abortion. There were many Second Amendment activists there who could be members of militias. The East District Baptist Church was picketing too. They've done some despicable things in the past, though they've never gone so far as killing someone. But then again, they've never gone up against someone who allegedly said she was the Daughter of God, so they remain suspects." He was carefully choosing his words. "There were also many people there who didn't appear to have any affiliation with any of the groups. We can't rule out they were criminals involved in sex trafficking, men who disagreed with Sera's stance on women's rights issues in various countries, or maybe one of Sera's followers

who felt like she'd turned against the cause because of what she
supposedly said."

"What do you need from me?"

"We'll need access to all of her computers and laptops, both in
her home as well as yours. Should the culprit be apprehended, any kind
of communication they had with Sera could be vital to the case. We
already have Meena Yun and Carla Ramirez's laptops, as well as Amy
Jones's."

My eyes narrowed. The intensity of my glare at the paperwork on
the sergeant's desk didn't disguise the anger I still felt toward Amy.

"I know this won't make you feel any better, but it took both of
Amy's parents and two officers to subdue her when she found out what
had happened. She was beyond distraught. I went to her home myself
to retrieve her laptop. Trust me, the knowledge of what she caused will
punish her for the rest of her life."

I thanked the officer, and he escorted me to the station door.

"Promise me they'll be careful with Sera's laptop. Her diaries are
on there, and I don't want to risk the files being damaged. I've never
read them. I don't know if I ever will. But now they're the only thing I
have left."

The sergeant nodded and promised he would be in contact the
moment they learned anything. He offered to have someone drive me
home, but I declined. I couldn't go home, knowing I wouldn't see her
or hear her voice. Instead I wandered the city aimlessly, not knowing
where I was heading—only that it was away from the apartment.

A selfish grief kept me from returning Aaron's phone calls. I
couldn't bear to speak to him, to hear his mourning or his anger. It
would only fuel my own, leading me deeper into dark thoughts of
despair and revenge. But I knew I'd have to face him eventually, once
he showed up at my door, unannounced as usual.

As I walked uptown, I saw a homeless man walking on the other
side of the street who, from behind, walked with a limp. He carried a
worn backpack but he was ahead of me so I couldn't see his face. For a
moment I debated whether to call out "Oscar" to see if he would turn,
but suddenly a deafening sound and a moving line of sirens passed me.
Police cars escorted three fire engines and several ambulances as they
battled through the late afternoon traffic. The sound gave me a cold
chill. I blocked my ears, but the flashing lights continued for what

seemed an eternity. I paused to think of the people who were in need of such a long cavalcade of emergency services. Unlike my Sera, could they be saved? By the time I looked back across the street, the man who I thought might be Oscar was gone.

I found myself back in Grand Central Station. Maybe I'd subconsciously chosen it as my destination. As I passed a newsstand, I noticed a handwritten poster advertising that day's *New York Times* that simply read "Standing By Sera." I placed money on the kiosk counter, tucked a copy under my arm, and found the bench where I'd discovered a baby twenty-four years earlier.

I opened the newspaper and found the tribute piece on the Op-Ed page with Dalyn's byline, where I began to read.

A Life Devoted: Sera Goodwin: 1990–2014

On Saturday, June 7, 2014, the world lost a woman who had become known as a savior—a title earned, in truth, by the actions she took to save the lives of countless women across the world.

I took a deep breath, unsure whether I was going to be able to read Dalyn's words. My eyes wandered up to the painting of the night sky over the concourse. I remembered a story someone once told me— that the sky, with its intricate constellations and stars, had been painted there in reverse by mistake. Apparently when the Vanderbilt family learned the ceiling was painted backward, they maintained that the ceiling reflected God's view of the sky, as if looked upon from above. The LED lights embedded in the ceiling where each star appeared must have been recently replaced, because when I looked up, they appeared much brighter than I remembered them.

I returned my gaze from the ceiling to the newspaper that rested on my lap. I read the words that ran below the photo of the smiling face of my beautiful, inimitable daughter.

At the young age of sixteen, Sera Goodwin dedicated herself to helping girls tackle the challenges of teenage life. Through the innovation and expansion of social media, she listened to troubled girls when they needed to be heard, advised them when they sought answers, and offered them understanding when they felt no one else could. To this day there are hundreds—possibly thousands—of parents in this country who have no idea it was Sera's hand that helped their daughters down from a ledge when they believed life had become too unbearable to continue.

I first interviewed Sera in 2008, two years after she began to harness the power of social media, expanding her own profile and website into a network of millions of young women across the world. It was her unwavering dedication and loyalty to these women that enabled her to achieve success on women's rights issues that many wouldn't have dared to attempt. In the following years, Sera built a formidable army of women and empowered each of them to contribute in struggles against sex trafficking, gender inequality, and violence against women. They also fought for equal opportunities for women in education, business, and politics.

Many described the millions of women who contributed to Sera's mission as "followers." But Sera never agreed with that title.

"These women don't follow me. They stand beside me. If anything, each of the millions of women that have contributed to the cause should be called a leader, since they have led other women out of lives that were, at times, hell on earth."

Together Sera and these leaders fought criminals and pimps. They confronted corrupt politicians and authorities. They challenged male-dominated institutions whose archaic opinions of women held them back from reaching their full potential. Sera believed every person who contributed to the cause became a light in a social darkness that many were too afraid to enter. Few would deny that Sera's light shined the brightest.

Some have tried to diminish that light and tarnish her reputation. In the days leading to her death, her critics alleged that she had declared herself to be the Daughter of God. Tragically, Sera was struck down before she could address the allegations publicly. Nor was she able to address the whispered speculation that she suffered from mental illness. Ironically, Sera herself likely would have turned these rumors on their head and taken the opportunity to shine a light on the plight and social stigmatization of mentally ill women.

Regardless of whether you believe she was mentally ill, a zealous social advocate, or even the true Daughter of God, there is no denying the incredible impact she made on the world. The women who stood with Sera in her battles remain devoted. They recognize that Sera didn't invent social media, charity apps, the concept of microloans, or online petitions. They know she didn't author the idea of hashtag activism, volunteering abroad, fundraising, or networking. What they do know is that Sera showed them that we already have the tools in place to make a difference and that the greatest challenges of the world are not impossible to overcome. She gave them the proof and evidence that we, as people, are the engineers of our own salvation.

Today you will see millions of women have changed their Facebook and Twitter profile pictures to a simple blue symbol: a short, vertical line running from the top to the middle of an incomplete circle. It is the same symbol found on nearly every power button on every television, phone, or computer. It's the international symbol for "stand by."

This symbol could be a gesture in recognition of the last line of the many blogs she wrote before she called her army to war. It could be a symbol shown in pride, confirming that, despite the allegations, they still stand by her. It could also mean they believe Sera is the Daughter of God, sent here to save women—the symbol signifying that they are standing by, awaiting her resurrection. Many have posted the definition of her name, pasted from baby name websites, to offer proof:

Sera: Hebrew—princess, winged angel. See: Sera-phim/ Seraphina

Whatever the individual reasons, the sheer number of people who have dedicated their identity to this symbol is a more remarkable tribute than I could ever hope of offering Sera today.

Since her death, an outpouring of love for Sera has been shown across the world on social media, and thousands of online tributes of condolence have appeared. Among the praise and hope for the future of her work, there is definite frustration. What if Sera had lived? What else could she have accomplished if that person with a gun, who ran like a coward, hadn't struck her down?

I only hope that the frustration, the feeling that a better future has been stolen from us, is turned into positive action. That was the core of Sera's message—don't wait for a miracle, because we've already arrived.

One of Sera's followers posted a most fitting tribute. She said Sera had "saved her life," though she didn't elaborate how. It read "If she believed herself to be the Daughter of God, don't we owe it to her to believe it too? It's a small price to pay for what she gave us."

Millions agree.

Standing by.

I wiped my eyes, but I had no tears left to cry. Dalyn's words were perfectly chosen and in my mind, I quietly thanked him for them.

I folded the paper and meandered away from Grand Central. As I walked, phrases from Dalyn's article reverberated in my head. I hadn't even considered how Sera would have responded in public to allegations of mental illness. I had tried so hard to protect her that the opportunity to defend herself never arose. Dalyn was right, of course. She would have deflected the question away from herself and used it as an opportunity to confront the treatment and stigmatization of women battling mental illness. She would have said they deserve respect and compassion, not judgment and contempt. They aren't "unbalanced" or "broken." They are whole.

Like Sera.

She embodied many of the struggles for which she fought. How could I not see that questions about her mental stability could have been another way to relate to women who desperately needed her help?

The slow walk home took hours. I walked with my head down, my form so exhausted I was unable to stride tall. As I walked through the East Village, I stopped in my tracks. On the ground, stenciled onto one of the paving slabs, was a blue standby symbol. I looked up and around me. The more I looked for it, the more I found it. It was painted on a white sheet that hung in the window of an apartment. It was painted on the glass of the bus shelter across the street. The walls holding flyers for local bands had been covered with papers that had the symbol printed on them. As I walked across the small side streets, I saw the exterior walls of the buildings, covered in graffiti, had a new addition. Huge blue standby symbols had been spray painted over the tags and street art. I marveled at the speed with which Sera's new identity had spread.

I arrived back at the apartment sooner than I wanted. For the second time in my life, I unlocked the door and found myself in a place that felt like an abandoned cathedral. I wandered to Sera's room and sat on the edge of her bed, my weight causing the stuffed lamb to topple off the pillow where she had left it.

The room smelled like her. It was the familiar scent of lavender and chamomile. I looked at the pillow Maria had given her and the ceramic bottle adorned with a bouquet of nineteen flowers that Miss Dee had given her, which sat on her dressing table.

Suddenly I remembered a third gift, given to Sera by the last of the three women to leave us.

The gold bracelet.

I walked to the kitchen island and opened the clear plastic bag. A white tag dangling from one corner read "Personal Effects" in block print on the front, with a telephone number and Sera's name on the back. Through the plastic I could see a smartphone, jeans, sneakers, and pink socks. I tore it open and poured its contents onto the kitchen table. I looked through her jeans, shook out her sneakers, and unrolled her socks. It wasn't there.

I took out my phone and called the number on the tag.

"Beth Israel Memorial Hospital," an operator answered.

"Could you please put me through to the morgue?"

"That line is busy at the moment. Please hold."

I paced the living room, waiting. The anxiety built inside me, matching the crescendo of the piano music playing on the line. The music broke, and the operator returned. "I'm sorry, sir, the line is still busy. Do you still wish to hold?"

"Yes, please." The music returned.

Of all Sera's possessions, the gold bracelet was the one thing I wanted—no, needed—to have. I'd never known her not to wear the gift since the day Maggie gave it to her.

The piano stopped again. "Morgue, how can I help you?" asked a harassed-sounding woman.

"My name is Adam Goodwin. My daughter, Sera Goodwin... she's there. I mean, her body is there... at the morgue. I've just opened the bag of personal effects they gave me, and a thin gold bracelet is missing."

"Sir, we're dealing with a major incident at the moment. There was a multiple-car crash in Midtown today involving a bus. We're dealing with a lot of fatalities. Can you please call back later?"

I must have passed near the crash site when I saw the line of fire engines, ambulances, and police cars earlier that afternoon.

"I understand you're busy, but please, she's my... she was... is... my daughter. I have to have that bracelet. Could you please... please ask someone to check her left wrist to see if she's still wearing it?" It was hard not to break down.

"It's very unlikely that—"

"I'm begging you, please.... Can you ask someone to look for me?"

There was a brief pause, then a sigh. I hoped it was one of understanding. "You said the name was Goodwin?"

"Yes."

"Hold on just a minute, sir."

One minute turned to five, which stretched into ten. Finally her voice returned to the line. When she spoke she sounded guarded, almost nervous. "Mr. Goodwin, have you already made funeral arrangements for your daughter?"

"I've started to. Why?"

"We had a shift change at five o'clock. The person working this afternoon hasn't updated the records. He was probably swamped by the fatalities involved in the crash, so he didn't get the chance," she explained. Still, I felt unsettled by the unsure tone in her voice. "Can I ask when the funeral home is due to pick up the body?"

"Not until tomorrow. Why?"

"Is there a chance they might have picked it up early?"

"I don't think— What's going on?"

A few moments of silence passed before she spoke again.

"Sir, your daughter's body, it...." She seemed to be unable to finish the sentence.

"*It's* what?"

"It... it isn't here."

The hairs on the back of my neck rose, betraying the sudden sense of calm that washed over me.

I watched as the handle of the front door slowly began to turn.

Author's Note

You can contact the author at greghogben@gmail.com.

Awareness is the first step.

This novel is dedicated to every person who follows @mydaughtersarmy on Twitter. Whether it was a retweet, a comment of support, or a word of encouragement, you have helped raise awareness of Women's Rights and LGBT equality. You are all advocates, and I thank each of you for your help over the past two years.

GREG HOGBEN is a British author based in Washington, DC. Greg is a human rights advocate with a particular focus on raising awareness of worldwide women's rights and LGBT equality.

E-mail: greghogben@gmail.com

Twitter: @mydaughtersarmy

Blog: http://www.huffingtonpost.com/greg-hogben/

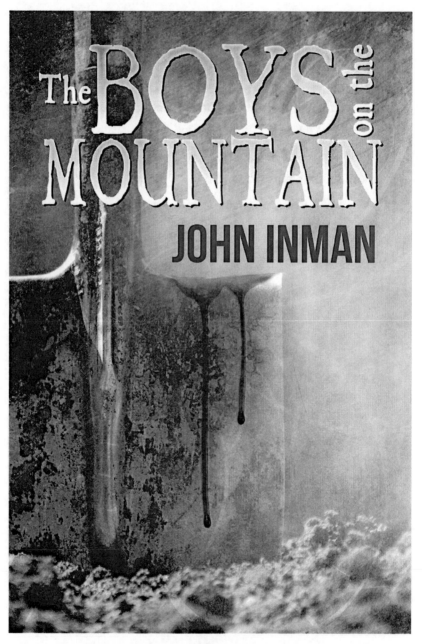

www.dsppublications.com

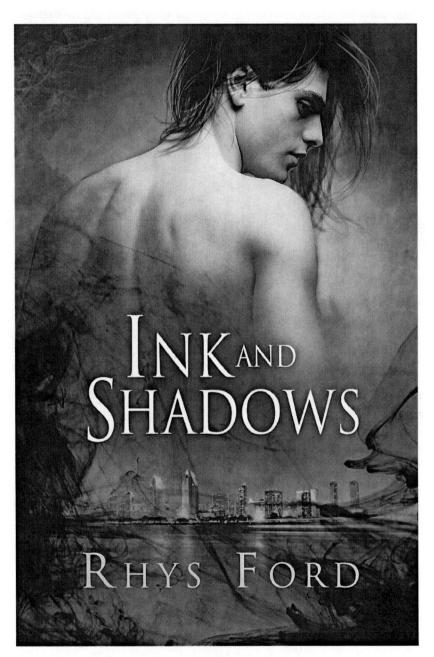

www.dsppublications.com

THIRD EYE

RICK R. REED

www.dsppublications.com

Vulnerable

The First Book of the Little Goddess series

AMY LANE

www.dsppublications.com